DRY ICE

BILL EVANS

AND

MARIANNA JAMESON

A TOM DOHERTY ASSOCIATES BOOK | NEW YORK

This is a work of fiction. All of the characters, organizations, and events portrayed in this novel are either products of the author's imagination or are used fictitiously.

DRY ICE

Copyright © 2011 by William H. Evans and Marianna Jameson

A Forge Book
Published by Tom Doherty Associates, LLC
175 Fifth Avenue
New York, NY 10010

www.tor-forge.com

Forge® is a registered trademark of Tom Doherty Associates, LLC.

ISBN 978-0-7653-6414-2

First Edition: August 2011
First Mass Market Edition: May 2012

Printed in the United States of America

0 9 8 7 6 5 4 3 2 1

To Karen Moser and Jody Novins, who know why.
And to my husband, who is simply the best.

—Marianna Jameson

This is dedicated to my four wonderful children,
Maggie, William, Julia, and Sarah. I love you more
than you will ever know.

—Bill Evans

ACKNOWLEDGMENTS

First I want to thank my partner in this techno-weather crime, Marianna Jameson. I truly appreciate her hard work, her style of writing, her wit and charm. Those are the things we share the most, along with a sick sense of humor, which make us great partners. We have made three great books together and I want to thank her for making that happen.

Secondly I want to thank Margaret Cheney for her great work, *Tesla: Man Out of Time,* which I relied upon for a great amount of background on Tesla the man. I also want to thank the Tesla Memorial Society of New York for their help in providing information on Tesla's life and times in New York City. They are trying to raise money to turn Tesla's building at Wardenclyffe, Long Island, into a science museum. Hopefully this book will help raise awareness about Tesla and generate more money for their goal.

Thanks to the Nikola Tesla Museum in Belgrade, Serbia, for their kindness and help.

I want to thank Jerry E. Smith for his book *Weather Warfare* and for his take on Tesla and the HAARP Program.

I want to thank the greatest editor in the world, Melissa Singer at Tor. I am so proud to be your weatherman every day. Thank you for making our words "sing." Thanks to Tom Doherty and the wonderful staff at Tor/Forge. I would especially like to thank Linda Quinton from Tor/Forge. I very much appreciate your wonderful support; you always show so much confidence in my work, which is a great feeling, and I thank you for your kindness and friendship.

I want to thank my wonderful wife, Dana, who has no problem telling me when the writing and my ideas stink. When she looks at me and politely says, "Okay, that's . . . that's okay," I know the work is great. I want to thank my children, Maggie, William, Julia, and Sarah, for their patience when I shut the doors to the den. I love you with all my heart.

I especially want to thank Nikola Tesla for giving me a great book. It is unfathomable to me that to this day, the recognition of Tesla's legacy is nowhere near the appreciation for the legacy of Babe Ruth in the game of baseball. Tesla was that big in his field. I truly hope that one day, future generations will come to appreciate the genius that was Nikola Tesla.

—BILL EVANS

In the course of researching and writing *Dry Ice,* I received the help and support of many individuals.

First thanks must go to Bill Evans for his fascination with the work of Nikola Tesla and his enthusiasm for this project.

Thanks to my buddy from my days in the aerospace industry, Ron Zellar, who is a creative genius when it comes to things that orbit this planet or otherwise exist in outer space, or don't actually exist at all. Once again, Michael Rowan was my go-to guy for everything that floats, flies, explodes, or salutes. Both of you helped immeasurably when it came to the science, both real and imagined. Richard Smith provided his usual stellar technical support and expert advice on all matters related to software and computers.

Thanks, too, to fellow author Barbara Caridad Ferrar, who was generous with sharing her insight into the mindset and outlook of a first-generation Cuban-American woman.

I offer my heartfelt thanks and deepest respect to the researchers on "the Ice" at the Dumont d'Urville Station, Princess Elisabeth Antarctica, Sky Blu Logistics Facility, Halley Research Station, McMurdo Station, and Amundsen-Scott South Pole Station, and the many others connected with the British Antarctic Survey, the Scientific Committee on Antarctic Research, and the U.S. National Science Foundation. You willingly put civilization on hold and your lives on the line to advance the cause of science and give the rest of us things to chat about at cocktail parties. I wouldn't change places with any of you, but I cannot thank you enough for your dedication and good humor, as well as your websites, diaries, blogs, photographs, and the other great information you have shared so openly. You rock.

Despite all the generous help from the subject-matter experts mentioned above, I know there will be errors. All mistakes are my own.

My favorite former spook and fellow author, Jody Novins, was once again invaluable for her willingness to share some insights into the world of capital-I intelligence, and for having a dark, sharp, and lovely sense of humor. Thanks, too, to author Karen Kendall for being my beta reader, for offering excellent advice on myriad topics, and for being able to make me laugh like no one else can. Agent and attorney Elaine English and author Laura Resnick provided lots of insight and assistance. I thank all of you for always being at the other end of the phone when I've needed you.

A little closer to home, thanks to my usual peeps: Nancy Mitchell, Pam Taeckens, Vicki Rowan, and Debbie Marsh, who always have my back, and to Cathy and Steve Vollmer, for describing what it feels like to be in the Oval Office. Thanks, also, to Maribeth Wonson, who was the high bidder at the CMS Fine Arts Auction and won the opportunity to have a character named after her in this book. It was a pleasure getting to know you and I hope you're pleased with your namesake.

The many talented and wonderful people at Tor/ Forge have my deepest thanks for their hard work and immense talent. Most especially, this book would not be what it is without the talent, insight, candor, and deeply appreciated patience of Melissa Ann Singer, editor extraordinaire and all-around fabulous woman. Thank you times a million.

Usually last on the list but always first in my heart are my husband and children, for whom I am very, very, very thankful.

—MARIANNA JAMESON

DRY ICE

1

CHAPTER

In the most remote location on the most remote continent on earth, the eerie landscape lay shadowless under a moonless sky as dark and vast as eternity. The high, empty, frozen plains of snow and ice cast up a feeble, hungry glow. The only light came from stars that glittered intermittently through the heavy cloud cover.

It was mid-March in central East Antarctica, and late in the evening of just another workday at the Terrestrial Energy Southern Land Array—TESLA—installation. The only sound to be heard, inside or out, was that of the wind, screaming at more than one hundred miles per hour across the empty, miles-thick ice sheet. The torrent of air slammed into the state-of-the-art research station and blasted across the large fields of radomes covering the many antennae that comprised the station's sole purpose and reason it existed.

The people of TESLA, twenty scientists and software developers and fourteen support staff, were the only island of humanity in this part of the earth's coldest, highest desert. Their nearest neighbor on that high-altitude plateau was the aging Soviet-era Vostok Base. Located as it was near the Pole of Inaccessibility—the most isolated outpost on earth—Vostok sat tantalizingly close to the South Geomagnetic Pole, the best place on the planet to study, monitor, and *alter* nature's electromagnetism.

The industrial giant Flint AgroChemical had chosen to quietly build the sleek, high-tech, $250 million TESLA even closer to that pole.

Flint's decision had left the Russians livid, the Americans astonished, and the Australians amused. The Chinese, aggressive newcomers to the Ice, still seethed with silent, stoic rage. One by one, those nations, and several others, had turned their polar-orbiting reconnaissance satellites toward TESLA to watch the goings-on.

Although the installation's antennae covered nearly one hundred acres, there wasn't much for the cameras to track—by design. Every antenna at TESLA was either buried under many feet of snow and ice, as was the Extremely Low Frequency field, or hidden under massive radomes. Some of the shelters were spherical, some geodesic; some low, others nearly two stories tall. Whatever their shape, the carefully crafted structures offered little resistance to the wind while protecting the delicate equipment within their walls. But that wasn't the only defense they provided.

The radomes frustrated the prying "eyes" of the multi-spectrum, high-resolution cameras trained on them from non-Flint-owned satellites. The complex composite materials used to build the radomes prevented snow and ice from building up on the surfaces while also preventing the units from emitting a heat signature. Their non-reflective surfaces bore a subtle camouflage pattern that rendered the large edifices nearly invisible during both the twenty-four-hour sunlight of the Antarctic summer and the deep-space darkness of the polar winter. No matter the intensity of the light directed at them, the radomes appeared no more sinister than the oddly carved snowdrifts surrounding them.

That invisibility was little more than a gesture really, a high-tech Bronx salute to those who made watching the installation a priority. Interested parties— competitors as well as nations—had antennae of their own that continually swept the earth's atmosphere, alert to the faintest of electromagnetic signals, which made it impossible for Flint to hide the signals TESLA sent out. The company's sole consolation was that no outsiders knew what the strange and heavily encrypted signals meant. Or did.

The vast arrays of receivers, composed of numerous shapes and configurations, captured communications from transmitters in precisely chosen locations the world over. This delicate but powerful network existed to gather and monitor vast quantities of minute data about the world's weather. The rest of the antenna arrays were powerful transmitters that sent forth data and commands to receivers and repeaters across the globe.

TESLA's control center and habitat sat not two hundred yards from the edge of the nearest antenna array. The elliptical, three-story structure stood tall above the ice plateau on massive hydraulic pillars. The exterior skin was the same dull, patterned covering the radomes wore, and a bracelet of windows encircled each of the floors. The garage unit sat at ground level between the pylons.

The station's long-legged, shallow-domed design was more functional than aesthetic. Too many early polar stations had been lost within mere decades to encroaching snowdrifts that slowly, inevitably, built up and then froze solid, encasing the stations in impenetrable prisons of ice. TESLA's sleek, aerodynamic design was cutting-edge, yet the entire installation resembled nothing so much as a 1950s cinematic concept of a futuristic moon station.

The scientists and developers living and working at the installation represented the pinnacle of their fields of study—artificial intelligence, informatics, agrometeorology, plasma physics, ionospheric mechanics, and other even more arcane subjects. They had willingly eschewed the pleasures of civilization to work at changing the way the world worked.

Literally.

A small cluster of the resident geniuses tapped away at their keyboards, working silently and nearly elbow to elbow in the "sandbox," the sequestered communal work area that occupied one end of the installation's high-security upper level. Some of the researchers were crafting new algorithms or speculating on outcomes, while others conducted white- and black-box testing of their software. Uniformly, their tasks were labors of love in a research endeavor never before undertaken by any private company. Governments had tried, but none had succeeded because none had had the leadership of a man as single-minded and intent on success as the one in charge of TESLA: Greg Simpson.

The existence of the Terrestrial Energy Southern

Land Array was an open secret within a small group of scientists, corporate executives, and American military commanders, but its true purpose was known to few. TESLA existed to influence the weather. Perhaps *control* would be the better word. Or *manipulate*.

Or *create*.

In the deliberate darkness of his office near the sandbox, TESLA's chief scientist, Greg Simpson, sat hunched over his keyboard, watching data stream onto his screen in real time.

It was always this way: the lights off, the room lit only by the soft glow of the bank of flat-screen monitors on his desk. The first time he'd brought a transmitter array on line—telling no one that he was going live, only that he was conducting a power test—he'd sought the darkness instinctively, perhaps to lessen the magnitude of what he was doing. But that unconscious, reflexive timidity had been quickly usurped by an almost otherworldly elation. Greg had come to believe that his actions deserved a reverence reserved for the miraculous, and he savored the experience alone, in this hushed gloaming that recalled cathedrals. And tombs.

Greg had always longed to apply the theories of the twentieth-century scientist and visionary Nikola Tesla to the greater world. To Greg, Tesla had always been both a genius and a virtual mentor. He revered Tesla as much as others had reviled the man. No, "reviled" wasn't the right word. The scientific community had dismissed Tesla as an interesting crackpot, part forward-thinker and part snake-oil salesman. But that hadn't stopped any of them from blithely cherry-picking his ideas. When Tesla died, the U.S. government had moved in like a strike force to confiscate his papers. They tested and even implemented his most immediately useful inventions. The rest had been left to molder.

When Greg had earned his own lab space, his own assistants, and just enough autonomy, he had begun refining and even testing some of the great man's less well-known theories. He used them to build his own reputation and then, as Nikola Tesla was never able to, Greg cashed in.

Greg typed commands on his keyboard and the sensitive mechanisms within certain of the radomes responded. Without so much as a click or a hum to compete with the roar of the wind on the other side of its shelter, a fixed, towering dipole array came to life. In other radomes, oddly curved dishes spun and tilted, some dramatically, some imperceptibly, moving into new positions that targeted specific coordinates in the sky.

The movements were timed and calibrated to the nanosecond. By the time each rig was settled in its place, alert and awaiting the next command, the generators in the low-slung power station on the near side of the antenna fields had achieved peak operational efficiency. Dedicated power boxes placed among the radomes ramped up to "go" mode, ready to supply the enormous wattage needed by the arrays. With a gentle tap of his finger, Greg executed the command. Mere nanoseconds later the fully juiced antennae emitted synchronous bursts of unimaginably powerful electromagnetic energy into the southern sky.

Instantly, though invisibly to the naked eye, the suddenly supercharged bands of the ionosphere, miles wide, began to shiver and shimmy, to warp and buckle as electrons and protons reacted, alternately colliding and repelling each other in ways that nature never intended. The effect was that of a massive earthquake in the atmosphere.

Seconds later, the secondary effect triggered, sending streaks of luminous greens and blues rippling through the clouds and across the endless black of the sky, flashing and shimmering like a kaleidoscope spun too fast. To any untrained eye, it would appear to be just another glorious display of the aurora australis.

The huge waves of energy snaked their way around the globe as TESLA's transmitters powered down and returned to "sleep" mode to await the next assignment. The installation's scientists dispassionately noted the direction, duration, and magnitude of the bursts, then moved on to other tasks.

Within hours or days, depending on where they called home, citizens of the planet would marvel at the beautiful spring weather, curse the autumn storms that pummeled them, or weep at the unfathomable devastation caused by nature's unpredictability.

The financial markets would churn, creating vast wealth for the executives at Flint. And, in the Pentagon, military leaders would smile grimly as field reports came in, for they had learned how to play God.

2

CHAPTER

Outstretched like a crabbed, admonishing finger, the skinny, steep-sided Wakhan Salient in the farthest northeastern reaches of Afghanistan pokes the sensitive borders of Tajikistan, China, and Pakistan. Though once part of the famous ancient trading route known as the Silk Road, traversed by the explorer Marco Polo, this long, rugged, narrow valley is a land forgotten by Time. Despite its proximity to politically touchy neighbors, the Wakhan Salient had for the most part been left in peace, in the care of peoples who had inhabited it for centuries; its terrain is too harsh and too remote to be useful to the Afghan government or the occupying forces of foreign armies.

Though steeped comfortably in their timeworn culture, the small, poor populations of Wakhi farmers and Kyrgyz livestock herders had welcomed the exploratory trekkers from Flint AgroChemical when they had arrived several years earlier. The Western strangers, rather rare in that part of the world, had shared grand tales of increased crop yields, paid-for infrastructure, and generators that worked.

While battles raged to the south, the farmers in the safe, pristine Wakhan uplands gladly entered the twenty-first century, courtesy of Flint. For its part, the company was doing little more than getting its foot in the door in a country that, once the war was over, would be hungry for stability, prosperity, and independence from foreign nations. The desperately short summers and excruciatingly cold winters of this high, remote, unforgiving valley made it the perfect test bed for Flint's latest line of genetically modified crops. If the project was successful, as Flint intended it to be, the company would redefine the world's understanding of the term "arable land." Along the way, Flint would ingratiate itself with national and local Afghan leaders and the new American president. The newly elected leader was a dove amid the Pentagon's coterie of war hawks; to the astonished disbelief of her military commanders, Commander-in-Chief Helena Hernandez wanted peace, rather than her administration, to reign in Afghanistan.

As if its executives had known ahead of time about the dramatic upheaval that would take place in the American political landscape, Flint had spent several years quietly making inroads with the Afghan agricultural ministry in Kabul. It poured money into the small, gasping, rural northeastern economies like it was water from heaven. The firm built infrastructure, literally and figuratively cementing its relationships with regional powerbrokers. The new occupant of the White House had been pleased and vocal about it—and the Pentagon stonily silent—as together they watched a single corporation do what an economic and military powerhouse could not.

Winter in the Wakhan Corridor had been unremarkable that year. As always, the wind was a constant. Bitterly, skin-searingly cold, it wailed mercilessly outside the isolated, cave-like huts that, until last year, had been reliant on yak dung for illumination and warmth. Those days of primitive existence were over; families that had been subsistence farmers for centuries now had enough heat, enough light, and enough food to satisfy their needs. Children spent their days in a newly built school instead of working in the fields, and adults could turn a spigot to get water instead of depending on snowmelt to quench their thirst and irrigate their crops.

Though it was the middle of March, there was no expectation of an early spring. Warmth was always slow to arrive in this land nestled tightly between the Pamir and Hindu Kush mountain ranges, but the scraped-raw beauty of the place made up for the winter's length. The night sky was strewn with stars, with no clouds to obscure their luminescence. Razor-sharp silhouettes of the mountains edging the valley wore their high snows majestically. Pale blue and glowing in the almost primeval darkness, the snowfields resembled nothing so much as an ethereal tiara settled delicately on the top of the earth.

From the other side of the planet, Greg Simpson decided to destroy the serenity of that beautiful night in the frigid highlands of northeastern Afghanistan as a lesson to Flint, and to the world. He was going to teach everyone the true meaning of the word *power*. And show them who held it. All of it.

His game of vengeance began with a rapid and unseasonable rise in temperature. The few brave hikers who venture to cross the Wakhan ranges every year know enough to climb by night, aware that at such altitudes the snow's hard surface crust softens quickly under daylight's strong, unfiltered sunlight. As the dawn broke that day, however, the endless expanse of hard snowpack had already become glistening mush. The softened snow blanketing the peaks began to melt, to trickle, then rush, then thunder down the steep, barren slopes, pushing rocks and mud ahead of it into the tiny settlements sparsely dotting the slim corridor. The farmers' fields, so miraculously prosperous the season before and already furrowed and primed for another bountiful year, were washed away. As were the farmers, their families, livestock, livelihoods. Their goodwill.

A short while later, in a place halfway around the world from the Wakhan, but just as rural and nearly as remote, Maggie Price drove her lumbering twenty-five-year-old 125-horsepower John Deere tractor under the roof of the carport. She turned off the engine and the vibrations she'd endured for the last four hours, and most of the four hours before that, stopped abruptly. She climbed off the beast to stand on shaky legs. It still sometimes seemed hard to believe that she'd traded in her three-year-old fully loaded 5-series Beemer sedan for a ten-year-old Bronco and this aging contraption, both of which had forced her to learn more than she ever wanted to about combustion engines.

The sweat trickling from beneath her favorite but ratty Australian bush hat was scraped away with a cotton-clad arm that left her forehead tingling in its damp wake. Another day's work done on her 400-acre farm. Her finally-certified organic farm. The farm that had been in her family for 206 years, give or take a few months.

Hers was the only family farm left in the western half of tiny Bullston County, Indiana. Make that the only piece of arable land in the county not already owned by Flint AgroChemical—not that those bad boys weren't trying every trick in the book to get their hands on it.

Maggie pulled off her hat and ran her calloused hands through her short, wet hair. Despite the cool, early-spring weather, the sun had been pleasantly hot in a clear sky until the last hour or so, and she was sweating like a just-run racehorse. Working alone, it had taken her days to get her fields plowed and planted. That was in between repairing the overhead field irrigation system that was on its last legs and taking care of the chickens, cows, horses, and one heavily pregnant sow. The dirty, unglamorous work left her exhausted in a way working on Wall Street never had, but she wouldn't trade a minute of it.

When Maggie had announced she was buying out her grandparents, she'd stunned everyone she knew, including her parents and siblings, all of whom were firmly ensconced in the sprawling suburbs of various large and interchangeable American cities. But the decision had been easy: she'd loved visiting the farm as a child and the thought of her grandparents selling it to the soulless behemoth Flint was more than she could bear.

The land was too good to be destroyed by Flint's chemicals and greed. Flint's local land acquisition executives—gangsters, in her opinion—had seen things differently, and had done everything they could to get her off the land. They'd filed frivolous lawsuits designed to bankrupt her, but she'd succeeded in having most of them thrown out. Knowing the local judges had helped immeasurably. They'd sprayed the fields that bordered hers so heavily with herbicides and fertilizers that it had delayed organic certification on part of her land for more than a year. She'd solved that by devoting a strip a few acres wide along the entire perimeter of her farm to native prairie grasses and had that area specially designated as a wildlife refuge, which forced Flint to back off on its chemical use. She'd filmed Flint aircraft flying over her land and spewing something over her fields. The local TV news station had been happy to air the footage before sending it up to their network and loading it onto YouTube.

As tiresome as Flint's war games were, Maggie knew the company would keep up its efforts to oust her from her land. She'd sworn to herself that she would keep fighting back until she didn't have any fight left.

She walked the twenty-five yards along the pasture fence to the house as she dislodged the foam earplugs that kept her sane while on the tractor. At the western horizon, a dim glow hinted at the setting sun that lay behind a thick wall of ominous clouds. They had begun to accumulate in the last hour, and they looked bad. Real bad. Low, thick, and heavy, clouds like that only meant one thing: a storm would be here soon. It would be a gullywasher. Maybe worse.

In the last few minutes, the sky had begun brandishing the greenish glow that too often presaged a tornado. News that twisters were forming in the area wouldn't surprise Maggie. It was the right time of

year for them and the unseasonable temperature fluc-
tuations the region had been experiencing in the past
few days were priming the residents for a big hit. Days
dawned warm and grew scorching by late morning,
and then the temperature would plummet twenty degrees in five minutes a few hours later. Sometimes, it
was a lather-rinse-and-repeat day and that sequence
would happen two or even three times. It was weird,
but there was no such thing as normal weather in this
part of Indiana, and there never had been.

Maggie had seen too often what havoc those roller-
coaster temperatures could do, how fast they could
stir up a tornado. And she'd seen the damage twisters
could inflict. In the last few days, there had been tornadoes all over the state, but most had been fairly
small and hadn't done much beyond tearing up fields
and blowing down a few trees.

*That may be the only upside to having nothing but
factory-farms for miles in every direction: there's no
one for the tornadoes to kill and no homes to destroy.*

The cynicism that had become her new best friend
brought a wry curl to her mouth as she clomped up the
quaintly sagging wooden steps leading to the back
porch—she couldn't bear to fix them, they'd been that
way too long—and sat on the top step to pull off her
mud-caked, steel-toed boots. They were a long way
from the Ferragamo pumps she used to adore, just like
her new wardrobe staples of heavy jeans, waffle-weave
thermals, and plaid wool overshirts were a far cry
from the Armani suits and Kate Spade bags she'd worn
with such high-powered pride.

They're just different uniforms.

Maggie peeled off her two layers of thick cotton
socks and let the cooling air waft around her bare

toes, then stood and walked into the small clapboard house. Ten minutes later she was back on the porch with a glass of iced tea in her hand, with clean shorts and a T-shirt on her freshly showered body.

There was a menacing stillness to the air now, a heaviness she didn't like. The sky was darkening rapidly, but not to the gorgeous purply blue twilight she'd gotten used to seeing. The color was edging toward a vicious, venomous green, backlit by an unearthly yellow brightness that defied logic.

The wind picked up suddenly, blowing hard. A pot of geraniums she'd just planted last week crashed off the porch's middle step and shattered. The large leaves served as sails as the plant swirled dizzily across the gravel drive, scattering dirt as it went. Maggie glanced at the heavy Bilco doors that lay near the corner of the house. They led to the root cellar, the only safe place in a bad storm.

Time to go.

Turning to the screen door, she whistled for the dogs. She'd last seen them cowering under her bed.

The wind gained strength steadily, its sound changing from a low moan to a high-pitched keening. Underlying it now were the first rising notes of the county's tornado sirens, which hit their drone-like crescendo in seconds and held it.

She whistled for the dogs again, but the sound died on her tongue as the sky commanded her attention. On the not-so-distant horizon, a thin black vertical line danced sinuously, maniacally, against the backdrop of the vertiginous clouds. Maggie's stomach dropped. On land this flat, the horizon was only about three and a half miles away. A tornado could cover that distance in a New York minute.

She bellowed for the dogs, knowing she—they—had to get into the storm cellar *now*.

The tornado grew as she watched. Wider, taller. She was frozen with awe for critical seconds until the adrenaline rush hit her brain and every synapse fired at once. As she turned to run for the safety of the cellar, the winds pummeled her, shoved her against the peeling wood siding of the house. Her head smacked into the edge of the door frame, setting sparkles of pain dancing at the edges of her vision. Ignoring the throbbing sting on her forehead, she ran along the porch, the wind urging her along, and leaped over the railing.

Holding on to the wood with one hand, Maggie flung out her other arm for stability. In that spread-eagled moment, her baggy shirt and shorts captured the stream of air blasting her from behind. She lost her balance—and gained momentum.

Stumbling, nearly cartwheeling as she fought clumsily to regain control of her limbs in the face of the merciless wind, Maggie passed the heavy metal doors that led to her only possible sanctuary. She couldn't turn back. The wind wouldn't let her. She knew then she'd never reach the strong cellar walls that would have sheltered her. She'd have to face the storm in the open.

Her terror was a thing alive. The air that bullied her was turning black, becoming thick and fragrant with the earth she'd plowed earlier. Fine particles of soil bit into her skin like the teeth of a thousand evil gods, lodging in her streaming eyes, her screaming mouth. The screech of the wind was wild, and sounded like the demons in the Hell she'd grown up hearing about. The rapidly dropping air pressure was making her eardrums fit to burst.

Her body slammed into the huge elm she'd climbed as a child, that her father and grandfather had climbed as children. The impact knocked the breath out of her, nearly knocked the sense out of her. She didn't care. The tree was solid and Maggie clung to it. The rough, striated bark scraped her cheek raw as she looked over her shoulder, turning her face into the wind. The nightmarish vision before her drove all thought from her mind.

A spinning, sucking cone of darkness moved toward her as if with a purpose, as if *she* was what it so angrily wanted to consume.

From behind the barn, a burst of flapping, alien color rose into the churning air. It took Maggie a minute to realize that the henhouse had exploded, and the chickens were being pulled into the storm. The roof of the barn tore away from its walls with a scream that was nearly human. Shingles and beams spun up into the sky as the barn wall nearest her began to shake and shimmy. One by one the wide boards came loose as if pried by unseen fingers and were flung into the raging river of wind.

Inside the destroyed barn, both horses reared wildly, lashing out at the sides of their stalls in their panic to escape. Two of the three cows had managed to break the loose halter ropes tethering them to their spaces along the milking wall. Loose tools and equipment, now airborne, slammed into them, stabbing, gouging, buckling them, making the maddened thousand-pound beasts crash into walls as they did their best to stampede out of what was left of the barn. Maggie watched in horror as the Holsteins were lifted off their feet and slammed into the solid fieldstone back wall of the structure. Whether they were killed or just stunned, the fight in them died and the cows' limp bodies were sucked into the furious sky. The third, her young, gentle Jersey, fought insanely against the rope that kept her in place until she, too, was picked up by the wind. The halter, the rope, and the ring it was attached to, embedded into the stone wall, held the frantic, flailing beast earthbound, but the wind would not surrender her. In disbelief, Maggie watched as the heifer's head was ripped from its body. Blood and tissue spewed into the storm as the carcass was carried aloft. The head, held together by its halter, smashed over and over again into the wall like a gory tetherball.

A roar like that of a jet engine filled her ears as the center of the storm bore down on her, and the tree Maggie clung to began to shudder and rock. Closing her eyes, she tightened her grip, snaking her arms and legs around the massive trunk and holding on to it with every bit of strength and fear left in her. Her mind was numb, too stunned even for prayer.

The tree heaved with the wind, buckling the ground surrounding it, and then the huge gnarled roots beneath her snapped, reluctantly relinquishing their century-long claim on the earth. Maggie opened her mouth to scream. Choking clods of soil filled her mouth, stifling her. The wind held her fast against the tree. Breathing became nearly impossible. Then the massive elm heaved again and began to fall. The aching rasp of roots being ripped from the ground surrounded her. She burrowed her body into the tree as if desperate to become part of it as the tree rose, then crashed to the ground. It began to slide.

The shed-sized root ball, finally unconstrained, provided an irresistible challenge to the wall of air pushing against it. The elm began to pick up speed as it skimmed the ground with Maggie still clinging to it, an inconsequential payload on a surface-hugging missile.

The roar of the wind now overrode all other sound. Maggie felt a ferocious pain as her eardrums burst. Breathing was a herculean effort. Her fingers were numb from the intensity of their grip on the tree; the muscles in her arms and legs were on fire.

An errant lightning bolt struck the ground nearby. The tree split in a violent explosion of fire and wood that flung Maggie into the windstream. Her first sensation was a stabbing shock, her second a miraculous peace. No sharp tree bark against her abraded, bleeding skin, no throbbing pain. There was just the wind that carried her—

The impact when Maggie landed knocked all the breath, all the life from her body. For a moment, her corpse lay face up, draped limply over the low stone wall of the pasture nearest the house. Then Nature flipped the lifeless shell of battered flesh to the sodden ground, where it flailed erratically for a moment. The wind caught its most aerodynamic angle and sent it skidding across the muddy, puddled pasture, just another piece of debris.

CHAPTER

It had been just under three months since she'd been sworn into office, and President Helena Hernandez had finally gotten comfortable in the large oval room, if not the larger-than-life role. Navigating the debris-strewn trail of not-so-natural disasters left behind by her predecessor, Winslow Benson, was perilous enough; doing it as the first female *and* first Hispanic—and a *cubana* at that—president only made the journey that much more exciting. Terrifying, if she wanted to be completely honest, which was something she hadn't been in decades, not since being sworn into her first term on the Miami-Dade school board thirty years ago.

Helena looked at her secretary, Maribeth Wonson, with a mix of confusion and disbelief. It wasn't yet five o'clock on Thursday morning, but she'd gotten up and showered an hour ago, then had a live radio interview with a German journalist. She'd hoped to go back to bed for half an hour, but Maribeth's words had just negated that.

"Say that again." Helena sat back slowly in her chair—John F. Kennedy's chair. It did make her back feel better. Not to mention what it did for her soul.

"The secretary of defense is on the phone. He'd like ten minutes."

"What does he want to talk about?"

"Afghanistan. There's been a setback."

This was what Helena liked about Maribeth: her perpetual serenity, her utter unflappability. When Maribeth was around, it always seemed okay to stop for a deep breath in the face of dire news. The downside was that Maribeth's face never revealed the true severity of a situation. The announcement of an imminent nuclear attack would likely be delivered in the same calm, quiet tone with the same pleasant smile.

Helena shifted her gaze from her secretary's face to the fireplace opposite her desk and then along the smooth, curved expanse of the room's pristine walls. Her eyes came to rest on the small modern bronze of Atlas that stood on a tall table outside the door to her private study. She'd asked for the sculpture to be placed there so she could remind herself that she was not the first person, nor would she be last, to feel as if she carried the weight of the world on her shoulders. She loved looking at it. The clean, hard lines of the Greek god's straining muscles and tendons seemed to impart their strength to her. She welcomed it as she continually, privately reassured herself that her presence in this room, her right to occupy it, was more than a victory of class or race or gender. Being here was an honor, a privilege, and an immense obligation. Privately, she also knew it was a tribute to her tenacity.

Just being in this room soothed her, although everything she did here impressed itself heavily upon her mind, and frequently her soul, an immutable burden. Helena prayed daily for the strength of Atlas. She would need it when she took this call. Her secretary of defense was no trusted ally. His appointment had been her first surrender to the reality of Washington politics; his approach to life and war necessitated a blatant compromise of her core values. She considered his presence in her Cabinet an expedient, and politically necessary, evil.

Helena brought her gaze back to Maribeth. "When's my next opening?"

"Now."

With a minute nod of her head, Helena replied, "I'll take the call."

She picked up the handset of the secure phone on her desk and heard the operator announce her presence on the line.

"Good morning, Ms. President. Thank you for taking this call."

"You're welcome, Secretary Bonner," she replied coolly. "What can I do for you?"

After a split second's hesitation, the former admiral cleared his throat. "A freak storm in northeastern Afghanistan triggered huge floods in a remote valley. The region is sparsely populated, and the damage is somewhat contained, but the government is concerned that the region's entire population may have been wiped out. It will impact the elections, ma'am."

Just hearing the word made Helena's eyes narrow. Delaying the elections was her SecDef's highest priority—in direct contradiction to her own. She frowned. "Floods? Isn't it still winter over there?"

"Yes, ma'am. We don't have a lot of information yet, but it appears that there was some unseasonable high-altitude warming that triggered a critical melt of the glaciers in the northern border territory. Two mountain ranges surround a long, narrow valley. We're still reviewing satellite data to get a better idea of what happened."

"Where did it happen? I mean specifically."

"The Wakhan Corridor."

Helena felt her mood plummet further. The region was the only bright spot in that grim, decimated country.

"*Was*" *is right*. "What's the situation on the ground?" she asked, picking up the fountain pen Maribeth always placed next to the phone. She uncapped it, drew a slash of blue on the memo pad nearby.

"It's obvious from the latest satellite comms that entire villages have disappeared. The recon teams we deployed hit the ground a little while ago and the images they're sending back show deep flows of mud and ice. None of the footage shows any survivors. Communications were wiped out." He paused. "I've already spoken to President Wardak, and let him know that, at his request, we will deploy additional units to assist his personnel in the search-and-recovery efforts."

"Thank you."

"If I may, Ms. President, I'd like to remind you that all of the Americans in the region are civilians. Most of them are from Flint AgroChemical. Intelligence estimates indicate there could have been as many as thirty of them in the affected region when the storm hit."

The president let out a long, silent breath. The secretary of defense's effort to refrain from gloating was obvious. Helena could practically feel his joy and loathing through the phone, and she had to fight the urge to let him know the latter sentiment was mutual.

Her administration's support of Flint's innovative agricultural programs in several deeply rural areas of Afghanistan had infuriated and disgusted Secretary Bonner and caused their first serious clash only weeks after his rapid nomination and congressional confirmation as secretary. The Afghan upcountry hit by the flood was more politically stable than most regions in that ravaged country. Bonner viewed any nonmilitary involvement there as dangerous despite knowing that the local populations weren't open supporters of the Taliban, and still lived a lifestyle more medieval than modern. He had been adamant that there was no reason to change that; bringing them into the twenty-first century would also bring them into the conflict, he'd argued. Providing new infrastructure and nurturing new wealth in the region in the form of crops and livelihoods would backfire by attracting the wrong element, and then his already stretched troops would have to be deployed to defend the long, treacherous, porous borders from newly interested parties, such as the Taliban, Al-Qaeda, and opium traders.

The discussions had been unpleasant, but Helena had not been persuaded by his arguments.

"What else?" she asked tightly. "What about the elections?"

She heard murmurings on the other end of the call, as if he were speaking to someone not on the line. "Ms. President, President Wardak just announced that he has postponed the elections until the situation in the Wakhan is stabilized."

"And how long will that be?" she snapped.

"He's suggesting two months at the earliest, ma'am. Most likely it will take longer than that. The area is very remote, as I said, and earthquake-prone."

Helena felt her temper rise and tamped it down before it shot to her tipping point. Two months would put the date of the elections right about at the time the military—*her* military commanders—had wanted them to take place.

How convenient. But how in the name of the Mother of God did he make it happen?

The thought startled her with its vehemence. She snapped abruptly upright in her chair.

Staring at Atlas, hard, Helena felt a cold finger of dread skitter across the back of her neck. Like people everywhere in the country—in the world—she'd heard the rumors about weather machines and rogue weather events after Hurricane Simone devastated the Eastern Seaboard and Katrina battered the Gulf Coast within months of each other.

The following year she'd gotten onto the House Intelligence Committee and had learned which of the scary, way-out-there stories were rumors and which were only called that to hide the eerie truth. In closed-door hearings, the committee had heard testimony that yes, Russia had had moderate success keeping rain from falling on their flamboyant May Day parades and that China, too, had been able to keep rain at bay to some degree during the Olympics. But the committee members had been assured by everyone who appeared before them that, despite small triumphs in line with what their Communist counterparts could do, the prospect of any nation using weather as a weapon was a far-off goal. Even the HAARP installation in Alaska, they'd been told, hadn't been able to accomplish that.

However, those assurances had been made years ago, when the other side of the aisle controlled the White House—and the flow of information on the topic was controlled by none other than then-admiral Frederick Bonner, who had risen through the ranks of the Navy as an atmospheric scientist before setting his sights on the Pentagon's E-ring. And since Helena had become president, there hadn't been a reason to broach the subject of weather manipulation.

Until now.

"Secretary Bonner, you described this as a 'freak storm,'" she said, scratching the words onto the memo pad.

"Yes, ma'am."

"And the region shares a border with China? I believe you called it 'porous.'"

"Yes."

"Could those things be connected in any way?"

His hesitation was slight, almost undetectable. Helena could picture the look of wary shock on his craggy, treacherous face. "Ma'am?"

"Would the Chinese stand to benefit from the destruction in this valley? Or from the elections being postponed?"

"Not that I'm aware of, ma'am."

It was coldly gratifying to hear such caution in a voice that, moments ago, had to conceal its jubilation. "Check into it and report back to me."

"You want me to— You think China did this? Made the storm?" he blustered.

Helena let a cold smile shape her mouth. "You sound incredulous. That I find disingenuous at best, considering your former job, Secretary Bonner." She paused. "I don't believe in coincidences. I would imagine you don't, either. Weather manipulation has been discussed for decades, and the Chinese have been playing with the idea as long as we have. I want to know what your experts think about my question."

"But—"

"I'll look forward to receiving your report as soon as you can get it to me."

Tess Beauchamp struggled to keep a pleasant expression on her face as she listened to her ostensibly worthy opponent spout war-mongering drivel.

Sitting under hot lights in an otherwise darkened auditorium wasn't the way she would have chosen to spend a gorgeous late afternoon in early spring on the quaint Mediterranean island of Malta, but she didn't have much choice in the matter. It was the last day of the invitation-only biannual NATO conference on advances in military weaponry. Tess was the main attraction for the conference's final and much-anticipated presentation: a face-off between two of the leading experts in the field of ionospheric manipulation. The topic was the latest advances in the use of weather as a weapon.

Tess and her opponent sat in comfortable chairs several feet apart from each other on the stage, separated by an Oriental rug and a pair of small tables bearing live plants and sweating carafes of iced water. The moderator of the debate sat center stage, looking as neutral and bobble-headed as a line judge at a tennis match.

While the chairs might have been comfortable, Tess was not and tried to subtly shift her position yet again, cursing whatever mental demon had possessed her to wear a skirt to this dog-and-pony show. Especially a skirt that came to a halt well above her knees.

The common-sense demon that assumed I'd be standing behind a lectern when facing a room full of men wearing brass baubles and campaign ribbons, not sitting with my ass at their eye level.

The organizer of the event, a charming, if slightly doddery elder of the weather-science community, had told her right before she went onstage that her opponent, a short, wiry, generally snide Austrian, had refused to stand next to her, insisting that they both be seated. Tess didn't need to be told the reason. She was six-foot-one in her bare feet, and Herr Twerp was a mere five-foot-four. He could make Nicolas Sarkozy feel tall.

So here she was, with her ass paralyzed from sitting in one position too long and with no hope of relief unless she wanted to give an auditorium full of NATO generals a crotch shot they'd never forget.

The worst part was that she was sorely tempted to do it.

"Dr. Beauchamp? Your final comment, please. One minute."

She nodded to the moderator, then made eye contact with Napoléon Lite. "If you'll allow me to be candid—" Tess ignored the smattering of laughter from the audience. "I don't take issue with your position because I'm a peacenik, as you so charmingly called me. I take issue with your position because it's based on a convoluted premise. You talk about the benefits of using weather as an offensive weapon, but if we use weather as a *deterrent* to conflict instead of as a *weapon,* the world at large will be better off.

"Poverty, as we've already discussed, is frequently a significant factor in the escalation of regional and even international conflict, and can be a clear precursor to declared war. And let's face it: wars aren't generally started over politics. That's just the hair spray and high heels. Wars are begun over borders, land, or natural resources; take one government in the mood to acquire, add a population made restive by basic needs not being met, throw in a natural disaster or two, or a few months of suboptimal weather, and you have a classic recipe for war."

Tess paused, gracefully pushing a long lock of blond hair behind one ear, and smiled at the man opposite her on the stage before continuing. "By regulating the weather for peaceful purposes in countries on the brink of an escalation of conflict, by operating in concert with ongoing humanitarian efforts, poverty could be radically diminished, which means wars could be averted. This approach does not have to be limited to places that are already in trouble. We have the technology to effect real change, positive change. And it can be applied everywhere. Anywhere," she said, leaning forward in her seat and only just refraining from pointing an accusing finger at him.

"Populations that are prosperous and happy have little incentive to disrupt their lives and civic structure and decimate their populations to support the high risks and no-to-low rewards associated with turning their surroundings into a war zone. To the contrary, prosperous societies are highly motivated to maintain the status quo. For the sake of a sound bite, I call my approach 'mutually assured prosperity,'" she finished as she saw the small red light blink on. She leaned back in her seat and folded her hands in her lap.

The moderator turned to allow Tess's opponent the last word. The little Austrian was already shaking his head vigorously. "I fear you are naïve, Dr. Beauchamp, and I know you are deliberately skewing my position. I am not speaking of war, I am speaking of technology. It is indisputable that we have the technology. It should be *used*," he said in his heavily accented voice, his finger stabbing the air for emphasis. "Call its use 'preemptive' or 'proactive' or 'offensive.' The words matter little. What matters is that the atmosphere, the weather, should be used as both a strategic and a tactical weapon to guard against rogue elements achieving any sort of critical mass in conflicts.

"We have seen, in Afghanistan and Pakistan, in Madrid and London and your own New York City, what these well-funded miscreants can do if left unchecked." He shrugged impatiently. "I agree that poverty can be used effectively to start wars, certainly. But it can be used to end them, too, because the hand that feeds a starving, war-weary population will be the hand of the victor."

You can't be serious. Bomb them, starve them, then save them? Tess bit her lip to keep from saying it out loud.

"And so I say," he continued, stabbing the air again with a stubby index finger, "that weather must be used strategically in terms of keeping enemies off balance. Even in happy, prosperous nations, there is always a segment of the population that gets greedy while the rest remain content, or at least complacent. As a tactical measure, using weather events—disruptions—to keep the populations focused on domestic concerns is critical. Droughts, flooding, cyclonic storms—they will keep governments' and populations' minds and money away from troublesome external issues they can't afford to support."

Like economic growth? You nasty little worm.

"And we will have to leave it there. Thank you both," the moderator interjected smoothly, and led the audience in a round of polite applause.

Tess turned off her microphone and unclipped it from the lapel of her suit jacket, then pushed herself to her feet as gracefully as she could, hiding a grimace as blood rushed painfully into her numb feet. She crossed the short distance between them and shook her opponent's hand with an outward show of professionalism, while secretly delighting in the small barrage of flashes from the approved press pool gathered at the foot of the stage. It was neither coincidence nor fashion sense that had driven her to wear three-inch heels today; it had been pure deviltry.

The thought of those pictures kept a genuine smile on Tess's face as she moved through the elegant but obligatory meet-and-greet reception that followed. She liked stepping out of the chaos of academic research and back into the knife-creased world of the military every now and then. She'd grown up on the grand poobah of Cold War military installations—the White Sands Missile Range—as the child of civilian employees, so she understood the mind-set. Not that she liked it. Both sets of her grandparents had worked on the Manhattan Project, her parents on Cold War "peacekeeper" technology of the nuclear variety. Despite the immersion and the indoctrination, Tess had never been able to buy into the idea that aggressor nations fought for peace. She'd always wanted to know what the side that was attacked was fighting for, but the people she asked generally sidestepped the question.

It wasn't a coincidence that she'd been drawn to what she'd initially thought—perhaps dreamed— would be a career in a gentle, incorruptible science:

weather. But by the time she was finishing her second doctorate, her eyes had been opened. Lucrative job offers had started to materialize. The interest governments and corporations had in weather manipulation had nothing to do with small farms or hardworking, sunburned farm families. No, corporations wanted to control the weather to keep their economic interests protected while knocking around those of their competitors. Governments' interests were even less defensible.

By then, though, Tess had big loans to pay off and a reputation that was beginning to shine, so she'd locked away her doubts, compromised a few values, and swore to herself that she would always direct her research toward good, peaceful ends.

But all too often she landed in situations like this one, where she was one of a few civilians in a room full of decorated, war-hardened military lifers, the only dove in a room full of hawks. Then she'd get congratulated on her latest theories—and told how they'd been applied. It wasn't always her idea of a good time.

As unobtrusively as possible, Tess made her escape from the party. It wasn't that she minded being challenged on her positions: she'd tell anyone who would listen that she firmly believed peace would inevitably trump war every time. She'd just been indoors too long and needed some fresh air.

She was staying in a boutique hotel only a few blocks from the conference center, so she walked, enjoying the warm Mediterranean sunshine and salt air. As she crossed the cozy, old-fashioned lobby, one of the clerks emerged from behind the ornate reception desk and hurried to her, pressing an envelope into her hand.

Inside it was a business card sporting the Flint AgroChemical logo above the name GIANNI BARONE, VICE PRESIDENT AND DIRECTOR OF STRATEGIC RE-SEARCH. She flipped it over, not surprised to see a few lines of strong, slanted script running across it.

I'll be at the Crown and Prince, three blocks from your hotel. Get directions from the concierge. Wear something comfortable.

Tess grinned, slid the card into the pocket of her jacket, and stepped into the single old-fashioned brass-grilled elevator. Fifteen minutes later, much more comfortable in a long, loose skirt, silk T-shirt, and low-heeled sandals, she left the hotel without talking to the concierge. She'd find the place on her own, and enjoy the chaos of the streets on the way.

Like so many modern cities with ancient roots, Valletta had become a colorful mishmash of crumbling stucco walls painted the hot colors of the sunset and bland office towers wearing concrete sheaths of mid-century gray. The few main roads were broad and lined with palms, but choked with cars, bikes and scooters, delivery vans, and the occasional eye-popping yellow tourist bus. And pedestrians, lots of pedestrians. Tess preferred to walk along the smaller streets and alleyways, where high walls and narrow lanes conspired to create their own shade. Parked cars slouched along the skinny sidewalks, two wheels resting well up onto the curb. Clay pots crammed with herbs and climbing roses hugged vividly painted doors peering out from intermittent niches.

As soon as her eyes adjusted to the pub's dim interior, Tess spied Gianni sitting at a small table against the wall, nursing an almost full beer. She slid onto the low stool next to him.

"That was some message. I think you reached new heights in brevity," she said, pushing her sunglasses up into her messy pouf of blond hair.

"I didn't think you'd mind," he said with an answering smile. "Can I get you something?"

She shook her head. "I had a glass of wine at the reception. That's enough for now. So, I'm dressed for comfort. What did you have in mind? A harbor tour by water taxi? A spin around the island on mopeds?"

"How about just a little walk so we can talk and take in the flavor of the city?" he asked, still smiling, and stood up.

"Sounds good. Aren't you going to finish your beer?"

Shaking his head, he replied, "It's warm. I forgot how hard this place tries to be authentic."

Out in the softening early-evening sunshine, they began to stroll along the thoroughfare, the sky just starting to go pastel and smudgy ahead of them.

"So, have you thought more about my offer?" Gianni asked, not looking at her.

"Of course," Tess replied, just as casually.

"Have you come to a conclusion? Are you ready to come stateside?"

She sent him a sidelong glance. "You mean 'to the dark side,' don't you? Antarctica is hardly stateside. The facility isn't even in American territory."

"The 'dark side'? That's a bit melodramatic. Even if that were the truth, it would be immaterial. Our facility has redefined the term 'state of the art.' You're going to love it."

"Oooh, I like it when you go all psychological on me."

"What do you mean?"

"I'm 'going to' love it?"

"A slip of the tongue."

"Uh-huh."

They stopped talking while they waited at a corner. When the light changed and they were back in the flow of foot traffic, Tess resumed speaking. "Okay, to be honest, I'm still thinking about it. But I like living in Europe. The pace of life is easy, the buildings are old, and Paris has been good to me. My apartment is great, my wardrobe is fabulous, my colleagues have finally accepted my accent, and I've learned to cook things I never imagined I'd ever want to eat."

"Sounds like heaven," Gianni said drily. "Come on. I fund half your research. It's time for some reciprocity."

His comment was true, but it still flicked at her ego like the tip of a knife. "You might fund me, but I'm still independent," she shot back a little too quickly.

Gianni said nothing, just laughed quietly. Tess rewarded him with a dirty look.

"Tess, none of us has ever been independent. Not when we were in school, not when we were at HAARP," he said, referring to the military research facility in Alaska where they'd met sixteen years ago. "And certainly not now. Since I've been at Flint, we've funded every grant you've ever proposed, even the green-weenie ones and the ones that went flat. All we'd like now is a little bit of your time. Exclusively."

She let out a short laugh. "A little bit? You said two years, minimum, with an option to extend it. That's a long time on the Ice," she pointed out. "It's not like you want me to give up Paris for Manhattan. You want me to give up my life in Paris to park myself in the middle of the East Antarctic Plateau. *Quel* bummer."

"You like being on the Ice."

"*Liked*. I'm older now and not as boy-crazy. And I have a heightened respect for creature comforts."

"TESLA is more comfortable than you can imagine. We need you, Tess."

She gave him a sidelong glance as they stopped at another intersection. "I don't think you've fully described that need. In fact, there are a lot of things you haven't described fully."

"Like what?"

"Like what is Flint doing in Antarctica anyway?" she asked softly, aware of the crowd around them. "The company started out hawking seeds and fertilizer, then Frankenfood, and then got into wind power before wind power was cool."

Gianni smiled but didn't answer until they began to move with traffic again. "The company has always been ahead of the curve," he replied, his voice casual and even a little amused.

"That's one way of putting it. Way back when, Flint would have had its pick of places to set up a wind farm test bed. Tarifa, Spain. Foote Creek Rim, Wyoming. Kenya's Chalbi Desert. Or any of a dozen other places from southern New Zealand to western Ireland to the coast of Norway." She paused and gave him a pointed look. "But Flint didn't choose any of those places, all of which are logical places for wind farms. It chose a scrappy, scrubby part of West Texas."

He replied smoothly, "Where's the challenge in setting up a test you know you'll pass? Besides, Flint had determined that it would be smart to put an energy generation facility near some place that needs lots of energy. And the Dallas/Fort Worth area was booming."

Tess rolled her eyes at him. "You never struck me

as a Kool-Aid drinker, Gianni, but it sounds like you've developed a taste for it. Are you telling me that Croyden Flint put adventure ahead of profits?"

"How about ahead of *immediate* profits? The primary issue then was applied research, Tess, not municipal power generation. That was considered a side benefit."

"One that paid off."

He grinned. "In spades. Flint's investment in research is always well rewarded by the new technologies it develops."

"So now the old man wants to conquer the last frontier?" Tess asked.

"There aren't too many challenges left on this planet. Naturally, we're looking into deep-sea exploration and exploitation, but . . ." Gianni shrugged expansively. "Flint strategists aren't stupid. With TESLA, we've capitalized on all that has gone before on the Ice—the invention of self-correcting support pillars with hydraulic lifts so installations don't get buried. Flying in materials just like the U.S. did when it built its big base near the Pole back in the late nineties. Hugely expensive, but worth it, to be in the best place to do what we need to do. So now we're the leaders of the pack. The rest of the installations on the Ice are stuck in the last century, doing passive research, observational research. We're doing the big stuff."

"The Belgians—"

"The Belgians." He snorted dismissively, almost under his breath. "You know what they're crowing about? That their new installation uses solar power supplemented by wind. That it generates zero emissions. You'd think they invented—"

"Hey, just a minute. They invited me to view the

mock-up. It's an impressive station. How can you knock it? What are you doing differently at TESLA?" Tess asked.

"Plenty. Why would anyone use solar panels on the Ice?" He shook his head in derision. "It's dark for nearly half the year, but the panels still have to be maintained. We, on the other hand, are fully supported by wind. Thirty high-yield vertical turbines running twenty-four/seven, capturing winds that routinely top forty and frequently exceed one hundred miles per hour. And it's all converted to hydrogen. Fuel cells do the rest." He paused and Tess gave him what he was waiting for: wide-eyed admiration. She realized her mouth was even hanging open just the slightest bit, and shut it immediately.

Gianni grinned at her and took her elbow. "I thought you'd be impressed."

"Well . . . yeah," she stammered as he steered her across the wide boulevard.

"We're at the bleeding edge of science and we have an endless source of clean power, Tess. That can't be too far off your idea of paradise. And we want you to run it." He paused and she let the compliment and all of its implications run through her.

As soon as they reached the sidewalk, Tess moved out of the throng of early-evening foot traffic and leaned back against a sun-and-shadow-dappled wall, brushing away the fingers of a twining vine attempting to entangle themselves in her hair. Trying to keep her game face on was too much effort and she finally let herself laugh, releasing the slightly stunned, slightly disbelieving joy that was bubbling through her brain and bloodstream. In a minute, she scaled it back to a broad smile.

This is it.

This was the opportunity she'd always hoped for and never thought she'd get. To be research director of TESLA, the most advanced weather research station in the world. It was akin to being handed your most improbable dream. She'd have absolute authority, absolute power—

I'll be the first person it won't corrupt absolutely. No. I'll be the first person it won't corrupt, period.

Tess closed her eyes and tilted her face to the warmth of the setting sun, letting herself become lost in the swarm of thoughts rushing through her mind. If she took charge of TESLA, she'd be able to put into practice all the ideas and ideals she'd been working toward for her entire career. She wouldn't just hypothesize, research, and teach; she could *do*. Make the world better, one stricken place at a time. She'd be able to prove to the naysayers, like that sneering little Austrian, that she knew exactly what she was talking about.

Cool triumph shot through her like quicksilver and she returned her gaze to Gianni, who stood next to her wearing a smile that bore its own brand of victory.

"The look on your face right now is one I've only seen in films. Usually lit by a warm spotlight and backed by a choir of angels. Or maybe just a flock of cartoon bluebirds flying in a holding pattern around your head," he said with a laugh. "Actually, you look like you could use a cigarette."

"It's that bad, is it?" she replied, unable to hide her delight.

"Worse." He paused. "So can I take that look as a yes?" he asked softly.

"Oh, man." Tess let out a breath on a laugh. "I . . . oh, man, Gianni. I need to think about this—"

He shook his head, his smile fading, and glanced down at his feet. "Think about what? Whether you really want what you've worked toward for twenty years?" he asked, sharp exasperation edging his quiet words. "Don't overanalyze this, Tess. It's simple. We want Greg out and you in." He shook his head again and raised his gaze to her face, his expression bemused. "You surprise me. I thought you'd jump at the chance to—" He broke off and shrugged.

The unspoken reminder of her troubled history with Greg Simpson delivered a sharp nick to Tess's ego, causing her excitement to dim. She took a quick, deep breath.

"Oh. It's been years since I've even thought of that . . . of him, Gianni," she said, as casually as she could manage. She pushed away from the wall and together they re-entered the stream of pedestrians. "I've never believed in revenge. In fact, I think it's pointless. So, while I'm overwhelmed at your offer, the thought of replacing Greg holds no particular thrill for me."

"You sound out of breath. Are we walking too fast?"

You jerk. This is not the way to persuade me. "I'm fine," she replied, forcing herself to return to her natural state of calm.

"Tess, Croyden has been looking for a way to bring you on board ever since that first grant proposal you wrote."

She looked at him. "That was years ago. He saw it?"

"He reviews all of them. He's the one who makes the final decisions on every grant."

"I didn't know that."

"You do now." He paused. "The bottom line, Tess, is that we want a change in the direction down there, and we want that change to be you. It's as simple as that."

"Gianni, nothing is ever that simple. I can understand why you want me in; tell me why you want Greg out. He's been there, what, six years? What's he doing wrong?"

"He's done nothing wrong," Gianni replied smoothly. "We just want him back at headquarters to head up a new project."

"Don't blow smoke up my skirt," Tess snapped, her delight of a moment ago completely gone. "He'll never agree to leave the Ice for a corner office in some suburban hell. Besides, it's April. You can't get there from here at this time of year. The travel window slammed shut well over a month ago."

"We can reopen it," he replied without hesitation. "Our fleet, our pilots . . . it's a non-issue."

Right. If they have no fear of death. Tess refrained from rolling her eyes. "Who's his second in command? Why couldn't that person run it?"

"It's Nik Forde."

The faint, remembered heat of an old romance warmed her face. "Oh."

"Is that a problem? Didn't your paths cross at HAARP before you, um, left?"

They not only crossed, they merged. She cleared her throat. "Of course it's not a problem. I know Nik. He's a smart guy. Why isn't he taking over? He's already there."

"Nik isn't a leader. You are."

"I'm not a leader. I've never led anything in my life," she countered.

"Maybe. But you were the only one of the postdocs who stood up to Greg—"

"That didn't happen for any noble reason, Gianni. It was an exercise in thoroughly justified, if slightly irrational, anger," she pointed out.

"No matter. You stood up to him when the rest of us, including Nik, sucked up to him and cowered if he so much as looked at us. If that doesn't make you a leader, it at least makes you a hero."

The overblown praise goosed her ego, and Tess tried not to laugh as they came to a stop at the curb. "I'm definitely not a hero, Gianni. Quit reading so many comic books. So, okay, last chance. If you really want me down there, you have to give me a good reason. A *real* reason."

Gianni didn't answer right away. They crossed the street and he gently steered her toward a small cluster of tables outside a bistro. They sat at a distance from the other patrons and after they'd ordered drinks, he met her eyes.

"Okay, Tess. You never heard this and I never said it," he began quietly. "For the past few years, some strange things have been happening in places they shouldn't and I think—no, I know—Greg is behind them."

The grave look in Gianni's eyes made Tess's breath catch in her throat and his words triggered an uncomfortably hot churn in her stomach. "What kinds of things?"

His gaze skimmed over her face before he answered her. "Bad things. Political things. Things we never authorized and never would authorize, Tess."

"You think he's . . . gone rogue?" she asked, unconsciously dropping her voice to a whisper.

Gianni shrugged, then nodded slowly. "Could be. I've been fielding some odd requests from NOAA and

NASA in the last few months. A few weeks ago, I got invited to speak to some program sponsors at the Naval Research Lab."

"Invited?"

"The request didn't leave me any room to refuse, but it was worded more politely than a subpoena." His voice was tight.

"Which program sponsors?"

He looked at her and lifted his glass to his lips, saying nothing.

"HAARP?" Tess asked, picking up the wineglass that had been placed in front of her. She didn't realize her hands were shaking until some of the wine sloshed over the side. She set it down and folded her hands, pressing them into her lap as she watched Gianni's face. There was nothing lighthearted about his expression now.

Gianni nodded.

"Why did they want to talk to you?" she asked.

"Seems they're not getting the sort of results from their equipment that they're used to."

A thrill shot through Tess. She rested an elbow on the patterned metal of the tabletop and set her chin onto her balled fist. "So, either they're being interfered with . . ."

"Or?" Gianni prompted her when she didn't continue.

"Or . . . it's ludicrous, Gianni. I can't even say it," she protested, leaning back in her chair, folding her arms across her chest.

"I want to hear it. Say it, Tess."

"Or the properties of the ionosphere have changed," she finished quietly.

Gianni lifted an olive out of the small dish the waiter

had left on the table. "Have *been* changed," he said before popping it into his mouth. "Greg's taken your research on plasma boundaries and warped it, taken your solar proton response algorithms and bastardized them. He's doing everything your esteemed opponent was talking about today."

"Why?" she hissed, outraged.

"You tell me. Personal profit? Because he can?" Gianni shrugged and reached for another olive. "You may not be the only person who could go to TESLA and change things, but you're the only person I'd trust to do it. Greg used your ideas to let the genie out of the bottle, Tess. You're the only one who can put it back."

It was approaching midnight when Gianni climbed out of the small launch onto the landing deck of the enormous power yacht *Game Changer,* which was moored within view of his hotel overlooking the marina at Portomaso. He walked up the steps to the main deck and entered the large saloon with easy familiarity. The barefoot gray-haired man across the room rose from his chair with a smile, extending his hand as he greeted Gianni with genuine delight.

His summerweight khakis were wrinkled and his silk shirt untucked and open-necked, but Croyden Flint's distinguished bearing and smooth, cultured voice bespoke his education and social rank. He was an American aristocrat, one of the last of that rarified breed descended from the pioneers of America's Gilded Age.

"Gianni, good to see you."

The older man's hand was warm and dry, his grip firm.

"Thank you, sir. It's a pleasure to see you again,"

Gianni said with just the right mixture of respect and obsequiousness.

"Have a seat. How did your conversation go with Dr. Beauchamp?"

"I'm pleased to report that she's agreed to come on board, Mr. Flint. I've already notified the office. We'll smooth things over for her with the university, maintain her apartment in Paris for her." He shrugged. "Whatever it takes for her to be comfortable with the move. She'll be with me when I return to Connecticut in two days," Gianni said, letting a smile cross his mouth. "She should be at TESLA within three weeks."

The chairman of Flint AgroChemical laughed heartily and clapped Gianni on the shoulder, then turned to cross the room. "Excellent. This will teach that damned Pentagon bomb-jockey Medev to try an end run around me. What does she know about the situation?"

"Enough to get her down there," Gianni replied, feeling relaxed for the first time in more than a month. "I had to tell her more than I intended to, but not enough to spook her."

"She's okay with it?"

"Not entirely. She's clearly uncomfortable at the thought of what Simpson might be doing, and she's got a do-gooder streak that she has trouble fighting. The point is, sir, that she's agreed to go and doesn't have any illusions about what she'll face when she gets there. She knows Nik Forde from her days at HAARP."

"Is that a good thing?"

"I don't think it's a bad thing," Gianni answered with a shrug.

"And Simpson?" the chairman asked, pouring two large drinks from a faceted crystal decanter that sparkled in the low light as if it were encrusted with diamonds.

"I'll have safeguards in place before I tell him, and that won't be until Tess is in the air, en route from Capetown."

Nodding his approval, the older man recrossed the room to hand Gianni a heavy snifter that fit perfectly into his cupped palm.

"Thank you, sir." Gianni paused to inhale the rich, heady aroma of the cognac. The fumes alone were intoxicating, holding within them the sweet, musty scent of decadence and extreme wealth.

Still in robust health at the age of seventy-two, the chairman was known for never drinking anything younger than he was. It was rumored that the cognac the old man kept on the yacht was nearly two hundred years old, rescued by his grandfather during World War I from a château that was later destroyed by the Germans.

I don't care how old it is; sharing it with him is nothing more than I deserve.

Enjoying a private sense of entitlement, Gianni waited until his host had taken a sip before indulging himself.

The chairman resettled himself in his chair and gestured for Gianni to do the same. "After you tell Simpson he's done, then what?"

"TESLA personnel will be informed of the change and, when Tess arrives, there will be a peaceful handover. She'll have Tate from Legal and Bamberger from HR with her, and two assistants—"

"Assistants?" Croyden raised an eyebrow.

"Security," Gianni said, his voice clipped. "Because it's a long flight from Capetown to the interior, there will be two crews on the plane. Dr. Simpson will be on the return flight, which will take off as soon as they've refueled. We don't expect them to be on the ground for more than two hours."

Croyden was silent for a long moment, staring at the deep amber fluid swirling in his glass. "How well do you know Simpson?"

"Pretty well, sir. I worked for him for ten years at HAARP."

"So you know what a nut he can be. And you think it will be that easy to get him out of TESLA? That he'll just go along without a fight?" Croyden asked, not hiding his skepticism.

"We hope it will be, sir, but we're prepared for some pushback. That's why we're sending Security, just to be on the safe side. They'll all be low-key, though, and won't make themselves known unless there's a need for it."

The older man frowned slightly. "Now it's starting to sound like a damned rendition. Just what do you think he's going to do?"

"We fully expect him to cooperate, sir, we're just taking reasonable precautions." Gianni paused and rolled the snifter slowly between his hands, warming the brandy and releasing more of its perfume. "It's an extremely sensitive situation and I won't deny that it has the potential for volatility. As you know, sir, before I came to you with this issue, when we were just beginning to have suspicions that something wasn't right, we brought in a team of psychiatrists to review Dr. Simpson's personnel profile. They determined that his emotional attachment to the entire concept of TESLA has shifted from reasonable to extreme. Their assessment held cause for concern on several levels, so I took the report to our director of security, and this is the plan she recommended." He took a sip, savoring it. "The crews will be fully briefed—"

"Not Tess? You're not going to brief her on the situation?"

Gianni shrugged. "I don't want to make her anxious. Besides, if Simpson does act out, it won't be her problem. The team going down there knows what they're doing and what they're there for."

Croyden's frown deepened. "I don't like the sound of this."

Gianni shifted forward in the chair to rest his elbows on his knees. "We don't have much of a choice, sir. We need Simpson out of there. We know he's carrying out assignments from the Pentagon, assignments that we haven't authorized and, in the case of Afghanistan, that both you and I specifically refused." He took a deep breath. "Please trust me, sir, when I say that no one's actions will be overt. Everything will be discreet and no one, including Dr. Simpson, will get the impression that he's being taken into custody. Even in the event of hesitation on his part, Dr. Simpson won't be harmed. The security team will be armed with Tasers and a variety of tranquilizers and sedatives, if needed. But all of that is only backup in the event of a worst-case scenario. Whatever goes down will be handled by the security team with a minimum of fuss."

"I'm not reassured, Gianni."

"There's no other way to handle this, sir. We asked him to come to Connecticut. He refused."

After a long moment, the chairman nodded, apparently satisfied. "All right. Anything else?"

Gianni paused briefly. "I think we need to discuss

what our response will be when the Pentagon learns that they've lost such a valuable asset."

"You mean when the secretary of defense finds out, Gianni. The Pentagon has no idea that it ever had such an asset," the chairman said with a smile. He lifted his snifter in salute and drank deeply from it without ever breaking eye contact.

After a split second of hesitation, Gianni returned the smile and the toast, ignoring the dark chill that ran through him.

CHAPTER

Three weeks later

Nik Forde sat in his small office on the top floor of the three-story TESLA habitat, listening to the wind howl on the other side of the inches-thick, impact-proof window to his left. The heavy blackout curtain was closed, as it had been for at least a month and would continue to be for much of the austral winter. He didn't keep it closed to keep out prying eyes—there were none—but to add a small extra layer of insulation against the brutal weather and to keep the light inside. The less interference the humans provided to their environment, the more pure the results of their work would be.

And he wanted his next effort to go off without a hitch.

Smiling, humming an off-key version of "Eleanor Rigby," Nik tapped away at his keyboard, responding to yet another email from his ex-wife, Eleanor Ryder—*Ms.* Eleanor Ryder, soon to be Mrs. Eleanor Ryder-Pentson—who had been the love of his life. It had been love at first sight, from the moment they met in the Harvard Coop—she a clerk, he a guest lecturer at nearby MIT—until the day she turned into a serious pain in his ass. That latter moment happened, not coincidentally, right about the time he'd taken a job in the very nerve center of the lower forty-eight, Washington, D.C. Right about the time she'd taken a job with a lobbying firm on K Street. Right about the time she'd met real power and real money and lost her taste for what she'd always affectionately called Nik's "geeky charm," preferring instead the oozy smarm of high-powered dairy lobbyist—Nik called him the Milk Man—Mitchell Pentson. Right about the time Nik decided to take off for the Ice.

Best decision he'd ever made.

"Sure, take his name. You never took mine. You said people would laugh, that Ryder-Forde sounded too much like a rodeo stunt. Well, I've got news for you, honey, Ryder-Pentson sounds like the kind of medical procedure you don't discuss over dinner," he muttered as he tapped away at his keyboard. "We'll see about the last laugh."

He checked coordinates on the screen to his left and typed them into the fields appearing on the screen in front of him. The high-altitude instability he was creating would push a wide swath of turbulence through the atmosphere over the Pacific Ocean, culminating in a strong, late-season tropical storm centered near the island of Fiji. Nik had been orchestrating weather systems for years, so whipping up this kind of storm was child's play. Or would be if the child were a prodigy with a pair of Ph.D.s trailing after his name.

He frowned at the screen. "I have a conscience. My intent is not malicious, it's—"

Leaning back in his chair, Nik looked at the ceiling

and the collage of photos he'd taped there. They were of nacreous clouds, beautiful and bizarre formations that only happen during extreme cold, when the nitric and sulfuric acids in the air mix with ice in the atmosphere to make huge clouds with the soft, blurred colors of mother-of-pearl. He'd taken the pictures himself a few weeks earlier as the Antarctic weather turned from autumn to winter. His office ceiling was the best place to keep them. Nik did a lot of staring at the ceiling while he worked.

"My intent isn't malicious," he repeated, "this storm is meant to . . . inspire . . . okay, it's meant to inspire fear. Healthy fear." He paused again. "Okay, it's meant to scare the hell out of her, but it's not going to bring down her plane or anything else. Yes, I'm being immature, if not petty, and yes, I'm doing it because I can. That's honesty. Done. No harm, no foul." He brought his chair upright and, with a delighted grin, tapped in the last few commands, instructing the computer to store the algorithm in a queue and activate it in twelve hours. Right when the Milk Man and the newly minted Mrs. Ryder-Pentson—a very nervous flier—would be cruising at 38,000 feet, nuzzling in their first-class seats. Unless Ellie had changed dramatically, they'd already be into their second bottle of Veuve Clicquot. The Milk Man would be celebrating the start of their three-week South Pacific honeymoon. Ellie would be trying to make it through the flight.

Nik turned to the third monitor on his desk, the one displaying the open email application, and began typing.

Ellie, have a great time on your honeymoon. I wish you and

He paused, running through all the descriptive phrases he'd like to use, and reluctantly settled on the only politically correct word.

Mitchell all the best.
Regards, Nik

With a single click, the polite and ostensibly friendly message flashed through cyberspace, heading for Ellie's iPhone, her office computer, and the laptop sitting on Ellie's desk in her—and formerly Nik's—historic town house in Alexandria, Virginia.

Sitting back, Nik let satisfaction wash over him as he addressed the screen. "Bon voyage, Eleanor. Good thing you got such a good deal on the hotel. Enjoy the flight. Let me know how that motion-sickness patch you'll be wearing works out for you."

Greg Simpson stared at the email on the screen in front of him. The reassuringly green logo—balanced scales bearing the earth on one side and a stylized lab beaker on the other—seemed to sway. The message's dark type blurred, its words merging into smudges as their meaning burned its way through his frontal lobe. His hands curled into fists.

You are not going to take TESLA away from me.

But he knew they were going to try. His refusals, his unambiguous, adamant refusals to step aside, to take on "new projects," had fallen on deaf ears.

This most recent message from Croyden Flint thanked him for helping Flint AgroChemical become the leader in the field of weather manipulation in one sentence and booted him out the door of TESLA in the next. The presumption and the arrogance in the brief note were a bitter dose to swallow, all the more because Greg knew the wording was so deliberate, so meticulously crafted for maximum effect.

"Help? No, I didn't *help* Flint become the leader in the field. I *made* Flint the leader," Greg whispered into the darkness of his office. "You supplied nothing but money, Croyden. Not the vision. Not the genius. Not the perseverance. Just the empty, lifeless dollars. And you'll see how far that gets you now."

Greg had spent decades at HAARP enduring Arctic winters, military supervisors, and government budget wars, all of which had been unpleasant but necessary means to achieving his goal. Trading one frigid Hell for another, he'd spent the last six years in the coldest, most inhospitable place on earth—the interior of Antarctica, a few hundred miles from the South Pole, where at the height of summer the temperature was negative thirty degrees Fahrenheit. He'd endured the continent's isolation, the desolation, the sensory deprivation, even the occasional lack of commitment from colleagues, and he'd triumphed over all of it just to get his creation to its current state. Developing and running TESLA was the culmination of his life's dream and his life's work. It didn't matter who paid for it, nor would it matter where Greg stood on the globe: TESLA was his. No one—nothing—could change that.

TESLA's powerful transmitters had gone fully operational just one year ago, but Greg had engaged in live tests for several years before that. Since then he, through TESLA, had been getting nature to do exactly what he wanted it to do, what Flint's executives wanted it to do.

And, increasingly, what the Pentagon wanted it to do.

That was about to change.

Greg swiveled to face the small screen of his personal laptop and opened a private email application that gave him a secure link to a top-secret military satellite set in a low-earth polar orbit. He patiently worked through the four password-protected portals that led him to the window he needed. The message he typed was brief and was encrypted before it was sent.

Call me. Now.

No greeting was necessary, no closing offered. The person receiving the message, a high-ranking officer in the Pentagon's E-ring, would not be pleased at receiving, rather than giving, an order, but Greg didn't care about that. Only his own displeasure mattered. His own fury.

To most of the fiscal-minded clowns occupying the C-suite at Flint, TESLA was the means to unimaginably vast power and unimaginably large profits, and nothing more. But the chairman, who'd learned his rapacious trade at the knee of his robber-baron grandfather, had never let himself be blinded by altruism, however warped. Croyden Flint had always known that the huge, secret array of transmitters whose development he was funding would not only micromanage the world's weather—its growing seasons, monsoons, droughts, and floods, even its earthquakes and tsunamis, when needed—but would have a second, even more secret purpose: for the right price, TESLA could be the Pentagon's shiniest new toy, its ultimate weapon.

And the unholy alliance had been forged.

Greg had discovered the truth about this arrangement a few months after the array came on line, when a deliberately bland, deliberately forgettable visitor had arrived for a quick and unforgettable visit, having nearly circumnavigated the globe to have a one-hour conversation with him. This high-level envoy from the Pentagon made Greg an offer he would have been a fool to refuse: occasionally, secretly, allow the military to sidestep its existing arrangement with Croyden Flint and come to him directly with requests. All he had to do was trigger an occasional weather or geophysical event when, where, and how the government asked him to . . . in exchange for whatever he wanted. Money. An invitation to become a JASON. A Nobel Prize.

He'd settled for all three, plus immunity. Irrevocable, complete, eternal immunity from any culpability for his actions.

And that had set him free.

Greg had been reasonably content in his role as the science director at the High-frequency Active Auroral Research Program, known as HAARP, the publicly acknowledged military installation in Alaska focused on applied ionospheric research. There, he'd had access to research materials he'd only dreamed of: the original papers of the most ground-breaking visionary in modern electromagnetics, Nikola Tesla.

Greg had studied the notes and drawings minutely, committing every word, every diagram, every equation to memory, and filling in critical gaps from his own knowledge and imagination. Over time, he'd drafted what he believed was the key to the most magnificent engine in existence: the weather. He'd kept his ideas to himself, burying small segments of his hypotheses in larger experiments that were then tested, but never letting anyone know that he was forming a larger, much different, focus. He'd heard too many stories—some real, some probably not—of how badly the government had treated Tesla, and the tales resonated too closely with his own experiences. He wasn't about to squander *his* genius.

Then Croyden Flint offered him the opportunity to devise the master plan for a new weather research installation, the first of its kind. The old man had promised him everything he'd ever wanted, if Greg would create a system that enabled Flint to exploit agricultural markets by controlling the ultimate means of production: regional weather on a global scale.

Greg had accepted the offer without hesitation, and he'd delivered the goods on time. After two high-intensity years spent planning and five more spent building and testing every aspect of the installation, the results had been perfect, inflating the wildest dreams of the executives and bringing to fruition Flint's three-generation quest for market domination. Then, a year ago, TESLA, fully operational and completely flawless, had been given the go-ahead to come on line.

The executives, immensely proud that their investment had been worthwhile, viewed themselves without irony as the most magnanimous of corporate stewards. By moving high and low pressure systems around the world, by stopping, starting, and diverting storms, TESLA allowed Flint AgroChemical to moderate rainfall, relieving pressure on critical water supplies. Delusions of godlike grandeur had the executives directing Greg's team to stave off floods and droughts, saving lives and reversing desertification. All the while, they crowed privately to themselves and one another about their ability to enhance sustainable worldwide agricultural food production.

By diminishing the awesome power of cyclonic storms, the executives saw their actions as selfless opportunities to give battered populations and economies a chance to recover and rebuild. Of course, Flint made huge profits every step of the way. From betting on weather-related outcomes in the stock market, to increasing sales of seed and the pesticides, herbicides, and fertilizers required to make genetically modified crops grow, to buying and selling those perfect crops grown under perfect conditions, the executives took advantage of every possible mechanism to reap their just rewards.

The chairman, who had always understood the larger perspective, saw to it that the company reaped the unjust rewards as well. Croyden took a great deal of pleasure in the downfall of Flint's competition as his enemies lost ships full of goods to storms at sea, as their crops and customers were lost to the capriciousness of nature, when prices for their primary crops went into freefall as markets suffered from surpluses due to weather that was too good to be true.

TESLA's atmospheric "adjustments," as Croyden liked to call them, were untraceable, and the operations were conducted so neatly and at such a distance from the firm's Connecticut headquarters, that they quickly became mundane; the consistently perfect outcomes came to be viewed as simply the well-deserved return on a $250 million investment in "agricultural research," as Flint's public relations machine modestly described it.

Greg's Pentagon visitor had warned him that the executives—that band of pathetic profiteers—wanted to oust him. Greg had dismissed the warning as a ploy; months went by in peace, months in which Greg worked for two masters, sometimes for the same ends, sometimes for opposite results. And then it happened. Flint had begun making noise about "bringing him home." He'd pushed back, of course, and that had ended the conversation. Until today, until a moment ago, when Croyden told him flatly that they were bringing him off the Ice, transferring him to the warmth of the corporate offices overlooking the Long Island Sound, where he would develop other projects.

Greg smiled. What fools they were, to think that he'd agree, to think there could be other projects of greater importance, of greater impact, than TESLA. Their lives were petty, as were their goals. But his only goal in life had been to master the weather. There *was* no greater goal.

And he'd achieved it.

He, Greg Simpson, and his handpicked team had harnessed the immense power of the earth, something Man had tried to do for millennia by offering up prayers and penance, by deploying methods ranging from live sacrifices to cloud seeding. For centuries, humans had understood that weather was a critical variable in the outcome of wars—both the military and political varieties. Across time and civilizations, the gods of weather and war had been beseeched by the oppressed and appeased by the victors. Geniuses and madmen alike had devised plots and plans in their efforts to affect the weather, but none had ever succeeded in wresting control of the weather from the very forces that direct it.

Until now.

Greg's team had turned Nature itself into the last, best weapon in the world's history, the ultimate force multiplier. Severe weather everywhere was created and steered, and then dissipated when the goal had been achieved—or the lesson learned. One large earthquake had shown the world that a self-proclaimed superpower really wasn't one at all.

Because of Greg Simpson, because of *his* genius, Flint was on its way to becoming the most prosperous, most powerful corporation on the planet . . . and America was re-establishing itself as the world's only economic and military superpower.

The small, bland, screenless communication device at the edge of his work space emitted a low buzz as it vibrated in its charger. Greg reached across his desk and picked it up.

"What's going on?" was the admiral's greeting in a voice that sounded annoyed rather than concerned. It pricked at Greg's ego.

"Your efforts have not worked," Greg replied. "I've just been told my replacement will be here in a matter of hours."

Silence on the other end of the phone confirmed for Greg that this was not news to the admiral.

"I'm sorry. We did everything—"

"No, you didn't," Greg said simply. "If you had done *everything*, this would have been settled by now. Instead, Tess Beauchamp has just taken off from Capetown, South Africa, in a Flint plane. I'm expected to hand over the keys to my kingdom and then head back to civilization." He paused. "You do know who Tess Beauchamp is. Third-generation government scientist. Recent sellout to the private sector." *Breakthrough re-*

searcher in agrometeorology and a leading figure in the field of applied informatics. Stupid bitch who bolted in the middle of a three-year fellowship with me fifteen years ago and nearly cost me everything because of it.

"Of course I know who she is. She spoke at a NATO meeting I attended three weeks ago. Listen, Greg, we can still fix this—"

"No, *you* listen to me, Admiral Medev," Greg said quietly. "You had the opportunity to 'fix' this. You failed. So I will fix it."

Alexander Medev's pause lasted long enough to make Greg smile with cold delight. "How?"

"I'm going to follow the most basic rule of engineering. I'm going to use the resources at hand."

"Christ Almighty. There will be a flight crew on that plane. Equipment. We can't—"

"I'm sorry, did you say 'we,' Admiral Medev? This isn't a collaborative effort anymore. *I* am going to address the situation as *I* see fit. Tess Beauchamp, Flint's new girl wonder, is *not* going to take over TESLA. I am going to remain in control, which makes her expendable. The plane and equipment can be replaced. The flight crew, well, those people are adrenaline jockeys, aren't they? That's what they signed up for, isn't it— risk, danger, adventure?"

Greg let the frigidity of his smile seep into his voice. "Anyone who agrees to fly onto the Ice at this time of year can have no fear of death. The window for flights closed six weeks ago. Everyone knows that no one should attempt to fly in until August barring a life-or-death emergency, which this isn't. There won't even be any internal flights for months. To send a flight in from Capetown now just for the sake of corporate politics is beyond foolhardy. And Flint's plan is not only stupid, it will destroy the project. We both know that."

"Let me—"

"Don't be ridiculous. You had the opportunity to act and, with your exquisite foresight," Greg said, sarcasm seeping through his silky calm, "you failed to do so. Now you're helpless, Alexander. If I leave TESLA, your career is over. You will lose your direct link to the array and you'll be back to fetching coffee for the real brass. The price of your weakness is that you've been taken out of the equation. I'm making the decisions now. Bringing down that plane is imperative. There is no other alternative. If that—" *bitch* "—woman arrives here, there will be questions raised that you and I long ago agreed must never be asked."

"Listen to me, Greg. I'll do whatever it takes. I'll pull strings and shut down the flight. That will give us time—"

"Haven't you been paying attention, Alexander? You're out of time. And luck. You can't stop the flight. The U.S. military has no jurisdiction over TESLA. The air fleet is flagged in South Africa specifically to keep you out of the mix. The planes belong to Flint and the crews are Flint employees. The ice we're sitting on is in Australian territory, as you know, and the Aussies are hardly going to interfere with our internal operations without a good reason. We've given them a lot of money to keep them out of our hair. So the harsh reality is that only Flint can stop the flight, and that is unlikely at this point. They've declared war on me."

"War? Greg, be reasonable."

"I'm being eminently reasonable, Alexander. You're the one panicking. Listen to yourself."

"Let me—for God's sake, you can't take out a plane—Flint won't like the publicity."

"Is that the best reason you can come up with? Given all that pungent desperation in your voice, I was expecting a morality play in three acts," Greg said with a smile that had grown wider during the call. "I have no fears of publicity. There won't be any. Flint won't allow anything to raise the profile down here, any more than you will. By the time news of the plane crash makes it into the paper, if it does at all, it will be on page fifteen, lower left corner, and the flight will have become a pleasure trip gone bad, an accident attributed to a sloppy crew operating in old aircraft during bad weather and without authorization."

After thirty seconds of listening to the admiral breathing heavily while trying to find new ideas, Greg nodded to himself. "I'll assume your silence implies consent. Thanks for your time, Alexander. I wish you much success in your future endeavors."

Greg disconnected the call, set the small unit back into its charger, and spun to face one of the large flat-screen monitors on his desk. In seconds, he'd pulled up a map of the Antarctic continent, then zoomed in to their small slice of it.

Their position, so close to the South Geomagnetic Pole, prevented him from creating weather too close to home, but a sudden Antarctic storm near the coast would be an occurrence so commonplace as to be hardly worth a mention. The fact that he had granted the pilot weather clearance she needed to take off would further allay any suspicion. After all, everyone knew not to fly if Greg Simpson, master of the weather, didn't give the okay.

The weather on the vast Central Antarctic plateaus was always bad in the winter. Vicious storms often started with no warning and could last from hours to weeks. Having a clear sky turn into a blur of blowing, blinding snow within thirty minutes was routine. He was merely going to ensure that such a storm blew up when and where he needed it.

Greg glanced at the clocks on the wall; it was four-thirty in the afternoon in Connecticut and here at TESLA. It confused the hell out of rookies to learn that each research station on the Ice kept time with its sponsoring country or the country on which it relied for replenishment and emergency services.

It was only in the Antarctic that anyone really became fully aware that time was nothing more than a human construct, a completely arbitrary measurement. In the austral winter, there were twenty-four hours of darkness, in the summer, twenty-four hours of light. Theoretically, all time zones converged at the Geographical Pole; a person could cross all the world's time zones in less than a minute by walking around the slim, flagged marker driven deep into the ice sheet.

Tess was scheduled to touch down on the installation's blue-ice runway in approximately eight hours, which gave him plenty of time to assemble the command sequence necessary to create category-five hurricane force winds in the upper atmosphere. Lowering the high-altitude temperatures enough to damage the plane's tires or freeze its hydraulic system would take slightly longer, but he had time. He could even wait to begin, if he wanted to.

He didn't.

Greg leaned forward, intently scanning the map in front of him. The only real challenge in the whole exercise was deciding which global coordinate would be best suited for the death of Tess Beauchamp and the winged horse she was riding in on.

Somewhere over water. Near a coastline, but too far out to scramble a rescue team.

He zoomed in closer, then closer still, until he could see the detailed faces of the harsh, wind-scoured cliffs of Queen Maud Land's long coastline. He clicked on a coordinate where the sea ice would be forming.

An excellent choice. The huge plane would pass over the area en route to TESLA. Between the treacherous winds and the dangers posed by the hardening sea, no rescue operation would be attempted. Not by sea, not by air.

Tess, over ice, with a twist of fate.

I'll drink to that.

5

CHAPTER

Her tall, slender frame folded nearly in half to fit in the seat, Tess Beauchamp sat in the cold, rattling fuselage of the huge Ilyushin cargo plane, trying to will warmth to her fingertips and some sort of enthusiasm to her brain. But it wasn't easy to get excited about heading into a war zone, even if it was just a corporate one. In Antarctica. In the throes of winter.

It was even more difficult knowing that what was waiting for her on the Ice was something of an emotional minefield.

Pushing farther into her eight layers of extreme-weather clothes, Tess tried once again to get comfortable. It was pointless. Her clothing left her feeling like a cross between the Michelin Man and the Pillsbury Doughboy. The ambient temperature in the stripped-down cabin hovered somewhere around not-cold-enough-to-kill-you; her "seat" was nothing more than nylon webbing slung between poles. She could hear nothing beyond the deafening thrum of the plane's engines—right through her earplugs. Comfort was a far-off dream at the moment.

Surely with all the technology the world had to of-fer and all the money Flint AgroChemical had on hand, there was a more comfortable way of getting to the South Pole than on a retired Russian military air-craft that was probably older than Tess herself, pi-loted by a woman who looked young enough to be wearing a Girl Scout uniform instead of a flight suit. The pilot had told Tess she was a former U.S. military officer who'd logged plenty of time flying in and out of Antarctica, but Tess was having trouble getting past the fact that she looked and sounded like some Disney tween princess.

The rest of the flight crew, the backup flight crew, and Tess's "entourage" from Flint HQ all seemed de-termined to keep themselves in the background. Tess hadn't interacted with any of them in Capetown other than the lawyer and the HR director, and had barely seen those two since boarding. One five-person flight team had disappeared into the cockpit and the other had strapped themselves into their seats and fallen asleep. The two Flint executives had spent much of their time huddled over their laptops. The two security guys hadn't said a word to her since they were intro-duced.

Tess knew she should have followed the backup flight crew's example and just slept, but she was too keyed up. She'd booted up her own laptop and once again reviewed the information about the personnel at TESLA. At this point, they had been airborne for more than six hours, having left in the wee-hour darkness of a South African night. In another couple of hours, Tess would return to the coldest, driest, and, right now, darkest place on the surface of the earth. But the climate wasn't what was bugging her. It was her host, or the man who'd be her host for the first five minutes, Greg Simpson.

Tess had good reason to despise Greg personally, but—although she'd never admit it aloud—she had to respect him, despite what Gianni had told her Greg had done with her research. Tess's reputation was growing and well-deserved, but Greg had been an icon in the field of weather science for decades. Their colleagues universally acknowledged that he was a genius when it came to understanding the physics— some said metaphysics—of the atmosphere. He'd been a legend even way back when she was an undergrad. She'd wanted to work for him since she'd first heard his name.

When the time was right, she'd shamelessly pulled strings of all sorts to be interviewed for the three-year HAARP fellowship Greg granted to one post-doc student each year. She'd wowed him in the interview and won the gig. She couldn't believe her luck. Working with Greg Simpson was the brass ring, the ruby slippers, the Holy Grail. And more than a little holy hell, as it turned out.

HAARP's location in Gakona, Alaska, was everything she'd been warned it would be—flat, cold, and boring—but the work was everything she'd hoped it would be: mind-blowing. Working for Greg had also been everything she'd been warned about. Greg was more than just a taskmaster. He was a single-minded, ego-crushing slave driver who didn't seem to need sleep, food, or downtime. And he never, ever let stupid human traits like compassion or empathy or understanding get in the way of his goals. She'd found that out firsthand when her grandmother had died unexpectedly.

Greg had been coldly accommodating when Tess said she needed to leave; despite the difficulties in getting from the interior of Alaska to anywhere in the lower forty-eight and back in a reasonable time frame, he'd extracted a promise from her that she'd be back in a week. Then her grandfather had suffered a massive stroke right after the funeral and had died the next day, leaving Tess and her family reeling from the compounded shock. Greg had quietly, surgically eviscerated her over the phone, going so far as to accuse her of fabricating calamities to take an unscheduled vacation, of not being able to cut it on the project. Then he'd demanded that she return in seventy-two hours or he'd pull her fellowship and kick her out of the program.

Somehow, Tess made it back before the deadline. She'd burst into Greg's office like a human tornado, like a fire-breathing Amazon goddess, and, towering over him as he cringed at his desk, had proceeded to inform Greg of her opinion of him. At a decibel level that nearly damaged some of the transmitters half a mile away. Using language so creative and profane that Kathy Griffin would have wept with jealousy.

Amid the loud, thought-drubbing white noise of the aircraft engines, Tess smiled at the memory of that day. Telling Greg off had felt *wonderful*. Emancipating. Cleansing.

She'd composed herself somewhat by the time the military police arrived, summoned by one of the people in the outer office who had "overheard" her rage. The MPs had escorted her to her quarters to pack up her belongings—and as she'd stormed down the hall, she'd seen the stunned, somewhat admiring, open-mouthed expressions on the faces of her colleagues. She'd seen the military cops biting their lips to keep from laughing as they followed her down the corridor.

But, despite Greg's best efforts to ruin her, the incident hadn't damaged her career. Not that Tess had hung around to find out if it would. She'd made a few calls and had gotten a job on a project as far away from Greg as she could possibly get: Antarctica.

Tess's smile turned wry. She'd been in her mid-twenties back then, just coming up for air after a grueling span of years spent getting two master's degrees and two doctorates. She knew now that it was more than grief and Greg's insensitivity that had set her off—and that it might be time to make peace with him—but the incident had worked out to her advantage. She fell in love with the Ice.

Antarctica was remote from everywhere—and everyone—on earth. An island continent that belonged to no one, the last land-based frontier on the planet. A place where the weather was beyond wild; where the environment and terrain were harsh, practically alien, but possessed a savage beauty that could seduce and kill in the same moment.

She'd heard that each research station had its own culture and as a group were borderline tribal, and the stories enticed her. She'd been steeped for so many years in hard-core academia and swampy personal relationships that never had a chance to flourish—including a nascent romance with Nik Forde that ended when her fellowship did—that Tess had needed some wildness, some challenges that would force her to live by her wits as well as her reason.

Antarctica had been the perfect antidote to Greg's toxicity. It was dangerous. Swashbuckling. And far, far away. Nothing about life on the Ice was ordinary; everything was extreme. Getting there was a marathon; adapting to the rhythmless pace of endless day and then endless night challenged both mind and body. Downtime meant spelunking through snow caves, climbing up the sheer ice faces of ancient formations, rappelling into virtually bottomless crevasses.

Tess realized she was smiling—a little ruefully—at the memories of that first trip. This one was her sixth and was completely different. One of the benefits of working with one of the world's largest and wealthiest corporations was the ease with which the transition had taken place. A smooth, professional "relocation team" from Flint had stepped in and taken over her life—arranging for her apartment in Paris to be carefully mothballed, hiring a service to keep her plants fed and watered and her bills paid, supplying her with made-to-measure cold-weather gear and anything else she thought she'd need on the Ice. All she'd had to do was pack what she wanted to take with her and hop on the luxurious corporate jet that whisked her from Paris to Greenwich, Connecticut. Once there, she'd been treated like royalty while being briefed on every aspect of TESLA.

Despite all the flattery and special treatment, Tess had kept herself firmly focused on the professional aspects of the task ahead of her, and had just as firmly avoided considering her motives for taking it on. She wasn't naïve enough to think that there hadn't been a lot of discussion in Flint's boardroom about whether, given her history, she should be Greg's replacement. She was equally sure that the executives had speculated on her reasons for accepting the job. But the answers were simple. She truly was the only person qualified to take it over, and it was a logical next step in her career. Government and academic positions had been her past and would be abundant if she wanted to make them part of her future. But TESLA was the cutting-edge present.

Tess glanced around again at the cargo plane's ugly, cavernous, utilitarian space. Fire extinguishers and personal-sized oxygen canisters were clipped to the walls, along with first-aid kits and some ominously unlabeled black boxes. Farther down the back, huge flat red panels hung snugly against the frame. They were the heavy-duty, inflatable life rafts. Not that she could ever imagine that a craft so flimsy could ensure anyone's survival in a body of water as cold and treacherous as the Southern Ocean as it was forming its massive seasonal expanse of ship-crushing sea ice. She shook off the thought.

The only good thing about the trip was that it was almost over. In good weather—a relative concept in Antarctica—the lumbering plane with its odd, glass-enclosed nose could make the trip from Capetown to TESLA in about seven hours. But in this kind of weather—in a word, dreadful—they couldn't fly as high or as fast. Frankly, she was surprised they were flying at all. But the weather had been okay when they departed and had remained so until well after they'd passed the BSR—the point Beyond Safe Return, when they were committed to keep going because they didn't have enough fuel to turn around and make it back to Capetown. But she'd learned that this odd-looking Russian plane was slightly more versatile than other aircraft because it sported

twenty-four low-pressure wheels instead of ski landing gear like most other Antarctic-bound planes.

Tess sighed and closed her eyes again, and tried
once more to get comfortable. In just under two
hours, they'd land on TESLA's blue-ice runway on the
East Antarctic Polar Plateau, and she and the equipment surrounding her would be off-loaded. She could
get out, stretch her legs, reacquaint herself with the
true meanings of the words *cold* and *dark,* then bundle Greg Simpson onto the plane and take over as director and lead researcher at TESLA.

And that, by all accounts, would make a lot of
people happy. Except Greg.

The installation was Greg's baby. His magnum
opus. Quite possibly his life. Which was exactly why
the company wanted him stateside.

Tess felt a sharp tug on her shoulder just as the
plane hit a patch of turbulent air that made her stomach lurch. Opening her eyes, she saw a blaze-orange
Michelin Man shape swaying in front of her and
glanced up to the person's face.

The first officer, long and lean underneath the flight
gear, was clinging to a strap that hung from the ceiling.

"A storm system just erupted out of nowhere about
two hundred miles ahead of us," the officer said, shouting over the deafening white noise of the engines. "It's
big. We don't have enough fuel left to climb above it
or go around it, so we're going to go through it. It's
not going to be fun. Put on your survival suit and then
stay strapped in."

Tess just stared at the man. "What?"

A look of unmistakable exasperation crossed the
officer's face. "Turbulence," he shouted, and pointed
to the other occupants of the stripped-down cabin.

They were all in various stages of putting on and fastening the closures on their neon-orange survival suits.

Tess's stomach dropped to her knees, or would have if she'd been standing. She swallowed hard. They were well past the BSR. And survival suits were only to be put on if there was a chance of a water landing.

Water landing.

That's what the pocket-sized pilot had said during her quick pre-flight briefing at the airport.

Right. As if Captain Cheetah Girl up there in the cockpit is Chesley Sullenberger and the wild, stormy, iceberg-filled Southern Ocean below us is the Hudson River on a good day.

Tess knew the sick anticipation growing inside her was pointless. The first officer was on his way back to the cockpit. Were it not for the bulky layers of cold-weather gear plus survival suit, the man would have looked like Tarzan as he grabbed the overhead straps and half-walked, half-swung his way up the aisle of the already pitching plane.

Grimly determined to think positive thoughts, Tess reached beneath her seat and pulled out the vacuum-packed bundle that contained her survival gear.

Shaking hands and a rolling floor did nothing to ease the task of dressing herself. She was already en-sconced in the bulky regulation ECW—Extreme Cold Weather—gear she'd put on at the airport. The parka, big clumsy white "bunny boots," huge mittens the Icers called bear claws, and a balaclava would now be topped by survival gear—the ultimate Antarctic fashion statement.

After Tess had suited up, she got up and weaved her

way along the short aisle to strap herself into a different seat, opposite the second flight crew. Their faces gave nothing away, but the casual, joking ease they'd displayed earlier in the day was gone, replaced by a quiet intensity that Tess knew ought to reassure her.

It didn't.

Tess's fight-or-flight instinct was in overdrive as the mild bumps and drops that had followed the first officer's warning grew into lurches and leaps that quickly became downright terrifying. Heart-stopping plummets ended with a jolt when the aircraft hit masses of air seemingly as solid as concrete. Then a steep ascent rolled to a halt with a shuddering motion followed too quickly by a twisting, tumbling, roller-coaster dive.

Eventually, and without warning, the rising and diving stopped and the plane began to roll sideways, nearly perpendicular, first one way and then immediately the other, as if manic angels were playing see-saw on the wings. With each abrupt motion, Tess's full weight was thrown against the straps bisecting her chest, then slammed against the hard seat-back. She brought her heavily padded hands up to clasp her neck, bracing it against whiplash. Her guts were in complete rebellion. Her body's sense of equilibrium was gone.

The bare walls of the cavernous fuselage ensured that Tess heard every squeal and creak as the tortured metal frame of the plane fought against the vicious combination of ninety-below-zero temperatures, screaming, churning winds racing around them at hundreds of knots, and near-constant lightning strikes. She knew the pilots would be coping with zero visibility, and while there were no other planes to collide with, the mountain ranges could be a problem.

She swallowed hard and wished she'd fastened the anchoring straps even tighter.

Finally, it seemed that the bucking and heaving were diminishing, and Tess wondered if her senses had been blunted by terror. She wiggled her fingers and toes, and focused on small visual details just to reassure herself that she wasn't hallucinating.

She wasn't. The turbulence, which had seemed to last forever, was abating. Feeling like she was awakening from a nightmare of epic proportions, Tess let her hands drop to her lap and slumped against the wall with her eyes closed, letting out a relieved breath. She wasn't sure how much time passed, but she didn't open her eyes until the flight was truly stable once again. Then she looked at the officers belted into the webbed seats across the narrow aisle from her. One of them caught her eye and grinned, then shouted—mouthed, really—"Are you having fun yet?"

Glad for any sign of emotion from them, Tess gave him the most genuine smile she could manage, pointed to the filled sick bags nestled inside a clear red plastic bio-bag on the seat next to her, then gave a thumbs-up. The fliers across from her laughed for a second, until the moment was destroyed by the distinct sensation of the plane descending.

No.

Falling.

Tess lurched sideways, toward the front of the plane. The huge crates and containers tethered to the floor and walls in the rear of the cabin strained at their thick straps as momentum and gravity conspired to push-pull them forward.

Tess could breathe only through her mouth, half

gasping, half gulping as she tried to combat the painful popping in her ears and ignore the uncomfortable pressure in her chest, the sensation of her stomach in a freefall.

Tess knew they shouldn't be descending—not this fast and not this soon. She didn't know how long they'd been enduring their aerial hell, but it couldn't have been long enough to get them to the installation. Past experience told her that the plane's fuel was measured precisely so that the aircraft typically landed with every fuel tank empty. Which meant there was no room for error. No room for detours. And there was no place to make an emergency landing. Even if they were over land, snowdrifts and crevasses littered the millions of square miles of the continent's empty, lifeless interior. Where they existed, landing strips were primitive: plowed ice fields that had to be cleared just before the planes touched down, scraped free of any drifts created by the endless and powerful winds.

But Tess was certain the Ilyushin was nowhere near a landing strip. It seemed far too soon. If they weren't still over water, then, at best, they were near the huge ridge of mountains that bisected the continent.

We're going to die.

To retain some semblance of sanity, Tess made herself recite every scientific and mathematical table she could remember, from the table of elements to the list of prime numbers. Just when she was certain she'd entered a state of hypnotic hysteria, she felt the plane shudder hugely, as if some giant hand had smacked it. Seconds later, the plane bounced. Hard.

Tess closed her eyes and screamed, knowing she'd never be heard over the ear-splitting squeals of the braking engines and anguished shrieks of straining metal. Wherever they were, they had to be hundreds of miles from any outpost of civilization.

She braced herself for the impact of the plane hitting the ground and breaking apart. The air on the Plateau, if that's where they were, would be thin, frigid, hard to breathe. It would rush into the broken, ruptured body of the plane, swamping them. Its freezing dryness would paralyze her lungs, but it would take a few minutes for her heart and brain to succumb. She'd be aware she was dying.

The second bounce was just as hard as the first, but not as high. The third came faster and was smaller still, and was accompanied by the distinct and unpleasant sensation of the aircraft fishtailing wildly.

Tess opened her eyes to see the flight crew across from her giving one another tight but clearly relieved smiles. There was even some nervous laughter as they began unstrapping themselves.

They were on land. The plane was definitely slowing as it coasted drunkenly along some surface that was hard enough and smooth enough—so far—to support it. With luck, it was the runway at TESLA. If not, then they were just lucky to be alive and intact. Damned lucky.

With hands shaking so badly from a combination of cold and fear that she could barely make them obey, Tess peeled off her heavy outer mitts. Every joint in her hands ached from being clenched in fists for so long. She forced her fingers to unbuckle the safety straps that held her in place. Cautiously pulling the foam earplugs from beneath her fur-lined hood and knitted hat, she listened to unfiltered sounds for the first time in hours.

The wind was howling, but the louder sound now was the high-pitched banshee wailing coming from engines in full reverse thrust.

"Where are we?" she shouted, her voice unnaturally loud in the stripped-down cabin.

A member of the backup flight crew shrugged. "I'll take Antarctica for a thousand."

Tess ignored the sarcasm. "Are we where we're supposed to be?"

The others looked at her and just blinked.

Right. Like they have any more information than I do.

She gave them a tight smile. The flight crew were on their feet, checking loads and preparing for debarking as if there had been nothing out of the ordinary about the flight or the landing. They even kept their balance as the plane skidded and swayed as it skated along the surface of the southern continent.

The engines were slowing. A few minutes later, the first officer emerged from the cockpit. White-faced and with fresh tracks of icy tears on his cheeks, he looked at Tess.

"Ma'am, we're at TESLA Base."

CHAPTER

"Incoming aircraft. All available personnel to the airstrip. Repeat, incoming aircraft. All available personnel to the airstrip."

The deadpan message that came at him through the speaker of the small walkie-talkie hanging from his belt made Greg's breath catch in his throat, his hands freeze on the keyboard.

The storm hadn't brought down the plane. Tess Beauchamp would arrive at TESLA.

He gave his body and his brain a moment to absorb the shock, and then immediately put aside the routine administrative paperwork he'd been completing. He sought another application, one of his own design, the one he'd mockingly named Dedication. His fingers tapped in his passwords in short, rapid staccatos. Seconds later, the program he thought he'd never have to activate opened on the screen before him. It represented years of ingenious tinkering and, for the last few months, serious, meticulous craftsmanship. As it should. It was, after all, his legacy.

* * *

"Repeat, incoming aircraft. All available personnel to the airstrip."

The calm voice coming through the speakers of the small radios carried by everyone in the installation was at odds with the absurdity of the message.

Nik Forde, assistant research director for TESLA, felt his heart stop for an instant. A plane making an unannounced landing at TESLA at this time of year? The spectrum of possible bad scenarios had no end.

He looked over at Dan Thornton, who was the installation's chief pilot, general mechanic for everything from the antenna arrays to the iPods, and an inveterate player of bad practical jokes. Dan was standing by one of the base library's huge, heavily draped windows. It faced the airstrip, the arrays, and, beyond them, the millions of square miles of ice sheet that made up the continent's vast, empty interior.

"Is he joking?" Nik demanded.

The burly Irishman shook his head at the reference to his fellow countryman Cormac O'Neal, who managed TESLA's fleet of vehicles and filled the role of air traffic controller when needed.

"Not that I know of," Dan replied, grabbing the radio clipped to his belt. "Cormac, it's too early in the morning for this shit. What the fuck are you up to? Hallucinating?"

If there was a way to work crudeness or cursing into a sentence, Dan always found it. Dan considered it part of his Irish charm. Nik figured it was more likely just the result of having grown up on the streets of Cork.

"Would you ever just shut your hole, Thornton?" came the barked interruption from Cormac. "I've a positive ID. It's an Ilyushin cargo plane with Flint's call numbers, and it's Carmel at the controls. She's fully loaded. Equipment and personnel. I just talked to her and confirmed it on radar. She's approaching the hundred-mile mark."

Nik frowned. Carmel McTeague was Flint's senior pilot. She knew how dangerous—how stupid—it was to fly to the Ice at this time of year. He got up from his chair and walked over to Dan.

"Oh, for fuck's sake, why didn't you—?" Dan began, still holding the small walkie-talkie radio near his mouth.

"Because I only just got the call, that's why," Cormac roared. "I didn't know to expect her. But she's aiming for us and she's going to touch down damned soon. So, she's going to need to find the fucking runway. She's come through a storm that would scare the balls off St. Peter, and if she's pushing tin with anything more than guts and fumes, I'll eat my fucking underwear. So get your big, fat, freckled arse down here, Thornton. Grab anyone else who's nearby. I need a crew out there to get the runway plowed and the cones up so Carmel has a chance in hell of finding the Ice before it finds her."

Dan, Nik, and everyone else in the room were already heading toward the stairs at a trot.

"Buggery bollocks, Cormac. It's the end of April. What's she doing coming here now?" Dan barked into the receiver, not willing to concede any ground for the sake of mere politeness.

"Ask her when she gets here. If she gets here." The terse reply ended the conversation.

Everyone in the facility who was conscious had heard the conversation, and two scientists and nine support staff were in the ready room pulling on their

ECW gear and grumbling when Nik, Dan, and the others entered the room.

Changes to the routine were not welcome at TESLA at the best of times. And an unannounced visit at this time of year was nowhere near the best of times.

"Does anybody know who's coming in?" Nik asked the room in general.

"How the hell would we know? Ask Greg," Mick Fender, who ran the growth station, aka the green-house, sputtered, his always thick Brooklyn accent deepening to near incomprehensibility in anger as he pulled on his layers. "The flight window closed nearly two months ago. Who in their right mind would be flying here now? No one, that's who. No one with a God-damned brain in their head, anyway. And now we all have to go risk our asses to get them. God—"

"That's enough, Mick. Carmel is flying the plane. She wouldn't do it if it weren't important. It has to be an emergency. No one would authorize it otherwise." The voice of reason was Kendra Ballew, the station's physician. "The important thing now is to get them on the ground safely. The runway hasn't been plowed since the last flight out."

Nik kept his mouth shut and reached for his second layer.

"Doesn't make sense, Kendra. An *incoming* emergency? Outgoing, I might understand—"

"It doesn't matter why they're coming, they're here," Dan boomed, closing down all arguments. He already had on his second layer of insulated clothing and was pulling on the third. "If we don't get the cones up so she can land, no one will ever get off that plane alive and then we'll never find out, will we? Now just shut up, lads, and get your arses out there."

The room was quiet then, but the level of annoyed tension persisted as everyone concentrated on dressing for the trek out to the runway, where the plane was supposed to end up if it didn't get blown off course or flip over on approach. Or just crash.

The East Antarctic Polar Plateau was hostile and unforgiving on a good day, so it was only sheer random luck that the dark sky above them was clear and blazing with stars. Just a few short hours ago, the frigid, deadly whiteout they'd been enduring for three days had ended, with the front that brought it in moving toward the coast. From what Cormac had said, the plane was coming through that same storm. Nik didn't want to think about it. Flying a plane through such weather was a suicide mission.

Nik concentrated on pulling on the huge, clumsy, but warm bunny boots. Getting the airstrip ready for the incoming plane wasn't going to be easy. The snowdrifts would be many feet thick and frozen into a solid mass. Just being outdoors was dangerous at this time of year. Nik had come to consider the cold almost a living thing, an invisible dragon with an odorless, burning, desert-dry breath that first seared, then paralyzed every bit of living tissue it encountered. It killed quickly, without mercy or conscience.

The ersatz ground crew finished suiting up and left the warmth and safety of the habitat for the garage space beneath it: a vast area mostly open to the elements. As fast as they could move in their layers of insulation, teams of station residents unplugged the polar vehicles from the heaters that kept them at the ready, and climbed in.

All of the vehicles, whether they moved on skis or tracks, had powerful headlights and rooftop strobe lights, all of which the drivers flipped on as they moved out. The convoy advanced toward the blue-ice runway more than one hundred yards away.

Keeping a firm hand on the joystick of the lumbering Delta—essentially a tractor with a multi-person cabin—Nik switched on the vehicle's global positioning system and the infrared head-up display on the dashboard. He was rewarded by only a faint blur on the screen. Even a hot engine stood little chance of projecting any significant heat signature in air so frigid. It was a grim joke that even with infrared equipment, during a South Pole whiteout only the magma pool of a live volcano could be seen clearly. If you were standing next to it.

It didn't take long for the convoy to arrive at the airstrip. Two members of the crew fired up the large JCBs, which were fitted with enormous snowblowers on their fronts, and began to chew up the drifts and blast the snow nearly one hundred feet from the runway. The rest began hauling out the reflective cones that would mark the edges of the cleared strip. The cockpit crew would be wearing night-vision equipment to help them see every speck of light available in the dark landscape.

Snow cleared and cones set, the crew reunited near the hangar, a grim and unwelcoming reception committee. Minutes later, the blinking wing lights of the Ilyushin appeared in the sky, growing larger as the plane approached a little too low and a little too fast. Its touchdown was rough, with a few hard bounces and some fishtailing, but no major mishaps. Its engines screaming in full-throttled protest, the plane taxied to a stop breathtakingly close to the hangar.

Then, the pilot coaxed the huge machine into the

brightly lit building at a crawl. Leaving it parked on the runway wasn't an option. The heat generated by the friction of the tires during the landing was just enough to melt the ice under them. Had the aircraft been left where it stopped for any length of time, the frigid temperatures would have caused the meltwater to solidify around the twenty-four huge tires immediately, embedding the huge cargo plane in the ice at the business end of the installation's only runway.

The lumbering Ilyushin with its odd, windowed nose came to a clean stop, neatly fitting into a tight gap between the installation's resident Twin Otter and Dash 7 aircraft. The massive doors fronting the building began sliding shut the instant the plane's tail cleared the entrance, but the wind continued to make its presence known with eerie, high-pitched whistles even after the building had been sealed off.

Nik pulled the Delta as close to the plane as he could manage and radioed the other convoy drivers that he had parked, waiting in the cab until every other driver had done the same. As much as they were a necessity on the Ice, the heavy service vehicles nevertheless posed a danger. Someone stopping their vehicle without warning or, worse, getting out of it before everyone else had stopped, could be an instant casualty. At this time of year, the station couldn't afford to lose a vehicle or a life. After the last one checked in, the drivers began piling out of the vehicles to make their way to the plane.

The presence of the Flint AgroChemical logo beneath the cockpit's starboard window confirmed that it was clearly a planned arrival, as Cormac had insisted. Which begged the question of why no one had been informed days ago. The impending arrival of a plane at any time of the year, especially now, was enough of a diversion to qualify as the news of the day for several days running, yet no one had heard so much as a murmur about this one.

The chief on the ground signaled for the pilot to open the aircraft door. A moment later the first survival-suited person clambered down the steel ladder, standing upright on the hangar's gravel floor for mere seconds before his legs gave out and he collapsed in a heap at Nik's feet.

That wasn't an uncommon reaction overall, and after a landing like the one they'd just endured—and the flight had probably been a doozy—Nik considered it understandable. At least no one was hysterical. Yet.

Nik helped the guy to his feet—he was tall, taller than Nik himself—and out of the way. Duffel bags were being flung out the door past the others who were climbing out of the plane. Moments later, the flight crews abandoned the huge plane to the tender mercies of the ground crew, who would off-load its cargo and get the Ilyushin ready for its eventual return trip—whenever that might be.

Nik shook his head as he climbed aboard the Delta for the trek back to the installation. It was a fool's errand to make the trip to TESLA at this time of year in the first place. Flying out could well be more dangerous. He shut the vehicle's door and, loaded with its human freight, the convoy began its slow return trip to the station.

Piotyr, another of the installation's science team, had the honor of driving the big Delta back to the habitat. Nik climbed into the backseat with three of the new arrivals. One of them was the first one down the ladder, the guy Nik had hauled up off his ass. He hadn't said a word or even moved since settling into his seat. He just kept his hands in his lap and his head down. Nik was willing to bet that beneath all those layers of ECW gear the guy was as tense as a bowstring. Or possibly unconscious.

We'll go with option one.

"So, it's just a sight-seeing trip, then?" he said—well, shouted—over the noise of the Delta's engine.

He watched one of the two shorter visitors smile tightly from behind a balaclava. The other laughed.

"Yeah, quite the dawdle." It was a feminine shout.

"Carmel? Is that you?"

The hooded head bobbed up and down.

"What are you here for?" he yelled, smiling at her. "It has to be something important."

"Delivering her," Carmel replied, nodding her head toward the bowed, silent figure next to him, "and some equipment. Some mail. Some food."

Her?

Nik blinked. A curious and not altogether pleasant sensation began in his stomach. He didn't know too many women who were that tall. In fact, he only knew one: Tess Beauchamp.

"Why didn't you let us know you were coming?" he asked.

The two women looked at each other, then back at him.

"What are you talking about? We were expected. The flight plan was approved."

Oh, really? Nik forced a smile. "I must be out of the loop."

"Yeah."

"How was the flight?" he asked.

"The worst I've ever experienced," Carmel said bluntly. "I've been flying heavies for ten years and bringing them to the Ice for six, and that's the worst damned storm I've ever driven through."

"Maybe you should take a different route home," he replied with a grin, making the pilot shake her head. He bent forward and lifted the furred edge of the tall woman's hood. "You okay in there?"

The hood moved up and down minutely.

"Welcome to the Big Chill. This isn't quite the welcome we usually give VIPs. Actually, we call them DVs down here. Distinguished Visitors."

The hood moved upward slowly until a balaclava-covered face appeared. What skin he could see was very pale and the eyes, large and long-lashed, looked hollow and exhausted. It was hard to tell in the dim light of the Delta's interior what color they were.

"I know. I've been here before," the woman replied.

"Huh?" he said.

Ooh, brilliant reply, Nik old boy. Especially if it really is Tess of the Endless Legs, whom you haven't seen in more than a decade.

The hood swayed side to side. "McMurdo. Wintered over about fifteen years ago. I've made a few shorter trips to other bases, too. Amundsen-Scott. Some others."

"In that case, welcome back to the Ice. And welcome to TESLA," he said, still not sure just who he was chatting with. "You'll like it better here than at McMurdo. The food's better."

The hint of a smile appeared on her mouth. "Is that all?"

"Well, I'm here. People consider me an irreplaceable asset." He stuck out his hand, still covered in the huge mitt. "Nik Forde."

The woman brought her own mitt to touch his in the polar-gloved equivalent of a fistbump, but didn't reply right away. He watched her eyes squint slightly, as if the face around them might have begun to frown. "I know who you are. It's me, Tess. Tess Beauchamp." Her eyes seemed to search his. "It's nice to see you again."

At the confirmation of her identity, Nik couldn't react fast enough to hide his surprise. A twitch of her eyebrow let him know she'd noticed.

They'd started dating right before she'd had to leave HAARP—well, started groping might be more accurate, he admitted. Then she'd blown up at Greg Simpson and left under a storm cloud of epic proportions, and he'd never heard from her again.

Which means she probably has no idea that I owe my career to her.

Her abrupt and frankly jaw-dropping exit, not even halfway through her fellowship with Greg, had given Nik his chance. He'd been Greg's second choice for the HAARP fellowship that year and had been paying his own way at the base just to get the experience. Greg had offered him Tess's place and Nik had jumped at the opportunity. He'd dug into the work without questioning his decision, or his boss's decision. Or contacting Tess, to let her know what had happened and to offer his condolences for the deaths of her grandparents.

Greg had worked him like a slave, which was the standard, accepted treatment for post-docs. Of course, when Nik had come back to work for Greg all these years later, the situation hadn't changed much. Greg was still an asshole and a slavedriver.

"Why are you here?" Nik asked, for lack of anything better to say.

"Nik, if you don't mind, I'd rather not talk now," Tess replied stiffly, then paused. "My sinuses are imploding from the altitude and my ears are completely blocked. My throat is raw because I spent most of the last hour of the flight throwing up, and I think I might have broken a few ribs during the turbulence because the seat harness was so tight. I'm in no mood to chat."

Nik nodded and watched her hood fall forward again as she bowed her head. He continued to stare at the garishly bright fabric as his brain churned with questions.

This didn't make sense. Tess Beauchamp, headliner in the industry, recent Flint hire, and one of the people at the very top of Greg's "people I loathe" list, makes an unannounced, late-season arrival on the Ice with an entourage in tow. At this time of year, it couldn't be anything as casual as a courtesy visit or a victory lap. Besides, as second in command, Nik knew Greg hadn't authorized any visitors—especially her—nor had he asked Connecticut for any backup or any new bodies. There were no openings on the team, no trouble, no one who had to be replaced, and yet the look she'd just given him had made it clear that *she* was surprised that *he* was surprised to see her.

Someone has to be on the way out.

And if Tess was the replacement, the candidates were few. With her background and stature in the field, she wouldn't be sent down here just to be one of the team. She was a specialist's specialist when it came to all things atmospheric. She probably had half the brass at the Pentagon, NOAA, and NASA, not to mention a few international agencies, on her speed dial.

Oh, crap. It has to be me.

Recollections of all the stupid pranks he'd pulled, all the times he'd seriously pissed off Greg, galloped through his memory. Trying to figure out which incident had sent Greg over the edge made Nik wince. Then he frowned.

It can't be me. Even if he wanted to get rid of me, there's no way Greg would ever work with her *again. No way in hell.*

His brain froze.

It's Greg. It has to be.

Nik slowly let out a breath. Everything was running smoothly at TESLA. There hadn't been any mistakes made—there had been a few weird tests now and then but no misfires or accidents, nothing that he knew of that would warrant Greg's removal. He knew there wasn't a chance that Greg had asked to leave. Which meant that Flint had reasons for wanting Greg out, and out *now*. Otherwise, the decision would have been made two months ago or six months from now, when getting a replacement here could be done safely. Instead, Flint defied all logic and common sense to get Tess Beauchamp here now, putting her and a plane full of people at risk. He shook his head.

Greggy, Greggy, Greggy, you abrasive, micromanaging prick, whatever did you do to piss off Croyden so badly?

The question burned a brand into Nik's gray matter.

When the slow trip back to the habitat ended, the passengers and their drivers disembarked in the garage and herded themselves into the ready room to strip down to their normal clothes. Then Kendra bun-

dled Tess and a few of the less robust other newcomers off to her office for a quick check.

Still silent and preoccupied, Nik left the ready room
and walked straight to the office of the only person on
the base who could provide the answers he was looking for.

7

A loud knock on his office door startled Greg. He immediately shut off his monitor. Although the door was shut and no one could see what he was doing, his reaction was instinctive. No one ever needed to know what he was doing or to disturb him while he was doing it. Anyone who worked for him quickly learned that. Interruptions of any kind were unacceptable unless something mission-critical was at stake.

It wasn't just his privacy—or in this case, his work—that he protected so fiercely, it was his mindset and his process. When he was deeply immersed in his work, the rest of civilization ceased to exist, and the transition back to the mundane world was difficult if it had to happen abruptly. He'd never explained it to anyone because few would understand. He'd accepted long ago that, in the course of the world's history, extraordinarily few people had been given the mental capacity and creative genius to operate on the intellectual plane he did; those who didn't weren't worth the time it would take to enlighten them.

Instead, he just insisted on his world running his way. It was the least that he deserved and it had proven time and again to be the best strategy. The routine success of his projects was uniformly due to his requirements; he kept everything and everybody running smoothly. Nobody ever had to worry about surprises. He knew those who worked for him muttered about control issues, that he was obsessed with his work. Instead of being offended, he was flattered. Most of the world's great thinkers had been labeled obsessive, if not by their admirers, then by their enemies. History had proven, however, that such words had had no effect on their achievements. Nor would the opinions of Greg's subordinates have any impact on the legacy he would leave to the world.

There was another, stronger knock on the door. "Hey, Greg, I need to talk to you."

Of course you do.

Tess had arrived, and had likely already caused the installation personnel to suffer an unexpected and unpleasant disruption to the usual smooth routine. It was an unforgivable breach.

Greg opened his eyes and glared at the still-closed door, his annoyance deepening at the flat bray of Nik Forde's Boston accent. Nik had joined the TESLA team three years ago and had quickly become the biggest thorn in Greg's side. Nik was no longer a postdoc who could be browbeaten into compliance. He didn't have to worry about getting a recommendation or whether his antics might damage his career. Nik was a top-flight scientist now, well respected by his peers and in possession of a reputation for employing creative approaches and daring solutions. He also had a reputation as a world-class smart-ass, and between his arrogance and his insouciance, Nik had refused to become merely another cog in TESLA's well-oiled machine. To Greg's extreme exasperation, Nik was forever questioning things that ought never be questioned, treating flippantly subjects that should be respected, and openly stating that he had no use for hierarchy or authority.

All of which should have made Nik a short-timer, but he'd proven to be too good at his job—and at dealing with bureaucrats—to replace. And he was Nikola Tesla's great-grandson. Greg knew he possessed some of that great man's papers—papers Nik couldn't even begin to appreciate.

The fool kept them in the open, framed and hanging above his desk. Greg had often visited Nik's office when the younger man wasn't there, expressly to study the documents. The information he'd gleaned had allowed him to fill in the last gaps in a theory that was ground-breaking in their field. Greg not only had the keys to the kingdom now, he had all the power that went with it. He'd learned how to bypass the boundaries of Nature—and subjugate her.

"Greg." Nik had taken to pounding on the door.

Taking the three steps to the door with stiff knees, Greg jerked it open. "What?"

Nik smiled and said, "Got a minute," in such a way that it wasn't a question at all.

"No," Greg replied, and began to close the door.

A hand shot out to stop it. "Sure, you do. A plane just landed. Perhaps you heard the announcement."

"I heard it," Greg said after a deliberate pause.

"Guess you were too late to the ready room to go out and help clear the landing strip, huh?"

"Yes."

Nik leaned one faded jeans-clad hip against the doorjamb and folded his arms against his broad, Polo-covered chest. "Well, guess what? The plane that landed—pretty hard, by the way—is an Ilyushin with the company logo on it. Go figure." He rubbed a casual hand over his stubbled chin. "Carmel McTeague flew it in. Everyone is kind of wondering why no one knew they were coming. Especially Carmel. She was expecting a welcome committee."

Greg said nothing, and didn't change his expression of cool indifference.

"Even after they passed BSR, no one warned them about the weather, so she didn't turn back or divert to Neumayer or SANAE. And guess what else? Since no one knew they were coming, we had to bust our asses to get out there and plow the runway in time. They all could have been killed a dozen times over." Nik fixed a hot gaze on Greg's face. "What gives?"

"The flight was canceled," Greg replied stiffly.

"Really?" Nik feigned surprise. "Someone should have told the pilot."

"Yes, someone should have."

Kicking the door shut behind him with a move better suited to a longshoreman than a Beacon Hill Brahmin, Nik stepped into the room, moved the files Greg deliberately kept stacked on the room's lone guest chair, and sat down. He slouched with his ass perched on the front edge of the chair, knees wide apart, arms refolded across his chest. His dark eyes glittered and everything about him bespoke aggression.

"Care to share what cargo was so important that it had to be delivered this long after the no-fly deadline passed?" he asked, his voice dripping with acid. "Or should I make that *who* was so important?"

"You'll be informed at the appropriate time."

"I'm second in command, Greg. I want to know why Tess Beauchamp just walked through our doors."

Greg stiffened. "Might I remind you, Nik, that if it hadn't been for me, you would be writing sleek algorithms for people who trade weather derivatives on Wall Street, instead of developing code that can alter weather systems. Yet you have the nerve to behave like this, to question me. I think you've forgotten your place."

"Hell, yes, I'll question you. Looks like I should have done it more often. And 'my place' isn't somewhere in the backroom with the boys, Greg. As assistant director, 'my place' is right here with you. So tell me what the hell is going on?"

"As I said, you'll be informed in due time. Surely you have better things to do than harass me."

Nik adjusted his slouch to a cockier angle. "Can't think of any."

"Nik—"

"From what little I've heard, that was a hell of a storm they flew through, Greg." Nik's voice had dropped so low that it met Greg's ears and went not a millimeter further. "Huge winds aloft, seriously low pressure at the surface. Know something else, Greg? I know you did it. I saw what you did when you did it. I just didn't know why." He paused. "So what was your goal? Did you want them to divert and be grounded somewhere for a few months, or did you want them to die?"

Greg kept his eyes on Nik's dark, accusing face,

kept his voice steady and calm as he replied, "This conversation is over, Nik."

Without another word, Nik stood up, turned on his heel, and left the room.

Other than enduring the flight from hell and the humiliation of climbing out of the plane on legs that could not support her weight, Tess's reintroduction to the Ice had been pretty much what she expected. The blast of frigid Antarctic air that assaulted her the instant the aircraft's door opened was the same; even inside the cavernous hangar, the wind was laden with snow that had strafed her like spray from a pellet gun. Her breath froze into a frosty ring around the mouth opening of her balaclava. The extreme dryness of the air had made her eyes sting and then water. The resulting tears on her eyelashes had turned instantly to crystals.

Antarctic bling.

She'd spent less than five seconds on the ground before being hauled upright and shoved into the huge tracked vehicle that had pulled up closest to the plane. Moments later, she'd discovered it was Nik who was playing host. She'd known it was him from the first word out of his mouth. That deep voice with the JFK overlay was one of a kind.

But Nik had disappeared upon arrival at the installation while she'd been hustled off to the clinic. Now, after being checked out by the curious but quite unamused base doctor, and made to drink a pint of Gatorade, she'd been released into the wilds of the TESLA habitat.

As warm welcomes go, this one sucks.

She headed up the tight, circular staircase outside the clinic door. At the top of the stairs, Tess paused to get her bearings. She'd studied the layout and photographs of TESLA, but she still wasn't quite prepared for the real thing. For openers, the installation looked nothing like any other polar research station she'd ever been in—and she'd set foot in most of them. From the outside, TESLA looked like a short stack of white pancakes separated by squatty wedding-cake pillars—not unlike other recently built stations with similar space-agey designs. It was the inside that set TESLA apart from the rest.

The interior held no hint of the usual stripped-down, bare bones, government-issue economy that inhabitants of other stations accepted as their lot because of cost and logistics. Even the new Belgian station, hailed as state of the art when it opened, was as inviting inside as an unfinished basement.

But from the first step beyond the ready room, it was apparent that neither cost nor logistics had been an issue in the design of TESLA. There was no open ductwork anywhere, no visible plywood or unfinished walls, no industrially spare furniture designed for functionality and built to take a beating. In fact, nothing about the place was the slightest bit utilitarian. In contrast, the lounge she entered at the top of the stairs resembled a public room of an elite, old-fashioned boarding school. Tess felt like she'd wandered onto the set of a period film instead of the world's newest, most high-tech polar research station.

The walls were paneled in what looked like real wood. Wing chairs and deep couches upholstered in rich fabrics sat in small clusters around polished tables. The furniture was elegant, solid, comfortable, and anything but institutional. Heavy draperies lined much of the exterior wall, presumably covering the continuous flow of windows that encircled each level. The floors were bamboo, stained dark and highly polished, and covered with thick Oriental-style carpets that looked like the real deal. The walls sported real art—some photographs obviously taken on site as well as paintings that could easily belong in a museum.

The atmosphere was one of studious calm. The presence of a real fireplace burning cheerily in the corner took her by surprise, but underscored the room's overall warmth and comforting coziness.

At the moment, the sitting room resembled a frat house on a Sunday morning, minus the smell of stale beer. Every person who was on the flight was present. She was apparently the last to join the group. Some of the crew were asleep, sprawled on the comfy-looking sofas or slouched in the wing chairs. A few sat at a card table, their heads resting on folded arms. The remaining ones were still upright, sucking on fresh mugs of coffee. One of the crew caught her eye and motioned to a tray on one of the tables, which held several insulated carafes and clean mugs.

"So, do you like it better than McMurdo?"

Her heart lurched at the low voice murmuring an inch from her ear. She spun around.

"Nik," she said, letting out a hard breath, "please don't do that. I'm still kind of jumpy from the flight." She studied the good-looking, dark-haired, dark-eyed, not-quite-as-tall-as-she-was guy standing there wearing faded Levi's and a hot-pink, short-sleeved Polo golf shirt. He was eying her just as thoroughly and apparently liking what he saw just as much.

You've aged well, Niky. Really well.

"Sorry." He smiled. "It's been a long time, Tess. How are you? You're looking good."

His smile was still pretty potent and, before she could stop herself, she brushed some loose hairs from her forehead, then tucked a few more behind her ear. "Thank you."

He laughed. It was a nice, familiar sound. Coming from a nice, familiar face. That sat atop nice shoulders and a trim, in-shape body that was a pleasant surprise. He hadn't been buff at Gakona. There hadn't been time or a place to work out. Clearly, there were both at TESLA.

His nice face and body report directly to you, Tess. So forget about it.

After a moment of nearly awkward silence, Nik extended his hand and they shook. "Welcome to TESLA."

"Thank you. I'm so glad to be here. I'd have kissed the ground out there if I hadn't known my lips would freeze to it."

"So that's what you were up to. I thought your legs gave out."

She smiled. "They did."

"Nervous flier?"

"Angels would have been nervous on that flight."

Nik laughed again, displaying straight white teeth framed by his easy smile. "I'll take your word for it. Where are you headed now?"

"To find Fred Tate and Tim Bamberger, who flew in with us, and then the three of us need to go to wherever Greg is."

"If they're not here, they must be in the dining room. You haven't seen Greg yet?"

"No, I've been in the clinic choking down electrolyte fluid," she replied with a wry grin. "But I do need to see him. Is he around?"

"He's in his office. I'll take you there. We can cut through the library to get to the dining room," he said, and led her out of the lounge.

Tess stopped short at the next threshold and looked at him, not hiding her incredulity. "Books? You guys shipped real *books* down here? Haven't you heard of e-readers?"

"You don't like books?"

"I love books, but it had to cost fifty thousand dollars a crate to get them down here. For that kind of money, I can live without the paper cuts."

"Come on, Tess. Remember how everyone bitched about the lack of them up at HAARP?" Nik laughed. "Greg remembered that. Don't get me wrong: he's still a colossal pain in the ass about most things, but then he demands something like this on our behalf and, well, it almost makes him human."

Tess glanced at him again, one eyebrow slightly aloft. It was a look meant to tell him that he was heading into awkward territory. He picked up on it immediately and gave a short nod.

As appalled as she was by what it must have cost to furnish the room—any of the rooms she'd seen so far—Tess had to admit she was soothed by the sight of all those hard-bound treasures. They really did make the place feel warm and friendly.

"Anyway, apparently he—Greg—decided that this eighteenth-century English country house look would keep the place cozy and keep people a little less stressed out. You know how he is; the pace we keep down here is close to your basic churn-and-burn doctoral program. Never rest on your laurels, keep asking, keep working, keep striving, question everything and everyone—except him." Nik gave her an easy grin.

"Is it working?"

"So far. Most of the team has been down here for more than a year, and we haven't turned into a reality TV version of *Clue* yet. No fights, no murders, no Mr. Green in the dining room with a bloody hammer."

Tess smiled. "I guess it's true that some things never change."

"Meaning?"

"You're the self-appointed neighborhood smart-ass."

"As ever. Gotta keep the tone light," he replied with a satisfied look.

She nodded, then returned her gaze to slowly pan the room. "So the whole place is like this? I mean, I studied the layout, but most of the photographs in the file were of the arrays."

"No. The work spaces are very high-tech and un-cluttered and bright. The personal quarters and common areas were designed to provide a visual and mental change from the work spaces."

"Does that work? Does walking down those stairs give you that 'ah, I'm home' feeling?"

Nik resumed walking. "In its own way. Given the hours we keep—which are self-defined and therefore pretty odd—it's nice to be able to literally leave the work behind when you leave the third floor. You pass through that high-security doorway and go from the twenty-first century back to a calmer one." He shrugged. "When your entire world is narrowed down to about twenty thousand square feet, every little bit of artifice helps."

"So, speaking of working hours . . . If you weren't expecting the flight, what was everyone doing up and dressed at four A.M.?"

"Like I said, we keep crazy hours. But, normally, not that many are up now. Today is a special day, though. It's April 27th." He glanced at her. "Ring any bells?"

"Will I be graded on this?"

"I'll give you a pass since the date would be different at McMurdo. Today is the last day that the sun will rise above the horizon here at the Pole. We'll be performing a little ritual later in the day, and we needed to prepare."

Tess laughed. "Ah, yes, the rituals. I won't ask. I'll just look forward to it."

"Actually, the truth is that our wake-sleep cycles are shot. I hope you're braced for Big Eye," Nik said, referring to the condition that afflicted nearly everyone who wintered over. Part insomnia, part attention-deficit disorder, with a few other more physical issues thrown in, Big Eye was the traditional name for the peculiar emotional fragility that frequently accompanied the complete disruption of the body's circadian rhythms coupled with extreme isolation.

"How could I forget about Big Eye? It's one of the joys of the Ice," she replied drily.

"It's not as bad here as it is at some of the other stations. We try to combat it. All the lighting is in the natural spectrum, and the fixtures are set to get brighter and dimmer to simulate daylight, twilight, whatever. It's Greg's attempt to keep everyone in sync. Here we are."

Nik stopped at the entry to a sitting room slightly smaller than the one they just left. This one sported a large-screen TV on the wall. The sofas and chairs in the room were more casual than those in the other room, and were suitable for sprawling.

The television was dark, and the only occupants of the room were the two Flint executives who had flown down with Tess. They sat side-by-side on a couch studying papers spread out on the low table in front of them. Greg was nowhere to be seen. Tess felt her mood, which had lightened considerably while chatting with Nik, become somewhat grim. Greg's conspicuous absence was not only a slap in the face professionally, but personally as well.

He should be here—somewhere—to greet us.

The two men stood up as Nik and Tess entered the room.

Tess smiled as she came to a stop near where the two men were standing. "Nik, I'd like you to meet Fred Tate and Tim Bamberger. Fred is Flint's deputy general counsel and Tim is the vice president of human resources for research and development. This is Nik Forde, assistant research director."

"Nice to meet you, Nik. Thanks for being part of the team," Tim said, shaking hands. Fred followed suit, then turned to Tess.

"Is Greg meeting us here?" she asked, forcing a smile.

"I've just gotten an email from him. Greg is in his office, expecting us," Tim replied diplomatically.

Nik turned to face Tess. "It's not unusual. Greg has always believed that rank has its privileges. He prefers having the mountain to come to Mohammed," he said lightly.

"In that case, let's party on," Tim replied, his voice so dry that it made Tess bite back a laugh. The four of them left the room.

* * *

"So," Nik said, stopping at the top of the circular staircase that had brought them to the upper floor, which housed the scientists' offices.

The corridor here at the top of the habitat was indeed, as Nik had said, a different world. The walls, floor, and ceiling were sleek, stark, and white. Abstract prints lined walls that were closely punctuated by anonymous doors that bore no nameplates or numbers, but each sported a small device that could read the strip on a smart card and another that read biometric data.

"Yes?" Tess replied absently, concentrating more on remembering how many doors she'd have to pass before finding Greg's office. According to the schematic she'd studied, his was the tenth on the left from the top of the staircase she'd come up.

"I think this would be a good time for you to answer the question I asked you out in the Delta," he said, his tone conversational and a little too smooth. "Why are you here, Tess?"

An odd mixture of amusement, annoyance, and even a little admiration ran through her as she looked into eyes that were dark, warmly familiar, and openly curious. His grin was charming and his voice meant to disarm. She glanced at the other men, who were watching her, probably for a cue.

"You're still adorable, I see," she replied with a smile that was slightly forced. *And dumb like a fox.* "You'll be brought up to speed, Nik. But I need to see Greg before I say anything."

Nik didn't miss a beat. "I'm not so sure he wants to be seen."

"That's his problem."

Her words weren't delivered sharply, but Nik raised an eyebrow anyway and gestured that they should continue walking.

Taking a surreptitious deep breath, Tess tapped on the door Nik had indicated led to Greg's office.

The door opened after a brief wait and then Tess stood face-to-face with Greg for the first time since that awful conversation fifteen years ago. Her stomach flipped at the sight of him.

He'd aged somewhat, but little about Greg had actually changed. He still had most of his hair and it was still thick and wavy, although the dark blond was well streaked with silver. His eyes were still bright blue and as warm as the glaciers ringing the continent on which the five of them stood. His clothing was still expensively geekish, his posture still steel-rod-for-a-spine straight.

Nope, not much has changed.

Tess met his gaze again and corrected herself. The look in his eyes was new. Harder, meaner— She stopped there, not wanting to start conjecturing.

What the hell. Crazier. *He looks wild on the inside.*

Something about seeing Greg standing there, rigid, made Tess unconsciously correct her own posture, adding another inch to the several she already had on him.

Not the best move, judging by the visible pulse that leaped suddenly at the base of his throat.

"Dr. Beauchamp. What a surprise to see you again." After a heartbeat's hesitation, Greg stuck out his hand.

Tess glanced at it, then looked at his face again. "Is it?"

He frowned at her.

"A surprise," she added, then took his hand, shook it once, and forced a smile. "It's been a long time, Greg."

His eyes narrowed at her familiarity, as she knew they would. "I see you have renewed your acquaintance with Dr. Forde."

She nodded. "Perhaps you remember Fred Tate and Tim Bamberger from corporate," she said, gesturing to the two men standing just behind her. "There are a few things the four of us need to discuss before—"

"Yes, we have much to discuss," Greg said, interrupting her. "But first I need to speak to the crew of that plane. Where are they?"

Tess's eyebrows shot up at his sharp tone. *That* plane?

"They're in the large sitting room," Nik answered smoothly.

Without a backward glance, Greg turned and began walking down the corridor, his movements abrupt. With mute surprise, Tess watched him go. There were a whole lot of things not to like about this situation. She glanced at Nik to see if he thought anything was out of the ordinary, but his expression hadn't changed.

"Well, that was pleasant," he said as Greg moved out of earshot. "It's nice to know that he's forgiven you."

"Ancient history."

"No way. I'm a constant reminder," he said with another easy grin. "You may not be aware of it, but I was first runner-up and got the crown and sash that you tossed at his feet."

She snorted—it wasn't quite a laugh—and said, "I imagine you gave him an equal and opposite set of headaches." She turned to the other two men. "Let's not be late for the show, guys."

They began retracing their steps.

"Is Greg normally this erratic?"

Nik looked at her in surprise. "Was he?"

Wasn't he? Hiding her dismay at his answer, Tess replied, "Maybe that's the wrong word. His departure just now was a little . . . abrupt. I remember him being more likely to order someone out of his office or demand someone come to him, than to dart away like that."

"'Dart'? What's with these words?" Nik laughed. "You weren't in his office, so he couldn't tell you to leave it, and the people he wants to see are in another room. They wouldn't all fit in his office."

Nik's non-answers struck her as somewhat disingenuous, so she smiled and dropped the subject, but filed away her questions. "You stayed in Gakona for a few years after the fellowship ended. How did that go?"

"I stayed there for about seven more years." He shrugged. "It was fine. I liked the money, I liked the work, and I liked the other researchers. Greg was the only thing I didn't like."

"But you came back to work for him again, down here. What prompted that?"

"Same things, pretty much. Bleeding-edge research, good people, great money. Greg's personality is really the only trade-off. His work ethic and ability to finesse the science haven't changed. They're still awe-inspiring. Given my history with him, I consider myself damned lucky to be here."

Nik's words held no hint of sarcasm, and Tess couldn't help but look at him with mild surprise. Which he noticed immediately.

"Of course, if you ever repeat that, I'll have to kill you," he pointed out.

She smiled. "So, it's been okay working for him?"

"Depends on how you define 'okay.' He's a complete prick on a good day. And I've never known anyone in such dire need of getting laid."

"A mental image I could have done without," Tess muttered as she heard the two men behind her stifle laughter.

CHAPTER

By the time they caught up with him, Greg was facing the flight crews, most of whom had gotten to their feet. Judging by the openmouthed astonishment on their faces and the white-knuckled grips some of them had on the mugs of steaming coffee in front of them, he had already launched into a diatribe.

Tess entered the room and stopped slightly to one side of Greg. Nik was a step behind her. The other two men remained standing near the door. The security team, which Tess hadn't seen since getting off the plane, stood leaning against the wall at the far side of the room.

"Sir, there's no way we would have been cleared for departure if someone down here hadn't approved the flight plan," Carmel McTeague said, legs braced, arms folded across her chest, apparently unfazed by the white-hot anger in Greg's eyes.

"Are you calling me a liar, Ms. McTeague?" he asked quietly.

"That's *Captain* McTeague, and no, sir. I'm suggesting that there might have been a snafu somewhere. Someone down here granted us permission to land and maybe forgot to tell you. Getting clearance is protocol, sir. I signed the flight plan and filed it. Approval was granted and your name is on the sheet."

Greg seemed to swell up, his face hardening into an unattractive mask of fury. "This is preposterous. You're accusing someone here of—"

This is going nowhere fast.

Tess cleared her throat and stepped forward. Everyone in the room turned to look at her. "Dr. Simpson, before this discussion goes any further, I want to speak with you privately."

Those glacial blue eyes shifted to gaze at her. Greg's brow furrowed; Tess assumed he was trying to cut her down to size.

Not gonna happen, cuddles.

She met his eyes calmly. The silence between them lasted long enough to have everyone in the room squirming except Nik, whose face wore its usual smirk.

"Certainly, Dr. Beauchamp."

Giving the fliers a quick, neutral glance, Tess followed Greg out of the room, the two executives on her heels.

Tess kept up with Greg as he walked briskly up the stairs and down the corridor. He stopped in front of one of the blank, unlabeled doors and opened it with the hard swipe of a smart card and gestured for her to enter ahead of him.

"Just Dr. Beauchamp right now, if you please," he said as Fred stepped forward. "You may wait here."

Tess let her gaze flick from Tim to Fred. "This won't take long. Just wait there, if you don't mind, guys."

Just inside the doorway, Tess stopped short, taken aback by what she saw.

The office was very small, as she'd expected from the schematics. The furnishings and equipment were standard and completely unremarkable. Three monitors, a keyboard, and a mouse—nothing more—sat on the shining surface of the desk. There was a small file cabinet in the corner; the bookshelves lining the walls were full to the point of almost overflowing. Every book was in perfect order, aligned at the edge of the shelves, just like his bookshelves in Gakona had been. Framed art and awards hung on the walls. A thick white rug covered the floor. A single chair sat to the right of the door.

The office was functional and neat.

But it was *not* the office of a man who would shortly be on a plane heading stateside.

She turned to face Greg. The cool appraisal in his eyes was more than a little unnerving.

"May I ask what you think you're doing?"

Tess watched him for a moment before answering, calculating her best response. Physically exhausted by the long, uncomfortable flight and still emotionally drained from the drama and sheer terror of the last few hours of it, not to mention the weirdness of the last ten minutes, Tess knew she wasn't at her best. Nevertheless, she was determined to get things out in the open, despite whatever convoluted head trip Greg was on.

"No, you may not," she replied calmly. "I won't play that game, Greg. You know why I'm here. Now why don't you explain this?" She gestured around the room.

He seemed taken aback momentarily, then his eyes went cool again. "What are you talking about?"

"This room. Your stuff. Were you intending to leave all of your materials for me?"

"Excuse me?"

"You haven't started packing. You know you're heading out on the return flight. Why isn't your office cleared out? I mean, *my* office."

He'd seated himself and taken a file from a drawer. He opened the file as he spoke; she knew he was attempting to dismiss her. "My dear Dr. Beauchamp—"

Despite her resolve, Tess realized that even after all these years, his voice, with its sneering overlay and the lock-jawed flatness of his Midwestern accent, hadn't lost its ability to abrade her nerves. Overplayed patrician scorn had always been his first weapon of choice, and he never failed to wield it with blunt force. Condescension oozed out of him like toxic sludge.

"Since you're no longer my research director and I'm no longer your grunt, I'd prefer it if you didn't speak to me in that tone of voice," she replied, holding on tight to her temper. "And please call me Tess."

He flicked his eyes at her and she saw something like amusement in them.

Overshot the runway. Damn it.

"Very well, *Tess*. Please, have a seat."

"No, I'll stand, thanks. It was a long flight."

A weird little smile appeared on his face, like that of a snake, complete with its own brand of repellent charm. It sent a ripple down her spine.

"How's your family, Tess?" he asked, pausing minutely before adding, "All still alive?"

"They're fine, thanks," she replied coldly.

"Our communications are state of the art—we have our own ground station—," he began, and she narrowed her eyes at the bizarre segue. He noticed that and paused. "After we've had our little chat, be sure to let your parents know you've arrived safely. Being the only child and all that." He paused again. "Are they still living down there in Mexico, off the grid, far away from the fruits of their labors? Or have they lost their taste for the simple life and moved closer to cooling towers and fallout zones?"

Tess felt her fingers curl into fists and immediately flexed them open, cursing the day she'd told him anything about herself. About her family. About the role her parents and grandparents had played in the nuclear arms race and the industries it had spawned. But he'd asked the questions in an interview and she, wanting to get the fellowship desperately, had been candid. Too candid. He'd used her candor against her whenever he wanted to rile her.

She smiled back at him, tightly. "Let's skip the pleasantries, Greg. And let's not insult each other's intelligence by pretending that you don't know why I'm here. Fred and Tim are waiting out there to facilitate the paperwork and the speechmaking. When that's over, you can hop on that big comfy plane and fly back to civilization."

A flicker of something—frigid rage?—in his eyes made her wary, then he folded his hands on his desk as he stared at her.

"I believe you've spent time on this continent, Tess, although not in the interior—"

Okay, the attention deficit disorder is something new. "I've spent time at the Pole, mostly at Amundsen-Scott," she interjected.

"Then you're aware that our weather here is significantly colder and windier, and much less predictable than at the coast," he said in the voice one would use to open a lecture in Meteorology 101. "Which means there is no guarantee that we'll be able to fly out as planned. Why your trip was scheduled for now is beyond me."

What brand of bullshit is this?

She didn't let her expression change. "Greg, you *do* know why it was scheduled now. Croyden wants you in a corner office in Connecticut *on Monday,*" she said bluntly.

He said nothing, just continued to stare at her with that creepy smile.

Tess stared back. "Why did you lie to everyone just now when the pilot—"

"'Lie'?"

"That's what I call not telling the truth. Do you have a different word for it?"

"It's a strong accusation to make."

It wasn't easy for Tess to keep her temper under control. "Look, I'm not here to play semantic games or any other kind of game; I'm here to replace you," she said very slowly and very clearly. "You are no longer in charge down here, I am. You and the entire staff here at TESLA know this. I was copied on all the emails sent to you by Gianni Barone, who is your boss and mine. I *know* you received those emails."

"Yes, *I* received the emails Gianni sent out, but no one else here did."

Tess stared at him. "*I saw the emails,* Greg. I know who they went to—"

"I run a tight ship down here, Tess. It's a high-stress workplace and the personnel here have the weight of the world on their shoulders. The pressure is remarkable. The ramifications of a single small mistake made here at TESLA would be far-reaching and likely disastrous. A wrongly calculated parameter, an unforeseen variable, or a random, unpredictable event can overleverage all of our hard work, transforming the outcome from a planned mission perfectly executed to chaos of unimaginable, even epic proportions."

The condescension returned to his face, his voice. "You understand the theoretical vagaries of chaotic systems, Tess, but do you know what we really do here? If you do, then you understand why it's necessary to keep intrusions and distractions to a minimum. It's critical that my team focuses on the work at hand. To that end, I have created a pleasant, comfortable environment in which they can operate free of outside disturbances."

His meaning sunk in seconds later and Tess couldn't help it; she felt her eyes widen in shock. "Outside disturbances like . . . email? You censor their email?"

"Censor?" Greg bristled at the word, then gave her that creepy smile again. "No, I monitor—I filter it. Yes, that's what I do. Just as we take pains to remove impurities from our air, water, and power systems, I take extreme care to filter out all communication impurities that could potentially damage our most important system."

"The most important system being the people here," she said, wondering if he was playing some sort of sick, nerdy practical joke. That was a long shot; he had no sense of humor.

"Yes."

"And one of the impurities you might filter out would be, say, a series of messages from the vice president of strategic planning in which he discusses a change in the administration of the installation."

"Yes."

A thin, icy needle of fear pricked her nerve endings as Tess held his gaze. "So, other than you, no one here knew we were coming? And no one knows that you're on your way out of here, or that I'm meant to be running things now?"

"That's correct."

"Okay. It's time to get Fred and Tim in here," she said, reaching for the door handle.

"Not quite yet, Tess." The quiet voice stopped her, and she looked at him. He looked back at her with unblinking, unwavering reptilian eyes.

Exuding a confidence she didn't feel, Tess let her hand drop. "There's not a lot more to say, Greg. You agreed to leave but now that I'm here, you've changed your mind."

"I haven't changed my mind. I never had any intention of leaving. I merely told Croyden what he wanted to hear."

"You don't have a choice in the matter. Flint wants you gone."

"Of *course* I have a choice in the matter. I'm here. The executive committee is not. And it all boils down to the fact that I don't want to leave," he said simply. "They never should have suggested it. They certainly should never have challenged my initial response. They had no right to do that."

"No right? Greg, they had every right. TESLA belongs to Flint. They paid for—"

"No, Tess. TESLA belongs to *me*," he whispered, getting to his feet. "I've been working toward this my entire life. Fifteen years ago, while you were looking backward and whinging about dead relatives and needing time to *grieve,* I was working toward *this.*" He lifted his hands toward the ceiling as if he were elevating a wafer during a church service, then lowered them in a slow, expansive movement.

Just the way he said it, so mildly, so calmly, made a small spider of alarm race through Tess's brain.

I'm the one that needs to be on the next flight out. I've been dumped headfirst into a bucketful of crazy. Damn you, Gianni.

Greg's eyes focused on a point on the wall above her head as if he were looking into the middle distance while addressing a crowd. "TESLA is *my* creation," he began. "I built this installation from the ground up. I made every decision from its very inception. I chose the design, the materials, the construction, the mission, and the personnel. Even now, I approve the menus and the movies and what kind of paper we put in the printers. Which operations we carry out and which operations we reject. *No one* contradicts me or supersedes me. Not even—" He stopped abruptly, and he brought his gaze to her face, staring at her and through her at the same time. "The decision to send you down here was the first challenge to my authority."

He leaned forward then, his eyes boring into hers. She had to will herself not to flinch.

"I've spent a lifetime working toward making this happen. I don't know what made them think I would turn it over to anyone. Especially you."

"Oh, honestly, Greg. Think about it. I'm the only logical repla—"

He waved her words away. "Don't talk to me about logic. You haven't put in your time."

Tess gaped at him, startled by his accusation. "Are you serious? How do you figure that? I've spent years—"

"You haven't put in your time with *me*. On *my*

projects. Working by *my* side. Learning what you need to know from *me*. I don't care who else you've worked with. *I* decide who gets to come here. No one as undeserving as you should ever have been allowed to set foot on this installation." He paused. "You're a quitter."

She brushed a sweep of her long blond hair behind her ear and refolded her arms across her chest. "I'm not a quitter, Greg. I just don't like to be abused," she said calmly.

He held up one long, slim-fingered hand as if to stop her comment in mid-air. "Nik Forde replaced you on that fellowship. His experience with me is the only reason he's here. Even so, that gives him no right of succession, and you're significantly less worthy of such a distinction."

Tess stared at her former mentor. "With all due respect, Greg, choosing a successor is not your call to make. This is a commercial, scientific enterprise, not a medieval fiefdom. Whether you like it or not, Croyden Flint and the board of directors own TESLA, and they want me to replace you."

For the first time since they began talking, fire lit Greg's eyes. Rage he must have worked hard to keep carefully hidden was there for her to see. He practically spat his next words at her. "You know nothing about what we really do here—"

Bad things. Things we never authorized and never would authorize, Tess. The properties of the ionosphere have been changed.

A cold pit of fear opened in her gut as Gianni's words came back to her. Maintaining her composure became more of a battle than a challenge.

"Then enlighten me, Greg. I've reviewed the entire

program: the mission, the installation, its operations, program goals, execution, successes, and failures. Tell me what I don't know."

The fire went out of him as fast as it appeared. His usual icy demeanor was back in place. "Why should I?"

"Because I'm in charge now. I want a smooth transition."

"You propose to take charge while I'm still here?" he asked after a brief, amused pause.

She lifted a shoulder and let it drop. "I'm already in charge, and you won't be here for long. You're leaving as soon as they get the plane refueled."

Greg watched her for a long, silent moment and then shook his head. "You're making a mistake, Tess. I'm as critical a component of this installation as the wind turbines or the phased arrays. TESLA cannot function without me."

The alarm Tess had felt a moment ago was tempered by a distant cousin to pity. Greg had an enormous ego; it was in keeping with his character that he'd see her as the undeserving usurper of all of his power, all of his work. Nor did it surprise her that he considered himself one of TESLA's vital organs instead of a replaceable cog. It didn't take a genius to realize that the thought of leaving TESLA had to be killing him.

Tess blinked. *Get a grip, girl. Greg Simpson bleeds liquid nitrogen and probably eats kittens for lunch. I refuse to cut him any slack.*

She pushed away from the wall. "Greg, I know you don't trust me with TESLA, but Croyden does, and that's what matters. I can only assure you that we'll make it work."

He looked at her blankly for a long moment, then

offered a bland smile. "Well. If you are so confident that you can replace me, it appears the only thing for me to do is to bow out gracefully."

Tess stared at him, almost breathless at the rapid change in his demeanor and decision. "Thank you," she said warily.

"Of course," he said with a slight, stiff nod. "Naturally, the staff, the programmers, and the other scientists will welcome you, although I feel obligated to advise you that this is a highly structured organization that places a significant value on routine and predictability. Attempts to disturb the status quo will not be met with any support from the team. You need that support when living in an environment as isolated and dangerous as inland Antarctica. But, of course, how you choose to behave while you're here is up to you, Tess."

While I'm here? Why does that sound so temporary? Cold distrust layered itself on top of her wariness.

He moved to the door and opened it, watching her from within that bubble of odd stillness. "If you don't mind, Tess. I have things to do."

"I'll survive, Greg. So will TESLA. Nik and the others will fill in whatever gaps you're referring to."

Ignoring her words, Greg looked into the hallway. "Gentlemen, I believe we need to talk?"

"Thanks for the chat," Tess said as she passed in front of him.

Greg's face was immobile, his expression cold, as if it were carved from the stone of those lethal cliffs she'd flown over just a few hours ago. "You're very welcome, Tess."

* * *

The meeting with the two executives from Flint was brief and mostly administrative in scope. Before they left his office, they confiscated his computers, his phone, and his smart card. He didn't mind. He didn't need them anymore.

Greg closed the door behind them and leaned against it.

The mere fact that Tess had arrived had sealed his fate, and when she hadn't backed down, he knew he'd had to accept reality. He was leaving TESLA. Oh, he'd played his part well; he'd signed the surrender. Though there was no longer any need to maintain his control, he would leave with his head high and his dignity intact as befitted a king dethroned. But he was not without power, nor was he without the means and the desire for revenge.

And he lusted for the taste of its sweetness.

He had already ensured that Tess would not bother him again. Not publicly, not privately. She and every money-grubbing, soul-sucking miscreant who had participated in the decision to send her here would be eliminated. Messily, dramatically, but inescapably.

It was all over, really. Much earlier in the day he'd embedded the software into the system and had set it to initiate as soon as a new password—Tess's password—was activated on the system. She'd be complicit in her downfall, and the world's.

All that was left for him to do was sit back in whatever five-star hotel Flint booked him into and watch his legacy unfold.

He removed a few mementos from the shelves, then glanced around the office. His eyes rested on a small framed quotation from Mohandas Gandhi. *Be the change you wish to see in the world.*

He smiled, congratulating himself on having lived true to those words, albeit in a way the great man never intended. He left it where it was, hanging over his desk, and completed his perusal of the room.

She can have the rest of it. And find out for herself that none of it will do her any good.

He left the office then, and headed toward his personal quarters.

9

CHAPTER

Outside Greg's office, Tess stood still for a moment, waiting for the sense of surreality to fade. Fred and Tim had searched her face with cautious glances, but she'd waved them into Greg's office with the assurance that she'd meet them in the dining room later.

The two other men remained outside the office after the two executives went in. She knew they were the security team that had flown down with her, but everything that had happened since she'd met them in Capetown had wiped their names from her mind.

"Are you okay?" the taller one asked.

Tess raised her eyes to meet his. "Fine."

"You don't look fine. You look—" He paused, and the other filled the void.

"You looked freaked out."

She smiled. "No, not freaked out. Just still tired from the flight. I'm sorry, but I don't remember your names."

The taller one pointed to himself, "Joe," then jerked his thumb toward his colleague: "Teddy."

"Nice to meet you again. And thanks for coming

down here." She paused. "Do you do this for every-one?"

"It's standard procedure when there's a transfer of power," Teddy replied. "Coming here is a better gig than accompanying some suit to a test farm in Iowa."

She laughed. "I've never been to Iowa, but I'll take your word for it. So do you stay here—" She stopped and indicated Greg's office door.

"Yes, ma'am. Unless you'd like one of us to accompany you somewhere."

"No, I'm fine. Just curious. I've never done this before. Walked in and taken over, I mean."

"It's a piece of cake," Joe replied. "Just give 'em hell."

Right.

She smiled and headed down the corridor toward the central staircase, inwardly cursing herself for letting her delirium at being offered the job get in the way of pressing Gianni harder on the issue of Greg.

When she was far enough along the curved hall-way that she could no longer see anyone, she stopped and leaned heavily against the wall.

I need food. And a sanity check. And to find out when that plane is going to get gone.

Glancing down the hall in both directions, Tess still saw no one, and took the opportunity to slide to a sitting position, eyes closed, the back of her head resting against the wall. Just for a minute. Just until she was thinking clearly.

It was futile.

One comment Greg had made overshadowed everything else that had come out of his mouth: "Do you know what we really do here?"

Her answer should have been an emphatic yes, but just the way he'd said it, the fact that he'd thought to ask it, told her that she probably didn't know the full scope of what went on at TESLA. And if that gap in her knowledge wasn't critical, Greg never would have mentioned it.

Tess blew out a slow, steady stream of air and took in another, then repeated the sequence and dragged herself to her feet so she could track down Nik or some food.

Or some answers.

She hadn't gone very far when she saw Nik leaning against the curve of the inner wall, hands thrust loosely into his pockets, watching her walk toward him. His normal, casual clothes—the hot-pink Polo and seriously worn blue jeans—reminded Tess that she hadn't changed out of the unfashionable but mandatory flight gear, which started with waffle-weave thermal underwear and just got better from there.

She slowed her pace and made eye contact, wondering what role he played in Greg's warped fiefdom. As she drew near, Nik straightened and gave her a half-smile.

"I'm beginning to wonder if you have a job," she said lightly.

His dark eyes flashed with amusement. "I do. I'm just not doing it at the moment. So, were you welcomed into the fold like one of the family? The prodigal daughter, perhaps?"

Tess slowed to a stop in front of him. "I wouldn't quite characterize it as a 'welcome.'"

"Greg doesn't like change."

"He never has."

"Where are you headed now?"

"I wouldn't mind finding a hot shower and a hot meal."

"I can help with both. Follow me," he said, turning in the direction she was headed. "I heard you speak at a conference a few years ago. In Moscow."

She smiled as they walked next to each other. "I've been to Moscow twice, both times for conferences in the same year. For one, I spoke about ionospheric echo boundaries. At the other, I debated climate change as the only outsider on a panel of chaos theorists."

"I attended echo boundaries."

"The other one was better."

"So I heard. Someone threw a chair."

"No, the chair fell over when he stood up to throw a punch. It connected, too. Not bad aim for an eighty-year-old. But I doubt the heart attack he had afterward was worth it," she added drily. "So why didn't you stop by to say hello?"

He gave her a sidelong glance, a rueful smile teasing at the corner of his mouth. "You were the most popular girl on campus. I couldn't get near you."

Tess laughed. "You should have tried harder. I would have loved to see you. I think I was the only girl on campus at that conference. With a speaking role, anyway. Were you waiting for me just now? Wondering if I'd emerge in a body bag?"

"Not really. I was heading downstairs and heard a noise. I waited to see if it was you. Do you mind if I ask you a blunt question?"

"It's apparently impossible to stop you."

He grinned. "Are you going to answer it this time?"

Tess felt her smile fade as she met his eyes. She slowed to a stop. "Yes, I'll answer it. But not here. Where's your office?"

* * *

Nik blinked at her as she stood there, facing him in the hallway in that flannel-shirted he-girl getup, her blue gaze meeting and holding his.

That was easy.

He cleared his throat. "Back there. I was standing outside of it when you saw me. But, hey, I can wait until you've had something to eat."

Tess shook her head, sending that long blond hair spilling over her shoulder. She pushed splayed fingers through it, then tucked some of it behind one ear. It was a gesture he remembered from the old days. It meant she was distracted and maybe a little edgy. Then again, she was hungry and tired and most likely had just gotten verbally slapped around by Greg. She had every reason to be edgy.

"Thanks, Nik, I appreciate that, but we might as well get this over with."

Get it over with?

He shot her an odd look but said nothing.

"Besides, I have to meet Fred and Tim in the dining room when they're done with Greg," she added. "This won't take long."

Maybe I am on the way out. "Okay," he said and motioned toward his office.

They walked in silence and came to a stop outside the unadorned door a few minutes later. Nik could feel her watching him as he swept his smart card through the sensor and pressed the pad of the middle finger of his right hand to the biometric screen.

"Nice touch. Did you think that up all by yourself?" she asked drily.

Nik turned to her with a grin that usually got him what he wanted. "Why be boring? Besides, it sums up my attitude to all the security measures around here."

"The security protocols aren't onerous. I think in some ways it must be easier to live in a top-secret vault than to work in one and then have to keep your nose clean for the other sixteen hours a day when you're in the real world," she said as she preceded him into the space at his invitation.

"Well, you have a point, but come on: no Internet connectivity? No attachments coming through on emails unless they're cleared by a censor? That's a bit over the top. The NRO and CIA let their people have outside connections."

"And they're hacked regularly."

Nik shook his head. "If we can't be trusted not to be stupid, we shouldn't be here." He walked past her and tapped the iPod on his desk, bringing it to life, before gesturing for her to sit in the chair wedged into a corner of the small, bookshelf-lined room.

"I haven't heard the Eurythmics in years."

Like, maybe, fifteen years? Since that first night we got a little inappropriate with each other?

He stifled a smile. "I'm lost in the eighties, what can I say?" He picked up the small remote control unit and increased the volume slightly, then met her eyes again. "But I didn't put it on to entertain you."

She blinked and a look something like . . . relief? . . . washed over her face. "You think your office is bugged?"

"I operate under the assumption that everything is bugged. Greg is one weird dude. That much has *not* changed," he said, settling into the chair behind his desk. "So, Tess, talk to me."

"Interesting decor." Tess lowered herself into the chair as she looked around the room.

"Thanks." Nik watched her eyes stop, then widen,

as she studied the set of framed pieces over his desk. It took her a minute to drag her gaze back to him.

"I'm here to replace Greg," she said simply.

"I figured it had to be me or him."

She smiled at him, her blue eyes clear and direct and slightly surprised.

"I mean, your reputation is . . . stellar, Tess. There would be no other reason for someone like you to be here," he said, hoping he looked less awkward than he felt.

Tess gave him a faint smile and crossed her legs.

Even in those crappy clothes, you look good. Damn good.

Blond and brainy was his favorite combination of traits in a woman. Adding a pair of huge baby blues and wraparound legs made the combination seismic.

"Okay, so . . . why?" he asked.

"Why what?" she replied warily.

"We might as well get it out in the open. Why you and not me? To run the show, I mean." The question didn't come out as smoothly as planned. Even he could hear the irritation, the bashed ego in his voice.

To her credit, Tess didn't look away. "I wasn't privy to those conversations, Nik. Gianni approached me with the offer. That's all I know."

He picked up a pen that was lying on his desk and snapped the cap on and off while keeping his gaze on her. "Come on. You never asked him why Greg's lieutenant, who's been here for years, who knows the site, the people, the project, the players, wasn't getting the spot, even temporarily, when it would have eased the transition? It didn't strike you as just a little odd, given the time of year?"

She said nothing.

"It's your turn to talk," he pointed out.

She leaned back in her chair, letting her head rest against the wall. "Do you really want to know, or do you just want to get your digs in, Nik?"

"I want to know."

"Okay. I don't know why you weren't chosen. I wasn't told. Gianni only said that Croyden Flint wanted me here. Can we move on?"

"No."

"There was a comment made about leadership skills, Nik, but it wasn't in the context of what you're asking."

"Croyden doesn't think I have leadership skills?" he demanded.

Tess lifted an eyebrow. "Like the ones you're displaying now?"

As annoyed as he was, Nik had the urge to laugh. He squelched it and kept his eyes on her.

"I don't know what Croyden thinks of you. Gianni said it," she continued. "But from what I've seen in your personnel file, you're still considered a loose cannon. A practical joker—"

"That can't be in the file," he snapped, mildly embarrassed.

"*Everything* is in that file. You know Greg is a lunatic for details."

"So why is he getting yanked?"

"Croyden wants him in Connecticut to work on other projects. Greg's known that for months. He kept refusing their suggestions that he return to headquarters, so they finally had to get tough. He wasn't told that I was on my way until I was in the air. It's a dreadful way to handle it, but they wanted him out immediately." Tess looked like she was about to say something else, then stopped.

"Hell of a way to do it," he muttered. "What a bunch of douche bags. When were we going to be told?"

"Everyone on staff here was informed at the same time Greg was, via email."

Nik thought about that for a minute. "Today?"

"Yes."

"I never—"

"—got the email. I know. Greg intercepted it." She paused, then added, "He told me he did."

They sat in silence for a while. She was apparently willing to give Nik whatever time he needed to absorb her words. Either that or she was falling asleep with her eyes open.

They're great eyes.

Down, boy.

"So where does this leave us?" Nik asked.

She paused, a slight frown creasing her forehead. "Define 'us.' "

Not a bad response.

Nik smiled. "Where does it leave the installation? Who's in charge?"

Every trace of a smile disappeared from her face and her eyes, and a coolness came into her voice, lowering it and making it stronger than it had been. "I am."

"Greg's stepped aside?"

"Yes."

Nik stared at her. "Seriously?"

"Yes. He'll be leaving shortly." She paused. "When he's gone, I'd like your help to make the transition successful."

"You haven't changed. No sucking up, just cut to the chase."

"What would be the point? I need your help."

Nik rubbed a hand along his chin, wishing he'd shaved, wondering if she'd noticed he hadn't. "Tell me what you have in mind."

Tess's light blue eyes were penetrating, and there was no mirth or softness in them. "Before I do that, I need to know if you're aware of anything that's happened here that might have made Croyden and the board want Greg out."

Nik pushed the thoughts of Ellie's flight to Fiji—and the storm Greg had sent to meet Tess's plane—out of his mind and leaned back in his chair. He folded his arms across his chest and looked at her. "No. He's the ultimate rule-follower. It's annoying as hell and, if anything, he's gotten worse since the array came on line. There are checklists for everything, two-person protocols for making changes, no one is allowed to do a freaking thing without Greg's approval. . . . So who's going to break the news to the gang?" Nik asked with a disingenuous smile and watched Tess's expression slip into a slight frown. She clasped her hands in her lap, so tightly that her knuckles went white. It was the only nervous gesture that he'd seen her make since she fell off the plane.

"I'll let Greg handle it if he wants to."

Nik gave a low whistle before breaking into a huge grin. "You got your Kevlar underwear on?"

"No, just the thermals, which I will shuck at the first opportunity."

"I'm happy to help."

She bit back a smile. "Thanks for the offer." Her face became serious again. "You asked how I want you to help. The first thing I need to do is avoid a turf war, Nik."

He shook his head. "I don't think that will be a problem. But I have to tell you that this change will come as one hell of a big surprise, Tess."

"I know it will, but I'm glad to know that you think they'll handle it. And if they can't—" She shrugged. "It goes on the TDB list."

"You mean TBD: the To Be Determined list," he said with a laugh.

"No, I meant TDB: the Too Damned Bad list. So, fill me in on what you do down here."

"What I do? Specifically?"

"Well, yes, but . . . what you all do," she replied, then cleared her throat, as if she were hoping to sound casual. "What TESLA does."

Nik's bullshit detectors pinged inside his head and he shifted his position on the chair. "You don't know?" he said carefully.

"I thought I did, but a few minutes ago, Greg implied that I didn't. Actually, he *told* me I didn't." She shrugged and forced a smile. "That's news to me. I've read everything that exists about this place—every technical report, every confidential memo—so if he believes there are things I don't know, that means there are things about this place that aren't committed to paper. Humor me. Tell me what they are."

Her light tone didn't fool Nik at all. He watched her for a minute before answering, slowly swiveling side to side in his chair, his gaze not leaving her beautiful, exhausted, but dead-serious face. "Our mission is simple. We improve Flint's bottom line by monitoring, predicting, and occasionally modifying the weather."

"Occasionally? Only the weather? And only to benefit Flint?"

Where are you going with this? "Yes, occasionally," he replied. "What else do you think we can do? And who else do you think we'd help?"

"I don't know, Nik. Maybe you could run a few things past me."

He shook his head. "Just the weather, Tess. We try not to micromanage things. We just send the weather Flint wants where Flint wants it."

"Nothing more than that?"

"Nothing more than that."

He could tell Tess wasn't satisfied with his attitude or his answers—*hell, I'm not too happy with her questions*—but she nodded at him and stood up. "That's good to know, Nik. Let's head down to the dining room."

CHAPTER

As Nik opened the door to his office, Greg's voice came over the small two-way radio clipped to Nik's belt, calmly asking all staff to assemble in the dining room in ten minutes. A moment later, Fred, Tim, and Greg emerged from Greg's office and joined Nik and Tess as they headed for the stairs. Fred fell in step with Tess.

"Well?" she asked under her breath.

"Not a problem. He signed where he was meant to sign. Hardly said a word."

"He never has been one for histrionics."

"He wants to make the announcement," Fred said, giving her a glance out of the corner of his eye.

"That's fine with me."

By the time they arrived in the dining room, TES-LA's staff and the flight crews had assembled and were waiting for them.

With a stance that oozed confidence, Greg planted himself in the center of the open space at the front of the room.

Tess sat at a table directly in Greg's line of sight with Nik on one side of her and Fred on the other. Tim and the two security men leaned against the wall near the room's entrance.

"This ought to be interesting," Nik murmured. "Or at least unforgettable."

Greg Simpson looked at the sea of faces assembled before him. They covered the range from Generation X to Geritol; most major ethnic groups were represented and the male-female ratio was nearly even. He'd always thought of TESLA as his little biosphere, the world in a microcosm—doing work that affected the macrocosm.

Some of the people facing him had been with him since the beginning, when he was at HAARP; some had been recruited in the planning stages of TESLA; some had been hired as the installation was being populated. It didn't matter how long he'd known them. They were his people, all thirty-three of them. He'd personally interviewed and hired each of them, from the chef to the mechanics to the doctor to the guy who ran the greenhouse. They were loyal, and he was utterly confident that nothing Flint's directors or Tess Beauchamp could do or say would change that. The flight crews stood off to the side, complete outsiders. But Tess, pompous, arrogant Tess, sat at the table directly in front of him, looking too calm.

He took a single deep breath and began to speak. "Thank you all for being so prompt. You all have other things to do, so I will keep this meeting brief. As you are aware, a short while ago, Dr. Tess Beauchamp arrived on an unannounced flight." He saw the pilot and flight crews exchange grim looks. "I will leave it to her to explain why her flight was unannounced and why she was willing to put herself, the flight crews, and all of you in danger to reach TESLA. Without further ado, I would like to formally introduce to you Dr. Tess Beauchamp, who will be replacing me, effective immediately, as director of research at TESLA."

His delight hidden, Greg watched startled surprise cross everyone's face. Stepping aside, he swept his hand through the space he'd vacated, indicating that she should fill it.

As if she ever could.

Sucking on a canister of Halon could not have left Tess's brain any more devoid of oxygen than Greg's blunt, accusatory introduction. She knew, and everyone else in the room knew, that he'd strung her up and left her swinging in a very strong wind.

Never fight with a pig in a mud puddle. You'll just get dirty, but the pig will enjoy it.

It was her father's favorite expression. Her mother's was much more succinct:

Well, Tess, what do you expect from a pig but a grunt?

Both sayings applied. Greg Simpson was clearly swine.

More slowly than she wanted to, Tess got to her feet and took a few steps forward before turning to face the small crowd. She waited for the quiet gasps and unquiet murmurs to die down, then cleared her throat and sent a look of sheathed daggers toward Greg as he took a seat at an adjacent table.

"Thank you, Dr. Simpson, for that . . . concise introduction." She took a deep breath as unobtrusively as she could manage. "As Greg said, I'm Tess Beauchamp.

Let me say first of all that it's a tremendous privilege to be here. In our industry, this installation is every scientist's idea of Disneyland, or maybe heaven. TESLA represents the most forward-thinking, cutting-edge technology and ideas on this planet, and I'm honored, deeply honored, to be here. The work you're doing here is reshaping the way the world works, making life better for many people, and repairing many ills suffered by the planet." She took another breath, willing her voice to slow. "My arrival was, as Greg said, indeed dramatic and, unfortunately, very, very dangerous. The effort to get me here put all of you at additional risk. For that, I apologize." Tess paused for a beat. "But I do have to thank Captain McTeague and her crew for getting us here in one big piece. I've flown in and out of the interior a few times, but I have never witnessed a more amazing feat of foul-weather piloting than I did today."

The expressions on the faces before her didn't change; they still ranged from curious to guardedly hostile.

Tough crowd.

Well, I'm tougher.

Straightening her already stiff spine, Tess held the pause as she made eye contact with as many of the people as she could. Some looked away, others took her effort as a challenge.

Here goes.

She let a faint, bland smile cross her lips. "I know now that my arrival was unanticipated by most of you. And that Greg's announcement is a shock—but I assure you that it was not intended to be. Emails announcing the change in administration were sent to all of you by the vice president of strategic planning,

Gianni Barone, informing you of this change. But due to a system protocol—" *Why am I saving your ass, Greg?* "—those messages were, unfortunately, never delivered to you."

Most of the people in the room were staring at Tess with doubt in their eyes, some with anger, but all were checking their reactions against those of the person next to them. Tess knew it wouldn't take long for one of the scientists to question her—she'd never yet met one who didn't speak his mind wherever and whenever it suited him to do so. She wasn't disappointed. Not thirty seconds passed before one guy, dressed a little bit like a throwback to the 1970s with his yoked, pearl-snapped shirt and graying ponytail, broke through the low buzz that had erupted.

"I've never had a problem getting emails from outside. Why are you saying this one was blocked? Who blocked it?"

From the corner of her eye, Tess saw that Greg had gone very still, sitting as rigid as a wall of ice in his chair, radiating an anger that was just as hard and just as cold. His eyes bored into her.

Scared that I'm going to tell the truth? Well, don't you worry. I will. Eventually.

Tess gave the questioner a small, tight smile. "What's your name?"

"Etienne Pascal."

"Thank you, Etienne. I'm glad you asked. I can't give you the answer you want right now. For the moment, suffice it to say that I know that it was, but I need more data before I present my findings. I'll welcome the question again and answer more fully when I've looked into the situation at greater depth." She let her gaze sweep the room.

"As you know, I've recently been named a vice president of special projects for Flint. Part of the reason Flint hired me is that the board of directors wants Greg at the corporate headquarters, developing new projects. They want me to continue the excellent work that he has begun here. Being here is the culmination of a dream—" She managed not to smile when she said it. "—and I have only the utmost respect for Greg's many years of hard work, devotion, and innovation, and for his creative genius, which has brought TESLA from a fantasy to reality."

Her eyes swept the room again, making contact with as many people as would meet her gaze. "Let me reiterate that I wish I had a better way to tell you this. I know it's a shock. I know that. But I am confident that together we can make this a seamless transition and continue TESLA's vital and exciting work. I'm looking forward to getting to know each of you. Until we get a chance to chat, I want you to know that I have an open-door policy. Don't hesitate to ask me questions. Stop me in the hall. Sit down next to me at dinner. Don't be shy." She paused for a beat. "Please join me in offering my thanks to Greg Simpson for all he's done."

Knowing everyone in the room was paying close attention, Tess looked directly at Greg and began to applaud. The others shuffled to their feet and followed suit while Greg remained in his chair, flushed and glaring at her. Then he stood up stiffly and faced his followers. The applause died immediately. The sudden silence in the room nearly vibrated with suppressed emotion as they all waited for . . . something. Greg offered a tight thank-you and a brief bow, then left the room without saying more and without making eye

contact with anyone but Tess. Trying to be as unobtrusive as possible, the two security agents followed him.

*Okay, then. One publicly humiliated narcissist is
now headed back to civilization.*

Nearly everyone came forward to shake her hand
and welcome her, but no one was effusive. Most were
cordial; a few couldn't manage to hide their hostility;
others were hesitantly sympathetic. No one lingered,
and in a matter of minutes, the room was empty of
everyone but Tess, Nik, Fred, and Tim.

"That went well," she said, forcing a smile.

"Sarcasm aside, it did go pretty well," Tim said. "You
didn't expect them to welcome you with open arms,
did you? Or for him to behave with anything resem-
bling grace?"

"No, but I didn't expect to be set up like that, either.
Tighten noose, release trapdoor, see body swing." She
paused and shook her head. "He's really a jerk, isn't
he?"

"*You're* asking that question?" Nik replied. "You
could've returned the favor by telling them he cen-
sored their email. Why didn't you?"

"I didn't see the point. I'm not vengeful, despite the
rumors," she said with a tired grin. "Sometimes I bite,
sometimes I bark, and sometimes I just move on. Besides, I have the emails and can show them to anyone
who doubts me."

"Well, let's get this show on the road," Tim said
after a brief, awkward silence.

"Right. Thanks, guys. Let me know when you're
ready to head to the plane," she replied, and the two
executives left the room with a nod.

"So, what about you? Are you still with me, Nik?"

"You're not the only one who plays it straight. I'll

let you know if I change my mind." He shrugged. "I mean, hell, why not be on your side? This is the most excitement we've had down here since the kitchen fire on Christmas Eve."

"I appreciate it, Nik. I'll see if we can't take that excitement factor a notch higher, then," she replied with a laugh. "I'm all for setting short-term goals."

Carmel McTeague, the pilot who'd flown the plane from Capetown to TESLA, strolled into the room with a certain amount of swagger in her approach. "That was some speech."

"Glad you liked it," Tess said.

"I'll give you a heads-up when we're ready to head back to the hangar. You know, for good-bye kisses and all that," Carmel replied with an irreverent grin. "I'm aiming for an hour. We've got Bessie all checked out and fueled up and humming, so we're just waiting on the guest of honor and his luggage." She paused. "And just so you know, Dr. Beauchamp—"

"Tess."

"Thanks. Just so you know, other than Nik here, these Teslans are not the friendliest bunch of Icers I've known."

"Thanks. I'll withhold judgment until I've actually met a few more of them." Tess turned to Nik. "Would you mind doing the honors?"

"I thought you'd never ask. Should we start with the townies or the gownies?"

"Townies," Tess replied. "They might be bigger pushovers."

"You've been away too long, Tess. There's no such thing as a pushover among those who winter over on the Ice."

* * *

"Nik, do you know where Tess is?"

He unclipped the small walkie-talkie from his belt and brought it close to his mouth. "She's with me. We're in the greenhouse. Do you need her?"

"Greg's gone to the ready room to suit up for the flight."

"Great, thanks, Dan." Nik hung the radio on his belt. "Shall we?"

Tess nodded and glanced at her watch. "Not bad. It's only been forty-five minutes. Looks like they'll take off on time."

"Carmel doesn't mess around. She's too used to the weather here. When she says 'wheels up in an hour,' it usually happens." He held the door to the greenhouse open so she could pass through into the corridor separating it from the rest of the ground floor.

Tess turned to shake the hand of Mick Fender, who managed the space.

"Mick, this place is amazing. You'd never know you were in Antarctica. It's a . . . biosphere in miniature. An entire farm in one thousand square feet," she said, looking past him into the small space lush from floor to ceiling with vegetables, herbs, fruit trees, and redolent with good earthy scents.

"Thanks," he replied, beaming. "Come down whenever you need a reality fix. Just walking around and breathing the air down here is therapeutic."

"I'm sure it is. I'll take you up on the invitation."

Tess and Nik let the heavy doors swing shut behind them.

"Flint should have put pictures of that in the files they gave me," Tess remarked. "It's incredible that anyone can make that happen down here. I mean, rabbits, chickens, pygmy goats . . . indoors? In Antarctica? I thought real books were a luxury. I can't imagine what the bean counters at Flint thought when orders came through for shipping cubic yards of *dirt* across the world."

"Considering the orders came in under Greg's pet project, I'd say they just sighed and paid them," Nik said with a laugh. "Yeah, it's a pretty cool place. Mick's a little quirky and can get touchy at times, but he's half botanist, half farmer, and total genius. And a veterinarian. Not bad for a kid who grew up in a walk-up in Brooklyn not knowing that chickens existed outside of shrink-wrapped grocery store packages. But if you need any surgical procedures done, make sure Kendra does them," Nik added drily.

"I'll keep that in mind. The ready room is down this corridor, right?" Tess asked, then pointed to the radio at Nik's hip. "I need one of those."

"You're right. I should have taken care of that already. I'll get you one as soon as we go upstairs."

They came to a stop outside the windowed door to the ready room. Tess could see that Greg was the only occupant. He sat on a bench, pulling on the layers of clothing he'd need to leave the habitat. Stepping aside, Nik opened the door and let Tess go in alone.

Greg glanced up at her briefly, then returned his attention to what he was doing.

"Have a safe trip," she said, hoping her tone was somewhere between pleasant and professional.

"That's outside my control," he replied, his voice as dry and cold and brittle as the air outside.

Okay. She cleared her throat. "Thank you for everything you've done here, Greg. It's a real tribute to your creative genius that you could bring an installation like this into existence. I think the transition will be smooth, although I know I have a steep learning curve ahead of me."

He looked up at her again, frigid amusement in his eyes. "You have no idea. But you now have what you've probably always wanted."

"That's not—," Tess began.

Greg ignored her interruption. "I leave you with the old admonition to be careful what you wish for because you will surely get it. You wanted to make a name for yourself in our small corner of academia, and you did. Now you want the power and the glory that goes with it—"

The patronizing sneer embedded in his words strafed her ego. "*No! That's not—*"

"But can you handle it?" He paused, then reached for the heavy insulated overalls. "It would be easiest on the staff if you use my office. I've only removed my personal effects. I've left all my files for you. I've been locked off the system, of course, but my computer is still in the office, and there's a copy of my hard drive on a set of flash drives in the top drawer of the desk. Nik will make sure you get set up with passwords. I've told Ron—" He looked up. "He's the lead programmer as well as director of IT. I've instructed him to delete all of my passwords from the system."

Five more minutes. Suck it up for five more minutes, and he'll be out of your life.

With an effort, Tess swallowed the overwhelming desire to defend herself and instead uttered a tight, barely gracious, "Thank you. I—" *God, how I hate you.* "Thanks for leaving everything for me, Greg. I'll do my best—"

"I didn't do any of it to make your life easier. I did it to ensure that this installation and the arrays continue to carry out their mission." He turned to look at the window on the door leading to the operations area. "It seems we've got an audience."

Tess looked behind her to see a small swarm of people standing in the corridor, chatting with Nik but clearly waiting to get into the ready room. "Is that the flight crew?"

"No, Tess," he said after a brief, belittling pause. "The flight crew is already at the plane. This is the ground crew. I don't want to keep them waiting. Open the door."

Though bristling at his imperious tone, Tess reminded herself again that these were his last minutes on site, and pulled the door open.

"Come on in, the water's fine," she said with a big, fake smile. The ground crew that would take him to the hangar and assist in the plane's departure crowded into the small room. She hadn't met all of them yet, so Tess just smiled and maneuvered to the door. "Godspeed, Greg, and I wish you all the best. I'll see the rest of you in a little while."

Fred caught her eye and she took a few steps to where he and Tim and the security guys stood. She shook their hands and offered quiet thanks, then backed out of the room and shut the door behind her.

Letting out a long breath, she looked at Nik. "Can I watch it take off from somewhere?"

He grinned. "Afraid it might not?"

Yes. "Of course not."

The huge plane held no cargo. Every sound echoed off the bare walls. Greg sat away from the incoming flight's crew members and the four other passengers— the two executives and their henchmen. He didn't need company. The noise of the plane precluded conversation anyway.

The massive engines revved and began to scream, then the plane began lumbering down the blue-ice runway. He shut his eyes as the aircraft lurched into the air, and then he smiled broadly, knowing that Tess herself would put his plan into action the moment she logged on to TESLA's internal network.

Everyone would realize almost immediately that things were going wrong, and they were smart enough to know *why* they were going wrong, but it would take them more time than they had left in this lifetime to figure out *how* those things were happening and how to stop them. And Tess, clueless, optimistic, open-minded Tess, might never figure out that she was the problem, that every time she logged on, she would be speeding up the actions he had planned for the world. Because before she could determine that, she would have to remember his words and divine their true meaning. It was all right there in the open, though, like a parting gift she didn't deserve. He'd been completely candid: he *had* done everything he could to ensure that this installation and the arrays would fulfill their mission. *His* mission.

11

CHAPTER

Nik ushered Tess into his office without any conversation. He didn't turn on the lights, but instead went to the far wall and pulled open the heavy draperies that covered the expanse of windows facing the airstrip. Tess stood next to him, battling a strange mixture of both elation and deep isolation that threatened to engulf her as she watched the plane slowly exit the hangar and maneuver into position at the end of the runway. The sight of it triggered a slow, wet, unwelcome burn behind her eyes; at the same time, it sent a powerful shot of adrenaline to her bloodstream.

I'm it. Greg is on his way to the U.S., and I'm here. She swallowed hard. *Please let things go right.*

From one hundred yards away, Tess could see the glow of the engines increase as the outbound pilot brought them up to full power. The plane began to move slowly, but in what seemed like only seconds, the huge, pale body of the Ilyushin was racing along the runway, its flashing wing lights sparkling on the slick ice beneath it. At last, the nose lifted and the wheels relinquished their grip on the earth. The plane rose steeply, slicing through the star-studded polar darkness as it banked sharply to the right. Then it disappeared from view.

Tess had expected the sense of elation to win out then, but she was wrong. The first emotion that assailed her as she looked into the vast, black depths of empty sky was something closer to fear wrapped in a smothering blanket of bone-deep aloneness.

"That's one chapter ended. Well, boss, looks like TESLA is yours now, warts and all."

Tess looked at Nik with a tight smile. "Before I completely believe that, I may need to talk to someone who saw him get on that plane and locked the door behind him."

Nik laughed as he flicked on his desk lamp. "He was on it. We'd have heard if he wasn't. So what now?"

She smiled and hoped it wasn't as shaky as she felt. "A shower and something to eat."

"That shouldn't be a problem." Nik reached for his radio and asked someone named Fizz to meet them in the large sitting room in a few minutes. Then he pulled the drapes across the windows and turned to open the office door.

Their eyes met and Tess felt a sharp jolt as the look on Nik's face changed from laughing insouciance to an expression of long-forgotten warmth.

She looked away from it.

"I'm glad you're here, Tess," he said in a voice not much louder than a whisper. "This is . . . it's going to be good. You've got all the qualities that Greg lacks and . . . well, you belong here. You'll shine."

The burn behind her eyes, which had only just begun to dissipate, became stronger and she glanced at the floor in a moment of self-preservation. She pulled in a deep breath and looked up, giving him a bright, false smile. "Thanks, Nik. It all happened so fast that it's still a little bit surreal, but I appreciate your good wishes and all the help you've given me so far."

After a second or two of awkward silence, Nick pulled open the office door and they moved into the corridor, stopping on the way to the sitting room to get the walkie-talkie Nik had requisitioned for Tess.

They had only been in the sitting room for a few moments when a thin, youngish woman walked in and approached them. Tess had seen her in the crowd when she'd made her speech, but they hadn't met yet.

"Ready to get settled in?" the woman asked Tess in a broad, unmistakably Irish accent.

"Very ready." Tess smiled and stuck out her hand. "Tess Beauchamp."

"Phyllis Reilly. Everyone calls me Fizz." She grasped Tess's hand and gave it a firm shake.

"It's nice to meet you."

"Likewise. It's a hell of a welcome you've had, if you ask me."

Tess looked at her in surprise. Part of her was a little startled at the casual response. The other part wanted to respond with "You don't know the half of it."

"Let's get you moved. Are those your bags?"

Tess nodded as the woman pointed to the two large duffels on the floor next to one of the couches. She realized that she hadn't seen them since they followed her off the plane. Someone had brought them up from the ready room.

"Is this all you've got, then? The two bags?"

"I travel light," Tess replied with a smile, then looked at Nik. "Meet me in the dining room in about twenty minutes. We'll continue with the meets and greets, then you can take me to the sandbox. If it's not too much trouble, I'd like to have temporary passwords by then."

"Not a problem. See you in twenty," he replied, and Tess returned her attention to Fizz.

"After you."

The younger woman picked up the larger of the two duffels and turned to face the door. "I've only just gotten your room ready," she said over her shoulder. "That's what I was up to when you were doing your meet-and-greets. I haven't cleaned out Greg's room, so for the moment I've assigned you to an extra room in the scientists' living quarters. It's never been lived in, so it ended up as storage. I just cleared it out. Are you ready?"

"Lead the way. Maybe you can solve a mystery for me, Fizz. Why are there separate living areas for the scientists and the non-science staff?" Tess asked as they moved into the library and continued through the installation and up the stairs. "Wouldn't it make more sense to have all the bedrooms together? I mean, for the sake of the layout—all the plumbing and whatnot?"

Fizz shot her a sidelong glance. "Sure, that would make sense. But it's not always logic that drove Greg. Did you ever see an old BBC series called *Upstairs, Downstairs*?"

Tess nodded.

"Well, there you have it: we're *Upstairs, Downstairs: On the Ice*. Class warfare without the bowing and scraping," she said with a wry grin. "We're the help, you're the talent. Most of us laugh about it, but there's a few of them—the scientists—who take it seriously. You'll figure out who they are soon enough."

"No, er, fraternization?"

Fizz let out a laugh. "'Discretion' is the key word there. Greg frowned on 'fraternization' in a big way. Said it takes one's attention away from work, which is the only gospel down here. Besides, you'll notice that the list of eligibles is fairly short, unless you're willing to settle. My opinion, anyway. Still, wintering over is a long time to behave yourself. I shudder to think of what some of these people must do when they go on holidays," she finished, almost under her breath.

Fizz stopped in front of a door and slid a smart card through the reader. At the sound of a low click, she opened the door and indicated that Tess should enter, then handed her the card.

"Oooh, nice. Better than any place else I've ever stayed on the Ice," Tess said, giving the small room a quick once-over. "A real bed instead of a bunk. A rug on the floor. Privacy. I'm impressed."

"We're not much on interior decoration down here, but I've gathered what I could. There's a private loo through that door, and showers are at the end of the hall. I'll leave you to get situated," Fizz said, placing the duffel on the floor near the bed.

Tossing her other bag on the bed, Tess turned to look at the woman. "Thanks, Fizz. This is wonderful."

Fizz hesitated, then let a grin cross her face. "Well, if no one else has said it, let me be the first. Welcome to TESLA, the nicest spot on the continent."

"Thank you."

"That was some introduction," Fizz continued, shaking her head. "I felt bad for you when His Lordship introduced you, but you seemed to handle it pretty well. I would've been tempted to drag the man bare-arsed down a gravelly road, but you kept cool.

Nothing else will come your way. Maybe some attitude, but I think you'll be well able for it."

"Greg and I go way back. I didn't expect him to welcome me with open arms," she said easily. "I just take things as they come."

"Best way to do it. So I'll go now and leave you to it," she said over her shoulder as she left the room. As soon as the door clicked shut, Tess pulled out her smartphone.

Gianni Barone was navigating the twisting roads of back-country Greenwich, Connecticut, on the way to his office when the phone rang. The name that flashed onto the on-dash screen of his Maybach had him pulling off the road into the huge gravelled and landscaped entrance to his neighbor's estate. He didn't want to be distracted by having to dodge enormous SUVs piloted by late-for-school teenagers on the narrow lanes while taking this call.

Throwing the car into park, he tapped the button that completed the connection.

"What's up?" he demanded before Tess could utter a word. "It's seven thirty. You landed at four. I expected to hear from you before now."

"It's been hectic."

"Are you okay?"

"I'm fine. Greg took off a little while ago."

Gianni blinked at the dark screen. "That's good," he said cautiously.

"You sound surprised," Tess replied.

"No, no, why would I be surprised? That was the plan. He knew he had to go."

"Uh-huh. The jig is up, Gianni. But we'll discuss that in a minute. The bottom line is that he's gone and I'm here. But there's bigger news down here. No one was expecting us."

"Say again?"

"Other than Greg, no one knew we were coming."

He frowned at the huge statue of Winged Victory perched in front of him in his neighbor's front yard. *Such subtle wealth.*

"Not possible. Everyone knew, Tess. You saw the emails. They went to the whole team down there. How could—"

"There are content filters in place on the local network, and Greg was the gatekeeper. Everything went through him. Or didn't. They truly didn't know I was coming. When we came into the habitat, I felt like a monkey on display in the zoo."

"How did you find out about the filters?"

"Greg told me about them. He said he didn't want upsetting news to distract the staff."

Gianni rolled his eyes in disbelief. *Crazy sonofabitch.*

"I'll get IT up here on it. We'll pull them down—"

"Don't bother. I'm sure the programmers down here can handle it. They do double duty as IT. But that's not the most important thing on my priority list. You need to tell me more about what goes on here."

Her words stopped him in the middle of a breath. Despite the repeated and increasingly pointed requests she'd made before she left, he'd been able to sidestep telling her the *real* reason he wanted her down there. He'd omitted any mention of the storm in Afghanistan, which, frankly, still sounded a little crazy even to him, and he'd been hoping his information was wrong.

"What do you mean 'what goes on here'?"

"It's—" She paused. "It's like I've stepped into some weird little fiefdom. I mean, okay, I knew it wouldn't be normal, given we're talking about Greg, and I know how he ran HAARP, but the extent of his social engineering down here is a little creepy."

Glad he'd been able to effect a course correction on her conversation, Gianni forced a laugh. "Social engineering? Come on, Tess—"

"I know it sounds dramatic, but I can't think of another name for it. Have you ever been here? It's not like any other station on the Ice."

"Of course it isn't."

"No, but . . . every need is met—the public rooms are like something out of Pemberley."

"Where?"

"Never mind. Everyone took Greg's departure so calmly. I'm not sure if I should be waiting for a revolution, or if they're all glad he's gone. Maybe they just don't care."

"Certainly, they all know what an asshole he is. They may well be glad he's gone."

Tess responded with a short laugh. "Well, don't get me wrong. It's not like there was a confetti parade when he made the announcement, but I didn't see any tears, either. Everyone kept a stiff upper lip, at least in front of me. But you'd think that since he's been the heart and soul of the place and his departure was such a surprise, things would be a little . . . disordered for a while. But everything seems fine. When I was making the rounds to meet everyone, they seemed okay with the transition. It's creepy."

"Were you expecting an armed insurrection? They're all professionals and it's a business decision. And they're probably giving you a honeymoon. Enjoy it while it lasts. If there's a reason they're not upset by his departure, you'll learn it in time. Have you hooked up with Nik Forde?"

A minuscule pause built before she answered and Gianni winced at his bad turn of phrase. He'd forgotten that they'd been rumored to be an item at HAARP.

"Yes. Nik's been very helpful. Funny. Same as ever, really. But very helpful."

"So, Tess, is everything good?"

"Yes."

Gianni frowned at the slight hesitation in her voice.

"Yes, it's all good," she continued. "I'll have a better grip on it when I've been here a few days."

He could still hear doubt in her voice and chose to ignore it. "I'm glad to hear it, Tess. I knew you were the right person for the job. Keep in touch, even if it's just a quick text, okay? Just until you settle in. Let me know if you have any other concerns about what you see or hear."

The silence on the other end of the phone stretched a little longer than it should. "I can't shake this feeling that there's something you aren't telling me, Gianni."

"You're probably just nervous because you're finally running a multi-million-dollar baby," he said, forcing levity into his voice as he stared out at the harsh, bright Connecticut sky. "Stay in touch, Tess."

Tess ended the call feeling less confident than when she'd placed it. But maybe Gianni was right. Greg was gone and she was in charge of TESLA and all the people who made the arrays and the installation work; that was enough to induce nerves in anyone. Of course, she thought as a huge yawn took her by surprise, it could just be that she was hungry and exhausted and more than a little overwhelmed by everything that had transpired in the last few hours—and weeks.

Enough introspection. There's hot water waiting for me at the end of the hall.

She wasted no more time and quickly settled into her new digs. Inside of ten minutes, her bags were emptied and her belongings put away. Then she gathered her toiletries and towels and headed for the showers. Given the tight water ratios every Antarctic base had to endure, she could take only a standard military three-minute shower—strip off, get in, turn the water on and wet down, turn the water off, soap up, water on, rinse, water off, get out—but it would be a shower. And, right now, that sounded awfully close to heaven.

Tess dressed in a hurry, pulling on the most sober outfit she had with her, though she knew it would generate looks and comments. It wasn't exactly standard Antarctic fare; nothing you could buy in Paris was. The fine black wool trousers fell in a long, slim line to the top of her low-heeled slingbacks and the loose, royal blue angora sweater draped over her curves. In Paris, Tess always wore a scarf with this outfit, tossing it artlessly over her shoulder, but she knew it would be way too much at TESLA. Nearly everyone she'd met was in jeans and T-shirts—two items she'd purged from her wardrobe when she'd headed across the Atlantic several years ago.

Grimacing as she looked in the mirror, Tess gathered her hair into a ponytail, gave it a few clever twists, and secured it with clips at the back of her head. It was a little messy and a little sexy, but mostly it was out of her way, which was the point. Then, she grabbed her laptop and headed for the dining room.

Since everyone at TESLA kept their own hours, food was always available, but the chef did what he could to maintain some semblance of normality by preparing meals appropriate to the time of day. Tess was just finishing up a quick, solitary breakfast of coffee, granola, and yogurt when Nik strolled into the room.

"Perfect timing," she said, setting her napkin on the table. She stood and brushed the creases out of her slacks.

"You clean up well," he said as he gave her a once-over.

She raised an eyebrow, not entirely pleased with the comment but deciding to ignore it.

"Thanks," she replied crisply. "I feel like a new person. I'd like to continue with the introductions. I think I've met all the ops and admin staff. That leaves the programmers and the science team."

Nik nodded, said, "You might have missed a few," then reached into his pocket and pulled out a walkie-talkie and a folded piece of paper. "This first line is your username. The rest are passwords, a different one for each system. You should change everything once you log in."

Glancing down at the list, Tess let out a soft laugh. "Power system: Bosslady01. Comms: DingDongGregIsGone!! Arrays: WeWillAlwaysHaveMoscow2008. God rights: HairyWart-on-satans-ass95." She looked up and met his grin. "You put a lot of thought into these."

"I wanted to make them easy for you to remember."

"Well done. They're unforgettable," she said, returning to her seat and turning on her laptop. "Let's see how well they work."

Nik sat down across from her. "That was what you called him, right? A hairy wart on Satan's ass?"

"I think it was actually an oozing wart on Satan's hairy ass, but that's just semantics."

"Is your room okay?"

"Wonderful. Luxury digs for an Antarctic outpost," she replied, her eyes on her screen.

"As I said, Greg didn't skimp on anything."

"Okay, so here goes. Power system," she murmured, and typed in her user name and password at the prompt. "Well done, I'm in. Give me a sec while I change it to something nowhere near as creative. There. Arrays." She glanced at the paper and keyed in the words, then glanced at the screen. "Okay, I'm two for two." She tapped a few more keys. "Comms. Done. Oooh, baby. Now we're cooking with gas," she finished with a laughing flourish.

The lights flickered so quickly that Tess blinked, and wondered if she'd imagined it. Then she saw the frozen look on Nik's face and knew she hadn't.

"Does that happen often?"

"No. That's the second time in four years. I think we'd better head to the sandbox—" His voice was clipped and his radio already in his hand when he was interrupted by a beep from the unit. It competed with a roar from the corridor outside the dining room.

"God damn it." The voice was male, Irish-inflected, and loud enough to make Tess jump. She spun around to see a large, long-haired, blue-jeaned, T-shirted man come crashing through the doorway nearest them. He charged at Tess and Nik, who were already on their feet, and came to a panting halt a foot away from them.

"Something wrong, Dan?" Nik's soft sarcasm made the other man suck in a loud, annoyed breath. "I'm not sure that you've met our new fearless leader, Dr. Tess Beauchamp. This is Dan Thornton. His official titles are base pilot and chief mechanic, but in reality, he pretty much keeps the physical plant running."

"I'm pleased to meet you," the Irishman said gruffly, then turned his gaze back to Nik. "Ay, I'd say there's something gone amiss, lad. That blip. What the fuck was that about?"

Tess's eyebrows rose at the man's vehemence, but she said nothing. Several people had gathered in the doorway and were watching the three of them intently, their faces tense and concerned.

"I don't know. We were just heading to the sand-box to ask the same question," Nik replied.

"What could it be, Dan?" Tess asked.

The Irishman looked at her. "It could be anything— a software glitch, hardware malfunction, something mechanical. I couldn't tell you. But we'd better get started looking for the answer."

"Radio the plane to ask—," Nik began, and Tess winced.

"I don't think that's necessary," she said as Dan replied, "It's well out of range already."

"Dan?" A female voice entered the conversation via their walkie-talkies.

"I'm here."

"It's Pam. I need you to go to the ground station."

"The what? Why?"

"The external comms just went down."

"What?"

"The external comms network just gave up the ghost," the woman repeated calmly and Tess's heart skipped a beat.

The worst thing that could happen at TESLA, at any Antarctic station, was for fire to break out. The second was a loss of contact with the outside world. For TESLA, in its remote location, the latter was particularly dangerous.

"I'll check it out," Dan growled into the radio unit, and looked at Nik, then Tess. "Now I've got to get back into all that fucking ECW gear I just shucked off, to go out to the fucking ground station to see what's wrong."

Tess cleared her throat. "You think something happened to the uplink?"

He stared at her, his blue eyes blazing, his face flushed, and she could tell he was trying to rein in his temper. "That might be part of it. I'd appreciate it if you would get the lads in the sandbox to start their diagnostics in the power system and the comms before I haul my arse back into the cold."

She met his eyes with a chilly look of her own. "Naturally, Dan. But while they're running diagnostics on the software, I think it's important to rule out that something *physical* happened to the power station. I'd like you to go take a look at it."

He let out a harsh breath. "Four fucking years into this party and when the lights go out, the first thing anyone can come up with is that my wires are suddenly shaking loose. In me arse they are. If you need me in the next ten minutes, I'll be in the ready room. And after that, outside."

Tess watched him turn around and walk toward the door, annoyance radiating from him.

Such fragile egos.

She turned to look at Nik as the two of them followed Dan out of the room at a slight distance. "Correct me if I'm wrong, but doesn't the external comms network include everything that connects to something outside of these few square miles of ice?"

"Yup."

"And all of it just went black?"

"Seems that way."

"You're very calm."

"There's no point in panicking. We've got layers of backups," he said, then brought the radio to his mouth. "Pam?"

The same voice that had announced the failure came on line. "Yes, Nik?"

"The backups kicked in, right?"

"No, actually they didn't."

He came to an abrupt stop. "What?"

"We're working on it, Nik."

"Thanks. We'll be there in a minute." He looked at Tess. "Are you okay?"

"Of course. There's a reason this happened, and we'll find it and fix it," Tess replied coolly, and took a deep breath to ward off the sensation of her stomach dropping to her weakening knees. There was nothing that would stop her racing heart.

They resumed walking and smiled reassuringly as they moved past the small clutch of concerned staffers. But as they began ascending the twisting stairs, Nik said in a low voice, "I'm not much of a believer in conspiracies, Tess, but I also don't believe in coincidences."

"I'm glad I'm not alone in that. What are you thinking?"

"I'm thinking that the power blip is connected to

the comms situation," he said, and paused. "I also think we can start looking for a causal relationship to that big old Ilyushin moving out of comms range."

"You think Greg did this?"

He said nothing for a minute, then met her eyes. "I don't like jumping to conclusions, but the timing is suspicious."

"But it's too perfect. He wouldn't have known exactly when the plane would take off, or when it would be out of range."

"True, but I think he also would have figured that even if he were still on the ground, you wouldn't have asked for his help."

Stung by the implication, Tess stiffened her back and ignored the comment. "I reviewed the comms systems on paper and saw the copy of the system they keep at HQ, but refresh my memory."

"We have two identical backups for every system. One goes to the vault—" He glanced at her. "You know about the vault?"

Tess nodded as they reached the top of the stairs and began to move down the hall. "In the ice beneath the installation, lead-lined, blast-proof, cipher locks."

"Right. The other backups are uploaded to one of our satellites and downlinked to a facility in Connecticut. Both sets of backups are heavily encrypted and streamed in real time. So if the uplink is gone, the vault copy is still running."

"So, everything can't be down, Nik."

"Everything external could be. If the backup had come on line, Pam would have said so."

"So we've lost the external network, the phones, the satellite links—what else?"

Nik frowned at her. "That's not enough? Tess, the

communications system is a silo, deep but narrow for security purposes."

"Which is one reason I've never liked the silo model. Being capable of losing everything at once is what I call one whopper of a vulnerability, Nik. That's not security, it's insanity," she snapped. "I know we have old-fashioned radio equipment for emergencies, and that wouldn't be affected by any network glitches. Tell me about that."

"Well, yeah, okay, we can transmit scrambled or open messages on all the bog-standard long-range frequencies, but I can't tell you the last time we used them for anything other than talking to incoming planes or people out in the field."

"So let's fire them up now," Tess replied as they reached the top of the stairs. "That's what they're there for. Get someone to dust them off and test them."

"Why? To send out distress signals?" Nik snorted. "Announce to the world that there's trouble in paradise an hour after Greg leaves? Do you have any idea what that would do to—"

Tess stopped and turned to face him. "Nik, when I was in his office earlier, Greg said to me that TESLA couldn't function without him. I'm beginning to wonder if he meant that literally rather than metaphorically. Did he ever say anything like that to you?"

Nik looked at her curiously. "Why would he have? I had no idea he was leaving."

"I'm just asking. Did he ever say anything like that to you?"

"No. He never gave any hints or indication that he was critical to the operation of the facility," Nik snapped, folding his arms across his chest.

"Thank you." She paused and looked him straight

in the eyes. "Look, Nik, I didn't appreciate your comment that I wouldn't have gone to Greg for help even if he'd still been on the ground. I'd like to set something straight. I have different priorities than Greg does, and my ego has a whole different set of drivers. I won't compromise TESLA for anything short of a full-blown and imminent catastrophe, but if that's what this becomes—and I don't think it will—the *people* here come first. Got that? The personnel are more important to me than the arrays or this building or Croyden Flint's corporate paranoia. So, if I determine that we need to issue a Mayday call on a short-wave frequency to get help, we'll do it." She paused. "I want us to walk into that sandbox presenting a united front. Is there anything else we need to discuss before we do that?"

She could see in his eyes that he was furious at being dressed down. *Too bad.*

"We've got radios in the planes," he said stiffly. "If all else fails, we can use those."

"Let's keep them in mind," she said, and resumed walking.

12

CHAPTER

Nik had somehow kept his jaw from dropping open as he saw Tess sitting there in the dining room. In this community where pressed khakis constituted formal dress, Tess was a vision. Her hair was up and sort of puffy, with little wispy strands dangling here and there. It was soft and feminine. The rest of her was pure dynamite. Her blue sweater was soft-looking, fuzzy, and clingy enough to show off the goods without looking slutty. It was begging to be touched—and would be, if he could arrange it. Then, when she'd stood up, he'd seen the rest of the package: dark pants that hugged every long, smooth curve just right. But her clothing, apparently, was the extent of the illusion of her softness.

"Okay, Nik, what do you keep looking at?" Tess asked as they approached the end of the hall. The door to the sandbox loomed ahead of them.

Startled, Nik brought his gaze to her face.

Before he could say anything, she rolled her eyes. "Listen, get over it. Quit pouting. And while you're at it, quit staring at my boobs and give yourself a rain-check on the flirting."

You make me want to bay at the moon. "For Christ's sake, Tess, I'm not pouting. Or flirting," he growled, then ripped his card through the sensor on the wall outside the door and waited. Instructions flashed onto the small screen and, obeying them, Nik pressed his left palm against the biometric reader. Sometimes he only had to press a specific fingertip to it, sometimes it required a retinal scan, sometimes a voiceprint. Sometimes a combination of several authentications. The infrequent visitors to the installation were inevitably frustrated by the protocols, but the security didn't seem cumbersome to the residents.

After all, they were entering C4—the command, communications, and control center for the array, the guts and brains of TESLA, and this was just part of the reality of their existence. His identity established, the door slid open with a soft shush.

"Hey, kids. Anybody hit paydirt yet?" Nik asked out loud, his voice like a shout in the hush. He let Tess precede him into the large, brightly lit room that was humming with low conversations and dozens of computers.

"It's about time," drawled a tall dark-haired be-spectacled guy who rose to his feet as they entered.

"Your call came over the radio the same time Dan walked in," Nik said, holding up a hand to ward off what he knew would be a well-deserved rebuke for not arriving sooner. "We're here, so you can fill us in. Everybody, sorry for the general nature of the introduction, but I want you to meet Tess Beauchamp. I know you were there for the handover earlier this morning."

Tess gave a brief wave to the room at large. "I'll

come around to meet each of you as time allows. I know you've got your hands full right now." She looked directly at the guy who'd risen as they walked in. "Can you give us a recap?"

"Sure. In a nutshell, we're fucked," he said pleasantly, walking out from behind the workstation and extending his hand to Tess. "Ron Zellar, lead programmer and commander in chief of the TESLA Optimists Society."

"Nice to meet you," Tess replied, giving him a wary grin as she shook his hand. "So what happened?"

"We went dark. Special effects included watching the external networks shut down like dominoes, one after the other, starting with the uplinks," he continued in the same calm tone of voice.

"All of them?"

"Yes, ma'am. The lights blinked out, the alarms came on, and general hell broke loose for a minute or two. I heard you sent Dan out to the ground station to make sure it's not a cable or wiring issue. Thanks for that. We've got another guy checking the hardware in-house. But neither backup came on line, which leads us to—"

"What? Neither one? Not even the local one?"

Nik noticed that, for all that forced smile on her face, Tess had gotten a little paler and her voice had gotten a lot quieter since she'd entered the room. He didn't feel so well himself. Despite all his smart-assery, even Ron was subdued—for Ron. The rest of the programmers might as well have been working in a morgue; there wasn't a Nerf ball in sight and not one of them was wearing earbuds. The room, which normally exuded an easygoing, lighthearted ambience, was as quiet as a cloister, and there was no levity in the air.

This really is not good.

Ron nodded. "Even the local backup, Tess. Everything has pretty much stopped talking to anything beyond the Pale. The arrays are still on line and we've pinged them successfully. Those networks are okay, so is the power system that feeds the arrays. Everything is in sleep mode, which is as it should be, and the tests we've run so far indicate they're alive and well and waiting for action. The habitat's life support and power systems are also okay. That power blip seems to have been a non-event, but we're running diagnostics as a precaution, anyway. So it appears that only the external systems have been sucked into a black hole. As far as we've been able to determine, everything on the ground is still talking to each other."

"That's good," Tess murmured. "What do you have people doing?"

"Well, Lindy, Fred, and Juno"—Ron pointed to a group that had been huddled around a single monitor when they walked in—"are continuing to test the ground-based systems. Nancy and Francene are trying to re-establish an uplink with one of the birds. Nangpal and Amil are working on the other. And I was just finishing up a game of Minesweeper." He smiled. "Rank has its privileges."

"Don't you ever get tired of being a smart-ass?" Nik muttered, catching Tess's eye to reassure her that Ron was only joking.

"Not so far." Ron looked back at Tess. "Actually, I'm reviewing the monitoring logs to see if I can find a clue as to what happened."

Tess nodded. "Sounds like you've got things under control." She looked around. "There's a conference room in here somewhere, isn't there? Could we have a quick chat?"

"It's over here," Ron said, gesturing to the back wall of the room. "Is this the part where you tell me I'm demoted?"

Nik frowned at him. "Ron—"

"Not yet," Tess replied with a smile, walking toward the conference room's open door. Nik followed them both and pulled the door shut behind him.

She stopped halfway down the length of the table and turned to look at the two men. "Ron, I appreciate your leadership on this—"

Nik wanted to roll his eyes. *Corporatespeak will get you nowhere down here. We're immune.*

"—and I want to thank you for keeping everyone calm and occupied," she continued, still a little pale but looking as unruffled as if she handled situations like this every day. "I'd like to bounce a thought off you. Nik and I have already discussed it. It's pure conjecture, and because of that I don't want it to leave this room. But what do you think about the idea that this isn't a random failure, that perhaps Greg pulled down the external comms network? That he planted some sort of logic bomb in the system?"

Nik almost choked as Tess calmly did the equivalent of waving a lit match near a fuel dump. Ron had been one of Greg's most trusted allies.

"Conjecture?" Ron replied. "I'd call it a given."

Nik stared at him. *What the hell?* "Why? Greg wouldn't do that. He knows how dangerous it is for us to be off line."

Ron shrugged. "Sure he does, but it's not his problem anymore."

"So you think—?"

"Don't try to approach it rationally, Nik. That's futile when you're talking about Greg. And I know what you're thinking, that I was the poster child for Teslan suckupitude for the last two years. I won't argue, but it wasn't due to hero-worship. It was more like morbid fascination, like watching a live-action lab experiment. I mean, how else would I have gotten him to tell me that he used to try to get as close as he could to the HAARP arrays when they were firing?"

"He did?"

"Nik, you knew that," Tess said, frowning at him.

"No, I didn't."

She rolled her eyes at him, and Ron asked too innocently, "Oh, do you guys know each other?"

Before Nik could answer, Tess replied easily, "Our time at HAARP overlapped. Go on."

Ron shrugged and continued. "Anyway, that's what Greg told me he did and, given the way he operated, I'd say he fried a few dozen mission-critical synapses standing out there in the blast zone, so to speak. To get back on point, there's no doubt that Greg has a lot of smarts and creativity, but the guy is as twisted as a ramen noodle and has about as much empathy. If he'd had any thoughts about the danger involved with leaving us dark, they would have involved only the danger to his career and reputation if he were unceremoniously yanked out of here and things kept ticking over as well as they had while he was here. It would relegate him to the status of a functionary rather than a visionary—no offense intended, Tess. But the truth is that, from his perspective, the rest of us don't matter except in relation to him. He's the sun and we're merely interchangeable satellites in orbit around him.

Classic narcissistic, sociopathic behavior. And that's why I can easily see him setting a logic bomb in place to knock us off line for a while."

"Just to make me look bad," Tess finished.

"Well, you do share a rather, um, colorful history with Greg—"

"You know about that?" Tess asked sheepishly.

"I'm sorry to be the one to break the news to you, Tess, but everyone in the industry knows about that," Ron replied. "You're sort of a legend in your own time. So certainly that could have fed into his actions, but how you end up looking would be secondary. His first goal would be to make himself appear irreplaceable."

"So you're already on this? You're looking for a command in the monitoring logs?" she asked.

Ron nodded. "Or a fault. Whatever it is, it's sure to be well disguised." He let out a breath. "For the record, everyone out there already thinks this is Greg's fault."

"What?" Nik asked.

"Nangpal mentioned it right after the shit hit the fan. No one argued."

"Is that why you don't seem too concerned?" Tess asked. "You don't think this is critical?"

"Well, it's critical, but I don't think it's a permanent failure. Greg is an egomaniac and an ass, but he wouldn't destroy the arrays, or the installation, or even the people here," Ron explained with an easy shrug. "This is his legacy. He won't ruin it."

"But it's in my hands now," Tess pointed out. "Whatever happens is on my watch."

Ron shook his head. "Doesn't matter. He won't let it tank under you. It would send the message that he left behind something that was substandard, and we can't have that."

"For the sake of argument, consider this: that he is a critical component to the operation here and shouldn't have been removed," Tess said quietly, meeting Nik's eyes.

Nik lifted an eyebrow. *Damn, I hope you're wrong.*

"Possible, but even Greg isn't that crazy. We'll come back on line as mysteriously as we went off. I'm sure of it, Tess," Ron said.

"But you just said that if nothing had gone wrong—"

"I know it's not logical. It isn't meant to be; we're talking about Greg and a whopping case of narcissitic personality disorder. Everything revolves around him. He took everything—every criticism, however slight—as a personal attack. So, if nothing had gone wrong, it would have belittled him. If things went catastrophically wrong, it would reflect badly on him. Either scenario would make him crazy. Crazier. It's all about image with him. So he has to scare us and test you, and maybe even do something to come to our rescue just to put you in your place, you saucy wench."

Tess couldn't hold back a laugh at his unexpected finish, but she recovered quickly. Nik wanted to roll his eyes again.

Being a little obvious, are we?

Ron looked at Nik as if he had heard the dark thought. "Speak up, Nik. You're chief general advocate for the devil."

Nik folded his arms across his chest and glared at him. "Thanks for giving me a chance to get a word in edgewise. I agree with what you've described. I don't have anything to add."

"I do," Tess said. "Until a few hours ago, I hadn't

seen Greg in years, but it was obvious when I spoke with him privately that he's changed. In this instance, I don't think the term 'crazy' is an exaggeration." She paused and looked at Ron, then Nik. "You can call me paranoid or overly cautious or whatever else crosses your mind, but I think we need to consider that he might have gone over the edge and is out for vengeance. If that's the case, whatever happens next will be much bigger than a comms blackout. And possibly more dangerous."

"And it will look like you're at fault," Nik added, watching her face.

She gave him a small, tight-lipped smile and nodded her head. "Of course. It wouldn't be any fun for him if it didn't."

Nik looked at Ron. "What do you think?"

Ron hesitated, then nodded slowly. "It's a good point. Far-fetched, but plausible. If he's finally snapped, it would be important to him that everyone knows exactly where to lay the blame—"

"So shall we agree to treat the blip and the blackout as Phase One?" Tess asked, looking from one man to the other.

"Yes." Nik looked at Ron, who hesitated for a moment, then nodded.

A sharp knock on the door interrupted the conversation. Nik, being closest to the door, pulled it open.

One of the programmers, Lindy, stood outside, pale and clearly in a state of mild panic. "Ron— I mean, all of you need to come out here. The phased array is powering up. It's not on the schedule and no one here gave any commands."

Nik wondered if Tess and Ron had the same sudden tightness in their chests. There was only one way an array could power up: if three people with the proper authorization gave the "go" command. One had to be either Ron or himself. Another was Tess. The backup alternate couldn't do anything alone.

Without a word, Nik, Tess, and Ron left the conference room.

Tess kept her imagination clenched as tight as her jaw as she returned to the large work space. The tension level was running higher than before, and the only sound was the furious tapping of keys. Several new people had materialized in the sandbox.

She followed the programmer, who had introduced herself as Victoria Lindquist—known as Lindy—to a workstation with twin monitors. One showed the stats for the phased array, some numbers ticking over slowly and others flashing so rapidly as to be incomprehensible.

"Does it usually power up this fast?" Tess asked.

"Never. It drains the system. We always power up more slowly," the other woman said. "This has to be some sort of override."

"Okay. First thing you need to do is get Dan Thornton back into the installation. He's out at the ground station. I don't want him out there if this thing is going to fire."

As Lindy began talking in low tones on her walkie-talkie, Tess straightened and glanced around, trying to spot Nik. He was in a huddle with a few of the people she'd met earlier. Ron, likewise, was speaking with a group of his developers. Tess looked back at Lindy, meeting her eyes, which were wide with controlled fear.

"He's already on his way back."

"Good. You were one of the hackers, weren't you?"

she asked, and watched the woman's face take on a wary expression.

"I'm sorry?"

"You hacked when you were younger, right? I thought I saw it in your personnel file. There are a few of you with that background. You're one of them, aren't you? You hacked a Russian—"

Another layer of tension crossed Lindy's face as she nodded. "That was me," she said quietly. "It was a long time ago and all the charges were dropped. What brought it up?"

"It impressed me. A lot. Still remember how to do it?"

A slow grin gave Tess the answer she was looking for. "I could give it a go."

"Forget that. I want you to give it all you've got. Find whatever is in there that could override the system and disable it. I want you to power down that array, and make sure it can't go live again unless we tell it to."

"Yes, ma'am," Lindy said, sliding into the chair.

Tess walked over to Ron and interrupted him with a pat on the arm. "Would you do the honors?"

"Nangpal Thompson, Amil Patel, and Pam Webb," he said, gesturing to the group he was speaking with. "Juno Blasi, and Jonah Teeter are in the back. Nancy Hagymasy and Debbie Huckfeldt are over there near Lindy. There are others, but they're not here right now. This is Tess Beauchamp."

She nodded at the group. "Nice to meet you. I'll look forward to getting to know you a bit better after this fire's out and we're back on line. I've told Lindy to throw everything she's got at regaining control of the array's power system. The same goes for all of you. If you've got a black hat in your history or ever wanted to wear one, put it on. I want you to get into every system—I don't care how: hack, crack, brute force, whatever it takes—and prop the door open. I have a bad feeling that even though we're not locked out of many systems right now, we may be soon. I want to avoid that. Give it your best," she said, making eye contact with each person in front of her. "I'm looking for speed, not elegance." She glanced at Ron. "I'm going to assume you don't have any problems with this."

"Let's do it."

"Good. Keep me posted." She left his side to join Nik. She'd met most of the scientists he was speaking with after her speech that morning. That seemed like days ago. "What's the latest?"

"Not so good. The command sequence for the array is right here. He didn't hide it," Nik replied.

"And that's a bad thing?" she asked.

"It is, because we've never seen it before," one of the other guys in the group—Etienne—offered. "Not outside of a test bed."

She leaned forward to study the code on the screen. She knew instantly that it was sloppy; the syntax was dense and clumsy, which was very unlike Greg's way of writing. Beyond that, it was just confusing, like reading a book in a language she barely knew. A few strings here and there looked familiar, but on the whole, it made little sense. Tess straightened and met the Frenchman's eyes. "Do we know what it's going to do? Where it's aimed?"

"I'm not sure," he said with a Gallic shrug. "The code is so convoluted and—"

"I can see that, Etienne," Tess said, interrupting him. "What I want to know is, if the array fires according to these command parameters, what is it capable of doing? Go out on a limb. I won't hold it against you."

The Frenchman was quiet for a moment, then gave another shrug. "Well, the general command flow follows the usual sequence for beaming into the Schlüchthofen band. But the intensity profile is strange and the capacitance settings are higher than anything I've seen at TESLA before. I'd guess that he's trying to cause a spontaneous recombination of ionized particles in the Schlüchthofen band," he said, referring to a recently discovered, extremely narrow, extremely potent ribbon of the ionosphere capable of producing magnified internal reflections, which meant it functioned much like a fiber-optic cable when certain frequencies crossed it. The signals became trapped within the layer's boundaries and would increase rather than attenuate as they bounced around the world. After a pre-set elapse of time, one of the other transmitter sites would send a paired beam into the same band, allowing the internally reflected beam back out so that it could do its work. Or damage.

Tess felt her heart stop for a split second, then thump erratically in her chest. She looked at Nik. "That means whatever action he's going for is geomagnetic," she said, her voice barely above a whisper.

"Let's not be coy, Tess. It means an earthquake," he replied, his dark eyes shuttered against any hint of emotion.

CHAPTER

Off the coast of the Mexican state of Michoacán, deep beneath the Pacific Ocean, the earth began to tremble. A powerful but short burst of energy pulsed against the tectonically fragile Cocos plate, rocking it and causing it to slide harder and faster beneath the North American plate. The deep oceanic trenches that snaked along the long western coastline of the Americas shook, their vulnerable walls and volatile hot spots responding to the motion with underwater landslides and lava flows.

The Sistema de Alerta Sísmica, a system of electronic sensors installed along the coastal subduction zone, triggered warnings that were transmitted immediately to receivers in Mexico City—or so that system indicated. In reality, however, those electronic receivers had gone deaf when they were hit by the same massive electromagnetic pulse that had tripped the submarine fault line and the sensors. No warning sirens went off across the vast and densely populated city; no piercing electronic shrieks alerted anyone to the disaster about to engulf them.

The temblor's first waves passed from the deep-sea fault to the coast in seconds and moved rapidly inland without pause. In little more than two minutes, the waves crossed hundreds of miles of countryside and reached the soft volcanic clay that comprises the sediment underlying Mexico City. Tens of millions of people lived and worked in the sprawling, crowded urban valley built atop a drained and ancient lake bed. None had time to prepare when the homes in which they were preparing to face the day started to shake and sway.

In the suburbs, screams split the morning. Clutching their children and whatever else they valued, people fled their homes for the ostensible safety of the streets and then froze with raw panic as they watched fissures form beneath their feet. The yawning, ever-widening chasms swallowed their neighbors and kin, their homes and cars, with an appetite beyond voracious. In the huge, sprawling city center, the hazy, smudgy blue sky rained boulder-sized chunks of concrete and warm, screaming bodies onto streets pregnant with growing piles of rubble. Billows of thick, choking dust rolled through the air and along the streets, hiding everything in their gritty depths. The particular and terrible vulnerability of tall buildings was there for all to see as they swayed like palm trees in sync with the earth's magnificent resonance before snapping off fifteen stories up and crashing to the ground like a child's toy thrown in a fit of temper.

For more than five minutes—an eternity—the earth shook beneath the terrified residents. Shockwave after shockwave assaulted the nation as, deep underground, the earth's crust broke in several places, sliding forward on a slow return journey to a molten state.

When the shaking in Mexico City ended, the true horror of the events began to unfold as people picked themselves up from where they'd hidden or been thrown, and began to emerge from their demolished homes. Across the entire enormous valley, heavy clouds of black dust saturated the air, filling already troubled lungs. Screams and cries from the injured, the dying, and the grieving were drowned out by the belated, helpless wail of sirens.

Streets of ripped and jagged asphalt stymied the efforts of emergency personnel. It was just as well; the would-be saviors had nowhere to take the wounded—or the dead. Too many hospitals had been damaged, if not destroyed outright, and the staff remaining within them had their own priorities to address.

Steel beams lay twisted on the roads and dangled precariously from the shells of the buildings they'd once supported. Mountain ranges of debris had amassed between buildings. Broken glass crunched underfoot; huge deadly shards rested propped against other objects at odd, often invisible angles, as if lying in wait to impale the dazed and unsuspecting souls who thought they had survived the worst.

Water gushed and geysered as huge mains and sewer lines cracked, then erupted beneath the roadways. Violent explosions rocked the remaining infrastructure as newly ruptured gas pipelines began burning. Hungry flames spread outward like the infernal circles of Hell, consuming everything that did not or could not get out of their way.

Tsunamis raced in all directions along the Pacific

coast and outward to the open sea. The scientists already tracking them from afar defined them as small but serious and predicted the sea-bound waves would lose their impetus by mid-ocean, fomenting no emergencies in the nations hugging the Pacific's western rim. Those governments monitored the western-moving waves with the mildest trepidation, ultimately deciding not to annoy their populations with sirens in the middle of the night for what could easily be a non-event by morning.

However, the towering waves roaring along the North American continent's edge ripped into the land with fierce, foaming energy to spare. Residents had no warning when the wave train entered the Sea of Cortés. Its force intensified exponentially as the mainland on one side and the skinny peninsula of Baja California on the other enfolded the waves in a tight embrace. The deep, joined basins and sudden, steep inclines of the submarine landscape worked together to compact the towering walls of water like a rapidly closed accordion, forcing them to gather into one another as they raced northward through the narrow gulf. The waves roared through the shallows and made fast, furious contact with the shore, ripping palm trees from their place in the sand and beachcombers from their place in the universe.

Near the southern tip of the Baja peninsula, just outside the sun-drenched coastal town of Los Frailes, a small army of household staff went about their daily work in Croyden Flint's massive seaside villa. Gardeners and housemaids alike had no time to flee when the first wave arrived; they were already statistics by the time that wave had receded. The furious waters kept moving up the gulf, hammering the coastline for nearly eight hundred miles and flattening everything in their path. The surging waves lost little force until they released the last of their fury on the sleepy towns scattered along the edge of the Sonora coast, home to thousands of acres of Flint's produce farms and processing plants.

The waves raced along the coast to the south of the epicenter as well, and few beachgoers were fortunate enough to survive their onslaught. The flat, manicured beaches of resort communities, the rocky shores of quiet towns, and the commercial piers and dockyards of bustling cities were slammed indiscriminately by darkly shimmering facades of water that crashed over them and then moved on. The size and power of the southern waves diminished gradually as they moved along their trajectory, crashing into the coast of Ecuador less than an hour later.

Meanwhile, in the heart of Mexico's capital, the day had begun with unrelenting calamity and epic struggles for survival. The full scope of the disaster would not be revealed for hours; the first pulse of energy had disabled the systems needed to receive and relay information, sending governments, armies, and diplomats around the globe scrambling to find alternate means to communicate with their Mexican counterparts. Meanwhile, in other parts of the country and abroad, people went about their business unaware of the doom that had fallen on millions.

As the sun climbed higher in the sky, burning through the everyday smog reinforced by the dense, suffocating fog of smoke and dust, the extent of the carnage was becoming unveiled. Those in the disaster-stricken region waited in vain for help from an outside world that was only beginning to learn what the dawn had wrought.

In a small house perched on a dramatic cliff overhanging a pristine beach on Mexico's Pacific coast, Larry and Gina Beauchamp clung to the frame of their bedroom doorway, not ready to die but too terrified to move. The remote bungalow they'd named Casa de Paz—House of Peace—had for ten years been their refuge from the world and a respite from their memories of decades spent devising the means to destroy the world. Now they lay—hung, really—on a floor that had been tipped to a forty-five-degree slope by the quake's first jolt, and to an angle even more acute by the next. Their bare feet faced the wall of windows that had brought thousands of sunsets into their home; their toes could find no purchase on the cool, slick, colorful tiles they'd laid by hand.

The specter of a slow and horrible death surrounded them as if it were a living thing, its voice clearly audible in the squealing wooden beams and grunting joints that were buckling under the stress of unplanned-for torsion. Tess Beauchamp's parents would never know that it was a man, not Nature, who had decided it was their time to die; they would never know that their only child's long-ago revelations had determined a madman's target, that her reappearance in his life had been the trigger.

They clung to crumbling hope and the slowly splintering lintel as the house dangled drunkenly over a freshly opened chasm in what had been immutable rock beneath their home. They whispered their love to each other and sent their prayers to the heavens as they tried to inch their way toward safety.

Gina lost her grip first, her neat, tidy fingernails catching in the soft wood and tearing off at the root. Her mouth was open in a silent scream as she slid, leaving Larry to endure the shushing of her large, muumuu-covered body and bloody hands as they crossed the polished tile. The altered weight distribution was enough to tilt the house past its tipping point, nudging the structure from precarious inertia to full and frantic motion. As she picked up speed, Gina at last began screaming, her voice primal and filled with terror. Larry's grip faltered then and gravity capitalized on the lapse. He careened across the floor through a thudding rain of roof tiles and adobe bricks.

With an almighty, ear-shattering crack, the groaning timbers surrendered and the house listed downward. It began sliding, then somersaulting past the raw walls of the new canyon before becoming wedged between them midway to the bottom. The combination of panic and injuries snuffed the life from the Beauchamps' bodies. The screams stopped. Their corpses crashed through the wall of splintered glass and fell heavily into the ferocious, foaming sea filling the virgin space below them.

14

Tess sat at the head of the conference table, looking at the tense faces in front of her. An hour had passed since the array had begun powering up, and mere minutes ago it had given birth to a pulse of energy that could—most likely *had*—rocked the world.

Nik was a mass of barely controlled tension, Ron was tight-lipped and unsmiling. A pale, wide-eyed Lindy fiddled with a pencil and wouldn't make eye contact with anyone. Etienne Pascal and Pam Webb, two of the scientists, were very still. Tess wasn't feeling her best.

If ever there was a good reason to have a belt of Scotch at this hour, this would be it.

"Tell me again about the pulse," Tess said, keeping her voice low and calm.

"Four thousand tesla units in the Very Low Frequency range directed at the Schlüchthofen band. Duration, ninety-one milliseconds. Followed by a second pulse thirty-two nanoseconds later with a duration of two hundred and three milliseconds. The third pulse lasted four seconds. Each transmission was aligned along slightly different trajectories."

The words chilled her blood. "And the impact?"

"A rupture in the central North Atlantic," Pam said. "Magnitude four on the Richter Scale."

Everyone at the table looked at one another with expressions ranging from doubt to incredulity.

"The north-central Atlantic?" Nik repeated. "What the hell is that about? It would cause tsunamis on both sides of the pond."

"Maybe not," Etienne replied. "Mag four is not that big, and the rock there is stable. There is no fault line up there. Iceland, yes. The Caribbean, yes. But the north-central Atlantic is a spreading center. Any earthquake there would more likely open a gap." He spread his hands in an acknowledgment that it made no sense to him. "If that happened, the water would rush to fill it, not rise up. It would pull down coastlines, no? Snap fiber-optic cables. Create havoc in the shipping lanes."

"Are you sure it was the Atlantic?" Tess asked, the information not sitting comfortably in her brain. "What would be the purpose of that?"

"Lowering the sea level and causing an uptick in the coastal real estate market?" Ron offered to the quiet group. "Okay, maybe not."

"No, *I'm* not sure it was the Atlantic," Pam replied to Tess while glaring at Ron. "But that's what the data show. The location doesn't make sense to me, either."

Lindy let out an annoyed sigh. "None of this makes sense, frankly. What's going on? Have we been hacked? I thought we were secure."

"We are—from outside threats. I think we've been hijacked internally." Tess knew her words would provoke a reaction, but she wasn't prepared for universal, silent acceptance. "Unless anyone has another idea," she added, looking around the table.

"There is no other explanation." Nik took a deep breath and met her eyes. "Given: The trouble started after Greg passed out of our airspace. Given: The comms blackout is thorough, not random, and not mechanical. Given: The arrays have never been programmed to execute without continual operator input. Until now. Given: We have been effectively locked out from controlling the arrays and contacting the outside world.

"Hypothesis One: Greg is fucking with us a little bit. Hypothesis Two: Greg has gone over the edge and is fucking with Flint big time. Hypothesis Three: Greg has gone over to the dark side and wants to flex all the muscle he's got." He looked at Pam. "Blowing a hole in the middle of the Atlantic would not be his style."

Pam looked at her hands for a long moment, then brought her gaze back to the group. "Okay, as long as we're engaging in the crazy, wild-ass-guess version of the scientific method, I'll throw this on the table: what if the problem is more granular than just feeding the arrays and the power system off-the-wall commands? What if the substrate of the system has been tampered with?"

"Meaning?" Tess asked, not liking the tension coiling like a snake in her gut.

"What if the geographical coordinates have been altered? Flipped, nudged, whatever. Set off by x degrees to throw us off."

"So we wouldn't know where the effects of the pulses were targeted," Tess replied, slowly.

Pam nodded. "If you want to make an earthquake, which is about the only thing that particular pulse pattern could do, you wouldn't make it happen where earthquakes don't happen naturally."

"You would if you want to shake things up—pardon the pun," Nik argued.

Pam shook her head. "No, Nik. If this is Greg's doing, he wouldn't be content with just scaring people. He's too results-oriented. He'd get more bang for his buck if he hit crustal zones that are already vulnerable to shifting. The pulses that just went out would do a lot more damage in the Pacific than the Atlantic because of all the active faults and subduction zones and—come on." She let out an exasperated breath. "You want some statistics? Try these: There are more than 450 volcanoes ringing the Pacific, and that doesn't even include the underwater ones, or the cinder cones, maars, and volcanic shields. I mean, take Mexico's Michoacán-Guanajuato volcanic field. It's a single magmatic system that covers fifty thousand square kilometers and includes—"

"We get it, Pam," Ron interrupted.

"Did you say Michoacán?" Tess asked at the same time.

"Yes, I did. And, okay, I'll shut up, but my point is that if Greg wanted attention, he'd go for the Pacific, or even the Mediterranean. The north-central Atlantic would be a non-starter."

Tess remained quiet, not liking the flick of new fear that one word had inspired. Her parents lived near Michoacán.

Nik shook his head. "Think about it, Pam. What does he crave more, the attention that an unexpected, totally unpredictable earthquake would bring, or the destruction that would ensue if the quake hit some-place it would be expected?"

"He'd want the damage," Pam said with quiet force. "And the attention that would follow. Flint monitors us, Nik. They already know what's happened and where and that, whatever happened, we did it. It wouldn't surprise me if a lot of other folks know, too. We're the only ones without a clue."

"Pam, I think your hypothesis about the substruc-ture of the code is worth investigating. Please keep me apprised of what you find," Tess said smoothly. "Nik, her other point that we could be the only ones who don't have a complete picture of what's going on is a valid one, too. We've been dark for about two hours. We know what the problem isn't, and we have a pretty good idea of what the problem is, and it's not going to be remedied quickly.

"I think we need to very strongly consider taking our situation 'public,' so to speak, and get some mes-sages out via the bog-standard radio frequencies, as you called them earlier." She held up a hand to ward off his objections. "I'm not implying that we need to send out a Mayday, but we need to let Connecticut know that we're wounded. They'll get in touch with Greg as soon as he touches down in Capetown. In the meantime, there isn't much we can do except what we've been doing. Continue the search-and-destroy mission for Greg's rogue code."

She rose to her feet, indicating that the meeting was over. A few glances between the others at the ta-ble let her know that not everyone was in complete agreement, but they were willing to get behind her, which said something, considering no one but Nik had ever worked with her before now.

As she anticipated, Nik stayed behind, shutting the door behind the last person to leave. "Are you sure about this?"

"As sure as I can be."

"Look, we don't have to transmit on the open frequencies yet," Nik said. "There's a pre-set signal that's transmitted to the satellites a few times a day when everything is okay. If that signal changes or is interrupted, it means there's trouble in paradise and the powers-that-be can take steps to determine the problem."

"Is it still working?"

"Nothing has indicated that it's not," he said. "But it's a passive signal, Tess. If we interrupt it, the only message they'll get in Connecticut is that there's trouble, which they already know. They know we've gone dark, and they know we've fired the phased array."

"Then they'll be expecting the signal to be interrupted."

"If we're in crisis mode. But if the signal continues, it will—or should—indicate that we're not in crisis mode yet. In other words, that we're handling whatever is going on."

Considering his words, Tess let out a long breath and dropped back into the chair she just vacated. "Has this ever happened before?"

"Never for this long. The power blipped for about two minutes about a month ago."

"Two *minutes*?" she repeated, wide-eyed. "Why?"

Nik waved a hand in dismissal. "It was nothing. Greg took responsibility. Said he'd goofed on a parameter."

Tess sat up straight. "He what?"

"He'd just fired the array and said he got something wrong."

"And you didn't investigate?"

"Tess, there wasn't any need to investigate. Greg knew what happened almost immediately. He put a report in the files."

"Well that 'report' never made it to Flint, Nik. Believe me, I would have seen it and read it if it were in the files."

Nik shrugged, annoyed. "Do you really need to focus on this right now? It was a minor glitch—"

"According to Greg."

"Yes, Tess, according to Greg, who caused the glitch and fixed it."

The situation was bad and had the potential to get much worse, and Tess was torn between wanting the security outside involvement would bring and wanting to prove herself capable of handling whatever Greg could throw at her.

"All right. We'll wait," she said slowly, meeting Nik's eyes. "For a little while."

Nik looked at his watch as he walked back toward his office.

Damn it.

He took a deep breath. It was pointless to try to fight off the mixture of guilt and nervousness that was assailing his conscience. The tropical storm he'd concocted in a fit of annoyance twenty-four hours ago, the one that was guaranteed to ruin at least the start of Eleanor's honeymoon, would be breaking any minute.

What the hell was I thinking? I'm no better than Greg.

The conversation he'd just had with the team in the conference room had shaken him. He was sure that everyone was a lot more concerned than they were letting on—he sure as hell was. The thought of Greg playing God just to get back at Tess, or at Flint, or whatever other motive he might be harboring was enough to chill his blood—yet he'd just done the same damned thing out of jealousy.

And that's all it really is, Nik, old boy, isn't it? Jealousy and a bruised ego. Ellie found someone who treated her better and you just can't take it like a man. You can't even pretend to be a mature adult where Ellie is concerned. You couldn't resist the temptation to make her cry. Nice going, Nik, you stupid ass.

It wasn't just guilt. There was a hell of a lot of helplessness built into what he was feeling. If he could undo it now he would, but he couldn't. That was the bitch about TESLA—there was no escape button to hit, no rewind, no pause. Whatever they wanted to make happen, happened. Most of the time, it happened just like it was supposed to, but sometimes Nature added her own surprise. That was never easy to take.

In the beginning, when they'd gone to live testing, and then had actually gone live, none of it had been easy to take. He'd fall into bed and try to block out the knowledge that everything he'd done that day would have both intended and unintended consequences; some people would benefit, others would likely be harmed. And he'd thought about leaving—a lot. Then the WinFly window had closed and he'd been stuck. Slowly, he'd gotten comfortable with what he was doing, with playing God; it had gone from being a job to being a challenge. He hadn't been alone.

Greg had known that everyone in the sandbox had serious conscience issues when what they did moved from the realm of theory to application. He'd skillfully and deliberately led them along the path from conscience-stricken to competitive; up until a little while ago, they had all been living comfortably in the same cozy rut, wreaking havoc for fun and profit. Sometimes Nik would realize they were like kids striving for gold stars or a pat on the head, but he'd get over it. Greg had been brilliant when it came to making what they did seem like a dangerous game, one step removed from reality. After all, nothing they did ever affected *their* reality.

We were all complicit. Now, we're all culpable.

He could kick himself for being such a clueless, adolescent prick. Now—when he couldn't do a damned thing to stop his own storm or anything more that Greg might have planned—Nik felt like he was waking from a coma, wondering why the hell he'd done what he did. It wasn't just Ellie his storm was about to terrorize, it was the hundreds of people on that flight. Everyone on any military, cruise, or container ships in the region. Islanders would be nailed as the storm broke up and dissipated across the South Pacific— and possibly a lot of them if the storm *didn't* break up and instead combined with some unforeseen variable and grew into something really big. Supercyclones weren't unheard of.

He shut his office door behind him and leaned against it for a long moment, feeling vaguely nauseated. Then he walked to his desk and woke up his computer, grimly determined to find out what Greg's code was doing and stop it before it could do any more damage.

CHAPTER

Eleanor Ryder-Pentson, the former executive assistant to and brand-new third wife of one of the most powerful lobbyists in the agriculture industry, looked at her left hand, which was clasped—partly in affection and partly in desperation—with her new husband's right hand on the armrest of their first-class seats on the inaugural Dreamliner flight from San Francisco to Fiji. It was an eloquent, telling tableau. His hand was so tanned, so rugged, so scarred and lived-in despite the neat, buffed nails; her hand was pale, smooth, and pampered. And it sported a pink marquise-cut diamond that would make Paris Hilton weep with envy.

The stone was huge, cold, and heavy on her hand. Wearing it still felt strange even after nearly a year. Ellie was sure she'd get used to it. Eventually. It was a bit more flashy—make that a lot more flashy—than she'd have chosen, if she'd been given the choice. But she hadn't been. With every ounce of diplomacy in her, she'd tried to explain that she generally went for simpler things. But Mitchell hadn't gotten where he was by taking no for an answer, so she'd acquiesced as gracefully as she could. After nearly a decade of wearing a plain gold band while married to a plain old man, Mitchell had said, she needed something with some sparkle and flash to suit her new life.

If Nik had heard that, he would have ruptured his appendix laughing.

She stiffened and caught her breath. *Get out of my head, Nik.*

"Are you doing all right, Ellie?" Mitchell's voice, so deep, so well-trained to convey exactly what was called for—in this case, kindness tinged with just a hint of condescension—reached her ears and went no farther. She turned to look at him, a tight, bright smile on her face.

"I'm fine," she said with considerably more cheerful confidence than she felt. He smiled back and squeezed her hand.

"Good."

A scrawny kid raised in the vast openness of central Wisconsin, Mitchell Pentson had learned early on that the last thing he wanted to do was spend his life shoveling snow off barn roofs for a few months a year and shoveling cow shit out of stalls for all of them, and doing it while denying himself every pleasure. Years of listening to his parents and their neighbors worry over every expense and rant about the cuts in government subsidies and land grabs by greedy agroindustrialists had taught him what true power was. He'd realized then that money was more important than loyalty because it could get you what you wanted faster. Using your brains brought bigger rewards than using your brawn ever could.

He wanted that money, that power, that influence, and a whole lot more besides. So he'd done whatever was called for to get himself into the University of Wisconsin, then Harvard Law, and then onto K Street. Still only in his early forties, he was already widely respected—or feared, depending on who you asked. And not just in his own industry, but in Washington in general. Several movers and shakers had suggested to Mitchell that he move back to the center of the country and consider running for office.

Ellie knew that Mitchell's mature, easy good looks hid a ruthless determination to succeed. He got what he wanted and rarely played fair. With his Common Man background and insider experience, Mitchell would do justice to any office.

"Happy?" Mitchell asked, his eyes scanning her face.

"Divinely." Ellie forced another smile and leaned forward to accept his kiss.

She hated to fly more than just about anything in the world. She hated to fly even more than she'd hated being single; more than she'd hated getting divorced; even more than she'd hated being married to Nik for that last year, which was saying a lot.

Yet here she was, cruising five or six miles above the biggest, deepest ocean on the planet. It wasn't a complaint, she assured herself, it was a sign of how much she loved and trusted Mitchell. He was wonderful and thoughtful, and there would always be topics on which they differed. Some, like this one, would be a topic she considered significant. He thought her usual mechanism for coping with flight-related stress—sleeping pills—was dangerous, and he'd made it clear that he didn't want to spend the first day of his honeymoon next to an unconscious bride. Good Champagne was his solution to her jitters.

Reluctantly, Ellie had agreed, and the first cork had been popped before business class finished boarding. She'd been smiling and sipping dutifully ever since because she wanted to please him, but Ellie knew there wasn't enough bubbly on the planet to turn her into a carefree flier. That's why, without telling Mitchell, she'd taken enough anti-anxiety meds to make water-boarding sound like a good time. But even that wasn't working.

She truly, truly wanted nothing more at this moment than to be on solid ground or even the deck of a ship or, failing that, unconscious. *Anything* would be better than enduring this hours-long feeling that each moment could be her last, that the natural laws of force and motion and momentum would succumb to the supremacy of gravity and she would fall out of the sky, hurtling to earth in a ball of smoky fire and screaming metal.

The thought became all too real a split second later, when the plane did one of those odd, startling little mid-flight plummets. Perfectly typical. Perfectly terrifying.

Ellie choked on a breath and instinctively squeezed Mitchell's hand as hard as she could.

He laughed gently and disengaged his hand to slide his arm around her. His other hand covered hers as it gripped the armrest. "Ellie, sweetheart, you're safer up here than you are driving home every night across those D.C. bridges," he murmured into her hair. "Relax. It's like hitting a bump in the road. Harmless."

"I know the statistics, Mitchell," she hissed, trying to sound reasonable and failing miserably, "but we're not on a road. We're in the air, over the middle of the ocean, thousands of miles from the nearest land mass. There are no bumps up here."

"Updrafts. Whatever. Darling, nothing is going to happen. Let's have some more Champagne," he said, reaching up to press the call button and then taking her hand again.

His easy gesture and soothing words were interrupted by the soft *bong* of the seat belt sign coming on, immediately followed by the click of an open microphone and the pilot's voice.

"Ladies and gentlemen, we've got a bit of high-altitude weather forming ahead of us. It's not unusual in the tropics to run into these upper-air disturbances. We're going to try to get above it, but things might get a little bumpy. At this time, I'd like to ask you to please return to your seats if you're moving about the cabin, and make sure your seat belts are securely fastened."

The flight attendants moved a little more quickly as they passed through the cabin, removing trays and empty glasses, and checking passengers' laps for compliance.

"Ellie, you're cutting off my circulation," Mitchell laughed, kissing the back of her hand as he disengaged her fingers.

"Oh God, Mitchell. I hate turbulence. I hate flying. I hate . . . this," she whispered, tightening her seat belt until there was no more give and wishing her seat had a chest harness like the flight attendants' seats had.

"Just breathe, Ellie. Slowly. Close your eyes if it helps, darling." Mitchell pulled her close, tucking her head onto his broad, warm chest just as the plane began to bounce and wobble.

"Oh God, Mitchell, I told you staying at The Greenbriar would be fine," she snapped. "We could have *driven* there. You wouldn't listen."

"Ellie—"

"Why did I ever agree to this?" she moaned into his shirt, her eyes squeezed shut, her body rigid.

"Shh, Ellie, Ellie, it's nothing. Just a little bumpy air." He ran a gentle hand over her hair.

Then, making a liar out of him, the plane jerked and swayed as wildly as a Wall Streeter on a mechanical bull. The gasps and muffled cries from around the cabin did nothing to console Ellie. She gripped the front of Mitchell's shirt in her hands, not even hearing the small sound of the fine silken threads snapping.

I'm going to die. I'm going to die. I'm going to—

The public address system came on again, more staticky this time. "Flight attendants, take your seats."

Oh God. Oh God. Hail Mary, full of—shit, shit, shit, what am I doing up here?

A scream built in her throat as the plane made an unnatural movement sideways, as if the hand of God was trying to slap it out of the sky. Ellie's mind went blank. She felt like she had the time she got caught in one of those awful, heavy Alaskan blizzards, when every human sense was smothered by white and cold and you couldn't tell if you were hallucinating or dying.

The aircraft made a sudden, steep plunge that felt like it would never end, as if the plane had been thrown toward the earth. Screams came from all corners of the plane. Even Mitchell stopped murmuring reassuring platitudes. She felt his body go rigid, his hands gripping her painfully, his fingers digging into her arms and back. Lightning strobed outside so brightly that it lit up the insides of her squeezed-shut eyelids.

The plummeting stopped just as suddenly as it had

started, as if that same awesome hand had jerked the huge jet to a shuddering halt. Braced to hear the hellish squeal of the plane's superstructure being torn apart, Ellie heard nothing but sobbing, cursing, and moaning. There was no thunderous crack as the composite frame fractured, no violent splash of icy salt water or ungodly roar of frigid, sucking air. Fully intact, the plane kept flying, buffeted viciously by winds that Ellie just knew were about to rip off the wings.

Death has to be better than living through this. Death would be peaceful. Death would be calm. Take me. I'm ready. I don't want to do this anymore.

Yet the massive jet, made puny by the magnificence of the storm, kept moving, as if it would never give up even such a hopeless fight. Over and over, the airliner lurched up through the sky at ear-popping speeds only to freefall again as if in mortal agony, the helpless victim in a sadistic game of atmospheric cat-and-mouse.

It didn't take long for the acrid stench of vomit to fill the cabin and, in sympathy with her fellow panic-stricken passengers, Ellie's stomach released its contents all over the beautiful, comforting man who had just sworn to be at her side through the good times and bad. And then the woman Nik had called a perfection-seeking, brass-balled bitch with a glacier where her heart should be the last time he saw her began to sob like a terrified child.

CHAPTER

The windows in Gianni Barone's office stretched nearly floor to ceiling. They were scrupulously kept clean and offered an unsurpassed view of the Greenwich Yacht Club and, in the distance, Long Island. The view and the office had only been his for a little over a year, since he'd been brought from the depths of mid-management into the C-suite at Flint AgroChemical as chief technology officer and vice president of strategic planning. Before that he'd been, well, not quite a grunt, but a mid-level executive who kept his hands dirty playing with the toys he'd helped create.

Gianni had come up through the ranks of the software development world, but not on the retail side or the Web side. His early employers didn't have pool tables and latte machines in the office, didn't take their nerdy *wünderkinder* on cruises on a whim, didn't sponsor intramural Nerf basketball tournaments with their fiercest competitors. No, during the years when the chic geeks were vying to see who could place the most outrageous demands on their employer, Gianni was working on the dark side of technology, for military contractors. No cushy offices, fancy food, or prima donna behavior had ever clouded his vision.

He'd started earning his chops straight out of college, working in top-secret installations that rivaled one another for re-creating the most Spartan workspaces: cavernous warehouse sites with cement floors and forty-foot ceilings from which dangled infant spacecraft mock-ups held together with duct tape and tinfoil, the coated wire of their guts spilling to the floor in Gordian tangles. He'd kept at it for a decade or so, burrowing deeper and deeper into the darkest recesses of the black tech world until he'd found his niche. In Alaska. At HAARP, the High-frequency Active Auroral Research Program funded primarily by the United States Navy. HAARP's multi-acre array of antennae held the promise of changing the world.

Weather "research"—a euphemism for the manipulation and control of the world's most chaotic and powerful system—was something Gianni had never considered getting involved with only because he hadn't known it existed outside of comic books and science fiction novels. When the Beltway bandits he worked for pulled him off a space-borne-weapon project to put out some high-end digital fires on HAARP, it was as if angels had started humming in his ears.

His new boss, Greg Simpson, hadn't had to persuade Gianni to remain on the tundra. Or to follow him when Greg left HAARP for Flint and TESLA seven years earlier.

By that time, Gianni had had enough of endless snow and ice. Connecticut sounded like heaven. The lure of a big salary and somewhere to spend it—like Manhattan—had enticed him back to the lower forty-eight and kept him there. Greg had been disappointed when Gianni had remained at the corporate head-quarters instead of accompanying the newly assembled team to the depths of Antarctica. As a trade-off, Greg had asked Gianni to become his eyes and ears in the halls of power. Gianni had accepted eagerly—especially since Croyden Flint had asked him, not long before, to keep a close eye on Greg.

Gianni leaned back in his desk chair, staring through the window at the yachts moving languorously in the distance. From the start, he'd understood the power that came with being a trusted source of information for the two most paranoid, power-mad people he'd ever met. Croyden held the kind of massive financial and political clout that could make anything happen and make it happen fast, but the power Greg held was exponentially more impressive. Should he ever get angry enough, Greg would be able to crush anything Croyden had planned.

At first, Gianni had tried not to let his position go to his head and had focused instead on maintaining an exquisitely delicate balancing act. But after spending time outside the tight orbit of Greg's insular world, and gaining entrée to Croyden's expansive one, Gianni had become annoyed at the sheer scope of Greg's ego and narcissism; his single-minded and increasingly vicious determination to get his own way; and his belief that he knew better than Croyden Flint what the company should do with the installation it had spent $250 million building and bringing on line. Greg was becoming a liability to the company and to Gianni's personal goal of becoming first indispensable to Croyden and, eventually, his successor.

Shortly after his arrival in the C-suite, Gianni had

been made aware of the firm's unique relationship—
dangerous, deeply intimate, and of long duration—
with the Pentagon. It had been initiated by Croyden's
grandfather, who had founded the company; Gianni
recognized immediately that it was a natural and mutually beneficial fit.

As a private company with virtually limitless resources, Flint could spend freely on research and development, unencumbered by congressional oversight.
Offshore, the corporation had even more freedom to
do as it pleased. But there were some things that even
money couldn't buy, and in those instances, Flint
turned to its five-sided friend for assistance. When lucrative regulatory, diplomatic, and intelligence favors
were bestowed, Flint was happy to oblige the Pentagon by providing custom-made weather, perfectly
crafted to resolve a vexing situation.

These days, Gianni was the man who made it happen. He was the man who took the meetings, who
made the deals, who decided if what the Pentagon
wanted would help Flint's bottom line—or hurt that
of its competitors. It had been a heady and rewarding
few months; being a puppetmaster was a rush beyond description.

But then he'd had to turn Admiral Medev down a
few times in succession. The decisions were war-
ranted and Croyden had backed him up: the rewards
weren't clear, the risks too high, the consequences
unfavorable. In hindsight, those refusals had to be
what set into motion the situation he now faced.

Gianni had been speechless with anger when the
denied weather events happened where and when the
Pentagon had requested. They weren't coincidences—
Nature didn't deal in coincidences like that, with pin-

point accuracy and impeccable timing. Croyden had demanded explanations. Gianni could offer him only two scenarios: the Pentagon had retooled HAARP to do what TESLA could do or had done an end run around him and had gone straight to Greg.

It didn't take long to figure out which was the more likely scenario.

Gianni had no illusions about Greg Simpson. The man was insane enough to take TESLA down in a blaze of irrational fury. He had the intellectual capability to do it. He had the technological and logistical means to do it.

It hadn't taken much to convince Croyden that Greg had to be shut down. It had been more difficult to get Croyden to agree to bring Tess on board as Greg's replacement. Ultimately, Croyden had accepted his word that Tess had qualities that would better serve Flint's purpose.

For instance, Tess would never willingly be the means to the military's ends. Despite owing her very existence to the Pentagon's war machine, she was a peacenik rather than a war hawk; her anti-war, anti-weapon stance was her biggest, probably her only, blind spot. Gianni was sure he could work it to Flint's advantage.

The sharp bleat of the phone on his desk pulled Gianni out of his reverie. He stopped to rub a brisk hand over his face before taking the call. He'd been staring at the water for too long. All that sparkle had made his eyes ache.

The small screen on the desk unit showed that the call was from Croyden.

"Damn it, you're on vacation. Can't you just disengage?" Gianni muttered before picking up the handset. "Yes, sir?"

"Any news?" the old man growled. He'd been in a foul mood ever since hearing that TESLA had gone dark.

"No, sir. The secure signals are still pinging and there's no evidence of distress or a disturbance at the site. The satellite images are extremely clear, sir. I'm concerned, but not worried. I'm sure it's just a glitch."

Best not to mention the enormous pulses TESLA's phased array had emitted that more than likely were the cause of the flogging of Mexico City.

"Was Simpson there when it happened?"

"No, sir. The plane had cleared the airspace about twenty minutes earlier."

"Glitch, my ass. If Simpson wasn't there when it happened, then he probably caused it. Have you heard from Tess?"

Gianni snapped upright at Croyden's comment, which echoed an earlier thought of his own. "Just the one time, sir, right after the plane took off with Greg aboard. It's on track to land in Capetown on schedule."

"Can you get word to the pilot?"

"Not at the moment. There are dead zones—"

"I know about the dead zones, damn it. How much longer 'til we can get in touch?"

"At least an hour."

"I want Simpson in custody the whole time they're on the ground. Until he's standing in my office, I don't want him to so much as piss without someone standing next to him. Understand?"

"It's already arranged."

"What do we do about the installation? How long do we wait?"

Gianni went still. "Sir?"

"Before we send people down there. An extraction team," Croyden barked.

"I don't think there's any reason to—"

"No reason to what? Panic? Intervene? Damn it, you're the one who convinced me he's gone rogue. Now you think that because the 'all clear' signal is still pinging, everything is fine? You don't think Simpson is smart enough to keep that going? God only knows what's going on down there."

Perching on the corner of his desk, Gianni studied his shoes—buttery brown Italian calf by Perry Ercolino—and tried to keep the exasperation out of his voice. "No, sir, it's not that. I strongly believe—I know—that anyone at the installation could disable that signal. If there's trouble, they're meant to."

"And if they're all in cahoots with him?"

"I can't see that happening. It would be against their best interests to keep TESLA off line."

"Then maybe they're already dead."

Gianni felt a chill shudder through him. "Greg Simpson isn't homicidal, Mr. Flint."

"Tell that to the Afghans," Croyden snapped. "What he did is mass murder."

Coming from someone who knows all about it. But it's different when it's profit-motivated, isn't it, Croyden?

Croyden cleared his throat and continued. "I'm touching down in Park City in about an hour. Call me when TESLA is back on line. I don't care what time it is. Tell Fred and Tim to call me when they get off that plane. I want to talk to that lying, two-faced sack of shit Simpson."

Gianni let out a long, silent breath. "I'll take care of it personally, sir. Enjoy your weekend."

* * *

"Got a minute?"

Nik looked up from his screen to see Ron standing in his office doorway, looking unusually grim.

"Sure. Come on in."

The younger man came in and carefully closed the door behind him.

"You look serious."

"Seriously perplexed."

"With something other than the comms problem?"

"You could say that."

"Sounds ominous." Leaning back in his chair, Nik folded his arms across his chest and met Ron's gaze. "What could be more important than getting us back in touch with the real world?"

"An impending change in focus."

"Go on."

Ron leaned his back against the door and adopted a wide-legged stance, as if bracing himself. The expression on his face went from a deep frown to a black scowl. "One of the test beds began running a brand-new set of algorithms, a series of simultaneous bursts that will run consecutively. It's bumped everything else off that machine."

The front legs of Nik's chair came down on the floor with a thud. "Say that again."

"You heard me right the first time," Ron said darkly.

Nik rubbed his unshaven jaw, giving himself a second to digest this. "Simultaneous *and* consecutive? So that's multiple parallels? Like a relay race?"

Ron nodded.

"Simultaneous *and* consecutive," Nik murmured, then looked up. "Anything else?"

"Multiple locations. It doesn't make much sense to me. I thought you might have some insight. I asked Pam and Etienne to look at it. I didn't want to alert the entire room."

"Did you tell Tess?"

"I came to you first."

"She's not going to like that."

"I'm not doing an end run, Nik, I came to you because I thought you might know something about it. I've been doing this stuff for years and I've never seen anything like this code. It—" He stopped and shook his head. "This is going to sound kind of nuts, but it looks like the code is trying to anticipate system capacity and estimate response times, only not the way we usually do that. This is more like 'here a blast, there a blast, everywhere—'"

Nik held up a hand. "Got it. No nursery rhymes. What made you look at the test beds?"

"I was going to take them off line so they couldn't be usurped," Ron answered drily. "Oh, the irony."

"Who else is on this?"

"Tommy Casey."

Nik was about to ask another question when a quick knock on the door stopped him. Ron pulled it open and instantly a dark, ponytailed head appeared in the widening crack.

"Hey, guys, the external downlink just came back."

Nik looked at Ron, who mirrored his consternation, then shifted his gaze back to Nangpal. "The downlink? Only the downlink?"

He nodded. "Yes, but not everything. Some things seem to be blocked, or scrambled. Weirdest thing I've ever seen."

"What do we have?" Nik asked, getting to his feet.

"Data streams from NOAA and NASA. Email. And CNN."

Nik stopped short and stared at him. "Did you say *CNN*? Is this some kind of joke?"

Nangpal shook his head. "I couldn't make this stuff up, Nik. Come and see it for yourself."

"I'll do that," he said, and lifted the walkie-talkie from his belt. "Tess? Please meet me in the sandbox." He let go of the button.

"Nik, I'm already here and waiting for you." Her voice was calm and cool, and Nik cringed inside.

Damn. Scratch one more demerit onto today's tally.

"She wasn't in there when I came in here," Ron said quickly.

Nik nodded and rose to his feet, his face betraying nothing. "I'll be right there," he said into the unit, then released the transmit button. "Okay, boys, let's go."

Greg sat in the gaping tunnel of the Ilyushin's fuselage as it roared over the Southern Ocean, both delighted with himself—his plans were well under way by now—and livid with Tess Beauchamp for surviving the trip south. The only part of the situation that made him smile was the knowledge that Tess would be the cause of all that was about to happen to the world in the next twenty-four hours.

Flint—and Tess—would pay a steep price for their interference with his life's work. It was more than likely that Tess had already begun to pay her price: by now, she was certainly an orphan, although she wouldn't have been informed of that yet.

But Mexico was just a test, merely the first place he would show his muscle. Whatever else happened would depend on Tess herself. If she were as clever as people thought she was, she would absorb the lesson quickly and realize that behaving like some sort of righteous prig, taking actions beyond the scope of her abilities, was causing all the harm. If she did that—which was unlikely—Mexico would be the only location harmed. But if she chose to try to elevate herself to his level, if she tried to outsmart him or outthink him and impede the progress of his plan, a more distressing outcome—global devastation on an unequalled scale—was assured. The blame for it would be squarely on her shoulders as the neophyte stepping into a giant's shoes.

He let his head rest against the wall of the plane and closed his eyes. His dreams would be sweet indeed.

17

Spring in Connecticut had been fabulous so far.
Swards of green so lush and verdant that they seemed artificial stretched in all directions, sliced here and there by discreet ribbons of freshly sealed asphalt and punctuated by majestic trees. In the country club's lavish clubhouse, foursomes of men—some quiet, sipping coffee, some already gregarious and loud and draining their third screwdriver—milled around waiting to be called to the first tee. The golf course was filling up in a steady, orderly fashion, as expected at 8 A.M. on a rare, unseasonably gorgeous Friday in late April. It was the boys' club ritual. The office, the board room, could wait; the golf course, and the deals to be made on it, could not.

As one of the oldest, most expensive country clubs on the East Coast, the Warrington Country Club boasted the most macho, monochromatic, and monied membership in the region. The combined net worth of the morning's players exceeded the GDP of nearly a third of the world's countries. Most of the men had grown up on the course and the members considered themselves a family, almost; all of them had either inherited their membership or had married into it. Women could only inherit memberships after the death of a member spouse—making Warrington widows a scarce and precious commodity.

Membership was strictly reserved for the blue-bloods: those gilded personages whose distant ancestors had been of the ruling classes of socially acceptable countries, whose less distant ancestors had ruled the free market, and whose families had for decades summered in Newport, wintered in Palm Beach, and spent the intervening months on New York City's Upper East Side with weekends idled away in Greenwich.

Castlelike Warrington Hall sat amid old-growth-studded acres of lush lawn that ended where the Long Island Sound began. There was no pier or marina, just a picturesque seawall topped with formidably jutting balconies that effectively precluded any approach to the grounds via the water. Members knew to drive in through the imposing gate, or arrive—appropriately clad—by way of the groomed riding trails.

The club made neither excuses for its policies nor exceptions to them. No one bought their way into Warrington. Not the young lions of Wall Street (too tacky), not politicians (too slick), not celebrities (too much trouble). The lone occasion upon which someone might be considered for a buy-in was if there was a large capital expenditure in need of funding. Then the membership committee was only too happy to quietly dangle a much-coveted membership, with its breathtaking initiation fee and annual assessments that were nearly as precipitous, in front of an eager outsider. For the privilege, the committee would take his money and even tolerate his presence, but it was understood among the members that no one would go out of their way to make the newcomer feel welcome.

It went without saying that Croyden Flint was a Warrington member; his grandfather had been one of the club's founders. And it was only by the grace of his well-funded and duly worshipped God that Croyden, accompanied by his children and grandchildren, was in his plane and on his way to his home in Utah that day rather than toiling on the still-pristine Alister MacKenzie-designed course.

Foursomes—all men; women weren't allowed on the course until eleven—were called at twenty-minute intervals. The congenial laughter and conversation deadened to a reverent hush at the tee and didn't resume until the pairs were in their carts and headed down the velvet fairway.

Not a man present cared about the nor'easter that had been battering the Atlantic coast from Bar Harbor to well south of Boston all week; there was no immediate risk to their happiness other than an annoying and growing accumulation of clouds. Their cottages in Nantucket and yachts in Newport were insured and, thus, didn't merit a thought.

By late morning, the Hall and its sweeping terrace that overlooked the eighteenth hole were packed with lolling families. Dowagers sat in the shade wearing Lilly Pulitzer while trophy wives clustered in the sun wearing as little as possible. Well out of maternal earshot, a battalion of imported nannies managed the toddling heirs.

The course remained full despite the lessening weather. The uninterrupted early sunshine had given way to huge puffs of picture-perfect clouds, and frisky breezes were playing occasional havoc with the longest drives. As the population on the greens and fairways, at the pool, and on the terrace and tennis courts had increased through midday, so had the wind, building steadily and slowly from light zephyrs to obnoxious gusts. Golfers on the front nine, just setting out—the mothers, wives, and daughters of the earlier players— were becoming hesitant. Most, though, pushed on rather than appear timid or weak in front of their peers and rivals. It was just weather, after all.

And then, within moments, their golden world changed. Clouds rolled in more rapidly than anyone had ever witnessed, and obscured the sun. Thick, heavy, and ominous, they looked like sculpted snow-drifts in motion under an eerie moonlit sky. A thousand shades of gray swirled dizzily overhead like a communal hallucination. Even the risk-takers tallied their scores and headed for the clubhouse.

The storm, from its start, was cataclysmic. Raindrops as large and hard as pebbles were flung from the sky in sheets of undisguised rage, creating instant torrents on the lush undulations of the greens and fairways. Hailstones, first the size of golf balls, then tennis balls, bounced off the grass, casting divots into the air. Ever larger spheres of solid ice fell from the clouds, smashing craters into the roofs of the speeding golf carts and sometimes into the delicate heads of their unlucky occupants. Multi-pronged spears of white-hot lightning struck the earth as if hurled by Zeus himself. Again and again, the sky exploded like the bellows of Hell, shattering the sound barrier and making the earth beneath tremble in response. Screams of abject panic caught in the throats of the living and the dying.

Those puny humans, often called the masters of the

universe, cowered before this display of real power. Through the deluge, the world glowed an otherworldly green as the grass and trees reveled in the surfeit of ozone and nitrogen nature was so violently disgorging.

More than one cart toppled while racing over the crest of a sodden hill and slid, scattering people who grabbed mindlessly for the PING and Honma clubs tumbling around them. The true nature of these status symbols made itself known as their metal shafts served as irresistible attractors to the myriad electrical leaders strobing from the molten clouds. In staccato flashes, terawatts of power punctured and scorched shorn lawns and helpless golfers alike, littering paradise with smoking patches of charred carbon, some of which screamed desperately for help that would be a long time coming.

The storm raged on, as if Heaven—perhaps Hell—had decided to empty itself on these pristine grounds. Warrington Hall's magnificent banks of leaded windows, expatriated from ancient ducal seats, shattered in the onslaught of hail and debris. The gales swept indoors to have their way with the decor and those persons sheltering inside.

Through the neighborhoods and the small, nearby burgs, walls of water rushed down inclines to collect in shallow, manicured hollows, surge through valleys, and wrench wider every available crevice in wood or stone. Trees that had survived both the American Revolution and suburban sprawl were torn out by the roots, crashing across streets and into mansions and bungalows alike. Terrified occupants ran for higher floors as homes, stores, and offices were inundated with rain and mud. Cars floated and spun as foaming currents gushed through streets. Caught off-guard, pedestrians struggled to walk against the wind and water, their resistance futile and occasionally fatal. Adult bodies bumped along in the sludgy, greasy flow until a vehicle or tree limb snagged them; smaller ones, some still in strollers, jammed the storm sewers.

Transformers exploded in paltry imitations of the lightning that provoked them. Power lines snapped, sparks spraying from the wildly snaking cables until the current died and the villages and neighborhoods went dark.

Through the bulletproof, floor-to-ceiling windows of his luxurious home nestled on high, open acres of back-country Greenwich, Gianni Barone watched the storm unfold and imagined the destruction taking place in the town. His decision to return to his house in the middle of the workday to retrieve a file had been a fluke, but now he was battling uncomfortable thoughts about Fate and Destiny. And Revenge.

The news about this morning's massive, devastating earthquake in Mexico had left a heaviness on his mind that he hadn't been able to shake. The suspicion that he and Croyden shared about its provenance was reinforced by the violence battering his town—Flint's town—made his blood freeze.

He reached for his smartphone, hoping that the cell towers nearby were still functional.

CHAPTER

Admiral Alexander Medev sat in his office in the Pentagon, riveted to the live footage of the carnage under way in Connecticut. The devastation unfolding on the screen was as horrifying as it was irresistible. It was sheer luck that any of the networks had a camera crew on the scene, but one of the talking heads who'd risen high enough through the ranks to comment on the news instead of report it had been taping a feature story on the plight of resurgent Wall Street recessionaires. When all hell broke loose with the weather, the reporter had begun providing a real-time view of what was happening on Greenwich Avenue.

The admiral was darkly entertained by the realization that, in a disaster, the rich die the same way the poor do. Horribly.

The buzz of his desk phone interrupted his morbid fascination. The name that appeared on the screen didn't surprise him.

"Medev," he said, his fingers wrapped tightly around the handset as he pressed it to his ear. His eyes strayed back to the television screen. Something about tragedy from a distance mesmerized him.

"Admiral, what the hell is going on?" Gianni Barone's voice was cold, calm, and very, very pissed off.

"What do you mean?"

"Don't make the mistake of playing me for a fool, admiral."

"Mr. Barone, I don't know what you're talking about."

"The storm in Connecticut. Did you order it?" he snapped.

The admiral sat up straighter in his chair and tore his gaze from the screen. "I didn't order anything, Barone," he hissed, as if he were not alone in his office with the door shut. "Why are you asking me something like that? Are you insane?"

"No, I'm not insane. I'll say it again, admiral. *Don't take me for a fool.* I'm watching the storm through the windows in my living room and it's only sheer luck that I'm not in the office—if the office is still standing. This storm defies every law of nature, so that only leaves two options: it came from HAARP or it came from TESLA. I'm asking you which one. I can assure you that I, that Flint, had nothing to do with it. Now, I want answers. Did you order it?"

"No."

"Who did?"

The admiral got to his feet in anger. "How the hell do you expect me to answer that? I can just assure you that I didn't. *We* didn't."

"Your assurances don't count for jack shit with me anymore, Alex."

"Look, I thought we settled our differences," Medev replied, lowering his voice to a furious growl.

"I told you I would back off, go through you first, and I meant it. When you nailed me, you nailed the department, and you know it. It was a fair fight and I lost. Okay? And because I lost, I've got a command performance for the Secretary of the Navy in half an hour and the topic is our black ops relationship with your company."

"I'm not interested in—"

"Well, get interested," the admiral snapped. "I'm guessing he's gonna chew me out just for practice. Don't expect me to cover your ass."

"You? Cover *my* ass? For what?" Gianni demanded, incredulous.

The admiral stared hard at the framed commendation on the wall opposite him. It was for valor and signed by a president who had understood the value of power. "From day one, this relationship has been a mutual use," he said. "We used you, you used us. You were the whore, we were your best customer."

"What's your point?"

"You changed our deal—"

"Not *our* deal. The deal was cut before either of us was on the scene," Gianni interrupted.

Alex Medev continued, "You slammed me and this office into view. The big dogs got a radar lock on me and now I'm out of God-damned chaff. Now we gotta help each other, Barone. You owe me."

"You must be joking. Help each other? *I owe you?* I don't owe you shit. And you're damned right I pulled the plug on that deal. What did you think I would do after finding out that you spent the last three months trying to fuck me over?" Gianni asked, his voice deadly calm. "For the last time: did the U.S. military order the creation of this storm?"

"I already told you we didn't. I didn't. Think about it. We have nothing to gain from—"

"Careful, or you'll drown in your own bullshit," Gianni snapped. "What are you going to put in that report Bonner wants?"

Medev went still. *No one is supposed to know about that report.* "What are you talking about?"

"What do you think I'm talking about, Alex? The report on Afghanistan that Bonner asked you to produce after he got his ass handed to him by the president. The one in which you dot every *i* and cross every *t* and make sure that no one learns anything about the provenance of that storm. *That* report. And don't even think of mentioning the name Flint in it, or I will personally come down there and rip you a new one."

"Barone, *we had nothing to do with that storm.*"

"I don't believe you. When is the last time you communicated with Greg Simpson?"

Medev rubbed his forehead against the throb that had begun to pulse inside there. "We contact him through you—"

"Admiral, *when is the last time you communicated with Greg Simpson?*" Gianni Barone roared through the phone. "We pulled him from TESLA this morning and shortly after wheels-up on his outbound flight, the installation went off line. Since then there have been two—two, admiral—events that could have been triggered by TESLA. I need to game up for the situation *we*—and that includes you, Alex—may be facing."

Admiral Alexander Medev, who'd fought, clawed, and brawled his way from ensign to admiral, never backing away from a fight or a gamble, swallowed hard, his throat suddenly so dry that he began coughing. It gave him just enough time to remember his last conversation with Greg Simpson.

I'm making the decisions now.

Medev felt his bowels surge sickeningly and fell back onto his seat as he realized Greg had taken TESLA rogue. The collar of his regulation shirt was clammy with perspiration and starch; sweat soaked his undershirt. He reached up weakly to loosen his tie before it choked him.

"Earlier today. Before dawn. The plane carrying Tess Beauchamp was en route," he rasped, breathing as if the oxygen in the room wasn't enough to keep him conscious.

"What did he say?" Gianni demanded. "What was his frame of mind?"

"He was furious with you, with Croyden. He said he was going to bring down the plane," he finished in a hard whisper. The stream of cursing that flooded his ear went beyond the breadth and depth of anything he'd ever heard aboard a ship or in a dockyard.

"What else?"

"He said he was making the decisions now. Not you, not us."

"What decisions? Was he talking about TESLA? Did—"

The admiral was taking huge, openmouthed breaths that stopped just short of being gasps. "He said he was going to address the situation as he saw fit. That sending Beauchamp to replace him was a declaration of war."

"Son of a bitch."

Medev leaned back in his chair, trying to breathe, to think.

"He was losing it, Alex, and you knew it," Gianni

said flatly. "You recognized the danger and made a game of it when you started going around me. *You* gave Greg the encouragement he needed to go over that edge. Now, you have to—"

"I have to go." With shaking hands, Medev tried to replace the handset in its cradle, missing by several inches without noticing. He sagged heavily into his chair, head back, clawing at the buttons of his regulation shirt.

This would cost him his career. He'd flouted orders; he'd gone independent, thinking he could cater to Simpson and keep him in line and keep TESLA in service to the Pentagon. Medev took a large breath, fighting to fill his lungs. Everything he'd been associated with, from that decoration on his wall to his chest full of ribbons to his family, would be tainted. His name, his record—

The admiral lurched forward, heart pounding, stomach churning, nearly falling out of his chair as he reached for his wastebasket. He made his target, for the most part, but still managed to spatter vomit all over his shoes and his knife-creased trousers. He pulled open the third drawer of his desk and reached toward the back. With violently trembling hands, he slid out the loaded .22 caliber snub-nosed revolver he always kept there—another small act of defiance.

The little gun was heavy in his hand. Alex stared at it through a blur of tears, seeing little more than a pistol-shaped smudge of darkness against his palm.

Gianni's voice was distant, coming out of the handset in bursts that sounded like he was shouting. The admiral ignored it.

He was a man of action. Too much a man of action, perhaps. He hadn't taken any time for reflection before defying orders and approaching Simpson directly; it stood to reason he wouldn't allow himself any time for reflection now. Only a coward would do that.

Medev cocked the hammer, then slipped the squat, smooth barrel into his mouth and twisted it to aim directly at the roof of his mouth and the brain beyond it. Then, made clumsy by the angle and his own desperate fear, he held the gun with both hands and squeezed the trigger.

The noise inside his head deafened him, the heat and smell of cordite burned his nostrils, but pain didn't come immediately. Neither did death.

He slumped in his chair, his vision gone crooked. He didn't know it was because one eye had been blasted from its socket, bursting like an egg yolk and mingling with the blood running down his face. The door slammed open and his assistant stopped short, looked at him, and opened her mouth in a scream he couldn't hear.

The admiral's vision clouded over then, just as the data from the raw and pulsing nerve ends registered in what remained of his brain. He wanted to join in the faint screaming now dully penetrating his damaged senses, but the gush of hot fluid in his throat prevented him. Hands were on him, moving him, but then the sensations stopped, the jolting, the pressure stopped. The sounds around him stopped, too, and he moved from chaos to endless silence.

Gianni stared at the storm raging beyond the huge windows of his home, knowing what the sharp crack on the other end of the phone meant. A female voice screamed seconds later, and he pressed the button on his smartphone to end the call.

He tried to summon remorse, even sympathy, but couldn't. It would have been easy to say his lack of response was due to the sudden shock, but he knew himself better than that. The reason was anger. When the shouting stopped, someone would realize that a phone line was still open, and would look to see who the admiral had been speaking with when he pulled that trigger. Gianni would be identified, and the questions would begin.

He threw the phone onto the leather couch and poured himself a Scotch.

19

CHAPTER

Nik, Ron, and Nangpal entered the sandbox to see Tess standing near Etienne's elbow as he sat at a workstation. She looked serious, her forehead creased as she stared at the screen.

"Pam was right about the geographical coordinates being messed up. That first set of pulses set off a huge earthquake in Mexico City. Knocked out communications for half the country. They're only just starting to broadcast footage," she said as the three of them walked toward her.

When they reached her side, she straightened up and Nik registered the annoyance in her eyes. He resigned himself to getting his wrist slapped.

"I realize old habits die hard, but you're all going to have to try harder," she said coolly and loud enough for everyone in the sandbox to hear her. "Next time anything happens, I expect to be informed first." She paused. "That's it. Nik, a moment?"

Oh, this will be pleasant. Nik followed her to the

conference room, opened the door, and let her pass through, then shut it and turned to look at her.

"Don't you dare play gatekeeper with me," she said in a low voice, her eyes spitting blue flames at him. "Do not even think of it. Do you understand me?"

"Hey—"

"No, Nik. I'm not interested in hearing excuses. What I am interested in is knowing what else you haven't told me."

He thought briefly about arguing, then just perched his ass on the edge of the table and folded his arms across his chest. "A while ago, one of the test beds began running a new set of algorithms that Ron thought—"

"Why did he go to you with it?" Tess looked like she was about to explode with anger.

"Oh, for Christ's sake, would you stop acting like there's a conspiracy against you?" Nik snapped. "We're in a very weird situation right now, Tess, and the people here are used to bouncing ideas off each other, not you. You've been here less than a full day, okay? He came to me because he thought that I, *as assistant research director for the past four years,*" he said pointedly, "might know what the algorithms were supposed to do. That's all there was to it. Clearly, it's not a secret, because I'm telling you now."

She glared at him but had regained her composure. "Go on."

"At first, Ron thought they were just being run to anticipate system capacity and estimate response time; we do that all the time, though these equations didn't look exactly like the usual ones. But that was only part of it." He paused, to make sure he had her full attention.

He did. All six-foot-one-inch-plus-high-heels of it. Her eyes were back to glowing as hot as cobalt 60 and she looked like she was about to jump him—not in a good way—if he didn't keep talking.

"And?"

"They seem to be aligning bursts on different arrays to effect events that are simultaneous and consecutive, in multiple locations."

"Simultaneous and consecutive? That makes no sense." She moved to the chair at the end of the table and sat down.

"They're strange commands, setting combinations of frequencies at all different ranges. There's no coherence to any of it because the full suite isn't there. There are definitely components missing, as if things are meant to be tested discretely as small executables. Every test bed is sewn up with them. Everything of ours that was in a queue was dumped."

Her eyes widened. "Just like that?"

He nodded.

"And no one knows what these new algorithms are meant to do?"

"I imagine Greg does," he replied drily. "Like I said, we're not seeing the full package. Frankly, it's the ugliest set of strings you ever saw. Convoluted, extraordinarily complex." He shook his head. "They're a mess."

"Okay. Let's back up for a minute," she said, folding her hands on the table in front of her and looking at Nik again. "The simultaneous and consecutive—explain that to me."

Nik slid off the table and into the chair to her left. "Multiple locations around the world. We don't know where; what looks to be the code for the coordinates is a mess of spaghetti code. Whoever wrote it intentionally made it difficult to decipher. Maybe the coordinates are randomly generated." He shrugged. "We haven't figured that out yet. With the geocoordinates disarrayed—"

"Not anymore."

"What?"

"When the comms downlink came back on line, the coordinate software reshuffled itself and everything seems to be back in order. I think Pam's a little wigged out about it."

Nik frowned at her. "And you're not?"

"Why would that get me stressed any more than anything else that's gone on since I arrived? I'm beginning to think I'm in Oz and Greg's the man behind the curtain," Tess replied drily. "It's crystal clear to me that Greg is playing with us, and he's never been one for fighting fair, Nik. Everything is a blood sport to him." She watched him for a moment, then continued, "That second set of bursts created an atmospheric event. Together, the two thirty-millisecond bursts of EHF reordered the bulk volume neutrality but left free-floating pockets of intensely energized, ionized particles. Big storm, Nik. *Bad* storm. Lightning deaths, flooding, bodies in the streets. You can see the footage yourself, courtesy of Greg."

"That's the one that hit Gander Bay?"

"That's where we thought it struck," she replied. "We were wrong. It hit the northeastern U.S. Ground zero was Greenwich, Connecticut."

For just a split second, Nik felt the blood stop running in his veins. "That has to be a fluke, Tess. That kind of pinpoint control—if it was even our storm—"

"It was."

"—is impossible. Even for TESLA."

She didn't say anything right away, just looked at him with a tight smile on her lips, a deep coldness in her eyes. "If you think so, Nik. Tell me more about the algorithms."

"They appear to command a set of events to occur simultaneously with one another in disparate locations, then another series triggers at a pre-set interval in the future from the first, in different locations. And so on."

Her expression became one of bemused fascination. "You don't know what it is?"

"Um, mass devastation on a global scale?" he asked, with no shortage of sarcasm.

"In a word, yes. It's also one of the things I was working on before I came here. It was for Flint, but classified—highly classified. Greg shouldn't have had access to any of it."

"Why were you working on—?"

"I wasn't aiming for the same outcomes. I was going for synchronous fronts to block storms, not to create simultaneous destruction."

"But he got at your research anyway, despite not having official access to it?"

"Seems like it. Gianni told me Greg had appropriated some of my other research. He must not have known about this. I'm sure he would have told me."

Nik leaned back in his chair. "Okay."

She watched him for a minute, then shook her head and gave a small, slightly thunderstruck laugh. "Nik," she said finally, her voice dropping almost to a whisper. "Don't you get it? This is one of the things Nikola Tesla wrote about, one of the things he theorized

about but could never make work, even on paper."
She dropped her gaze to her hands, which were folded
on the table in front of her. "I went to Belgrade. I got
permission to view his archived papers. There were
only hints in them, so I petitioned the CIA—" She
glanced up at him. "I shouldn't be telling you any of
this, so if you squeal on me, I'll have to kill you. But
they let me into their archives, Nik. They let me look
at the papers they confiscated when Tesla died.

"What I found there dovetailed with what I saw in
Belgrade. Greg saw them, too. His name was on the
register at Langley—can you imagine? The CIA still
has paper registers in their archives?" She took a deep
breath. "What I saw still wasn't complete. But somehow Greg seems to have cadged together some of the
missing information."

She paused for a moment, staring at her hands
again, then met his eyes. She was smiling, her eyes
alight with a different kind of fire. It transformed her
face from pretty to . . . intriguing.

"Nik, this is what Tesla was working on when he
died. It was . . . he was so close to a breakthrough.
I think Greg put the final pieces together."

It was as if someone had flipped a switch in Nik's
brain. There weren't any words left in his mind; her
statement had erased them all. He could only stare
at her, realizing after a minute that his mouth had
dropped open. He closed it.

"Nik, did you hear what I said?" she asked, frowning at him.

"Yes."

"Do you agree?"

"I don't know what the hell you're talking about,"
he confessed.

She blinked at him again and he watched the crease in her brow deepen. "*You don't?* But you're—" She stopped.

The old burn flared to life, hot and painful as ever, and Nik glared at her.

"I'm what?" he ground out.

Tess blinked at the sudden anger in Nik's eyes.

Uh-oh.

In her excitement, she'd forgotten what she'd meant to keep to herself—*another* thing she'd meant to keep to herself.

It's too late now. He knows I know.

She folded her arms in front of her and gave a tight, one-shouldered shrug. "Well, you're Tesla's only living male heir, right?"

"How do you know about that?" he demanded.

"I've heard rumors over the years that you were named for him," she admitted. "And it's in your personnel file. But I would have figured it out anyway, Nik, when we stopped in your office for a second this morning and I saw what you had on your wall." She paused. "I don't know too many guys who keep handwritten Serbian love poems framed in their office."

He frowned at her. "You read Serbian?"

"And French, Italian, Russian, and Greek. We always had a lot of foreigners traipsing through WhizMer," she said, trying not to sound defensive. "Plus, I studied Serbian for a few months before I went to Belgrade so I'd know what I was looking at when I saw Tesla's papers."

"He sent the poem to my great-grandmother," Nik said stiffly. "It was his favorite."

"They were friends?"

Nik looked at her without saying a word.

"Hey, you know all about my sordid past," she pointed out. "You made out with me fifteen years ago in Greg's office while he was out doing his special snake dance through the dipole array. I even let you feel me up. I think that qualifies me to get a little insight into your background. Especially considering that it may have just taken on some global security significance of potentially epic proportions. Kind of a tit for tat, as it were?"

She could see that he was suddenly fighting back a grin.

"Your tits were great back then."

Well, I asked for that, didn't I?

"They're even better now," she retorted. "But we digress. What I need to know is how Greg put the pieces together. His name wasn't on the register in Belgrade, Nik, it was only at Langley. That means that I've seen more of the old guy's work than Greg ever did, but I couldn't put the pieces together. Apparently, Greg did. I need to know if there is anything you told him or showed him that you haven't told or shown me."

He let out a slow breath. "Nikola Tesla *was* my great-grandfather," he said slowly, as if the words were being forced out of him. "I know the legend is that he was celibate, famously so, but my great-grandmother was a force of nature. Irish, with a big brain and a pretty smile. She was his secretary when he had a lab on Fifth Avenue in New York City. The lab burned to the ground one night and she, ah, helped him through his grief, which accounted for the appearance of my grandmother."

Nik's words inspired the same tingle Tess had felt

when she'd been reading the great man's papers. "Wow," she murmured. "Did they get married or anything? I mean, if all the biographers got the celibacy thing wrong—"

"No marriage. Great-granny was a suffragette, apparently, and remained single. As did my grandmother and my mother. It was an all-female household until I arrived," he replied. "Happy now? Can I stop?"

"Are you kidding? What are the other things on your wall?"

"Just some early sketches. His version of a particle beam weapon, circa 1899 or thereabouts."

Tess felt her mouth drop open. "Can I see them?"

"Now?"

"Yes."

He shrugged. "Let's go."

He held open the door for her and, ignoring all the startled looks as they passed through the sandbox, they left the control center headed toward Nik's private office. "So were you named after him, too?"

"No," she said with a smile. "You're not the first person to ask me that, either. I was named after my grandmother Thérèse. It morphed into Tess when I was little because the neighborhood kids didn't want to deal with the French pronunciation. I thought about going back to it while I lived in France, but by then I'd been Tess too long."

Once inside the office, he took the frames from the wall and handed them to her.

She took them from him gently. "These must be worth a fortune," she breathed.

"They would be if I ever wanted to sell them," he said, his voice as dry as the air outside.

She sat down on the lone chair in the room and

took her time studying them, then held one up. "Do you know what this one is? What it's for?"

"No, they're all jumbled. They're strays, not a full set of anything."

She looked at him, then blinked. "Did you say 'all'? You have more than these two?"

He nodded. "They're layered behind those. I didn't have time to get them all framed."

Tess could feel her pulse kick up a few beats per minute. "May I?"

He shrugged. "Go ahead."

She turned over the frame. The brown paper had been slit and taped shut. "So I'm not the first."

"What? Let me see that." Nik took it out of her hands and stared at the neat seam as if he'd never seen it before.

Their eyes met then and neither said a word. He handed the frame back to her.

Okay.

Tess slid the papers out and studied them, one at a time, then reluctantly returned them to their not-so-secret hiding place. She handed the frames to Nik, who replaced them on the wall.

"Thanks."

"Did they do anything for you?"

She smiled. "Not much. They really are just a collection of mismatched sketches." She paused. "Tesla once said he wanted to devise a superweapon that would put an end to all wars. That's what I've read, anyway."

"The family stories support that," Nik replied tightly, and sat down at his desk. "And yet here we are, you and I, trying to get Greg to stop playing with the game-changer great-granddad never quite created."

"The irony of it all. Is that what you're thinking?"

"Not quite."

Tess flashed him a look of contrition. "I know I pushed it, Nik. Thanks for trusting me." She paused. "I won't repeat anything—"

"Thanks for that," he snapped.

"Look, I'm sorry. I didn't know it was a sore spot. I mean being related to him. If I had, I wouldn't have mentioned it."

"It's not a sore spot. It's just none of your business. It's not anyone's business but mine."

Annoyed silence hung thick in the room for a long moment, then Tess sighed and leaned back. "With all due respect, I beg to differ. Your heritage is more than just your business, Nik. You're the last carrier of the genes of Nikola Tesla. That sort of puts you up there with Caroline Kennedy's children and Princes William and Harry—"

"Oh, for Christ's sake, would you just—"

She glared at him, frowning. "No, I won't drop it, if that's what you were going to say. The man was an icon, Nik, and way, way ahead of his time. He was also undisputedly a genius—"

"Don't leave out 'delusional' and 'suffering from dementia,'" he interjected bitterly.

"Oh, to hell with that. That happened because he didn't know enough about what he was messing with and let himself be exposed to too much of a good thing, as in electromagnetic radiation," Tess replied, dismissing his words with a roll of her eyes. "In fact, that's probably where Greg got the idea to hang out in the antenna fields while they were—"

"Tess—*boss*—with all due respect," he ground out, openly mocking her, "shut the fuck up, okay? It's *really* none of your business."

"No, thank you, I won't. I want to know why you haven't capitalized on it, Nik. The man was famously and openly celibate, and yet here you are. It's documented. You could have—"

"I could have what? My own reality TV show?" he snapped. "I don't need any bullshit from you about my family tree. The identity of my great-grandfather has always seemed to me to be a private matter. I'd appreciate you taking the same view."

Tess sat for a moment in silence. "I apologize for bringing it up. I didn't mean to upset you."

"You already said that. Apology accepted. Are we done now?"

"Maybe."

He let out a frustrated breath. "Okay, I have a question for you. What the hell is WhizMer?"

She cocked her head and squinted at him. "It's what we called the White Sands Missile Range."

"Who's 'we'?"

"Me. My family. All the kids on the range." She stopped and shrugged. "I thought you knew. I guess I never told you."

"Told me what?"

"That you're not the only one with familial baggage. I'm not the long-lost heir to scary particle-beam blueprints, but I *am* third-generation spooky in my own way. All four of my grandparents worked on the Manhattan Project. That's how they met, and how my parents met—they grew up together. I was born on the Missile Range. I don't mean nearby, I mean *on*. My mother was out doing some field work when I decided I'd drunk enough amniotic fluid. I was delivered fifty yards outside the base hospital by a geologist assisted by a radiation specialist. I grew up on WhizMer, too."

"The military did surface testing of nuclear bombs there. They let people get pregnant?"

She lifted an eyebrow. "Kinda hard to stop them. Anyway, it was a unique childhood. My first complete sentence was 'It's need to know, mom.' In school, the standard excuse, because it was usually true, wasn't 'the dog ate my homework,' it was 'my dad was helping me and started making notes on the back of the page, and now it's top-secret, so I can't turn it in.' It was like growing up in the dark because of all the security protocols," she said, trying to wipe the stony expression off his face and maybe get him to smile.

"I got a security clearance when I was twelve so I could go to my mother's office and empty her trash can to earn my allowance. And to top it all off, my first and only summer job during college was at the Skunk Works—the place where they tested and built the Stealth Bomber. I'm still not allowed to list it on my CV," she said with a laugh. "So, are we even now? Can we get back to talking about you?"

"No," Nik said, his voice flat with finality.

"Wrong answer. Does Greg know about great-grandpappy? Has he seen these?"

"Seems like it. That backing was fine when I moved down here." He let out a harsh breath and looked at the ceiling again. "I always figured he knew, and that's why he tolerated me."

His words sent a shiver down Tess's back.

"Does he think you channel the genius of Nikola Tesla?"

"No, I'm pretty sure Greg thinks that *he* channels Tesla's genius." Nik stood up and took two steps away from the desk to lean against the wall. He thrust a hand through his hair, then shoved it into the front pocket of his jeans. "It's more likely that Greg assumed I have some insider knowledge of Tesla's theories, but he never asked."

Tess cocked her head and looked at him, squinting just a little. "It's not far-fetched."

"The man died nearly seventy years ago."

"But you have the sketches. Do you have anything more?"

Nik shrugged casually. "My great-grandmother worked for him for years, and maintained a close relationship with him after she left. Rumor has it she was with him when he died."

Tess didn't let her excitement show. "I never heard that."

"Maybe that's because only my mother ever said it."

"Does that mean there *is* a cache of documents that no one knows about?"

Nik shrugged and dodged the question. "My grandmother always said that her mother told her that she made extra copies of the important documents in case something went wrong. Tesla didn't even question it."

"*And she kept them?* My God, Nik! Where are they?"

Nik frowned at her. "You just saw them."

Tess folded her arms in front and hugged them tight against her ribs. The question wouldn't budge, weighing on her mind like a dull ache. "Okay, listen, Nik. We both know what's done here. You mess around with the world's weather so that fields planted with Flint-engineered crops stay healthy through to harvest. They get enough rain, enough sunshine. Meanwhile Monsanto, ConAgra, Cargill, Bayer, and the rest of the competition don't feel the same sort of love." She looked at him. His face was neutral. "Right? Their farms and factories and test fields get trashed by the biggest can of environmental whup-ass the world is ever likely to see. Custom-made by you."

"That's twice you've said 'you,'" Nik interrupted, defensiveness seeping into his voice. "Aren't you part of this, too? As I recall, you're a vice president of Flint now."

The comment caught her off-guard. Tess pulled herself together instantly and brushed a lock of hair from her face, then returned her hand to its fisted position under the opposite arm.

"You're right. I'm part of it now. We control the weather. Or did until a few hours ago," she said, her voice careful. "And I'm not happy about the change in status. We've lost control of the comms, the software test beds, and the arrays, Nik. Greg's got logic bombs popping out of the software like ass cheeks at Hooters. We don't know where to look next. We're chasing shadows. All we know is that the arrays are doing big, very, very bad things to the outside world. We can't tell anyone what's coming and not just because our comms are down: we don't know what's going to happen or when or where." She paused, glaring at him. "Why can't we figure out what he's up to and how to counteract it, Nik? What are we doing wrong?"

"What we're doing wrong is approaching this like scientists who are rational and sane: two things Greg isn't."

"I can accept that. But back in the dark ages, Greg wrote very elegant code. Very clear and streamlined. *This* is dense, complex, and confusing. That bothers me. Greg doesn't write crap code. Ever."

"Not usually," Nik said.

"Explain that."

"There have been a few occasions since the arrays came out of testing a year ago."

"What did the crap code do?" she demanded.

"I don't know. But it was outside the spec of what we normally do here. None of us had seen anything like it before. Not since HAARP."

Chills shot through her and Tess knew that her eyes had gone wide. Her pulse tripled, and all she could do was stare at Nik's dark, shadowed, unsmiling face.

"You do remember what we were doing up there, don't you?" he asked, his voice mocking. "Building 'enhanced communications capabilities' by bouncing electromagnetic signals through specific regions of the atmosphere's upper strata. Even back then none of us believed it, Tess. We all thought it was weapons testing."

"No, we didn't, Nik. I didn't. I wouldn't have—," Tess protested.

He cut her off with a look. "Come on. Remember how the experiment designs were always altered when they came back after testing? And we weren't allowed to know the results?"

"That's not so unusual—"

"Tess, take off those rosy glasses. Don't you remember standing outside in the dark, freezing our asses off as we watched the sky erupt with all those weird, streaking lights and oddly shaped clouds? You know there's no way in hell they were the result of long-range radio signals, and they weren't the aurora. They only happened when the arrays fired, Tess." He paused. "You used to say that the sky looked like it was warping and fracturing. Well, that's what happens here, too. And you know TESLA's signals aren't comms and they aren't benign."

She said nothing for a moment, just looked at her hands. It wasn't until years after she'd left HAARP that she'd begun to link the dates of world events with some of the "tests" she'd devised. She'd realized with no small sense of disgust that she was a contributor to the next generation of "peacekeepers," the way her parents and grandparents had been. The clouds she created weren't mushroom-shaped and the fallout wasn't radioactive, but the destructive capability was infinitely greater. "Yes, I remember. I promised myself that I'd never again be involved with weaponry."

"Let's see. I'll bet you also thought that Flint's goals were benign."

"No, Nik. Not benign. But there's a long stretch of road between 'not benign' and deadly."

"It gets significantly shorter when profit is involved," he said bitterly.

She stared at him, at his dark eyes utterly devoid of any humor, any lightheartedness. They were cold and grim. "You've changed, Nik. Not for the better. Why?"

He grabbed a piece of paper from the recycle bin, scribbled a short list of words, then handed it to her.

Aceh. Sichuan. L'Aquila. Samoa. Haiti. Afghanistan.

The six words hit her like a fist. The paper fell out of her nerveless fingers and fluttered to the floor. Tess looked at him, unable to express the horror she felt. Together, those six events had claimed nearly three-quarters of a million lives.

And Nik had just taken responsibility for them.

Tess brought an icy, shaking hand to her forehead to brush away a stray hair, or pretend to. "You made these happen?"

"We realized afterward."

She took a deep breath. It didn't steady her nerves. "How long after?"

"January of this year. I spent two weeks in Sydney. I hadn't been off the Ice in a year. So for three solid days, I just surfed the Net, catching up on the news."

"What made you look into those?"

"There were times when Greg would put out some strange code—upload it, run it—and it pissed me off that he wouldn't explain himself. I was supposed to be in on everything he did. So I kept those dates in the back of my mind. When I saw what had happened in the world, I made the connection."

"What did you do about it?"

"I confronted him. He denied everything." Nik paused. "Tess, you don't look so good."

"I don't feel so good," she admitted. Her voice sounded kind of wispy and breathless, even to her. "I'll be okay in a minute."

"The altitude may be getting to you. Besides, you're exhausted. You had a long and harrowing trip and then walked straight into a crisis. When's the last time you slept?"

"I don't remember. And I forgot about the altitude. You're probably right. But I'm okay."

"How long has it been since you've eaten?"

"What time is it?"

"Four-thirty."

"In the afternoon?"

He nodded.

"Then I think it's been about six hours."

"So throw low blood sugar into the mix. Want to continue this conversation over coffee and a sand-wich?"

"Thanks, but let's just keep going. I'll be fine. So the dirty code that's running now—?"

"It's very similar to what Greg was doing when each of those six events happened."

"How did you see his code? I mean, the earlier stuff."

"I hacked his files," Nik said bluntly.

She gave him a faint smile. "I'm impressed. Did he ever find out?"

"Not that I know of, but that's not the point. I don't know exactly what he's doing this time, but the magnitude of whatever he's doing is far greater than any of those events."

"Oh God." Tess paused as a deeply unsettling combination of fear and sadness welled up inside her. "Nik, I feel like I'm in an asylum. Or on the set of *CSI: Antarctica*." She paused for a moment, then continued. "Let's see if I have this straight: Greg isn't just the antisocial jerk we all love to hate, he's a mass murderer. And Flint ordered him to commit what amounts to genocide, repeatedly, using TESLA."

"I never said Flint, Tess."

She stared at him. "Then who?"

He shrugged. "Two of those events—China and Afghanistan—have strategic importance—"

"Strategic importance for whom?"

"The U.S. military. The earthquake in China was right before the Olympics, while we were in beta-testing down here. The floods in Afghanistan happened right before their elections. By then we were up and running." He paused and leaned forward, bringing his face close to hers and speaking softly. "*We* did it, Tess."

A shiver ran through her, the kind that as a child she had ascribed to someone walking over her grave. *How appropriate.* "Are you absolutely—?"

"I have proof," he said harshly, and Tess caught her breath. "It's all in the monitoring logs for the array. I think the results were much more intense than intended. I can't accept the idea that the Aceh tsunami was an intended result. What I can see happening is that we were supposed to hit a remote spot on a volatile fault line; it would have been an easy win, and easy to assess the impact. But either he didn't do enough research on that section of the fault, or his computer modeling was wrong, or he just set some incorrect parameters. He wrote all the code himself so I can't say for sure."

"Do you remember how he reacted when he heard about the tsunami?"

Nik looked at her. "Yeah. Everybody was pretty shocked, but he just went white, then red. Then he left the room."

"Nobody connected any activity from the array with the earthquake?"

"There was no reason to suspect anything. He covered his tracks. The code was uploaded in advance, and the arrays fired when most of us were either partying or asleep. Or gone. There was a skeleton crew here. It was Christmastime. Summertime. Downtime," he said with a shrug. "I left a few days later for my vacation. I confirmed the timing by reviewing the monitoring logs when I got back. He couldn't have planned it better, Tess."

"What about the other ones? They happened at different times of the year."

"His control got better with subsequent events and I think he became much bolder about not hiding it. The Sichuan earthquake was big, on an active fault, but inland. The damage was dramatic but contained.

L'Aquila was still more contained. Samoa was barely a blip." He paused. "I don't know what Haiti was meant to prove."

"But Nik . . . No one knew? *No one* connected the dots?"

"We were busy with our regular work, Tess." He gave her the shadow of a grin. "We're not responsible for every bad thing that happens on the planet, you know."

"What about Afghanistan?"

"Unambiguously political. Maybe he had a new client."

As she stared at him, the universe seemed to narrow to a single view: Nik's face. "Are you— Who do you work for?" she demanded.

"Don't freak out. I'm no spy. I work for Flint. I don't know if I can say the same about Greg."

"Why haven't you told anyone about this?" she demanded.

He looked at her. "Like who? Somebody is asking him to do this, Tess. Someone is bankrolling him. Maybe it wasn't Flint and that's why he was yanked. Maybe it was Flint and they really do want him doing other things. Maybe this is just Greg's idea of fun."

"It wasn't Flint," she replied, remembering Gianni's veiled allusions to Greg's actions.

A knock on the door cut off whatever Nik was about to say. He opened the door. Ron stood at the threshold.

"They cracked it," he said, walking in and tossing a small collection of papers on Nik's desk. Nik shut the door behind him as Ron continued, "The coordinates flipped out again so they don't make any sense, but these are big events scattered all across the globe.

Mother-freaking huge events of a magnitude we've never attempted. Nobody out there can decipher the commands, but the frequencies—," he said heavily, his usual bantering tone gone. He brought up a hand to rub his eyes, then let it drop and looked at Tess and Nik. "I'm not being overly dramatic to say this really could be Armageddon."

The three of them stood in silence for a moment, absorbing his words.

"So let's assume that Greg is working for someone other than Flint. Who would want large-scale, simultaneous, consecutive events run in a dozen different locations?" Nik asked.

They were quiet for another minute. Tess closed her eyes as the reality became clear to her.

"I can only think of one person who'd want that, Nik," she said, her voice low.

"Who? Bin Laden? Chávez? Putin?"

"Greg." She looked up at him. His doubt was evident. Ron's expression hadn't changed.

"Tess . . . no. Come on." Nik stared at her. "That's crazy. He's going to traumatize the planet because he's been replaced?"

"Because he's been replaced by *me*."

"Sounds plausible to me, Nik," Ron said quietly. "Nobody blinked when Nangpal said he thought Greg was behind the comms crash and the power blip, and no one else could have commandeered the arrays. He's already trashed two locations. This is just another step on the same trajectory."

Nik glared at him. "Greg 'acting out,' yes, I can see that. But taking down the whole world because he's pissed off? Sorry, you're overreaching."

"Think about it, Nik. He has always liked to make

his point with a sledgehammer when a scalpel would suffice. And now he has the opportunity to make one that Croyden Flint can't miss. I think he's gone rogue and those events in the queue are going to be successively bigger and uglier than what he's already done."

"So Flint is the target?"

"It makes sense, doesn't it, that either the man or the company or both could be his target?" Tess replied. "Flint owns a lot of farms in western Mexico, and Croyden has a home in Baja. The headquarters is in Greenwich, and Croyden has a home there, too. The best way to get Croyden Flint's attention is to hit him in the bottom line. And what better means of doing so than to use Croyden's most expensive investment as a weapon against him *personally*?"

Nik moved away from the wall to perch on the corner of his desk, one leg swinging freely, a dark scowl on his face. "So what now? If we go with your hypothesis that Greg's acting alone, we haven't exactly cracked the code of what's going to happen."

"I know that, Nik, but it gives us a framework. It will help us focus." She ignored his rolled eyes. It was getting more difficult to ignore his obstinacy. "So, I need to know one thing straight up: Who out there"— she motioned to the door—"are his true believers?"

"We're all adults here, Tess. Intelligent ones," Nik replied drily. "Everyone here now knows Greg was a few ticks off the dial from Normal. *No one* at this installation would knowingly participate—"

"Are you sure that no one would go along with him? Are you *sure*, Nik?" she interrupted.

"Tess, all of us—including you—are here for the same reason. For the adventure and the work. We know what we're doing here is not 'cutting edge' stuff.

It's not 'bleeding edge.' It's *over the horizon* stuff, practically science fiction. We put up with Greg's bullshit because the 'wow' factor beat grading undergraduate papers, fighting for tenure, and sitting on dissertation committees. No one knew what Greg was doing."

"You did," she snapped, and saw Ron's eyes widen as Nik's face became suffused with an ugly flush. "If either of you have the slightest doubt that someone out there isn't thinking clearly, I want them locked out of the sandbox and the system immediately. Understood?"

Nik stared at her. "Do you always stir up this much shit?"

"Honestly, Nik, I've never worked in a place where there was this much shit to stir up," she muttered under her breath. "I have to get something to eat. Let's go."

CHAPTER

By late Friday night, Greg was comfortably installed in a small suite at the five-star Bay Hotel in Capetown overlooking a white-sand beach fringed with palms. It was almost midnight, and he had a glass of wine resting on the table next to him. His feet were up on the railing of his private balcony as he reveled in the warm, wet air of autumn. He wasn't going to let the reality of the two-person security team—backup for the goons who'd been on the flight with him—ruin the ambience. He'd informed them that they would stand their watch outside his door, not within his sight. He'd put a rapid stop to their protests and Fred and Tim, his other babysitters, had reluctantly acquiesced.

He should have called Croyden by now; those executive lapdogs had requested and then demanded that he do so. He hadn't. Gianni had called, demanding that Greg get on the phone. He'd refused that, too, opting for a shower and a nap first, and then a meal.

That's when the velvet gloves—if that term could even be applied to the way they'd been treating him—

had come off and they'd started making their puny threats. He'd just smiled. Nothing could faze him now. The game was already under way. The Mexican earthquake had been his opening salvo. The storm in Connecticut was intended to let Croyden know that no place on the planet would be safe. Every x hours— x being determined by Tess's activity on TESLA's networks—the world would experience another outrage, and Croyden would be treated to another show of Greg's power. The earth would be ravaged. It would be the last, greatest reality game: *Survivor: Earth*.

By now, the Teslans could see the havoc the arrays had begun to wreak, and they'd have figured out that more was to come. But he'd ensured that no one at TESLA would be able to hack his code and stop it, and no one would be able to bring the installation back on line. He'd foreseen that possibility back in the early days, when he'd been designing the program. At least half the programmers and most of the scientists had some hacking in their backgrounds; some of them had been good at it. But letting them win was never an option. He'd built the system to respond to every attempt they made, to every keystroke they entered. Every input would alter the code, usually with the effect of speeding it up, sometimes by ratcheting up the intensity. And if someone somehow managed to get too close to actually deciphering his code, they would trigger the last, best geostorm civilization would ever see.

He picked up the handset of the hotel phone on the table beside him—why be secure?—and, with a smile, directed the operator to put him through to Croyden in Park City, Utah, where Gianni had said he was vacationing with his family. Then Greg settled back in his chair and lifted the wine to his lips, enjoying it with every sense.

He'd been extremely thorough. He'd found every one of Croyden Flint's many residences and then had moved on to identifying every Flint-owned entity from coast to coast, from continent to continent. He'd looked at every corporate unit, every field test station, every farm, every chemical and manufacturing and processing plant. Then he'd done the same for all of Flint's largest competitors.

Certain areas—the southern and central United States, huge swaths of Canada and central Europe, northern Iraq, southern India, the plains of South America—were dense thickets of Flint-owned enterprises. Destroying Flint—the man and the company—was an eminently reachable goal.

The call was picked up on the other end.

"I believe you wanted to speak with me, Croyden," Greg said silkily in response to Croyden's gruff greeting.

"What the fuck are you up to?"

Greg smiled at the starry sky above him. "Well, at the moment, I'm sitting on a balcony in the moonlight overlooking Camps Bay Beach, enjoying an excellent Meritage and breathing soft, fresh, unfiltered air for the first time in months. What are you up to, Croyden?"

"Whatever you're doing, Simpson, we'll stop you. I'll personally crush you," the older man growled with a vehemence that made Greg laugh out loud.

"Croyden, don't you understand? Your opportunity to do the right thing has passed. Crushing me would be futile and accomplish nothing of value. There is only one way to stop what I have planned for you, and that is to destroy TESLA, to obliterate it and the people there. We both know it's a step you would never take. You're powerless for, perhaps, the first time ever, and all because of a decision you made. How does it feel?"

"Listen, you—"

"No, Croyden, I'm done listening to you," Greg interrupted calmly. "You just sit back and enjoy your surroundings. Springtime in the mountains. Such a lovely time of year. I have to go now."

Greg disconnected the call, then informed the operator that he wasn't to be disturbed. He settled back into the soft cushions of the settee and glanced at the watch on his wrist. It wouldn't be too long now before the sweep of devastation would resume. With a smile only marginally warmer than the ambient outdoor temperature air at TESLA, Greg took another sip of wine.

The clouds had formed slowly over the coastal Pacific in the middle of the previous night and had settled over the always thirsty lower San Joaquin Valley just before dawn. The rain was gentle at first: heavier than a mist, lighter than a drizzle. It was the perfect type of rain to have this early in the growing season. Young crops stood up to it, soaking it in and thriving on it. From Fresno to Bakersfield and all the way across the wide, wide valley, nearly to the foot of the Sierra Nevada, millions of acres of overworked ground absorbed the rainfall greedily. The soft moisture swelled the particles of soil and filled the minute air gaps between them.

There had been few grumbles as the farm workers began another long day. The low, heavy clouds and warm showers would be a welcome change from laboring under a sun that had become relentless over the past several weeks.

In the small, plain buildings that held the field offices of Flint AgroChemical's many test farms and experimental stations, none of the site managers, crop specialists, or agricultural engineers gave the rain a second thought. It was just Nature doing what Nature did best. They didn't care as long as it didn't ruin their weekend.

"Are you sure you want to do this?" Nik asked as he accompanied Tess to the dining room.

"Yes. Since everyone's probably gathered there already for dinner, it will be a little more relaxed than if I call a special meeting. Word will get to anyone who's not there."

"That's not what I meant."

She sent him a look. "Please tell me you're not implying that I should keep the staff ignorant, Nik. They need to know what's going on. I mean, I no sooner arrive and Greg leaves and our comms go dark, and then every scientist and programmer goes into a huddle in the sandbox. I'm sure information has been leaking out to the rest of the staff all day. It's only right that I tell them what's going on. I should have done it hours ago." She paused and sniffed the air. "Am I hallucinating, or do I smell roasted lamb? In the old days on the Ice, wintering over meant canned or frozen everything, and we all shared cooking duties. Everything started to taste the same after about three weeks."

"Ewan is a phenomenal chef," he told her as they walked into the dining room, which held scattered tables of various seating capacities. All wore linen tablecloths and proper place settings. Nearly every table was filled with people in various stages of dining. "Food first or The Talk?"

"The Talk. I'm starving, so that will guarantee I'll keep it brief." She walked to the center of the room. The chatter died as every eye turned toward her. "Hi. I'm sorry to disturb you, but I'd like to give everyone a quick update on our situation.

"We're still off line as far as our communications uplink goes, as I'm sure you know. Ron's team is working very hard to determine the problem and—well, no, that's not completely accurate," she said and paused, then continued more carefully. "We know what happened. The system didn't crash by accident or because of anyone's mistake, and it has nothing to do with the equipment. The communications network was brought down deliberately, probably by a command or executable placed in the code."

She took a breath. "In addition, the arrays appear to have been placed into an alternate control scenario. The science team and the developers are working very hard to contain and correct that situation as well as restore full communications. That's about all I can tell you. Or," she corrected herself with a smile, "rather, that's about all I know at the moment.

"I'll keep you updated as things change. In the meantime, I want to assure you that all the systems that sustain the habitat are operating as they should be and we're not in any sort of danger. We have an emergency backup communication system if we need it, which I don't think we will. If you have any questions, feel free to sit down and ask me, or stop me in the hall. *Bon appétit.*"

"Tess," came a voice from the far side of the room. She looked around to see Mick from the greenhouse with a questioning look on his face.

"Yes, Mick?"

"Who put the command in the code that brought down the communications?"

She hesitated for just a minute. "We're pretty sure Greg did."

"*Greg?*"

She nodded. "You might have gathered from his manner this morning that he wasn't happy about leaving. He fought Flint's decision to bring me down here and tried to keep the information from you," she finished with a tight smile.

No one else asked any questions and the buzz in the room resumed and gathered strength. Tess joined Nik at the entrance to the area where the food was set out.

"'Alternate control scenario'?" he said under his breath. "Did Gianni teach you that one?"

"No, I thought that up on the fly. I realized that I don't know who on the administrative staff knows what about what we do down here. I didn't want to give away the farm. Telling them that our multi-million-dollar rainmakers are behaving like a remote-controlled LEGO project didn't seem like a good idea."

"Well, that was a good catch. Everything is need-to-know around here, and the powers-that-be decided long ago that the admin and ops people don't need to know much. I'm not sure even Dan does," Nik said, making his last statement lighthearted and loud enough for Dan to hear as they came to a stop next to him at the buffet.

"You're not sure Dan does what?" he said, emptying a small ladle of gravy over the slices of lamb on his plate.

"Nothing. I was just busting your chops," Nik said easily, reaching for two plates and handing one to Tess, who had closed her eyes and wore an expression that was nothing short of rapture as she breathed in the rich, heady fusion of aromatics and roasted meat.

She murmured, "Oh, who knew you had to head south to get to heaven?" in a voice that Nik had never heard used in regard to food.

Nik sat back in his chair and shifted his torso first one way, then the other. He felt stiff and creaky after sitting in front of his computer nearly without a break for the last four hours. They were working in the conference room and Tess sat nearby, working on her own laptop. Nik found it remarkable that she seemed not to have changed her position in at least the last thirty minutes, or for much of the evening, for that matter. And damned if she still didn't look good.

She'd been alternating between working in the conference room and the sandbox all day and hadn't taken any time to install herself in Greg's old office yet. She'd laughed it off, saying she needed to do a "vibe cleanse" first, but Nik suspected she just wanted to get integrated into the group as quickly as she could. Setting up her work space in the conference room and leaving the door open most of the time—two things Greg had never done—had already impressed the sandbox inhabitants.

"This stuff is amazing. Sick, twisted, and clearly written by a genius," Tess murmured for what had to be the hundredth time. They were reviewing the monitoring logs of all the data and commands that had been fed to the antenna array in the hours since Greg had been alerted that Tess was on her way to TESLA. She'd already perused Greg's paper files and the flash drives he'd left for her to see what she could find that related to Nikola Tesla. She hadn't found much.

"You know, I used to think I'd get turned on by a woman who could read this stuff and like it. But you're reading code like it was a novel, and I'm getting a bit concerned. That's not normal," Nik said bluntly, getting to his feet and stretching, half hoping she'd watch.

Tess glanced up then, a grim look on her face that did nothing to hide the excitement in her eyes. "Greg is a monster, Nik. And my response is normal. This code *does* read like a novel. It doesn't have any dialogue or adjectives, but action? Insanity? That's here in spades."

"It's machine code, Tess."

"Come here and look at this."

He walked to where she was sitting. She scrolled up the screen, then stopped and tapped her finger against it. "Okay, take this burst of activity in mid-March, just about a month ago. Crazy code, much like what Ron's been talking about. Well, these lines seem to indicate that they had to do with steering—"

Nik squinted at the screen, then looked at her. "No, they don't."

"Sure they do. It's buried and it's clever, but it's there. Anyway, just accept it so I can move on—"

"Wait a minute—," he protested.

Tess rolled her eyes. "No, just hear me out. Here's this teeny, tiny burst of atmospheric activity down here on the tundra—"

"We're not on a tundra. It's an ice sheet," Nik pointed out.

"I know that. So down here on the ice sheet, there's this pulse—" She drew her finger along the screen beneath a line of characters. "And here's the *atmospheric* monitoring data from NOAA," she said, pulling up a different window. She ran her finger down a column of numbers and stopped about halfway through. "It's right here. An amalgamation of heightened solar proton events caused an increased polar cap absorption of HF radio signal transmissions and significantly limited Antarctic communication capability." She looked at him triumphantly. "This is the blip you mentioned. He was testing ways to smack down TESLA, Nik. He was trying to cripple the love of his life and make it look like an accident. How's that for sick?"

"But he didn't cripple us then, and that code isn't what ran today and pulled us down," Nik pointed out.

"You told me the comms blipped a month ago." She tapped the screen. "This is what did it. So he knew it worked, and he must have tweaked it. And if he could do that locally with one microburst, imagine what he could do with a bigger one. He could take out every installation on the Ice." She snapped her fingers. "Like that. And this string—" She flipped back to the window displaying the commands for the HF array. "Look at that. A little more bashing around of the solar flux peak absorption differentials and—" She went back to the cached NOAA data and scrolled down several pages. "And a day or so later there's a beauty of a cyclone in the Central Pacific, in an area a little north of where the usual commotion is at that time of year. No big whoop, right? *Wrong.* I get email news updates from all kinds of people and, wait, let me find it—" She opened her email application as she spoke.

"You save them?" he asked, incredulous.

"I save everything. Here we go," she replied. "Said storm just happens to coincide with some Russian naval war games, resulting in one seriously pissed-off bear and, no doubt, a bunch of delighted American admirals. Coincidence?"

Nick looked at her, resignation in every cell as he walked back to his chair, sat down, and tilted it to lean against the wall. "Gimme a white flag. I surrender. This is proof that—?"

"That Greg is serving two masters."

Nik said nothing for a moment, waiting for the icy chill that ran down his back to dissipate as he watched the blue fire crackling in her eyes.

"The second being the U.S. military," he said at last.

"It makes perfect sense. They kept him fed, housed, and entertained for, what, twenty years? I'm guessing his departure from HAARP wasn't so much a divorce as the start of an open marriage. Sequestered down here at TESLA, with Flint paying his bills and no one looking over his shoulder, he could keep playing with the Pentagon brass and Flint would never know."

"So Greg is the Pentagon's secret whup-ass weapon?"

"Looks like it."

Nik sighed. "What next?"

"I'd like to shut things down."

Nik gaped at her and nearly lost his balance as the chair's front legs landed on the floor and skidded. "Did you just say 'shut things down'? Are you *insane*?"

Clearly startled, Tess blurted, "Yes! No, sorry, I thought you were going to say 'serious.' No, I'm not insane. I'm asking."

"You want to power down *the whole installation*?"

"Well, no, of course not. Just the arrays," she replied

hastily. "We don't control them. We can't even keep them in 'sleep' mode. It's untenable, Nik. We can't just keep wringing our hands every time they power up. They're destroying things. *We're* destroying things." She let out a frustrated breath. "Look, don't take this the wrong way, but you guys have built up some sort of an emotional distance to what you do. I mean, you've seen the footage from the flyovers in Mexico City, you saw what happened to Greenwich. We're killing people, Nik, and maybe not just strangers." She let a pause build, then stood up and walked to the door to close it. She turned to face him. "I'm trying not to think about this—I know I need to focus on the situation here—but my parents live on the central Pacific coast of Mexico, Nik. Right on the cliffs. Greg knows that. The epicenter of that earthquake wasn't far from the coast. They could be hurt or—"

"Don't think the worst, okay? It doesn't help anything."

"My point is, Nik, we need to get rid of that detachment, that sense that we have time to fix this. We don't. We have big events queued up. We don't know what they're going to do or where they're going to do it, but we know they're going to be big. We've got to make this personal and do something *now.*"

"It's not like we can flip the big 'off' switch down in the basement," he said, not holding back his sarcasm.

"Sure there is. The power station."

He stared at her. "You're serious."

She nodded. "Why can't we?"

"Do you have any idea what's involved with doing something like that? No, Tess. It's no-go."

"Excuse me?"

"Tess, it's a last resort."

"Let's ask Dan what's involved."

Issuing a heavy sigh, Nik called Dan on the radio and the two switched to a secure frequency. "Tess and I are batting around a few imponderables, Dan," he said, his gaze hard and fixed on Tess's face. "What's involved with powering down the fuel cells?"

"What's involved for you is primarily just a lot of swearing and arguing on my part. The rest of it would be my problem. But I was just about to track you down. The sensors out there near the hydrogen tanks are showing some readings that aren't making me feel all warm and cozy. An H_2 release is all we fucking need."

Nik turned a little pale, then closed his eyes for a minute. "This isn't one of your jokes, is it?"

"I wish."

"Keep us posted." He set the radio on the table and met Tess's eyes. "A hydrogen release. I don't even want to go there."

"You don't have to. Greg wouldn't mess with that. He doesn't know the first thing about chemistry."

"You sure?"

"Yes. I mean, not that kind of chemistry. It's probably a wonky sensor or a false reading."

"Yeah, we get a lot of those. You know: all this crappy equipment," Nik replied, heavily sarcastic.

Tess rolled her eyes. "Oh come on, Nik, a hydrogen release could blow this entire place to smithereens. The explosion would be visible from space, for heaven's sake. Greg wouldn't do that."

"Glad you're so confident, Tess." He sighed again. "Assuming we're not facing a hydrogen-enriched Armageddon scenario and we were able to power down

the arrays, we'll be saying good-bye to our careers.
We may never be able to get them back on line."

She stared at him. "That's my point, Nik. We can't
think about saving our careers right now. We can't
think about preserving TESLA. We need to stop the
pulses before another one is turned loose on the world.
Ron discovered an established periodicity. The first
three bursts were six hours apart. We're coming up on
the magic number and I'd bet dollars to doughnuts
there will be another one. I'd like to postpone it, Nik.
Permanently. No matter what it takes."

21

CHAPTER

The soft rain that had begun eight hours ago over north-central California had not let up. By the time children got off their school buses that afternoon, the ground was well-soaked and the fields that had been dry for so long were covered with shallow pools of standing water. Creeks were running higher, the river was flowing clearer, the landscape was looking fresher.

That's when the storm changed. The raindrops became steadily bigger and began to fall harder and faster. There was no wind and not much thunder. Just rain. Lots and lots of rain.

The loud, incessant pounding of water against roofs and gutters and roads kept valley residents home on date night. Bored children moped about weekend activities that would have to be postponed. Their parents wondered whether what they'd been planting, or weeding, or harvesting would survive the onslaught.

The answer was making itself known in the encroaching darkness. Groves of towering walnut and almond trees maintained their staunch, but weakening grip in increasingly sodden ground while across the valley, orchards full of softer fruit barely tolerated the torrents. Branches laden with peaches, plums, and half-grown apricots bent toward the earth as the rain pummeled their fruit and suffused their wood with too much of a good thing. Beneath acres of cherry trees, the earth was awash with muddy blossoms.

Field after field of cotton plants sagged, then toppled to the ground. Tens of thousands of acres of young and maturing food plants—corn, tomatoes, lettuce, melons, strawberries—that had been carefully nurtured for weeks, that had been teased up to the edge of fecundity by sunlight and chemicals and irrigation, began to list sideways in the fields. Well before the farmers and the field hands turned in for the night, their crops lay flat in the mud, turning to pulp under still-heavy skies, a bumper crop of wasted money and wasted time.

Roads between fields became wide ribbons of mud. Equipment was mired where it had been left. Along the miles of paved highways connecting the small towns that dotted the valley, first the low spots, then the flat stretches became too dangerous to cross. Creeks began to overflow their banks. The soil had been so dry for so long that it couldn't absorb the rushing water fast enough; and so it just dissolved and was swept away. Across hundreds and hundreds of square miles, people slept fitfully or not at all, knowing their homes, their livelihoods, and their futures could be sucked into the mud or washed away by the very water for which they'd been praying so hard.

The rain became heavier.

Livestock grew restive and even a little panicked by the constant thunderous tattoo on their enormous barns' metal roofs and the foul, muddy water rushing along the floors, swirling around their hooves. In the *colonias,* the shantytowns that sprouted every growing and harvest season at the edges of fields, soaked residents huddled, tightly packed, in trucks, trailers, and more flimsy shelters. In the small towns, residents fared little better. Aging, poorly built homes and apartments, crammed beyond capacity with tenants, revealed their flaws as the deluge seeped through ceilings and the cracks around windows. Water heavy with silt and soil began to flow under doors and lap against foundations. Even in the better areas, second floors became the only viable escape routes as roads turned treacherous or simply disappeared from view.

One after another, small canals, catchment pools, and drainage ponds all over the valley overflowed their banks and barriers, sending floods rushing wherever gravity beckoned, washing away whatever was left in the fields—along with any hope of economic or crop recovery. The big river and its tributaries at first absorbed the heavy volume of water crashing along their courses, but at last, they, too, began to rise beyond their boundaries.

Well before dawn, the airwaves were full of dire reports of flood stages and crests, talk of sandbags and levees. Flash floods, disaster kits, and evacuations. Damage estimates were already in the hundreds of millions and still rising.

Downstream, secretly delighted communities braced themselves for the unexpected bonanza of so much needed water.

22

CHAPTER

Fucking hell." Nik stared at the screen, believing and not believing what he'd just discovered. "Hey, Tess," he said, then looked down the table to where she was sitting. Or had been. She was slumped over, forehead on the table, sound asleep.

He stood up and stretched, not bothering to be quiet. Not waking her up wasn't an option. He couldn't leave her here, and he wanted to knock off for the night. But first he had to deliver the latest blow.

Walking to where she sat, he shook her shoulder gently. They'd been working in virtual silence since they'd argued about shutting down the arrays, so he had no idea how long she'd been like that. But, judging by the lack of response, she'd been out for a while.

"Hey, Tess. Wake up."

She moaned a little but didn't give any other indication of re-entering a conscious state.

Too damned bad, darling, this won't wait.

He carefully shut down her computer and slipped it into its case. Resisting the temptation to snoop was easy. Not only would it not have been right, it would have been traceable. And he didn't need any more trouble in paradise right now.

"Tess, come on, hon. You gotta wake up and get out of here."

She murmured something he couldn't make out. He shook her again, lightly.

"Tess."

Her head came up slightly, her face tilted to his. Her eyes were still closed. Her mouth was . . . beautiful. She was beautiful.

No, she's irresistible.

Not bothering to fight a smile, he lowered his face to hers and kissed her. Softly. Nicely. Conservatively. On the mouth.

Tess became conscious slowly, but not so slowly that Nik could pull back in time to avoid the half-slap, half-shove that she gave his face. He landed on his ass and was still clearing his head by the time she was standing over him, not entirely steady as she slipped her feet into her shoes. While glaring at him.

"Just what the *hell* do you think you're doing?" she demanded. Her eyes were burning with annoyance.

"Clearly, I was being a jerk," he began, getting to his feet as far from her as he could manage. It wasn't much, given the size of the conference room and the length of her reach. "No harm intended. I couldn't wake you up, so I—"

"So you thought it would be a good idea to kiss me?" she hissed. "What are you, some sort of arrested adolescent?"

He winced. "Apparently."

"Well, don't try it again," she snapped, then paused. "We're in enough trouble down here without—" She let out a long breath that seemed to carry her anger with it. "We're in enough trouble without adding any more complications to the mix," she finished more calmly.

"Got it. Sorry."

"Okay. So what time is it?"

"About midnight."

"Great," she muttered, and looked down at her clothes. "If anyone is out there roaming the halls, this isn't going to look good. I look like I slept in these."

"You did," Nik said with a repentant smile. "That's better than the alternative, isn't it? That you were in the conference room with me but not in your clothes?"

Tess flicked her eyes to him. "Thanks. I'll point that out to anyone who asks."

He took a deep breath and absently rubbed a hand along the back of his neck. "Listen, Tess, I've got some news. You'd better sit down."

"What's wrong?"

"You are," he replied slowly, watching her face. "About an hour ago, I went back into this morning's monitoring logs to see if I could find a smoking gun."

"I thought Ron had someone do that already."

"He did, Tom did it before noon. But either he didn't go back far enough, or he didn't see what I just saw."

She let out an annoyed breath. "Knock off the suspense, Nik. What was it? A logic bomb?"

"Oh, yeah." He met her eyes. "Named Tess Beauchamp."

Tess blinked. "What do you mean?"

"You're it. When you logged into the system, a small series of executables triggered, sending a bunch of drone codes into every system."

Tess stared at him, feeling the blood drain from her

face and her knees start to shimmy. She lowered herself into the nearest chair. "I did this?" she whispered, her voice shaky.

He gave her a minute to absorb it, then nodded. "Clearly, Greg had the code in the system in advance. I don't know how far in advance. Could be weeks or months. I didn't look that far back. But, early yesterday before you arrived, there was a very small burst of activity done under an override. Logged by Greg. He uploaded a very small piece of code. It's encrypted so I can't see it, but I imagine it was the instruction to deploy when you logged on."

Tess stared at him in silence.

"He didn't hide that he did something, but he was careful to make sure we couldn't see exactly what he did," Nik continued.

"Because if we could, we'd be able to undo it," she said softly.

"Precisely."

"Oh my God." Tess fell rather than leaned against the back of the chair. "What a . . . there isn't a word for someone like him."

Nik shrugged. "That's all I have for you at the moment. I suggest that we keep this to ourselves. Telling the others wouldn't help anything, and might just create more tension, which is the last thing we need."

She nodded and rose to her feet, steadying herself against the table. Taking a deep breath, she forced a smile onto her face. "On that happy note, I think I'll turn in."

She didn't make any move to leave the room though, and they studied each other for a moment. Then Nik shrugged. "Your room is next to mine. Mind if I walk with you?"

She hesitated for a split second, then shook her head. "Not if you don't mind escorting a mass murderer down the hall," she said lightly.

"Don't say things like that, Tess. You're one of the good guys, regardless of how Greg manipulates you." Moving past her cautiously, Nik picked up her laptop and handed it to her, then pulled open the door. He motioned for her to precede him into the deserted sandbox, and then the corridor. The door quietly slid closed behind them.

Tess began walking down the hallway. The lights had dimmed as Nik had told her they would, and the space was lit only by the soft glow of night-lights that punctuated the darkness every few yards. Shadows clung to the curved walls in odd patterns. The entire floor was absolutely silent and slightly eerie, and Tess was glad for Nik's company. It only took a few minutes to reach their rooms.

As they stood outside their twin doors, Nik gave her a tired, friendly grin and shoved his hands into the pockets of his jeans. "Well, welcome again to Paradise South." He paused. "It's been a hell of a first day for you, Tess."

"Feels like it's been more than just one," she muttered. "What I wouldn't give for a martini right now."

"I don't have any gin, but I do happen to have a bottle of good brandy that's begging to be opened."

"You have booze?" Tess whispered, feeling her eyes widen. "I thought this place was as dry as Meridian, Mississippi, on a Sunday morning."

"Well, it is. But, just like Meridian, it's only dry if you don't know where to look." He swiped his smart card through the reader outside his door. The lock clicked and he pushed open the door, allowing her to enter the room first.

Tess was pleasantly surprised by Nik's room. It wasn't any bigger than hers, but it had personality. Dark blue walls were studded with framed art, mostly photographs of cloud, snow, and ice formations. There were several photographs of people she didn't recognize. The bed was a double and sat high, with drawers beneath it, just like the one in her room. A night table and a small table and two padded chairs completed the furnishings. It was comfortable and almost cozy.

"Very nice. Are all the rooms like this?"

He nodded as music she didn't recognize filled the room with soft, low instrumentals. "Personal quarters are the only private space we have, so Flint did them up pretty well, catering to our individual taste as much as possible." He flipped on a small table lamp, turned off the overhead light, then opened a narrow pocket door that slid silently into the wall to reveal a small closet. "Have a seat."

Sitting at the table would have required her to duck beneath his arms as he reached into the closet, so Tess gingerly seated herself on the edge of the bed. Nik set a wooden box on the table; it contained a pristine bottle of French brandy. He reached up again and produced a pair of crystal snifters in a padded box.

"Proper glassware and everything," she said with a smile. "I'm impressed."

"I like to do things the right way," he replied with an answering smile as he cracked the seal on the bottle and poured two short drinks. Handing one to her, he lifted his own. *"Santé."*

Tess smiled at him over the rim. *"Živeli."*

Nik's eyebrows shot up as he lowered his glass. "That's a Serbian toast."

"I know."

"I thought you said you could only read it."

"I don't recall saying 'only.'" She lifted the goblet to just below her nose and breathed in the heady fumes. "Oh, Nik, this smells divine."

"Taste it."

She took a small sip and closed her eyes, letting the cognac roll and swish gently throughout her mouth before allowing it to slide slowly down her throat. "This is utterly gorgeous."

He grinned. "I'm glad you like it. Listen, don't let what I just told you freak you out."

She gave him a look. "Of course not. Mass destruction is such a trivial thing."

"I mean it. It's done. We have to keep moving forward."

"I know that, but Nik, has it occurred to you that if I tripped the trigger, I could be setting off something every time I log on?"

"Yes, it did, and you're not. Once I saw that code execute following your log-on, I went back and looked for exactly that sort of thing. I didn't find anything."

"I'm not convinced, but thank you for looking for it." She shook her head. "What a scumbag."

"Oooh, such strong language," he said, teasing her. "You called him an oozing wart on Satan's hairy ass for less than this."

She smiled, touched that he was trying to cheer her up. "True. Maybe it's time he graduated."

"To what?"

"Maybe I should just call him Satan."

"Seems to fit."

A comfortable silence grew between them.

"Penny for your thoughts?" she asked.

Nik laughed quietly and set his drink on the table, then leaned a shoulder against the wall, crossing his arms in front of him. "I know I should be thinking about more heavy issues but, truthfully? I'm wondering why you're really here. Not in my room, I mean at TESLA." He shrugged. "I mean, why you? Of all people, why you?"

Tess slipped off her shoes and curled her legs beneath her, leaning on one hand, holding the brandy loosely with the other. "Gianni said I was the logical choice, presumably because of my research. I've recently become known as a good storm stopper. The flip side to Greg, I guess. Given what's going on down here, I'd say that Gianni made a good choice."

"I can't argue with that." Nik's dark eyes were looking straight into hers and the message in them was unbusinesslike and unmistakable. "You look like you could use a little TLC right now."

"I could," she said with a laugh, then looked away. She took a deep breath and another sip of the brandy, then brought her gaze back to his face and his eyes, which had grown warmer and darker. "Getting romantic is a really bad idea, Nik."

"I couldn't agree with you more," he said, pushing away from the wall and taking the few short steps to reach her. He took the snifter out of her hand and set it on the bedside table, then helped her to her feet. "But sometimes you get really good results from bad ideas," he murmured, his mouth close enough to her ear to send a warm flush through every cell in her body. His arms slowly encircled her. Her own crept around his neck.

"Not going to happen, Nik," she whispered. Her lips grazed the rough stubble on his chin. *Oh my God, he smells good. He feels even better.*

"I'm a gambling man, Tess. And I'm willing to bet we're about to get naked together."

"You think?" Tess breathed, and would have laughed, but his lips were trailing hot, slow kisses along a dangerous trail that led to her mouth, rendering her unable to engage in even the most basic multitasking.

"Think what?"

"That we're about to get naked," she said against his lips.

"Of course I do. Don't you?" His voice was barely audible.

Yes. Yes!

"No, Nik. I don't," she said softly, reluctantly. She slipped her arms between them, placed her hands on the front of his shirt, and applied gentle pressure. He released her immediately, but his eyes were still torrid and his smile still dirty.

"Good try, though," she added with a grin. "Thank you for getting my mind off the other stuff. And by the way, you haven't lost your touch."

"Let's not talk about touch, Tess," he said with a sigh as he handed her the drink he'd taken from her a moment ago and leaned against the wall once again. "So, how about those Red Sox?"

CHAPTER

In Connecticut, Gianni Barone sat in the darkness of his home office, smoking the in-case-of-emergency cigarettes he'd stashed in his desk when he'd given up the habit years ago. The moon was full, sitting in a sky so clear that it looked like it belonged in a movie.

It was almost three in the morning. Nearly twenty-four hours had passed since he'd heard from Tess. Flint's army of tech support wizards had spent much of that time running test after test, trying to determine what had taken TESLA off line. Battalions of Flint's weather and terrain analysts—and the security group—had pored over hundreds of new satellite images in an effort to answer the same question. But the answer he was looking for wasn't forthcoming. No one could offer him any explanation other than whatever the problem was, it lay within TESLA's security perimeter.

From the minute TESLA had gone off line, Croyden had been breathing fire at him, blaming Gianni for everything from Greg's attitude shift to the blackout to Medev's death. The smirking, sneering telephone conversation Croyden had had with Greg hadn't improved the old man's mood. At least Greg was halfway back to the States. Gianni had insisted that the U.S.-bound flight take off early in the morning to get Greg stateside as soon as possible.

There is going to be an ass-kicking like no other when I see him.

He took a deep drag on the first Marlboro Red he'd smoked in five years. The harsh burn of the smoke entering his lungs was like the handshake of an old friend and, as such, he held on to it for a minute.

It had ceased to matter to Croyden that Gianni had kept things humming at TESLA as Greg went down the tubes, that he'd found the perfect replacement for Greg, and that the array was beating all expectations in terms of benefitting the company and trashing the competition. It didn't matter that the whole project was moving toward profitability faster than even the most optimistic estimates had predicted.

In thanks, Gianni had become the whipping boy. Greg blamed him for the selection of Tess as his replacement. Croyden blamed him for Greg's attitude. And Secretary Bonner had had a few choice words for him on a secure call late this afternoon. With Medev gone, Flint's relationship with the Pentagon was in tatters and probably beyond repair.

He took another drag and blew a stream of blue smoke toward the ceiling.

It's time to start thinking about the future.

On the other side of the country, the northern mountain air had been engaged in a metastatic churn for the last twenty-four hours. Overnight, Thursday's heavy clouds had cleared and the storm that had trailed them had stopped unexpectedly and was parked on one side of the mountains. The other side, home to Park City, Utah, was graced with a surprising, blindingly clear sky for Friday morning's first run. The multitude of spring-break skiers packed into the gondolas and the lines waiting for them had been in high spirits, laughing at the turn in the weather that had the TV weather guys stumped while keeping this bastion of sportsmen, socialites, and celebrities a paradise for one more day. Sunny skies, easy breezes, and deep powder, with the promise of more snow overnight, had resort managers beaming and their personnel working overtime.

By noon, the well-heeled skiers still on the slopes and those lunching on the balconies overlooking them were reveling in the warmth of the high-altitude midday sun. Jackets were off, and, in some cases, shirts. The temperatures continued to climb and by late afternoon the conditions on some of the more exposed trails had become slick. Experienced shushers handled it; the inexperienced and the show-offs kept the Ski Patrol and emergency care centers busy with breaks and sprains. A few black diamond runs and the bunny hills were reluctantly closed due to unsafe conditions.

When the sun slid below the high horizon, the expected slide in temperature didn't happen and the town officials' initial glee turned to more-than-mild concern. The warm air lingered, in defiance of local memory and natural order. Hotel executives frowned while, oblivious to the worries of their profit-minded hosts, guests lingered outdoors, enjoying their drinks in the oddly warm night air and wondering idly what the skiing would be like tomorrow. Sheriff's deputies patrolled the streets, braced for a long shift filled with shouting revelers who had no need for an early night and no reason to remain sober.

Not long after the town was finally asleep, the stalled storm began to move. Slowly pushing their way over the Wasatch peaks, the still-heavy clouds encountered the warm air.

It began to rain.

24

CHAPTER

Helena Hernandez had already become used to the near-constant stream of people and interruptions.

But when getting dressed at five A.M., I should be allowed a sacrosanct moment.

With a sigh, she acknowledged the tap on her dressing room door. It could only be her personal assistant. "Yes?" she said, pulling on the U.S. Merchant Marine Academy T-shirt that she favored for working out.

"Ms. President, I'm so sorry to bother you, but Ms. Wonson would like to see you for a moment."

"Thank you. Send her in."

The door opened and Maribeth walked in, in a suit, hair in place, makeup flawless, not at all discomposed by seeing her boss in sweats with no makeup and her hair heading in all directions. "Thank you, Ms. President. Candy Freeman called a few minutes ago. She would like to see you as soon as she can."

Helena was the first president in the nation's history to have a national security advisor focused solely on the atmosphere and environment. Candy Freeman was one of the few people she could trust to sift through the hysteria and hyperbole that infected every mention of climate and weather. Candy had spent twenty years at the Central Intelligence Agency, first as a weather analyst, then as a supervisor, and eventually as a chief in the directorate of technology and research. She'd brought the nerdy weather research group from career-killing obscurity to career-making prominence, and was leading the way in the emerging world of counter-eco-terrorism.

Candy had cemented her reputation by maximizing her team's skillful intelligence-gathering and analysis of Hurricane Simone a few years earlier; their behind-the-scenes response to the recent undersea methane release in the Caribbean had been not only impressive but critical to saving millions of lives. Among those intimately familiar with both crises, there was wide agreement that Candy was one of the unsung heroes. In the court of public opinion, though, there hadn't been any heroes, only villains, and the government's half-hearted response to the disasters had been the tipping point in the downfall of the previous administration.

Whatever it was Candy wanted to talk about now, it couldn't be good.

"When's my next opening?" she asked, tying her workout shoes.

"Now. Your schedule is already overbooked. She asked if you could meet her in the Situation Room."

Years spent in the public eye had given Helena the ability to avoid showing surprise under the most trying circumstances, but nothing had ever been able to quell the jump in her gut at the sound of certain phrases. "Meet me in the Situation Room" was one of those phrases.

"Did she say what she wanted to discuss?"

"That storm in Connecticut yesterday afternoon and the floods in Central California."

"What about them? I've already declared each area a federal disaster zone."

"She wouldn't tell me, Madam President. She said I wasn't cleared."

The president's secretary is cleared for everything.

"Who else will be there?"

"Defense, NDI, NOAA, and—" Maribeth glanced at the pad in her hand. "Someone from the Office of Ionospheric Monitoring."

Helena frowned at her secretary. "Is that NASA?"

"Pentagon," Maribeth replied, then looked up and shrugged. "I never heard of them until yesterday. That admiral who committed—"

"Oh God. Don't remind me."

"Yes, ma'am. He worked there."

Wonderful. Helena kicked off her shoes and shimmied out of her workout pants, motioning for Maribeth to hand her a pair of casual pressed slacks hanging behind her. She ripped off the T-shirt and threw on a cotton sweater. Slipping into a pair of loafers, Helena left the room in search of a hairbrush.

Minutes later, the president entered the main conference area in the Situation Room suite, casually dressed, barely coiffed, and flanked by an aide. Nodding at the small group standing around the table and the larger group lingering near chairs that lined the walls, Helena noticed that the flat-screen monitors lining the walls were alive with images of the aftermath of each of the storms. The scope of the damage was unfathomable.

The storms had been incredibly severe, destroying the heart of each community like a well-aimed bomb, then spreading outward in every direction. Video feeds from the ground, helicopters, and satellites showed the destruction in varying degrees of horrendous detail.

News footage showed the displaced residents wearing the same dazed, disbelieving expressions the nation had seen on the survivors of hurricanes Katrina and Simone as they stood weeping, surveying the complete destruction of their lives and neighborhoods, and sometimes their families. It didn't really matter whether the cars upturned or floating in the muddy waters were Buicks or Bentleys, or whether the flattened homes had been huge and priced in the millions or tin-roofed shacks. The shock and horror and sense of loss were the same.

Helena took her seat at the head of the table. Before the others had seated themselves, she turned her eyes to Candy Freeman, possibly the only woman in her administration shorter than herself.

"What do you have?"

"Weather manipulation, ma'am," Candy said without preamble, her deep, West Texas accent sounding curt for the first time ever. "I've got a meeting in a little while with a man who might be able to help us out. His name is Gianni Barone. He was the last person to speak with Admiral Medev before his, uh, accident. Barone is an executive with Flint AgroChemical." She paused minutely. "He's in charge of their weather manipulation division."

"I didn't know they had a weather manipulation division," Helena replied drily, not liking the plunge her stomach took at Candy's words.

"Most people don't. They call it their 'climate research working group' when they refer to it at all, which isn't often. We've been watching them for a while. I'm still gathering information, but it appears that we may have even done a little business with them."

Helena stared at her. "Say that again."

"We might have availed ourselves of their services. Not the administration, ma'am, or at least not yours, but possibly the Pentagon. I've got to get more data on that."

"Please do."

"This group, Barone's group, isn't like the research groups at other agribusiness conglomerates, Ms. President. Flint isn't just funding studies to try to find the best conditions and locations for growing their crops." Candy shook her head, setting her fluffy blond curls into motion. "Flint has been quietly engaging in active and expensive types of applied research. For years they've been hiring upper-atmosphere experts and other geniuses, like high-level software developers with deep experience in aerospace navigation, military weaponry, and high-end communications systems. They've hired hardware guys who've built next-generation weapons as well as some who've designed and built deep-space telescopes and other data-gathering equipment."

"Why?" Helena interrupted. "Flint's core products are seeds, poison, and Frankenfood. Everything the environmental lobby loves to hate. What are they up to with weather manipulation?"

"They have a vertically integrated business model. In this case, it's literally vertical—ground to sky. Besides the things you mentioned, Flint has farms, fisheries, you name it. If it's edible, Flint has a hand in producing it. As such, they've gotten into a lot of risk management lately. They offer consulting—"

Helena barely refrained from laughing. "Okay, I'm a city girl to my core, but, Candy, risk management consulting? For *farmers*? I don't even know what that means."

"It can mean a lot of things." Candy shrugged. "Advising farmers about the latest practices or products to avoid crop failures, blights, or diseases, whether they're raising plants, animals, or fish. Flint also has a very low-key financial arm. Disaster insurance, weather derivatives, that sort of thing."

Helena felt a chill settle at the back of her neck. "They use the financial markets to bet on natural disasters and the weather," she said tightly. It wasn't a question.

"Or against them," Candy added. "It's not a new thing, ma'am. Enron started doing it years ago." She paused. "We know Flint is doing atmospheric testing. They built a base in Antarctica a few years ago, very hush-hush and state of the art. They persuaded Australia to hand over some strategic real estate, which really pissed off the Russians, who are already nearby, and the Chinese, who were negotiating for the same spot."

"What's the attraction?" Helena asked.

"Isolation, for one. It's a thousand miles from any coastline. Very difficult to get to from anywhere. They have a fleet of planes—*Russian* planes—specially equipped to make long-haul flights, and flight crews that consist of ex-military personnel with polar flight experience. They typically fly out of Capetown, South Africa, instead of Christchurch, New Zealand, like nearly all other U.S. interests. In other words, they've been pretty obvious about not wanting anyone to know what they're doing. That folds into what I think is the bigger reason for their secretiveness, which is that their little slice of heaven is critically near the South Geomagnetic Pole."

"We have a base *at* the South Pole, don't we?"

"Yes, we do, a small one. But the South Pole is just a geographic marker, and the ice it's on moves about ten feet a year. Then there's the South Magnetic Pole, which is somewhere in the Southern Sea off the Antarctic Peninsula. The pole I'm talking about, the one Flint is interested in, is the South Geomagnetic Pole, which is the best place on the planet to study—or interrupt—the earth's natural electromagnetism. And the talent they have sequestered down there on the Ice is a stellar group, ma'am. They pilfered several of our people from HAARP." She stopped. "Ms. President, do you know about HAARP?"

Helena met Candy's clear gaze. It was as cold and hard as the ice she was talking about. Blond, pretty, confident, *Anglo*—women like Candy had always intimidated her. Granted, it was easier to shrug off these days than it had been in high school, and college, and early in her career. All she had to do was remind herself that she was the leader of the most powerful country on earth.

Helena merely lifted one eyebrow in response to her advisor's question. "I do. I was on the House Intelligence Committee and was contacted regularly by the tinfoil-hat crowd."

Others in the room twitched their mouths to avoid a smile. Candy grinned openly.

"Yeah, well, in this case, some of those Reynolds Wrap Wonders might be on to something. Flint's Antarctic research station is called the Terrestrial Energy Southern Land Array, TESLA for short, which is kinda cute because in the early twentieth century, Nikola

Tesla did all kinds of research on harnessing and directing ionospheric energy."

Helena held up a hand. "Wait. That office of—what was it?"

"The Office of Ionospheric Monitoring," Candy supplied.

"That's it. Someone from that office is here, right?"

"He's waiting in the wings over at the Pentagon."

"What do they do?"

"I'll get to them in a minute. If I could just explain something else first, Ms. President, with your permission."

Helena nodded for her to continue.

"Nikola Tesla did a lot of oddball stuff, high-end, wow-factor research like building a lightning tower out on Long Island. But he also did some things that were less well known, even a little scary, like building a particle-beam weapon. He came up with the idea of using the earth itself as a transmitter for radio and other electromagnetic signals. That idea eventually morphed into the ELF grid in the upper Midwest." Candy cocked her head questioningly, asking without asking if Helena knew what she was talking about.

I've only been in office two months and have been busy rebuilding the nation's economy, international reputation, and a few major cities. I might have missed a few details.

"Go on," was all she said.

Candy nodded once. "Yes, ma'am. ELF stands for Extremely Low Frequency. It's a range of radio frequencies in the electromagnetic spectrum that can be used to transmit messages over long distances. But instead of the regular sort of antennae, like dishes or dipoles, the physical system for ELF is a huge underground grid of transmitters that we use for, among other things, staying in contact with our submarines when they're deeply submerged. The grid covers hundreds of square miles of the Upper Midwest because at those frequencies, the wavelengths are measurable in miles. The subs trail receivers a few miles long to pick up the transmissions—"

"Are you getting off track, Ms. Freeman?" Helena asked, feeling as if her brain were starting to swell and press against the inside of her forehead. Unfortunately, science had always had that effect on her.

"Yes, ma'am, a little. Okay, back to Tesla. The man, I mean. He also messed around at the other end of the spectrum—and again, I mean that literally. He pioneered the idea that the sky, the atmosphere itself, could be used as a giant transmitter to bounce signals around the earth. Fast signals traveling long distances with no interference. Well, we've tried that, and it works. It's why we built HAARP."

Candy tapped a long fingernail against the polished surface of the cherry conference table. "This is where the conspiracy-theory whackdoodles come into it. Their undies are in a permanent bunch. They swear that messing around in the atmosphere causes everything from the ozone hole to the Northern Lights, from earthquakes to erectile dysfunction and PMS. They say we use radio waves for mind control and weather as a weapon to punish uncooperative countries, and they get more creative from there."

She paused and folded her manicured hands, with their hot-orange nails, in front of her on the heavy table. "Trouble is, some of what they say is close to accurate, ma'am, at least when it comes to HAARP. We think that at Flint's TESLA base, they've taken it a few steps closer to the edge of woo-woo, that they actually *can* manipulate weather—move weather systems, stall them, even create them."

Helena felt a disturbing flutter at the base of her throat as her pulse kicked up a few beats. She held up a hand, indicating Candy should pause, then motioned to the aide standing nearby. She scrawled *I want the Afghan report from SecDef Bonner ASAP* and nodded at the aide, who nodded back and immediately left the room.

The president returned her attention to Candy. "You think that Flint might be behind yesterday's storms." It wasn't really a question.

"Yes, ma'am."

The room was silent except for the soft susurrus of temperature-controlled air breezing through the ceiling vents and the very faint background hum of the white noise deliberately introduced as a security feature. Helena kept her eyes on Candy and the cloud of blond curls that framed her gracefully aging Barbie-doll face. The only thing that didn't mesh with the national security advisor's carefully constructed aura of ultimate femininity was the look in Candy's eyes. It was unmistakably challenging, though not disrespectful.

"Why would Flint do it? This kind of destruction"—Helena motioned toward the screens—"can't serve their interests. Besides that, it's criminal. And if they transcend national borders . . ." She left the sentence unfinished.

"You're right, Ms. President. It doesn't make sense. They own or control a lot of the Central Valley. Their headquarters are in Connecticut. And there are reports that Croyden Flint and his family flew to Park

City late this week for spring break and there's a weird spring storm brewing there. That's why we want to talk to Gianni Barone."

"Couldn't these just be unfortunate coincidences?" Helena asked after a moment.

"My staff and some other atmospheric agencies checked out the build-up to the storms. Weather is an inherently chaotic system and, therefore, vulnerable to an infinite number of variables that can effect changes with no warning, but these storms were all highly atypical. And our monitoring equipment picked up irregular and very powerful electromagnetic pulses coming from TESLA prior to each incident."

Helena's eyes trailed back to the large video monitors lining the walls. The devastation was almost incomprehensible. That it might have been deliberate made her mind reel. "Do I understand that you think these storms were somehow instigated by Flint's equipment in Antarctica?" Helena asked carefully.

"Yes, ma'am."

"But they've destroyed Flint holdings."

"Yes, ma'am."

Helena looked at her deeply for a moment, not saying anything. *This is like* The Twilight Zone, *only weirder.*

"So are we talking about big mistakes or are we talking about eco-terrorism?"

"Eco-terrorism," Candy said with no hesitation. "A man named Greg Simpson has been running the TESLA installation since its inception. He used to run a program at HAARP and has been on intelligence radar screens for years. He's meticulous, bright, and very, very driven. He's a JASON," Candy explained, mentioning the little-known, elite group of hand-picked scientists who consult for the government on everything from nuclear weaponry to . . . whatever the government wants them to investigate. "A few years back, Flint offered him a blank check and full control of the TESLA project. He walked away from HAARP without a backward glance. Bottom line, ma'am: he's got more than just brains in his head, he's got a lot of classified information in there, too, bundled up with a lot of ego and attitude."

"Meaning what?"

"He could be susceptible to compromise or temptation."

"Is he stable?"

"No."

"Dangerous?"

"Could be. There's a lot of firepower down there."

Helena tried to keep her mind off the anger pulsing in her blood. "You said that the Pentagon has made use of the equipment down there. What for?"

"Thank you for asking, ma'am. Let me introduce you to someone who may have an answer to that." Candy picked up one of the remotes on the table in front of her and pointed it at the only dark monitor in the room. The screen lit up with the larger-than-life-size image of an impassive face of a graying, crew-cutted man with one star on the collar of his Navy uniform.

"President Hernandez, I'd like to present Vice-Admiral Deekins, acting director of the Office of Ionospheric Monitoring. Admiral, your commander in chief," Candy said, drawing out the last words.

The man rose to his feet and saluted. "Good morning, ma'am."

"Good morning. Be seated, Admiral Deekins, and please accept my condolences on the death of your colleague."

"Thank you, ma'am."

Helena murmured, "Ms. Freeman, please continue."

"Admiral, we were discussing the storms that trashed Connecticut and California recently. They're something of a sensation on the weather wonk websites. What can you contribute to the discussion? Has your group found any atmospheric anomalies linked to them?"

"No, ma'am."

Helena felt a flicker of annoyance at the terse, confident reply and glanced at Candy's face, which was unchanged.

Either she's really good, or she's setting him up. Or both.

Helena returned her gaze to the screen.

"Nothing, admiral?" Candy asked.

"No, ma'am."

"Are you familiar with Flint AgroChemical's TESLA facility, admiral? In Antarctica."

"I've heard of it."

"Could you explain to us what it does?"

"It's a private concern operating within another nation's sovereign territory. I believe they conduct atmospheric research. I don't have any more specific knowledge than that."

"Admiral Medev was speaking with a Flint executive when he died. Why? Does your office work with Flint?" Candy snapped, her tone as sharp as the shard from a broken bottle.

The admiral's cold eyes and clenched jaw betrayed his irritation. He was clearly not used to being addressed in such a way. "To the best of my recollection, this office does not. Perhaps they were friends."

Candy opened a file on the table in front of her, then leaned back in her chair, one slim, bracabletted arm resting easily on the table. "Could be. Admiral Medev and Mr. Barone worked at HAARP for a few overlapping years. As did the man who designed and runs TESLA, Dr. Greg Simpson. Please tell the president what HAARP is and does, admiral."

"Ms. President, HAARP is a large dipole antenna array in rural Alaska that utilizes the ionosphere as a conduit for transmitting military communications."

"Is that all, admiral?" Candy asked, her voice dripping with sarcasm.

"I could be more technical, but if you're not intimately familiar with what riometers and digisondes do and how fluxgate and induction magnetometers work, there's no point in that. If you want me to validate all the nonsense about HAARP that's on the Internet, I can't do that."

"Is TESLA just HAARP 2.0?"

"I can't say, Ms. Freeman. You'd have to ask someone at Flint."

"Thank you, admiral." With a click from the remote, the screen went dark. Candy turned to Helena. "Ms. President, I assure you that HAARP is more than a glorified radio station."

She beckoned to a man who'd been sitting quietly at the edge of the room, out of the line of sight from the computer-mounted camera she'd just shut off. He stood up and saluted.

"Ms. President, I'd like to introduce Admiral Teke Curtis. He was with the Office of Ionospheric Monitoring and recently began working for the Secretary of the Navy. He also worked at HAARP while Greg Simpson was there. Gianni Barone was Admiral Curtis's direct report."

The president nodded at the officer, who completed his salute with a sharp snap of his wrist. "Please join us at the table, admiral. What is your take on this situation?"

The man stepped forward and took a seat several places away from Candy.

"I agree with Ms. Freeman, ma'am. The Internet is full of outlandish rumors about HAARP, but some contain shreds of truth. The HAARP array does transmit massive amounts of energy into the atmosphere, primarily the ionosphere. Fully ramped up, it could knock satellites out of orbit and planes out of the sky and disrupt communications worldwide. It could make people crazy on a big scale. We don't do any of those things, but the capability is there." He paused minutely. "TESLA is different. It has numerous arrays that transmit at a wide variety of frequencies. Its capabilities are far greater than HAARP's. Our intelligence indicates that TESLA is capable of causing wide-scale atmospheric events with significant terrestrial consequences on a global scale."

Without looking away or letting her expression change, Helena let the officer's words sink into her brain for a moment before replying. "Do you think TESLA has been compromised?"

Admiral Curtis was silent for a long moment. "I do, ma'am."

"By whom?"

"That's hard to say. Our surveillance satellites haven't recorded any unusual occurrences. A plane landed there approximately twenty-four hours ago and departed an hour later. There has been a sharp uptick in electromagnetic activity since then. Very strong activity."

"Could any of that recent activity have caused the storms we're discussing?"

"Yes, ma'am."

"Ms. President, would it be possible for the three of us to have a private conversation?" Candy asked smoothly.

"Certainly."

Helena stood up and so did everyone in the room. She walked toward an unobtrusive door near her chair. An aide materialized to open it and Helena, Candy Freeman, and the admiral walked into a small, informal sitting area. Helena ignored the seats, turning to face Candy and Admiral Curtis the moment the door was closed.

"Teke, please describe what you discovered about the relationship between Admiral Medev and Flint," Candy said, her voice warmer than it had been in the larger room.

Teke Curtis looked at Helena, his dark eyes grave. "The office had a long-standing relationship with Flint, Ms. President. The program was highly classified and for a long time things were handled personally between Croyden Flint and Admiral Bonner, now Secretary of Defense Bonner."

Helena felt her irritation level rise at the mention of her Cabinet secretary's name.

"The results were very effective but deliberately low-key, ma'am. When Admiral Bonner retired, Admiral Medev became responsible for liaising with Flint, and Croyden Flint installed Gianni Barone on the Flint side. Barone took a tougher stance on our requests than Croyden Flint ever did, possibly because he and Medev never got along, not even back in their days at HAARP. It appears that, in response, Medev began dealing directly with Greg Simpson. Covertly."

Mother of God. Helena was silent for a moment, looking at her hands as his words sunk in.

"Where did Medev's requests originate?"

"Some came from higher offices, ma'am. But some appear to have no official origin."

"So he may have been acting alone?"

The admiral nodded.

"Have there been incidents . . . orchestrated by him since I took office?"

"We've confirmed one. The floods in Afghanistan in late winter."

It wasn't easy for Helena to keep her cool in the face of his admission. "You know this for a fact?"

"Yes, ma'am."

Treason is such an ugly word. "Anything else, Admiral Curtis?" Helena asked, eager to get out of the room and into planning mode. She had a Cabinet to clean out.

"Yes, ma'am. Gianni Barone was in Malta during a recent NATO conference, and met with a scientist named Tess Beauchamp. She's a weather researcher who also used to work at HAARP. Immediately after the conference, she left her job in France and returned stateside. According to the state department, she flew to South Africa about a week ago and left there for Antarctica on a Flint plane late Thursday. We believe it was her plane that landed at TESLA yesterday."

"Why is that significant?"

"We believe she replaced Simpson," Candy said. "The same plane took off about an hour later to return to Capetown and we have an unconfirmed report that Simpson was on it." She paused and looked directly at the president. "We think TESLA has gone rogue, Ms. President. Either Greg Simpson is still running the show remotely or Tess Beauchamp is working with him."

"What makes you think he's 'gone rogue,' Candy?"

Teke Curtis cleared his throat. "If I may, Ms. President. Greg Simpson is a classic narcissist. He thinks he's infallible. When he runs a project, he goes through staff like water through a sieve until he has a team that follows him blindly. I've seen how he operates."

Candy leaned forward. "Greg Simpson is like Dr. Evil without the laugh track. He's buttoned down, smart, OCD, sociopathic—and mightily pissed off, ma'am. Mightily pissed off."

"Let's bring in the others on this conversation," Helena said coolly, and walked back toward the door.

CHAPTER

Park City residents and guests alike were awakened before dawn on Saturday by the flash of lightning and the crash of thunder—and the sound of hard, vicious rain beating against the slate roofs and redwood siding of the town's multi-million-dollar structures. Incredulous faces stared through windows, watching the powder they'd skied on the day before turn into slush and then into puddles. Streams rushed along the sides of the roads.

The combination of rain and warmth began to drill holes in the snowpack throughout the mountainsides that surrounded the village. Layers of months-old snow, some coarse and some fine, some dry and some wetter, absorbed or gave way or deflected the rainwater. The water moved through the hardened pack; in some places it slid over impermeable ice lenses and in others found narrow pathways through which it percolated to the base.

Hours of this wet barrage fomented a result that was cataclysmic, though not immediately visible. Huge sections of the mountain's snowfield went isothermal: enough water had penetrated to the base of the snow-pack so that the layers upon layers of dense, compacted snow now rested atop a thin film of meltwater. Encouraged by wind and gravity, the season's solid mass of many feet of snow began to lurch, then slip, then glide down the sides of the hills.

By noon in Park City, the road to the airport was crammed bumper to bull bars with mud-spattered shuttle buses, sports cars, and luxury sport vehicles bearing irritated, petulant vacationers. Every car sported rooftop carriers full of now-pointless skis. The thwarted travelers sat in the stalled traffic and tele-phoned, texted, and Tweeted their frustration, but their actions did nothing to speed their departure. They remained, oblivious, in harm's way.

The avalanche descended on the town without warning. Thunder from the storm masked its roar; the rain- and warmth-spawned fog conspired to hide the rushing gray wall of wet, heavy death as it slid into and over the town at hundreds of miles per hour. Tim-bers cracked and walls crashed onto people sitting in-doors in front of blazing fires or glowing screens, onto families lingering over lunch or partiers recovering from the night before. Screams were smothered by the choking weight of the gushing slush. Buildings col-lapsed, their stones and snapped beams and shattered roofs tumbling and bouncing in the streets' filthy tor-rents. Cars were thrown, buried, or crushed; the luck-ier occupants died instantly.

In less than half an hour, the catastrophe was com-plete. The storm front had moved on, its fierce power spent. The sun came out. The tiny, once-wealthy town had been completely destroyed, and lay buried now under many feet of heavy snow and grisly debris. The playground of millionaires had been transformed into a deep, sucking sea of mud and carnage. All was silent except for the rhythmic thudding of news helicopters and the distant wails of approaching emergency vehicles.

Croyden Flint lay pinned in the back of the stretch Hummer he'd hired to take his family to the airport. His daughters, their husbands, and his grandchildren lay around him, some screaming, some moaning, some ominously silent. The stench of death was in the air, mingling with the metallic smell of blood and the must of wet wool.

The limo was on its side, tipped nearly upside down. The temperature inside the cabin was dropping. Filthy, slushy water flowed steadily through the gaping hole where the windshield had been. The water cascaded over the upended steering console and flowed around the heads and shoulders of broken bodies that lay on what had moments before been the interior roof of the car. Croyden watched helplessly as his family drowned around him, as their bodies thrashed and then grew still. He was next.

Wedged in the twisted wreckage, unable to move, Croyden Flint could only close his eyes in horror as he felt the icy water wend its wet fingers through his hair and drive its slow needle-pricks of cold into his scalp, his forehead, his eye sockets, and, finally, his nostrils.

26

CHAPTER

G reg relaxed in the plush seat of the Gulfstream jet, ignoring his unwelcome entourage of Flint flunkies while flipping through the latest issue of *Greenwich* magazine. Its slick, glossy photos of slick, glossy people made him want to laugh. He'd rocked their cloistered world; he'd given those smugly smiling people, who lived pointless lives in ostentatious houses, a wake-up call. And it had been nothing more than a by-product of his interest in Croyden Flint. Croyden's homes had all been targets: the mansion in Greenwich, Connecticut; the huge clifftop estate in Mexico; the getaway "cabin" in Park City; and the big house in California's Central Valley. He'd known Croyden Flint would be at one of them during this northern spring weekend. And if he hadn't been, if he was still alive, then he'd be around to watch the rest of his empire crumble. Literally.

This widespread destruction was Greg's magnum opus. Flint, the Pentagon, even other governments probably already knew that he was behind the destruction and were scrambling to figure out what would happen next and how to prevent it.

They can try all they like. It won't do any good.

Greg smiled, stretching his cramped muscles as he leaned back in his chair. The next event would be unparalleled if it happened as it was supposed to. Given his previous success, Greg had no reason to consider that it might miss its mark. But then, the target was so much larger this time—not some rural hick town, small ski resort, or suburban retreat. His next creation would affect an entire region, an area that bridged two continents and spanned innumerable warring histories. And the nation that would bear the brunt of it had a troubled past and a manic present; thanks to Greg, soon—very soon—Israel would face a devastated future.

The timing would be perfect. The storm would flatten one of Flint's most prized projects and some of its most productive agricultural lands and would coincide with a visit by America's new defense secretary—and Croyden Flint's lapdog—Frederick Bonner.

With any luck, the storm will flatten Freddy, too.

"Where are you headed, Teke?" Candy asked casually as they left the White House.

He glanced down at her. "My office."

"Can I give you a lift?"

"Crystal City isn't exactly on the way to Bolling Air Force Base."

"I feel like taking the scenic route."

He laughed and climbed into the back of the town car that was waiting under the portico.

"We're taking the admiral to the Pentagon, Jimmy," she said pleasantly, then depressed a button to raise the divider and flipped a switch to turn on the white noise.

"How did you manage to get an office outside of the West Wing?" Teke asked.

"I told them I didn't like the commute," she said breezily. "I live in Alexandria and have been heading out to Langley all these years, so I didn't really like the idea of coming all the way into the District and dealing with that traffic. So we settled on Bolling. It's secure enough for them, and close enough to the Wilson Bridge for me."

"So what did you want to talk about?"

"I need the low-down on TESLA. All the stuff you didn't want to tell the president."

"Simpson's a nutbar," he said bluntly. "His file ought to be about a foot thick by now."

Candy smiled. *Slightly larger, but who's measuring?* "I'm told the station is inaccessible until their summer, which is six months away."

"That's correct, except in emergencies."

"Like Tess Beauchamp?"

"If Simpson wasn't on that outbound flight, it will be a cage match. They hate each other."

There was a brief pause. "I'd like to watch what's going on down there a little more closely."

"Do you mean that metaphorically or literally? With eyes in the sky or on the ground?"

Candy turned to look out the window. The Potomac was sparkling in the waning moonlight. "Whatever will get me more information and put us in a position to assist."

"Fuck."

"Gesundheit," she replied silkily.

"If you're thinking of deploying a team, Candy—" Teke stopped and shook his head. "TESLA is a thousand miles past nowhere. There's no possibility of surprising them. There's no way to set up a base camp anywhere near it."

"I know all that. Darlin', I need a solution. I think we need someone in there. Maybe a few someones. And we might need them right quick. Lord knows what else our little friend is planning. How can we get people there if we need to?"

Teke's look was grim. "It's a thousand miles inland, so subs and ships are out. The hundred-mile-per-hour winds and sudden white-outs rule out small planes and choppers. It's too damned cold for them, anyway. And it's too far to make it with tracked vehicles unless we fly them in with us."

"What's left?"

"A human air drop."

"Sounds good."

"I don't recommend it." Teke let out a hard breath. "Candy, what you're asking for is complicated and dangerous. We don't have the right sort of people on that side of the planet, and we can't get them there from here quickly enough."

"I have friends who can handle that little wrinkle."

He paused and looked at her deeply. "Do you outrank me?"

Candy smiled at him. "I'm not sure. Would you like me to find out?"

"Not really." Teke let out a resigned breath. "I'll make some calls."

"I already asked the Agency and the ONR to see if there's someone local who might be able to help. Some of those people Greg took with him when he left HAARP might be loose assets. Who are you thinking of calling?" she asked sweetly.

"My A-team," he replied drily, giving her a look.

"Oh, mercy, Teke, you don't mean Curly and Moe, do you?" she said with an edge to her voice that was accompanied by a roll of her eyes.

"Admirals Rowan and Hormann are excellent tacticians, dedicated, highly decorated officers, and creative thinkers."

"They're also your buddies from college—"

"It was the War College, Candy," he ground out.

"Doesn't matter. I've heard the stories. Something about a silver mylar balloon carrying thrusters and a circuit board. Got you all in trouble with the Park Police, I heard. Didn't it land on the South Lawn of the White House at midnight?"

"The steps of the Capitol at five A.M.," he corrected.

"A distinction without a difference. What can those two clowns bring to the table?"

"They're hardly clowns. Rowan spent fifteen years running or commanding subs and just got a third star on his collar. Hormann turned down a chance to teach at TOPGUN so he could stay in D.C. It's a tribute to both of them that they've managed to retain a sense of humor after this long."

"Bless their hearts," she said too sweetly, then paused and became serious. "I really need a plan, Teke. One that will blow the garter belt off our commander in chief. Just in case she asks."

Teke stared at her for a moment, then nodded and looked out the window. The rest of the trip was spent in silence.

"Nik. A moment?" Ron said over his shoulder as he walked past him into the conference room.

Nik, who was sitting at a spare workstation in the sandbox, looked up from his computer, which was just booting up. "Tess isn't here yet and I haven't had my first cup of coffee. Can it wait?"

"I wouldn't advise it."

Nik followed him, shut the door, then leaned against it. And waited.

Ron turned to face him with an expression that was uncharacteristically concerned. "Something's going down, Nik. It's not good. Worse than what has already happened."

Nik pushed away from the door as the day's first adrenaline burst hit his bloodstream. "What's up?"

"I couldn't sleep much last night. I kept thinking about what Tess said about Greg possibly doing this for reasons of revenge or just insanity. So I started looking a little closer at some of the code in his algorithms for the Extremely High Frequency array. It's the latest one to flip into pre-warm-up mode. Take a look."

Taking the few short steps to the table, Nik peered at the screen of the laptop Ron had brought in with him. On it was the interface for the command queue for the EHF array. It overlapped windows showing the command queues for the other arrays.

The code was full of strings that Nik had never seen before. He glanced up at Ron. "What is this?"

Ron shook his head after replying with a shrug. "I'm not sure. It looks like he's done some sort of crude crypto on it. Swapped out meanings or—" He lifted his shoulders in another shrug.

"Is this the first time you've seen it?"

"Pretty much. Until yesterday, I didn't usually check Greg's work," he replied drily, causing Nik to bite back a grin. "The problem is, none of this makes sense. The coordinates are still bogus, but they're set to a different scale than the other events were, the ones that have already happened."

"How so?"

"A lot of these coordinates are in the oceans. Open ocean, miles away from anywhere. What's the point of that?"

"Beats me," Nik muttered, remembering what Tess had said many hours ago about war games being interrupted. "Do we still have access to the system?"

"Depends on what you mean by 'access.' Everyone can log in, but nothing happens. Everything I've tried to put in for the last twelve hours has been rejected. Doesn't matter what it is. And the coordinate system, the timing system—they're all wrong. Nothing means what it should."

"I thought you cracked that yesterday."

"We did. It changed again." He met Nik's eyes. "That doesn't happen by accident."

"Have you tried inputting anything new? Just as a test?"

"Yes."

"Did it take?"

"No. But I don't like the way these coordinates keep changing. He's brain-fucking us."

"Well, we might be screwed anyway," Nik said as he straightened up. "Tess wants to power down the arrays."

Ron's eyes widened. "That's a bit extreme."

"That's what I said. If we don't want to do that, we have to come up with Plan B."

"We don't have a Plan A yet."

"Put it on your list," Nik said as he turned to leave the room. "I've got to get Tess in here."

27

CHAPTER

For the last ten days, the weather in the belly of the Mediterranean had been unusually torpid for mid-April. Tourists from Britain and Germany and places farther north were delighted to spend the hot, dry, still days roasting themselves on the beaches of Ibiza and Sardinia, and pass long, late, wine-filled evenings on flower-bedecked balconies from Marbella to Barcelona. Farther along the region's other coastlines—Nice, the high instep of Italy's boot, the beaches of Tunisia to the cliffs of Tripoli, even up the Dalmatian coast—the weather was close to perfect. Everyone was happy.

Yachtsmen at the helms of sleek, tall-masted, wood-hulled beauties were the first to notice the change. After drifting easily near the slim, imposing Strait of Gibraltar for more than a week, unwilling to venture into an oddly becalmed Atlantic, they welcomed the freshening breezes. They cut their idling engines, ran up the sails, and enjoyed the ancient, still romantic rush of seeing broad sheets of canvas fill with salt air and billow into round, sensual fullness.

Glad as they were for the sea change, it didn't take long for those same mariners to sense that Nature was behaving with more than simple vernal capriciousness. Their barometers, both the electronically fed and the timeworn devices reliant on mercury, were unsettled. All across the region, something was amiss, and the wisest among the sailors aimed their bowsprits toward the nearest port of call. Those less wizened or just less wise accepted the challenge blowing their way, never considering they might live to regret it—or not live at all.

The wind stiffened overnight and the temperature dropped. Barometers began to fall. And fall.

Tourists awakened to heavy skies similar to the ones they'd left behind in Copenhagen, Basingstoke, and Bonn; and to winds that bit through their optimistically lightweight holiday clothing. By noon, lightning rent the sky. Cold rain pelted sideways from dense black clouds that seemed close enough to touch. Visitors huddled, grumbling, in the cramped living rooms of their vacation rentals or the pubs of their hotels. Shops pulled in their awnings. Cafés closed.

By midnight, the salty waters of the Mediterranean were battering seawalls and assaulting beaches with waves that topped ten feet. Scores of uprooted palms lay across streets and cars; centuries-old olive and cedar trees stood at awkward angles against the onslaught, already stripped of both their equilibrium and their most majestic limbs. Cell towers and bell towers toppled; streets flooded. Beleaguered mayors of wounded coastal cities and near-dead villages hovered over battery-powered laptops, tapping out emotional pleas for government aid and for tourists not to desert them in this time of need.

Television meteorologists across the region were bemused by the spring storm's existence as well as its growth and intensity; none of them had predicted this early Mediterranean hurricane—or Medicane, as the more hip of the fraternity called it. Yet even as they discussed its strange provenance, the unnamed storm grew like a sea monster from a myth.

As it widened its reach, the hurricane's forward speed increased dramatically. In defiance of the odds and the laws of Nature, its convection tower expanded vertically and horizontally, battering both the Tunisian coastline and the ankle of Italy's boot as it churned a broad, vicious path across Sicily and left a decimated Malta in its wake. Once in the open basin that stretched from Libya to Greece, its path momentarily unobstructed by either islands or continental promontories, the storm gained even more strength.

It skirted Crete and then, roaring like a beast mortally wounded and seeking revenge, it lunged toward the region's most tense coastlines.

Beirut, Damascus, Tel Aviv, Gaza—all were crushed by the fierce, awesome power of winds topping 110 knots and laden with rain that pelted both ancient walls and modern edifices like the lethal, scattering spray from an Uzi. Flint's hundreds of acres of orchards, which stretched along the coastal plain of the Middle East, were flattened; millions of dollars of fruit were pulped into the earth. Farther down the coast, the company's newest endeavor—a hard-won, much-lauded, state-of-the-art desalination plant intended to bring freshwater to a thirsty region—was ravaged by the storm, its solar-power plant destroyed beyond repair.

The area's famously restive populations, though

accustomed to the random violence of humanity, were unprepared for the indiscriminate brutality of the storm. The people had no option but to retreat until the winds stopped keening and the rain wore itself out. When the sunshine returned, a sodden, broken world lay before them and the grim task of recovering got under way.

As soon as secure communications were restored, the U.S. secretary of defense, shaken but safe in the embassy's heavily reinforced underground shelter, called Candy Freeman, demanding to know what actions were being taken to stop Greg Simpson before he could strike again.

It was still dark outside—dark and cold—at 6:30 A.M. in Washington, D.C. Gianni fought the urge to stamp his feet to keep the circulation going as the armed military police officer ran his driver's license through a scanner, then frowned at the screen and tapped a few keys. Gianni's arms were folded tightly against his chest to ward off the wet chill as he stood at the entry gate to Bolling Air Force Base. He was there to meet with Candy Freeman, who'd sent a team of FBI agents to wake him up a few hours earlier.

The agents had been polite. They'd offered to let him call his attorney, but Gianni had seen his attorney's Old Greenwich home—or, rather, the wreckage left in the place where the house had stood just a few days ago—in some Internet footage and had opted not to call. So he'd been gently placed in the back of a Bronco next to a third agent for the trip to the airport in White Plains. Getting there had been an adventure. The roads were nearly impassable. The power was still out and the only light came from the Bronco's headlights, the moon, and the harsh flash of battery-powered traffic barriers. It was just as well. Gianni didn't really want to see what had happened to the formerly picturesque Merritt Parkway.

The airport was dark and silent. Silhouettes of wrecked planes dotted the landscape. The SUV pulled up to a small jet parked on the tarmac and Gianni was ushered onto it. The plushness of the little jet surprised him. One of the FBI agents onboard noticed him staring and said, "It belonged to a South Florida drug dealer. We nailed him under RICO and got this as a bonus."

"Ah, that explains the ambience," Gianni replied pleasantly as he took his place in a seat that appeared to be upholstered in ostrich. The seat belt—dyed lizard—had a scratched, utilitarian chrome buckle, which seemed really out of place. Gianni looked back at the agent.

"They used to be gold-plated, with diamonds. They were sold off."

Gianni smiled.

All in all, it wasn't a bad flight. The coffee they offered him was probably Maxwell House instead of Starbucks, but it was hot and caffeinated and had woken him up. So here he was, a mere two hours after opening his front door, freezing his ass off in decidedly unscenic southeast D.C.

It's amazing how efficient the government can be when it wants something.

At last the cop returned his license and waved Gianni and the FBI agents through the gate, where an escort waited in a nice, warm car.

Inside the main building, things went a little faster. Badges were issued and smart cards were swiped.

Gianni and his entourage stepped through the metal detector and toward the elevator. The doors opened almost instantly.

Seconds later they stepped into a deeply carpeted hallway lined with potted plants and some seriously nice art. His escorts—both FBI and military—remained silent as they walked about halfway down the hall and stopped in front of a door identified by a brass plaque that bore no title, just a last name and an initial: C. FREEMAN.

Gianni entered the anteroom alone and was greeted by a smiling assistant who directed him to have a seat, then picked up the phone. He'd barely sat down when he was told that Ms. Freeman would see him now.

His first up-close look at Candy Freeman was not what he expected. Gianni knew her by reputation and had seen pictures and occasional news footage of her, so he knew what she looked like. But he hadn't expected the wattage of her smile to be so high, nor the energy level in the room to be so apparent. Especially at this hour.

She came out from behind her desk, walking easily on the highest heels he'd ever seen on a woman outside of New Jersey, and shook his hand with a grip that made him wonder what her forearms looked like. Her suit wasn't basic Beltway attire. It was well cut and fitted, but short-skirted, and of an orange so deep and bright it reminded him of a South Pacific sunset.

"Mr. Barone, thank you for making the trip down to Washington. It's always so much nicer to chat in person, isn't it?"

Her honey-thick drawl was soft and feminine, and between that and her Southern belle manners he had to fight an urge to laugh. Everything was at odds with the rumors he'd heard about her, which included many dark deeds done for the CIA.

"Thank you for inviting me, Ms. Freeman," he said, not bothering to mask his sarcasm.

She ignored it. "My pleasure. Let's sit over here. Would you like something to drink?"

A double Scotch, neat. "Coffee would be fine, thanks."

She walked to the door, opened it, and said something quiet to someone on the other side, then returned to where Gianni stood. Candy gestured to the pair of wing chairs that faced each other across a low table. They sat.

Opposite him, a window framed the many-hued lights of Reagan National Airport strobing the air and sparkling off the still-dark Potomac. The view was a little bit fairy-tale-ish, but the last twenty-four hours had been so surreal that he took it in stride.

The woman from the outer room came in bearing a tray with a silver coffee service, a china·cup and saucer, and a frosty can of Dr Pepper next to a crystal tumbler. She was followed by another woman who settled into a chair near the door and placed a small notebook computer on her lap.

"Thank you, Margaret. Mr. Barone, this is my assistant Joely," Candy said, with an airy wave toward the woman in the chair.

The door closed softly and Candy leaned forward to pour some coffee from the ornate silver pot into the china cup, then handed the cup to him. "I hope you won't mind me getting right into the topic, but I really need to know what's going on down at your TESLA installation."

The calm, casually uttered statement left Gianni

speechless for a moment. "Could you be more specific, Ms. Freeman?"

"Do I need to be, Mr. Barone?" she asked, her eyes
making direct, unwavering contact with his own. "I'm
talking about the storms."

Gianni sat back in his chair. "Do I need an attorney?"

"I can't imagine why you would. You're not under
arrest."

"I'm in custody."

She smiled. "You might want to consider it protective custody, considering how many governments have
been asking us some very unusual and rather pointed
questions in the last few hours. It's only a matter of
time—and not much time—before they start kicking
ass and looking for a culprit." She paused. "Now, how
about we get to the point. We know what TESLA
can do. We know that this great nation of ours occasionally partakes of Flint's . . . largesse. We know you
were the last person to speak with Admiral Medev
before his untimely demise, and, in fact, that the call
hadn't even been completed when he met his unfortunate end. The big question in certain circles is what
you two gentlemen were talking about that provoked
such a dramatic response."

Gianni ran through several possible answers before
deciding that he didn't need to court more trouble; he
and Flint were already in deep. "We were discussing
the storms."

"Were you also discussing their provenance?"

"Some of the recent activity at TESLA could have
provided the trigger point for the atmospheric agitation that contributed to the storms," he said cautiously.

Candy shook her head from side to side slowly, the

look on her face scornful. "Activity and agitation. Such nice words," she said quietly. "We'll get back to them in a minute. Let me ask you another big question that's floating around town, Mr. Barone. Why would Flint want to destroy its own headquarters and a large portion of its most productive cropland, not to mention several cities in which its CEO owns homes?"

Gianni took a deep breath. "If the storms originated from TESLA, and it appears likely that they did, they were unauthorized."

"But someone *is* authorizing them," she pointed out. "Unless your equipment can do this on its own."

"These actions are not authorized by Flint," he said firmly, starting to get annoyed.

"So we'll call it unauthorized devastation. What an odd expression. How frequently is devastation authorized?"

"Ms. Freeman, I don't appreciate your sarcasm," he snapped. "Flint is a company lots of people love to hate, but nothing the company has ever done—*ever*, in its hundred-and-forty-year history—has been done with malicious or destructive intent. Whatever is happening now is not happening at the direction of the company."

She leaned forward, popped the tab on the can of soda, and poured some into the tumbler.

"Is Greg Simpson still in charge?" Her kittenish tone was gone.

He hesitated, not pleased at playing mouse to her long-clawed cat. "No. We've replaced him."

"With Tess Beauchamp?"

"Yes."

"Where's Greg?"

"En route from Capetown to Greenwich on one of

our corporate Gulfstreams. They touched down to refuel in France a little while ago."

"He's still onboard?"

"No one got off the plane."

She nodded. "I'd like you to have him land here, in Washington, instead. I'll have someone make the arrangements. Let your people know to expect a call."

"You're going to take him into custody?"

Candy's mouth tilted into a smile, but her eyes remained cold and serious. "Surely you didn't think we'd release him into the wild? Have you spoken with Tess since she landed there?"

"Once. Briefly."

"Why only once, with all that's been going on?"

Gianni pulled in a deep breath. "Because TESLA went dark shortly after Greg departed. We have not been able to re-establish communications with them."

"Ho, that's not good."

"No, it isn't," he snapped. "I'm getting tired of this pointless banter, Ms. Freeman, so if you're about done—"

She smiled again. "Oh, I'm nowhere near done, and this is anything but pointless, Mr. Barone. But if you'd like to change the way this conversation is going, I'm willing to work with you on it." Candy leaned an elbow on the arm of the chair and rested her chin on her loosely closed fist. "Our files on Greg Simpson go kind of silent after he left HAARP. I want you to tell me what he's like now and what he's been up to lately."

Gianni set his untouched coffee back on the tray. "He's been working on proprietary systems. His personality is much the same as it's always been."

"Why did you replace him?"

Gianni smiled. "I want immunity from prosecution, Ms. Freeman. Full and unconditional."

She raised an eyebrow. "I've already made it clear that you're not under arrest, Mr. Barone."

"I don't care what you want to call it. If you want me to say anything more, *anything,* Ms. Freeman, tell me what I want to hear. If you have to wake a few people up, go ahead. I'll wait."

"Make a note of that request, Joely," she said calmly, looking past him. Then she returned her gaze to his face. "The Attorney General has authorized me to offer you full immunity from any federal prosecution arising from Flint's actions in this regard, Mr. Barone. Please continue what you were saying."

"Greg was making his own decisions, using our arrays for purposes not aligned with Flint's goals. The event that tipped me off to what Medev was doing was the landslide in Afghanistan in March. He'd asked us to do that and I said no," he said quietly. From the corner of his eye, he could see the Washington Monument stabbing the brightening sky. "When it happened, I realized Medev had gone directly to Greg. I worked backward from that and discovered it wasn't the first time." Gianni paused. "Ms. Freeman, I get the feeling nothing I've said so far has surprised you. I'm wondering why we went to such extremes to place TESLA in Antarctica when we have the same level of privacy as we would have had were it in Newark."

"Perhaps you chose Antarctica because it doesn't smell as bad as Newark," she replied with a smile. "Don't worry about what we know. Was the side deal the only reason you decided to replace him?"

"I didn't need another reason. Greg was using TESLA as a weapon of mass destruction, proving that he'd become dangerously unstable. In a small, isolated environment like TESLA—" He shook his head. "I couldn't afford to wait. I did what I could, put the best person in place as quickly as I could. And I can assure you that if what's going on can be stopped, Tess will stop it."

"'If,' Mr. Barone?"

"I can't offer any guarantees. I can only tell you that the team down there is exceptional."

She paused, thinking about that for a moment, then shifted in her chair, kicking off her ridiculously high heels and tucking her legs underneath her on the seat. "What's your plan?"

Gianni looked at her, feeling the acid eating through his stomach lining. "I'm sorry?"

"What is Flint doing? What if there are more disasters in the chute? Are you going to disable the arrays remotely? Take TESLA off line?"

He shook his head slowly. "No. There's no way to disable the array or take it off line remotely, short of destroying it. It's a contained system, heavily fortified."

"So your plan is to just wait and see what happens?" Candy Freeman demanded. "Do you have any idea where this is going to end?"

"No." He leaned back in his chair and glanced out the window. The sky was lightening and the Potomac was edging from black to dark brown. The airport lights were less startlingly bright. "We thought we'd addressed every contingency. This sort of occurrence—"

"Let's just call it 'terrorism' and be done with it, Mr. Barone."

Gianni nodded. "Nothing like this ever occurred to us. Our focus was on preventing external attacks."

"Does the installation have defensive capabilities?"

"No. The equipment was never the primary concern; the software was. There's a continuous backup to a secure vault beneath the habitat. If certain required protocols aren't performed as scheduled, the system will lock down. Everything topside will be degaussed automatically."

She thought about that for a minute. "Let's go back to the unauthorized devastation for a minute. Have we seen the best TESLA can do with these storms— Park City, Greenwich, etc.?"

"No. And TESLA didn't only produce those storms," he replied. "It triggered Tropical Storm Ayala, although I'm not sure how that fits into the picture."

"I haven't heard of that one."

"The South Pacific, about a thousand miles from Fiji. It blew up from nothing to a pretty wild state very quickly yesterday afternoon. Predictions are that it will become a typhoon later today. It isn't threatening any major land mass yet, but it easily could."

"I'll keep my eye on it. What about the Mediterranean? Secretary Bonner seems convinced that TESLA was involved."

He looked at her. "I haven't heard anything about that."

"A huge hurricane sprung up out of nowhere and ripped down the middle of the Mediterranean, then slammed into the central and northern coasts of Israel a few hours ago."

Gianni felt his eyes widen and he caught his breath, feeling as if someone had sucker-punched him. "Where?"

"Everything from Tel Aviv to Haifa is trashed. Damascus sustained some serious damage, as did points farther north, but Israel seemed to be hit the hardest, according to early reports."

He rubbed a hand over his face. "We just completed a three-hundred-million-dollar desalination plant near Haifa. Secretary Bonner was going to bring it on line today."

Gianni swallowed hard, then looked at Candy and decided to give her everything she wanted. There was no point anymore in holding anything back. Greg had clearly decided to destroy Flint and anything that came in his way. "TESLA caused the earthquake in Mexico City."

"Are you serious?" she demanded, showing the first hint of surprise since he'd walked into her office.

He nodded wearily.

"You have to explain that to me."

"The planet is just a spinning ball with a powerful magnet at its core, and tectonic action is controlled by geomagnetic waves."

"Okay."

"Greg hypothesized that if we could control the atmosphere's electromagnetism, there was no reason we couldn't control the earth's geomagnetism. Everything TESLA does is based on a very simple idea, Ms. Freeman. The arrays direct pulses of magnetic energy with specific signatures to specific locations in the atmosphere, the earth's crust, or, if there was a reason to do it, into outer space or into the oceans."

"What happens in those scenarios?" she asked warily.

"Directing it into the earth, as you've seen, creates tectonic action. Earthquakes. Volcanoes could be triggered. Tsunamis." He shrugged. "If we direct it into space, the immediate, short-term results would be the crash of communication grids—"

"Whose?"

"Anyone's. Everyone's. The type and amount of energy TESLA can produce could knock nearly everything in low-earth and mid-range orbits right out of the sky. That would be most of the telecommunication satellites. Telephone systems, anyway. Iridium and other satellite constellations—gone. They might blow up. They'd certainly go dark. It would happen in minutes. The waves of energy wouldn't stop there. They'd continue to propagate out, crashing things in higher orbits, geosynchronous. Maybe not everything would be destroyed, but enough would. It would be a global communications disaster. I don't know what would happen as the energy continued to travel through space. Depends on what the initial burst is, which frequencies are used, how powerful it is. It could affect smaller orbiting bodies—"

"Such as?"

"Comets, asteroids, meteors." He lifted his hands and let them drop. "The moon."

As he said the last word, Gianni watched Candy Freeman go pale.

"The moon?" She shook herself, as if to pull herself together. The effort wasn't successful, judging by the grip she had on the padded arm of the chair. "Are you serious?" she said again.

He nodded slowly. "I'm serious. I just don't know if I'm right. It's an educated guess. I never spent much time thinking about what that energy would do if used outside of the ionosphere. That's outside TESLA's spec. We discussed it briefly in the context of an accident, but that's it. TESLA's max output, under the worst circumstances, would be . . . bad."

"Bad?" she repeated sharply, then looked away, licked her lips, and took a sip of her soda. "How bad?"

Gianni noticed that her hands had a tremor that wasn't there before. "Real bad."

"You also mentioned the energy could be directed toward the earth. The oceans. What fresh hell would that bring to the mothership?" she asked more calmly, setting the glass on the table and meeting his eyes again.

"As I said, earthquakes, volcanoes, tsunamis," he said flatly. "How big would depend on the magnitude of the energy burst."

"The pulses could be directed anywhere?"

He nodded.

She paused. "Just out of curiosity, Mr. Barone, has this been tested? Or is this just a theory, like what you said about outer space?"

"It's not just a theory," he replied slowly.

"You've produced earthquakes besides this last one in Mexico?"

He nodded and closed his eyes. "At the request of Admiral Bonner and, presumably, the last administration."

"Where?"

"China." His throat felt thick suddenly and the word came out strangled. He met her eyes, which held shock and disgust.

"Which one?"

"Sichuan, 2008. And Haiti, 2010. The tsunami, 2004," he said, his voice barely audible to his own ears. "That was the first geomagnetic test. It was just a small pulse, but there were some miscalculations—"

"Ya think?" she snapped, then collected herself immediately and stood up. "Gianni, let's stop here. To be perfectly candid, this has been one hell of a chat. More enlightening than I had anticipated or hoped, and more disturbing than I'd expected. I suppose that goes with the territory." She managed to give him a tight smile. "Thank you very much for coming. I've made arrangements for you to stay at a hotel. You can get some sleep, and some food, and then we'll continue this conversation later. I'll be in touch." She looked past him to her assistant. "Jo, call a car to take Mr. Barone over to the Ritz Carlton." Candy looked back at him. "Let me know if you need anything. I'll see you in a few hours."

Gianni shook her hand and allowed himself to be led out of the room. The same stone-faced agents who'd brought him down from Connecticut escorted him to the elevator. Just as the doors were about to slide shut, a very tall man wearing starched Navy beige walked past him and casually made eye contact.

The glance was quick, over in an instant, but something in the man's eyes left Gianni with a decidedly sick feeling in the pit of his already roiling gut.

CHAPTER

Teke Curtis walked through the anteroom, knocked once on Candy Freeman's office door, then let himself in. The chair behind Candy's desk was turned toward the window that framed the sun's early-morning glow over the District of Columbia.

"Thanks for listening in, Teke."

"No problem. This has been a hell of a day so far," he said drily as he crossed the room and walked around the desk to perch on the wide windowsill, partially blocking her view. "Nothing but doom and more doom in the forecast."

Candy was slouched down awkwardly in her chair. She flicked her eyes up to meet his and he was stunned at the hollow look he saw there.

"I don't think I've gotten all of the story yet."

Saying nothing, Teke stretched his legs out in front of him and crossed them at the ankle.

Candy leaned her head against the back of the chair. "I'm not even sure what I'm supposed to be focusing on right now. The thought of weather being the new 'nuke' is one I thought we wouldn't have to face for a few more years. But here we are. A few 'miscalculations' caused the greatest disaster of the last, what, fifty or so years? Maybe more? Hundreds of thousands died from that tsunami. Tens of thousands dead from that Chinese earthquake. Two hundred thousand in Haiti. And that's just what he's admitted to. There could be more. And Bonner ordered all of it." She shook her head. "Am I unpatriotic if I say I hope something heavy and sharp fell on his head when he was cowering in that cozy embassy bunker this morning?"

"He was just the man in charge, Candy. If it hadn't been him, it would have been whoever was in his place," Teke said bluntly. "What Flint does at TESLA is what we've been trying to do at HAARP for decades. Since the first battle ever fought—when Cain picked up that rock and knocked the shit out of his goody-goody brother—warriors have wanted a weapon that gave them an unassailable edge. Natural events similar to the ones TESLA can produce have changed the course of world history. The eruption of Krakatoa broke the back of the Dutch influence in Southeast Asia and arguably helped Islam flourish. A cyclone hit Pakistan in the early 1970s and pretty much sealed the deal on statehood for Bangladesh. You could even argue that an earthquake helped bring down the Sandinistas in Nicaragua."

Teke gave a one-shoulder shrug and continued. "Now the disasters are custom-designed. The 2004 tsunami reset the political landscape in Aceh and Sri Lanka and even caused peace to break out for a while. Katrina pointed out some glaring issues in our own domestic politics and policies. The earthquake in Sichuan nurtured some much-needed political unrest in

China's interior. All the shit going on in Haiti for decades was reset to zero. And the landslides in Afghanistan gave the guys in the E-ring a hard-on of epic proportions because it neatly and completely trashed the plans of their brand-new female commander in chief." He walked around to the front of Candy's desk and sat down in the chair Gianni had recently vacated. Candy twirled around to face him.

"Come on, Candy, we both know that the homegrown response to any disaster can seriously affect domestic politics and even social and economic stability. It's also a given that any disaster presents political bodies farther afield with myriad opportunities to 'get involved' in the situation. Remember Cuba offering the U.S. assistance after Katrina?" he said.

"Please go on, professor."

He nodded. "Take what Barone said and look at it from the angle of ill-gotten gains. Sure, a half million or so people died because of that tsunami, but that was just the price of progress. That event gave Bonner and Flint—and Simpson—proof they could make the earth release a burst of energy measuring about 32,000 megatons. That's not small potatoes."

"No, it isn't. And we're going to make sure that that sort of progress is stopped. Handling Bonner is going to take some delicacy, but Simpson is going to be in our custody the minute he touches down on U.S. soil. In fact—" She leaned forward and depressed the intercom button on her phone. "Joely, honey, I need you to make a few phone calls. I need you to get the tail number of the Flint Gulfstream that's currently en route from France to the U.S. with Greg Simpson aboard. I want it intercepted by a couple of our whup-ass jets ASAP and escorted to someplace nearby, then

I want some of our guys to greet Dr. Simpson as he exits the plane and get him chatting. You let me know what the plan is when it's all set, sugar."

Candy leaned back in her chair. "Everything I've heard makes him sound just as nasty and just as crazy as a rabid dog, but I don't think we can do an Ol' Yeller on him. Much as that would solve a lot of problems." She closed her eyes and let out a long breath. "Lord above, Teke, the sun is barely up and I already feel like I've been shot at and missed and shit at and hit, if you'll pardon the expression." She paused. "You know Tess Beauchamp. What is she capable of?"

"She's smart. I mean street smart, and tough enough, for an academic. What do you need her to do?"

"I don't know yet. I think the first thing should be to get that array off line somehow. With that off the table—"

"That's a lot," Teke said, interrupting her. "It couldn't be done surreptitiously or probably even attempted without their full cooperation. I'd guarantee there are fail-safes and trapdoors built into the system architecture precisely as safeguards against accidental or deliberate attempts to pull it down. If Simpson is as nuts as people think he is, he'll have put logic bombs into the software. Those things are damned hard to find before they trigger, which makes them a narcissist's weapon of choice. They can be set to execute if an action *isn't* taken at a certain time or under certain circumstances, or if a certain action *is* taken. It's like laying mines in cyberspace. You only know you've found one when—"

She opened her eyes and looked at him. "Please don't give me any gory minefield visuals, Teke. I've got enough bad images in my head this morning." She paused. "I get what you're saying about the narcissism, but it just doesn't sound like he'd do anything destructive to the system. I get the impression that he'd sacrifice the planet before the software."

Teke raised his eyebrows. "You think he's *that* crazy?"

"I haven't heard anything to make me think he's sane."

A tense but companionable silence grew.

"When do you meet with the president?" he asked.

"Soon."

"What are you going to tell her?"

"Damned if I know. I'll think of something on the way."

Tess entered the sandbox and said to no one in particular, "Nik just called me. Is he still in the conference room?"

Lindy nodded. "Hey, Tess, before you go in there, have you seen this footage?"

Tess walked over to her workstation and set down her laptop. "What footage? I haven't logged on yet today."

"There was a hurricane in the Mediterranean overnight."

"In the Mediterranean?" Tess leaned over Lindy's shoulder to watch the streaming video. The devastation was extensive and heartrending. She felt her stomach drop. "Did we do that?"

Lindy glanced up at her. "What do you think?"

Tess shook her head, then straightened up and walked to the conference room. Ron opened the door when she knocked. The expression on his face wasn't a good one.

"What's wrong?" She stepped into the room and immediately closed the door behind her.

"Ron just found more commands in the queue that don't mesh with the mission. We don't know what the hell they are or what they'll do, and we're still locked out." Nik stood up roughly and the chair he was in skittered backward. "Fuck this. We have to hack the array control system."

"Oh, pipe down. Can't you even say 'good morning'?" Tess snapped, setting her laptop on the table and booting it up. "We haven't been able to hack the comms system, and the control system is way more dense." She looked at Ron. "What is everyone out there supposed to be doing other than watching what we did to the Mediterranean last night?"

"That's another fucking mess," Nik muttered.

Before anyone could comment, there was a short tap on the door, then it opened. Pam stuck her head in. "Got a minute?"

"Lots of 'em. What do you have?" Ron replied.

"Bad news."

"Come on in," Nik said, leaning back in his chair. "This is Bad News Central."

She came through the door and leaned her slight frame against it, then gave a nervous laugh. "You're not going to believe this."

"Try me," Tess suggested.

"I've never done this to myself before, but I was just reviewing the activity log to remind myself of all the things I've tried in terms of trying to get the arrays back under our control. I noticed that every time I entered something, small lines of that goofy 'Greg code' appeared in the log." She looked at each one of them.

"The array control system has become heuristic. For every thing any of us do, there's a change made in the system by Greg's code. And it's all encrypted. It looks like the same thing has been happening in the comms code."

"Holy shit," Nik muttered.

"I'm with you on that," Ron murmured and looked at Tess. "It's your turn."

Tess flashed a look at him, then returned her eyes to Pam's flushed face. "I'm not sure what there is left to say."

"Well, we can't stop what we're doing. It won't help anything. Whatever is in the queue is going to execute. We have to keep hacking at the systems and hope we can break in," Nik said forcefully, watching Tess.

"Agreed." She looked at Pam's kind, worried face. "It's critical to get the communications network bright again."

"But those commands—"

"We still need to find out what the commands in the queue are meant to do, but we can't tell anyone or warn anyone about them until we get the comms up."

Pam nodded and left the room. Tess waited until she was gone, then closed the door.

She looked at Nik. "I want you to check in again with Dan to see if those sensors checked out—"

"What sensors?" Ron asked.

"The ones on the storage tanks. The hydrogen storage tanks," Nik said bluntly. Ron's face paled slightly.

"And I want you to dust off the 'In case of emergency, use 110-year-old technology' radios just in case we need them," Tess finished.

"Don't bother. They won't work," Ron said.

Both Tess and Nik looked at him in surprise. "Why not?"

"Jamming signals." Ron looked from one to the other. "They came on when the comms went down. I thought you knew that."

"No, I didn't. How could I have if no one told me?" Tess demanded.

Ron shrugged. "Sorry."

Tess rolled her eyes and paused briefly to log on to the system with the new passwords Nik had given her. "When the arrays fire, those signals would be obliterated."

"They go off when the arrays fire and come right back on when the arrays go to 'down' mode."

Tess snaked her hands through her hair and tugged viciously at the roots.

"What are you doing?" Nik asked, frowning at her.

"Getting some blood to my brain," she ground out. "Ron, is there anything else you thought we knew and clearly don't?"

"I don't know, Tess."

She stood up, folded her arms tight to her body, and started to pace. "Seems like we have one card left, and it's not an ace. We have to shut down the all-clear signal."

"That won't do a damned thing to help us, Tess. Flint will scramble an extraction team, but we don't need a plane full of guys with guns coming through the door. We need hackers, Tess. Or somebody to meet Greg at the gate in Westchester with a syringe of sodium pentothal."

She stopped pacing to look at him. "Nik, if we don't stop the signal, all we can do is cross our fingers and hope that the governments of the countries we're trashing don't decide that turnabout is fair play."

"Yeah, or keep trying to get into the system and take back control of it," he snapped.

She let out a hard breath and was about to reply when the lights flickered for just a fraction of a second. The three of them stared at one another through a suddenly dense silence. Instantly, Tess unclipped the walkie-talkie at her waist and asked everyone to meet in the dining room. By the time she walked in with the gang from the sandbox behind her, the rest of the staff was waiting for them.

"I don't have a lot of news, and none of it is what I'd call good," she began, giving the assembled group a tight smile. "But you need to know what's going on. In a nutshell, the control system for the arrays has been completely hijacked and a series of commands has been locked in. We don't know what those commands will do, we can't change them, and we can't get access to the system."

She paused and let her blunt words sink in as she looked around at the faces in front of her. They were a pretty stoic bunch, but she could see fear in some of their eyes.

Here goes.

"Some of you know and some of you may not fully know what we do here at TESLA, so I'm going to tell you. We manipulate the weather and induce some geological activity." She paused as she saw the admin staff register varying degrees of surprise, shock, and unease. "We can make things happen, and prevent some things from happening, anywhere in the world. The whole reason this installation came into existence was to use

the weather for benign and beneficial purposes—
mostly to improve Flint's bottom line by sending good
weather to areas where the company has agricultural
interests. That mission was changed. The arrays are
now beyond our control and TESLA is doing things
to punish—" She shrugged, palms up in front of her.
"Flint? The world? We don't quite know. We do know
that our arrays, operating under code embedded by
Greg before he left, are responsible for the big storms
that have happened across America and the Mediterranean, and the earthquake in Mexico."

The expressions on the faces before her now reflected disbelief mingled with dread.

"I want you all to know that I—we—are now operating under the following assumptions: that the outside world has probably realized it's under attack from
our arrays and that there will be a response. I don't
know what kind of response." She ignored the few soft
gasps that followed her words. "I am also assuming
that the people at Flint HQ are working very hard on
our behalf. There may be Flint people on their way to
us already," she added hurriedly as she saw a few pairs
of eyes start to shine with tears.

"We're running diagnostics on the power system to
determine what caused the blip we just experienced.
I'm concerned, but there's no reason to panic. That being said, we must prepare to face our worst-case scenario: a full power failure. I want everyone to review
emergency and survival procedures in case we need to
initiate them."

One of the women toward the back of the small
crowd let out a sob that she quickly stifled.

"I know this is nerve-wracking. I know you have
questions. But I've just given you all the information

I have. You need to stay focused on what *is* happening and don't speculate about what may never happen." Tess paused. "Okay, that's all I have. We'll reconvene at noon for an update. If you need me before then, I'll be in C4. Thanks." Tess turned to Nik and Ron. "Let's go."

CHAPTER

The installation became a small, buzzing hive feeding off its own fury at Greg's betrayal and everyone's fear of the possibilities. Then, shortly after Tess concluded her talk, the arrays re-awakened and sent out their first set of simultaneous bursts. The pulses they emitted caused the atmosphere to bend and writhe with energy it could barely contain. And when it stopped, chaos erupted around the globe.

Lightning strikes were not uncommon in the vast, wet highlands of Roraima, the northernmost and least populated state in Brazil. The region was home to little more than dense tropical rain forest; the strikes were of negligible concern to anyone. Heavy, year-round rains generally eliminated most fires before they could pose serious risk.

That morning in late April proved different.

The strikes were abundant and huge, searing the air as they hurtled between earth and sky. The sounds that followed by mere seconds would have made any listener certain that the atmosphere itself was splintering. Each forked sword held tens of thousands degrees of heat; within minutes of the storm's conception, the ever damp floor of the tropical forest was dry enough to combust.

And combust it did. Massive balls of fire erupted as trees exploded, the dense moisture in their tissue converting instantly to steam as the bolts of lightning blasted them with temperatures that existed nowhere on earth other than in the deepest pools of subterranean magma.

Few noticed or cared that the rain forest was burning, sending up billows of heavy black smoke, enough to block out the midday sun, because the eyes of the Americas were turned to places more populated, and more devastated.

It was morning in Los Angeles. The sun was up, and the major arteries snaking through the city and around it were already becoming clogged with cars, trucks, and buses heading in every direction. Although it was a weekend, elevators and escalators across the vast metropolis nevertheless carried workers to their offices in the myriad towers that punctured the skyline at all points of the compass. Beaches were filling with tourists. Malls were coming to life. No one was thinking of the stresses and strains that had been building along the San Andreas Fault since its last really big release just over 150 years ago. The Big One had become little more than a myth to residents and a joke to outsiders.

But when the precarious balance that kept the Pacific and North American plates pressed against each other shifted, no one was laughing.

When the first wave, the compression wave, hit the region, the sound was thunderous and heard by everyone who was outdoors and by most who were not. The transverse waves followed almost immediately, making buildings sway and the ground roll. And roll.

The tallest buildings had no chance of survival; their height overpowered the ability of any stabilizers to counteract the sideways slide of the earth on which they stood. Even bridges built to withstand severe torsion were not built to withstand what hit them that morning. They twisted and buckled like cheap toys, crumbling onto the pancaking layers of roadways below. Planes roaring along the runways of the area's many airports lurched into drunken skids as the tarmac moved beneath them. Others flipped as brand-new gaps in the pavement caught their landing gear. People stampeded out of buildings only to become unwitting targets for the rubble that fell from shattered buildings and billboards and utility poles.

The shaking went on for what seemed like a small eternity, while across the world other horrors awaited other peoples as one of the planet's most complex and extensive tectonic plate margins began to roar.

Along the Makran coast of Pakistan and Iran, underneath the northern Arabian Sea, continental plates began to rub against each other. It only took a nudge to the huge transform fault that bordered the world's largest accretionary prism to set them in motion. Waves of intense energy moved easily through the deep, thick layers of sediment, rocking the seafloor and the land and the cities that bordered that sea, and giving birth to a giant wave.

Along the entire coast, residents had settled into their late evening routines. No one was prepared for the unspeakable havoc that erupted when the shifting earth pushed the massive wall of water toward land. The wave rushed the steep continental shelf with a speed that left those who saw it awestruck in their final moments. The sea-born monster rose above the cities and broke, slamming buildings to the ground, snapping the hulls of thousands of docked ships waiting to be loaded with the region's liquid black gold. Water inundated huge petroleum tank farms and luxury high-rises, washing away the dreams and lives of countless souls, sucking every remnant of their existence into its dark depths.

Farther out, the earth's motion awakened long-dormant hot spots and ignited substances locked away by Nature for millennia. Fire shot skyward from the waves and lit the night as submarine mud volcanoes erupted with a violence reserved for apocalyptic legends. Newly released plumes of methane and other gases shook the very air with their explosions and sent flames to towering heights.

Aftershocks continued to rock the region and the complicated shifting of the underwater landscape triggered submarine landslides that, in turn, created tsunamis that raced in all directions.

As the seafloor beneath them heaved and shifted, drilling platforms collapsed, their spindly open towers swaying in dizzy arcs before falling artlessly through the air. With screams of tortured steel, the mighty superstructures were torn apart and crashed into water already patchy with thick, growing islands of heavy crude.

* * *

Along the northern coast of Western Australia, a sky that was clear and shining one minute shivered in the next and conjured a massive cyclone that roared onto the unsuspecting populace like a wild dog. Residents of the territory fled the onslaught of water and wind, seeking futile sanctuary indoors. Its winds as dangerous as razor-sharp teeth, the storm set its grip on the sleepy coastal cities and shook them until their fight was gone.

Rain poured from the sky as though from a faucet. Winds circled and slashed and shrieked with Hell's own fury. The white sands of the incomparable Cable Beach were sucked away as waves assaulted the shore, stealing whatever they chose. Rising flood waters swallowed coastal cities and towns. Farther inland, sewers and natural waterways alike filled beyond their capacity and spilled over, wreaking their own havoc.

Things not securely anchored to the earth—cars, palm trees, foolhardy humans—became unwitting missiles thrust along erratic trajectories. And when the storm passed, almost as quickly as it had come, survivors emerged, dazed and shocked, and wondering what unholy nightmare had befallen them.

CHAPTER

"O kay, I feel like I'm playing a game of Risk. Or chess," Nik muttered, breaking the tense silence in the sandbox.

They were the first words—make that the first non-profane words—that Tess had heard him say in hours. Since the blip early that morning, he'd been either cursing under his breath or roaring invective while staring at computer monitors and tapping at keyboards. Tess wasn't much for swearing, but she was tempted. She hadn't come all the way to Antarctica to spend her time hacking her way into a cache of definitions for a whole bunch of gibberish commands that would be deadly once they executed.

The last set of bursts from the array had made everyone in the control center go pale. The power emitted was beyond awesome and the lights that had appeared all around them in the sky were psychedelic—and terrifying.

But what truly frightened the Teslans was watching their power flicker again.

Tess had immediately gotten on her walkie-talkie to reassure the staff that there was no damage to the installation. It was the truth. What she didn't broadcast was that the diagnostics revealed that the flickers were just deliberate scale-downs in power output: pranks placed in the code courtesy of Greg. She couldn't discern any purpose behind them other than to instill fear.

Now, though hours had passed, the room still hummed with tension. Someone had finally turned off the streaming video link to the news shows after the images of the latest round of catastrophes were shown—and burned into their brains.

Banter was no longer tolerated by anyone. Instead, the air in the control room was filled with the clatter of keystrokes as the scientists and software developers worked side by side to wrest system dominance from Greg. Each of the would-be hackers had taken a different line of attack as they tried to get into the core systems, but although everyone was eager to crack Greg's code, they'd come to realize that blunt force would only cause more trouble. Every keystroke had to be considered. A premature power grab would be foolhardy—they had no way of knowing what security traps were embedded in the software, or what they might do. It was like trying to navigate a minefield. Blindfolded.

Tess broke the silence with an "Oh boy," and abruptly sat back in her chair as she stared wide-eyed at her screen.

Ron swiveled to face her. Nik stood up and walked the few steps to where she was working. "What?"

Tess glanced up at them, then pointed to the screen. "Anyone secretly entertaining doubts about whether

Greg is a genocidal maniac can stop now," she said, her voice shaky. "That's the command queue. And if what you all figured out about the system timing for the array is right, then that line of code"—she tapped the screen—"is going to execute not several hours from now—local time—as it appears. It's going to happen much sooner and it's going to be big. Really, really big."

Both men leaned over her shoulders and squinted at the screen.

"What is that?" Ron asked.

Tess looked up at him. "I don't know exactly, but the bursts are sequential. Just like last time, there are four command sequences all timed to execute nearly simultaneously, then there are four more set to happen x time after that. I haven't figured out what x is yet, but the timing is, again, nearly simultaneous. Step back, fellas. I need some air." She stood up and wrapped her arms tightly around her waist in a move that was both protective and designed to press against the stabbing pains in her stomach. "The geographical coordinates just reshuffled again, too. We'll have to figure out the methodology of the new notations. You know, is north south now, or is it east or west? If we can't figure it out ahead of time, we'll have to piece it together as things start to happen."

"What things?" Lindy asked. She was sitting at the workstation next to Tess, and had abandoned her task to watch them. As had everyone else in the room.

"I don't know. Big things. And they're going to go off like a string of firecrackers." Tess managed to give her a weak smile. "Something tells me he isn't sending sunshine where they want rain."

"We have no idea where it's going to happen?" Etienne asked.

She looked at him and shook her head slowly, feeling the situation weigh upon her so heavily that she had to fight the urge to sag to the floor. "No, but based on the range of coordinates at first glance, it looks like . . . everywhere," she said, her voice gone quiet. "The best I can figure it is that if you take the equator, the International Date Line, and the Greenwich meridian, you effectively divide the globe into four segments. The last set seemed to include one event in each quadrant. It looks like that's going to repeat. He's into equal-opportunity destruction."

"Well, that narrows it down. I think I need coffee," Ron said somewhat weakly as he stood up. "With a splash of cyanide."

"Hey, none of that," Tess said, brushing the air between them with her hand. Then she sighed. "I'll join you. I need a momentary change of scenery."

They left the sandbox together and hadn't gone but a few feet when Fizz Reilly came charging up the stairs and stopped in front of them.

"The radios aren't working," she said, slightly out of breath. "The walkie-talkies."

"What do you mean they're not working?" Ron interrupted, sliding the small device at his hip out of its belt clip and fiddling with the buttons. Tess checked her own. The power lights on all of their units were lit, but the units were making no sound. Not even static.

"I mean that none of them work," Fizz snapped. "They were fine five minutes ago, and then nothing. All channels are down."

Tess stared at her, wondering if she were hearing Fizz correctly. "But we secured that system."

As the three of them stood there, the units crackled back to life.

"Well, look at that—," she began, and stopped when she saw both Ron and Fizz slowly raise their heads to look at her. Ron looked grave, Fizz a little alarmed.

"Well, they work now." Tess smiled uncertainly. "It was just another blip. I'm sure it's just like the other ones. Nothing to worry about."

Fizz cocked her head at Tess and then moved it from side to side slowly. "We don't have blips here, Tess. Ever. You may not be concerned over those power blips, but everyone else is freaked out. And now the local communication is flickering in and out of life?" She took a breath. "I don't know what goes on in there"— she pointed to the sandbox door—"but I know how the rest of this place operates. There are backups for everything, and backups for the backups. Our local communication network is a critical system. It doesn't just go down for no reason."

"I understand that, but it's electronics, Fizz," she replied tiredly.

"No, Tess, Fizz is right," Ron interrupted. "These radios are on an independent, local system, not connected to anything else. Just like the power system."

"If it's independent, why are you looking so grim?" Tess asked, a little bewildered.

"Because Greg's letting us know he's tunneled his code into everything, Tess. He's letting us know that nothing is safe. With another set of crazy-ass commands ready to execute, we need to double down and find a solution," Ron said.

It might have felt like the middle of the night, but it was only the middle of the afternoon. Teke Curtis stood near the large conference table in the Situation Room, hands at his sides, looking around idly and wishing like hell he didn't have to be here.

"Penny for your thoughts, big guy."

He swung his head at the deep voice so close to his ear and grinned at sight of Mike Rowan, fellow career naval officer and frequent partner in crime.

"How's it going?" Teke said as they shook hands.

"I'm still living the dream," Mike replied, quickly surveying the room. "Where's your girlfriend?"

Teke frowned. "What?"

"The blonde."

"You mean Candy Freeman, the national security advisor?" Teke asked drily.

"Is that who she is? I thought she was a tour guide," Mike said absently, and Teke stifled a laugh at his deliberate blandness.

"She's over there, but I wouldn't let her hear you say that. In fact, you might be better off if she doesn't see you."

"Shit. Too late. I pinched her on the ass as I walked in," Mike replied. "So where's Hormann? He's coming, isn't he?"

"Should be here any minute."

"So we're here to cover your ass, right? Is it a speaking role or just a walk-on?"

"We'll see how it goes."

"Hey, kids."

Both men looked over their shoulder to see the man they were waiting for.

"Hey, Chris."

"Mike, Teke." The taller man gave Mike a cursory glance. "Did you get a bad haircut, or did you give up growing hair for Lent?"

"Gosh, what a deadly sense of humor, Chris," Mike replied, then stopped and squinted at the other man's uniform. "What's that?"

"What?" Chris asked, looking down at his chest.

"No, on your collar. Oh, it's only *two* stars," Mike said, but before the other man could respond, Candy Freeman walked over. Mike said hello to her, then strolled to the other side of the room, leaving Teke fighting a smile and Chris simmering.

"So the gang's all here," Candy said, nodding at Chris. "What are you up to?"

She'd changed her clothes before they left her office at Bolling, and was now wearing an uncharacteristically sober business suit. Teke knew that when the Queen of the Technicolor Wardrobe wore black, it wasn't a good sign.

"What else would I be doing except contemplating life and its many wonders?" he replied easily.

The president entered, followed by at least two Cabinet members, several security advisors, and a few assistants. President Hernandez glanced at Teke, nodded at Candy, and continued across the room to take a seat at her desk. Candy, Teke, and the president's entourage settled into the comfortable chairs arranged around the table.

"Candy, I believe you have some information on the situation developing at TESLA," President Hernandez said.

"Thank you, Ms. President. We've confirmed that the storms in Connecticut, Park City, Central California, and the Mediterranean were triggered by the TESLA installation," she said calmly, "as were the earthquakes in Mexico and Los Angeles. We're continuing to investigate other significant events that have happened in the last thirty-six hours. Gianni Barone, an executive from Flint, is cooperating with us and he's confident that the installation has gone rogue. He believes that TESLA is not under the control of the personnel on site but is being controlled by Greg Simpson. Simpson is currently en route to Annapolis Naval Air Station on a corporate jet that's being escorted by two F-18 Super Hornets. He'll be met by FBI and CIA personnel when he lands and brought to the District for questioning."

"Will that stop the madness?" the president asked drily.

"That depends on what, if any, information he provides, ma'am. We anticipate that the atmospheric and terrestrial havoc will continue."

"For how long?"

"We don't know."

"What is Flint doing to regain control of the situation?"

"They're trying to re-establish communications with TESLA and determine how to disable the arrays. There isn't much more they *can* do."

Teke watched as the president leaned back in her chair and looked at Candy with an expression that was well on its way to becoming legendary. Piercing, cool, and unwavering, Helena Hernandez's gaze could bore through titanium.

"What can *we* do?" she asked bluntly. "Could something be done to make a catastrophic equipment failure look like an accident?"

"Ms. President, if you don't mind, I'll let Admiral Curtis field that question."

"Go ahead, Admiral Curtis."

"We could destroy the arrays, but I would strongly

caution against that, ma'am. The risks to the personnel are too high. The entire installation is just a few hundred acres, and the arrays are close to the habitat. If the life support systems are damaged, they're in serious trouble. They have nowhere to go."

"What are our options? Can the arrays be taken off line?"

"Ma'am, if that were possible, I imagine it would already have been done."

The president kept her gaze fastened on him. Her voice was very calm. "I'm not referring just to powering down the installation. I'm asking about taking it *off line*. Remotely, if necessary."

The room was silent for a long minute as Teke stared at the president's serious, unwavering expression.

Holy shit.

Teke kept his gaze trained on the small woman at the head of the big table. Anyone tough enough to be born in the shallows of Miami Beach to a mother who'd just waded ashore from a boat with nothing but rags on her back, and rise up to be sworn into the Oval Office sixty years later could probably face down anyone and win. Even a psycho scientist named Greg Simpson.

"If you're asking whether we could destroy the arrays, ma'am, the answer is yes. Using fighters or bombers at this time of the year is out of the question. There are no staging locations and the weather conditions are too risky. But remotely, via satellite?" Teke shrugged. "Sure. It would take a while to get an armed bird into the correct position and orbit, but we could zap TESLA with some electromagnetic pulses that would incapacitate it. Snap, crackle, pop. Or we could take the big bang approach and launch missiles from one of our subs, but, likewise, it would take some time to get them into position. Both options put the people at TESLA in jeopardy."

"How much time would it take to get a satellite or sub into position?" the president asked, ignoring his last statement.

"We could have an armed satellite in position within five hours, ma'am. We have an attack sub, the USS *Texas*, in the region transiting from Perth. It carries both conventional and nuclear Tomahawks," Teke replied, hoping the big *n* word would make her change course. "However, we can't use conventional weapons. Their maximum range is six hundred miles with a top speed of five hundred fifty miles per hour and the TESLA base is one thousand miles inland. The nuclear Tomahawks have a longer range, about fourteen hundred miles. Based on how close we can get the sub to the coast due to the buildup of winter sea ice, the flight time would be approximately three hours from launch to target. I can have my staff draft scenarios and run estimates on the collateral damage to the environment and to the installation—"

"Don't forget about the Tridents, Teke."

Teke looked over his shoulder at Chris Hormann.

"Thank you, Admiral Hormann," Teke replied curtly. "A Trident missile would be an option, ma'am. It's a submarine-launched ballistic missile with multiple nuclear warheads. It has a range of seventy-five hundred miles with a top speed of eighteen thousand miles per hour. We have an Ohio-class sub carrying D-5s on deterrent patrol in the Indian Ocean south of Diego Garcia, which puts it well within range. Once launched, a modified low trajectory D-5 launch could be on target from the southern Indian Ocean in under ten minutes, ma'am."

The president frowned at him. "Let's keep nuclear missiles off the table for the moment, Admiral Curtis. The environmental fallout—no pun intended—would be extreme and we have international treaties to uphold. I'd prefer to do it without fireworks if we can help it. The media coverage—images on Google Earth—"

"With all due respect, ma'am, the environmental fallout would be less than you might imagine," Chris interjected smoothly.

Teke controlled his surprise as he looked at his colleague and friend. *You want to nuke Antarctica?*

Chris sent the president a reassuring smile. "We could send in a D-5, set up an airburst at ten thousand feet. It would take out the troublemakers, melt some ice—maybe down to bedrock, maybe not—but that would be about the extent of it. Even with the high winds. You see, ma'am, when you nuke a city, all kinds of things become irradiated: metal, concrete, dirt, living tissue. But you can't irradiate oxygen and hydrogen atoms, which is all water is. Even in a nuclear reactor, it's not the water that gets tainted; it's the stuff *in* the water—particulates and whatnot—that get irradiated. Antarctic ice is pretty pure, so if you melt it and blow a few icebergs worth of the resulting water vapor into the air and it gets carried a few hundred miles, it's not the same as if it were tons of irradiated and airborne dust from an urban blast. There's just not much to contaminate down there, ma'am. I think it's a viable solution."

"Thank you." The president looked at the room's other occupants. "Other options?"

"I'm not so sure about the nuclear option, Ms. President," said a familiar, laid-back voice and Teke jerked his head around to see Mike Rowan leaning forward at the table, hands folded in front of him. "I suggest considering a HALO drop."

The president looked at him. "Who are you?"

"Admiral Michael Rowan, ma'am. HALO stands for High-Altitude, Low Opening, Ms. President. It involves dropping a Spec Ops team into the installation. We send a Delta Force team over there on the Peregrine Hypersonic Transport. We drop 'em above TESLA at 20,000 feet. Takes 'em two or three minutes to land. One bounce and in they go, assess the situation, do whatever they have to do"—Mike shrugged—"blow up the arrays, extract the people, stay for lunch, whatever.

"Meanwhile, we scramble a support team to McMurdo. Once the Spec Ops team has the area secure, the support team comes in on a C-17 and evacs everyone to McMurdo and then to Christchurch. They'd be having a pint of Speight's in some pub about twenty-four hours from now."

The room stayed ominously silent and after a minute, the president looked at Teke. "What do you recommend, Admiral Curtis?"

Teke hadn't felt such stabbing pain in his gut since his appendix burst, but he ignored the feeling and met the president's eyes. "I prefer to use human assets whenever possible rather than a nuclear missile, ma'am. While the nuke would present a faster solution, I think it would be overkill. I have a team in Christchurch on alert since early this morning. It could be deployed to McMurdo now." He paused. "It's risky, but the HALO drop has merit, ma'am."

The president nodded once, then looked at Candy.

"Put together a plan. Whatever you need," she said simply, signaling that the meeting was over.

The room began to empty. Once in the wide corridor outside the room, Candy, Teke, and Chris Hormann stopped and waited for Mike Rowan, who ambled toward them with a grin.

"Score," he said under his breath as he reached them and then, in a trademark move, he lifted two fingers to his lips; took a deep, triumphant drag from an imaginary cigarette; and blew a long, satisfied breath toward the ceiling. Teke smothered his laugh with a cough.

"A HALO drop?" Chris said quietly. "Why the hell would you push for that, Rowan? It's homicide."

"What's the problem? Those guys are trained for it. They *live* for the chance to do something like this. Why not make everybody happy?" Mike replied. "Besides, it's a better option than disappearing the South Pole. I mean, for one thing, there's no playbook for it; nuking the polar ice cap was never a scenario that came up in the war games at Newport, Hormann. The penguin threat scenario just never seemed credible."

"How about we call it a draw, fellas?" Candy Freeman turned to Chris Hormann. "Weren't you a pilot?"

"Yes, ma'am," he said.

She turned to Mike Rowan. "And you were on subs?"

"Yes, ma'am. Seventeen years."

She turned back to Chris. "Then what were you doing pushing a sub-based intervention and what was he doing talking about air drops?"

"They always try to beat each other at their own game," Teke answered.

Candy looked at him for a moment, then shook her head. "Whatever floats y'all's boat," she said, then shifted her gaze back to Chris Hormann. "I hope you were right about all that 'can't irradiate water' stuff, because it might come down to that. And this is no time for a pissing match."

In Dallas, April is one of the months the locals look forward to. There's a tingle in the early-morning air, and by afternoon the weather is nice enough to leave the windbreakers and sweatshirts at home and break out the new flip-flops and T-shirts.

No one, tourist or local, complained when the afternoon temperatures on Saturday started to rise beyond what the weather guys had foretold. Texans like their heat, and it was a great start to a perfect spring weekend.

The next morning, though, people started to murmur about too much of a good thing. Overnight the temperatures had continued to climb and when dawn arrived the plants were dry of dew and the residents were damp with sweat. The rain that had been predicted never appeared. The wind that always blew a steady stream from the west had disappeared, leaving the air still and hot. Temperatures continued to rise.

By the time church bells had started ringing on Sunday morning, the mercury was past one hundred. Pastors watched their flocks wilt in the pews and shortened their sermons. Coaches across the area lost count of the players who were passing out on the field. Outdoor activities and events were cut short across the region as both the faithful and the profane wondered what the Good Lord was up to.

Seeking relief from the dead heat that had settled

on the day like a woolen fog, people stayed indoors in droves, closing drapes and blinds and turning on the air conditioners. The sudden, unanticipated surge in power consumption crashed the electrical grid for the entire Metroplex; windows were once again flung open as residents sweltered in their stifling homes. Frazzled parents gave up the fight to keep their fractious children out of cold, dirty backyard swimming pools not yet cleaned and shocked for summer. Farmers watched their nascent crops wither in the blistering sun, the morning's irrigation having proved to be a pointless exercise.

People seeking cool destinations fared no better than those who stayed home. Every nearby lake was abuzz with boaters and JetSkiers seeking relief from the heat while shallow waters near the sandy, man-made shorelines were dense with bodies. Lines of stopped vehicles, their hoods up, their bellies steaming, queued along the sides of roads in all directions as their owners fretted under an unrelenting sun. The brave and the foolhardy among them left the dubious protection of their cars in search of shade and shelter. They walked toward uncertain refuge with slower and slower steps, stumbling along asphalt highways striped with tar softened by layers of dizzy, shimmering air.

As the day went on, not the merest wisp of a cloud marred the traitorous, celestial blue sky, and the sun turned lethal as it continued to heat the land and the people on it.

CHAPTER

Tess entered the conference room with Nik close behind. She whirled to face him as he shut the door.

"Okay, look. I feel like I'm at the top of a really tall roller coaster that's poised for a dive. It's a sensation I've never liked," she began with no preamble, her voice grim and a little rough. "We're watching the world fall apart. We can't stop it and we're no closer to determining what's next in store. The blips have put everyone on edge and tempers are starting to fray, including my own, and emotions are starting to run high. Kendra is passing out anti-anxiety meds like they're candy. Despite all that, what I need to do right now is assess our security." She looked at him. He looked as exhausted as she felt. "We've been off line for more than forty-eight hours, during which time we have assaulted countries all over the world with extreme weather and other unnatural disasters. Let's you and me talk about retaliation in real terms and in real time."

"Tess, by this time, Flint, if not the U.S. government, has figured out that something is seriously wrong down here."

"Yeah, I get that, Nik," she snapped. "But you don't turn a polar station dark and not send up the emergency flares, which I wanted to do but I let you persuade me otherwise. My decision. I accept that. But now we have to consider what they *don't* know, which is whether we've been taken over by terrorists, whether we're all in cahoots with Greg, or even whether any of us are still alive. They have no idea what we're doing down here except messing up the entire world, and we have no way to let them know that we're trying to make it stop."

"Tess, you said we had to brace ourselves," he said, making an obvious effort to keep his voice calm. "Maybe we have to take it to the next level. Code, I don't know, Red. All Systems Go. Send up the flares, stop the pinging. Whatever."

"We're past that stage, Nik. I don't think anyone will care that we've stopped the pinging." She paused. "I'm thinking the odds are way too high that we're going to be on the receiving end of a military intervention by U.S. forces or someone else's if that next set of commands executes." She paused again. "My God, Nik, just looking at the code makes me sick. The sheer magnitude—"

"There's not going to be a military intervention," he said flatly. "There are no troops for thousands of miles. They can't drop a bomb on us. It's Antarctica. There are treaties—"

"Why couldn't they? Think about what Greg's done," Tess said, feeling her anger start to bubble over. "He—make that *we*—have caused huge earthquakes. Catastrophic storms. Wildfires. Tsunamis. At least one cyclone and dozens of floods. And then there are the spin-off events, and all that death and destruction." She took a deep breath, then continued more calmly. "Why wouldn't the countries where this stuff is happening consider those to be acts of war? They know we're doing it."

"They also know we're civilians."

"So is the Taliban. And Al-Qaeda," she snapped.

"Thanks for the comparison," he shot back. "Think about it, Tess: they'd go for the arrays before they'd go for the installation."

"Is that supposed to make me feel better? How could they take out the arrays without killing us? They surround us on three sides and they're only a football field away. Greg was an ass to build them so close to the habitat in the first place," she hissed. "He had to have the exterior walls lined with lead, for heaven's sake."

"On the bright side, that will help absorb any blast."

"Stop being such a smart-ass, Nik. What if whatever they drop on us lands on the runway? Or the wind turbines? Then what? I go from being the new boss to collateral damage in two days?" she demanded.

"Clearly," Nik snapped. "But they wouldn't blow anything up, they'd disable it."

"Great. With what? A death ray I don't know about?" Tess threw her hands into the air and let out a hard breath. "Look, the point I'm trying to make is that I don't want them to do anything to us or to the arrays. Ugh." She pushed her hands through her hair.

"Okay, let's assume that they know that Greg was acting alone—"

"That's a leap, Nik. Besides, I don't think anyone cares at this point whether Greg acted alone. All that matters is what TESLA is doing," she pointed out, then closed her eyes for a moment and took a few deep breaths before opening them. "Okay, rant over. We both need to get back out there. The only logical thing to do is to keep on hammering away at the code and hope that we're not condemning the entire world to a premature death." She walked to the door and, her hand resting on the door handle, turned to him. "And Nik, stop the pinging."

"You just said it was pointless."

"I know. But at this stage, letting them know we're alive and in trouble might be our only means of saving ourselves."

She opened the door and re-entered the sandbox.

Greg had spent the last few hours of the flight asleep. He roused himself only when the flight attendant awakened him with the news that they were on the final approach for landing and his seat needed to be upright. He stretched, then raised the window shade—and caught his breath at the sight of a military jet flying parallel to them. Glancing down, he realized the scenery below them was all wrong. They were over open water and the land in sight was neither Long Island nor Connecticut. He looked over at Fred, who was watching him with a cold smile.

"What is that jet doing out there? Where are we?" Greg demanded.

"There are two of them, actually. They began escorting us about forty-five minutes ago, and at the moment, we're over the Atlantic," Fred replied.

"That's not Long Island down there," Greg spat.

"No, it's not. It's either Delaware or Maryland's Eastern Shore. Depends on exactly where we are.

There was a change in the flight plan. Some people in Washington want to talk to you."

Greg, who'd never before encountered true fear, felt everything in his body go still. "I have immunity."

"Really?" Fred asked without much apparent interest. "Then maybe when the FBI and CIA agents take you off the plane, they're just going to turn you over to one of the other countries you've destroyed. There are enough of them, some less civilized than others when it comes to matters of law enforcement. Saudi Arabia and Iran, for instance. If nothing else, you'd be assured a speedy trial. Probably followed by a public decapitation or hanging." Fred shrugged. "As my eleven-year-old is fond of saying, right now it sucks being you."

He's bluffing. "They can't turn me over to anyone."

"Of course they can. You're the only suspect for a whole catalog of crimes against humanity."

Greg felt his composure begin to slip. "Are you coming with me?"

Fred's smile widened. "You look scared, Greg."

"*Are you coming with me?*"

"Why would I?"

"You're my lawyer."

"No, I'm not. I'm Flint's lawyer. If I go anywhere with you, it would only be to make sure you don't incriminate Flint."

"Croyden—"

Fred's smile faded, replaced by a cold hardness that turned his face into a mask. "Croyden is dead. His car was trapped in the avalanche in Park City. He and his whole family were killed, thanks to you. Which is the real reason I can't be a spectator at your grilling by the feds. I need to be in Connecticut as part of the transition team. I might be able to spare someone to come down here a little later in the week."

The sensation of dampness was making itself known beneath his clothes, and Greg felt his face grow warm. He pushed back against the encroaching fear and surreptitiously slid his palms along the thighs of his trousers. "They have nothing on me."

"Even if that's true, which I doubt, be assured that very soon they'll have everything that Flint can possibly provide them, Greg. The company will cooperate fully. In fact, Gianni has been working with them since the storm hit Greenwich. There may even be a team of feds on their way to TESLA by now."

Greg felt the blood drain from his face and leaned his head against the seat. *It's too soon.*

Fred pointed out the window. "See that smoke in the distance? A freak electrical storm triggered a wildfire in the Shenandoah National Forest two days ago. Being April, it's not quite wildfire season. Took the Park Service by surprise, apparently. It was a hell of a storm, and it's a hell of a fire. There were lots of springtime campers and hikers in those mountains. The body count is already approaching triple digits." Fred looked Greg straight in the eyes. "The worldwide body count is well into the millions and not all precincts have reported in, as they say. Does that matter to you at all?"

Greg said nothing, then simply closed his eyes.

Too soon, he heard the full thrust of the wind screech against the upraised flaps and then, moments later, felt the soft bump of the landing. He opened his eyes and looked out the window. It didn't look like any airport he'd ever seen.

"Welcome to Annapolis Naval Air Station," Fred said coldly.

The plane taxied for only a short time, then came to a stop. Greg noted that the engines were idling, not shutting down.

He watched the flight attendant open the door and drop the steps. Two men in business suits and two women in khakis and windbreakers entered the cabin. One of the women made a beeline for him.

"Dr. Simpson, I'm Special Agent Gray. I'd like you to come with me now, sir," she said.

Greg looked up at her. "And just where would you be taking me?"

"To FBI Headquarters, sir. Please stand up."

Greg was acutely aware that all the people he'd been traveling with—the Flint executives and security teams—had remained seated and were watching him with avid, silent interest. The two flight attendants, the pilot, and the co-pilot were clustered at the front of the plane. Glancing over his shoulder, he saw that the security people were actually grinning. He returned his attention to the agent standing in front of him. "Why are you taking me there, Agent Gray?"

"There are a lot of people who'd like to speak with you, Dr. Simpson. Please stand up."

"I'm due in Connecticut."

"Dr. Simpson, we can do this the easy way or the hard way. I can assure you that going down those aircraft steps is not easy when your hands are cuffed behind your back. Please stand up," the agent said, her voice betraying no frustration.

Reluctantly, Greg stood up and moved toward the doors. From the corner of his eye, he saw his luggage being taken out of the hold. The two men and the other female agent preceded him down the steps; Special Agent Gray followed him. He was escorted to one of three large, black Suburbans parked in a line. All five of them climbed in. He was seated between the two FBI agents in the second row of seats. The two others sat in the front.

No one said anything as the car began to move across the tarmac. As they made a turn onto a road, he saw the Gulfstream taxiing slowly toward the runway.

The silence in the White House Situation Room was dense with tension. Every chair at the long conference table was filled and there were more ribbons and brass in the room than there were left at the Pentagon. It was the third time in two days Candy had been here and the second time in several hours.

Under other circumstances, I might say this is getting old. I wish.

Candy had never minded being center stage but, at this very moment, with the president's famously intense attention focused on her, she would have preferred to be in the wings.

"Have you initiated your plan, Ms. Freeman?" the president asked.

"Yes, ma'am. A Special Operations team has deployed to TESLA aboard a Peregrine Hypersonic Transport aircraft. Admiral Teke Curtis is accompanying them as an advisor. They'll be over the installation in five hours and the team will be dropped from twenty thousand feet. A C-17 specially reinforced for polar emergencies carrying support and medical teams is en route from Christchurch to McMurdo Station. They should be touching down in about two hours and will refuel and deploy to the Amundsen-Scott South Pole base, where they'll remain on alert for immediate deployment to TESLA as needed."

"What's going on at the installation?" the president asked.

Candy let out a slow breath. "It's hard to say. They've been dark for about fifty-five hours. We're attempting to contact them using alternate methods. Greg Simpson is on the ground and in FBI custody here in Washington. We have confirmed that Croyden Flint died in the Park City avalanche. The board of Flint has authorized Gianni Barone to make all of Flint's resources available to us. A Flint plane is en route from Capetown to McMurdo as backup for us."

"The U.S. Navy needs Flint's backup?" the president asked with a cool lift of an eyebrow.

"Technical support, ma'am," Candy replied over snide chuckles from around the table. "The Flint crew knows TESLA: the winds, the runway, the people. We might need that intel."

"Is the array still active?"

"Yes."

"So it could fire again."

"Yes, ma'am. It appears to be firing at six-hour intervals. The intensity has escalated with each event and the only areas not hit so far are Asia and Russia."

"What if it fires when our men are in mid-air?"

A silence grew that Candy knew she had to break. "Depending on the specifics, we could lose some assets," she said, hating the dispassionate, sanitized language that was part of their code.

The president studied the faces around the table. "We can't afford to wait and see what happens. We don't need to speculate about what might happen if

Moscow, Beijing, or Pyongyang gets hit with something." She looked directly at the representative from the Joint Chiefs of Staff. "What are our options? In real time."

"The *Louisiana,* an Ohio-class sub equipped with Trident D-5 nuclear missiles, is on alert, ma'am, and within range. The *Texas* is also within range for its nuclear Tomahawks. Or we can fight fire with fire and blast them with some electromagnetic pulses from one of our satellites. We'll have one in position within an hour."

"What will happen to the people down there?" the president asked, her voice quiet and calm, her face impassive.

"There will be collateral damage with any of the options, ma'am. We can't get around that. The pulse would create the least amount of physical damage, but the results would be no different for the personnel."

In other words, they'll die horribly no matter what.

It seemed to Candy that the unspoken words echoed in the room.

The president's eyes came back to her. "Candy, keep me informed. Let me know when your team—" She stopped for a moment. "We'll hold off for now on exercising the other options. If the situation changes, I'll reconsider."

"Yes, ma'am," Candy replied, getting to her feet as the president did.

Without another word, President Hernandez left the room.

Helena took the stairs back to the Oval Office. She hadn't had a moment to work out in the last few days and was starting to get twitchy. The distance from the Situation Room to her office was as good as ten minutes on a StairMaster, which was better than nothing.

Maribeth was waiting for her.

Helena slid behind her desk. "All set?"

"Yes, ma'am. Secretary Bonner is in the anteroom."

"That was fast."

"He's only just arrived back from the Middle East. He came here directly from Andrews."

"Thanks, Maribeth. Show him in." The president sat back in her chair.

Frederick Bonner strode through the door like the military leader he was, yet he was clearly jet-lagged and clearly annoyed, but keeping the latter in check. "Ms. President," he said as he came to a stop near her desk.

"Hello, Frederick," she said easily. "We need to discuss that Afghanistan report."

His eyebrows rose at her abrupt introduction. "I'm happy to do that, Ms. President. When would you—"

"Now."

"Now?"

"Yes. Is that a problem?" Helena asked.

"Well, I'd like to read it again to refresh my—"

"I really don't think that will be necessary, Frederick. I've read it and I've spoken with some people about it. The consensus is that it's a great piece of fiction."

She watched his face darken with anger. Having dealt with him many times while she was in the House and the Senate, Helena knew that his response was multi-layered. He didn't like being spoken to like that, and especially not by a woman. Even if that woman was his commander in chief.

"It's not fiction, Ms. President. It's a full and accurate accounting of the situation."

"No, it isn't, Frederick. There's no mention of Admiral Medev in it, or Croyden Flint, or TESLA, or Greg Simpson," she replied, sitting forward to lean on her forearms. "That makes it incomplete at best and, as I said, fiction at worst." She paused. "Are you aware that all the trauma happening in the world the last two days has pretty much been triangulated to TESLA?"

"No, ma'am," he said stiffly.

"Then you must be out of the loop," she snapped. "Simpson is in FBI custody, claiming that he has immunity from prosecution, thanks to you. Would you care to explain why he's making that claim?"

The look in the secretary's eyes was priceless. All those years of battle-hardened living hadn't prepared him for seeing his career flash before his eyes at the words of a woman nearly half his size. And that woman was relishing the moment, relishing the mixture of fear, caution, and fury that had settled on Frederick Bonner's craggy, aristocratic face.

"Can I speak with him?"

"No. You can speak with me. Did you offer him some sort of immunity? And, if so, in return for what?" she asked.

"I can't answer those questions right now, Ms. President."

"I didn't think you would, Mr. Bonner," she said, deliberately not using his title. "But here's something you can do for me. Present me with a letter of resignation before my press conference, which is in"—she glanced at her watch—"about forty-five minutes."

His eyes widened and he opened his mouth to speak, but she just shook her head.

"Game over, Frederick," she said. "You serve at the pleasure of the president, and I'm no longer pleased. Under extreme pressure from the party, I nominated you. It was against my better judgment because I didn't trust you. And you have fulfilled my expectations." She paused. "I'd like you to know that your cooperation in the matter of Greg Simpson and TESLA will go a long way to helping me decide whether I direct Justice to include you in the investigation. In the meantime, you have a letter to write."

Five hours had passed since the arrays sent their last pulse into the atmosphere. It had been nearly that long since Tess had asked them to begin making preparations to deal with a worst-case scenario. Everyone in the installation was on edge; the easygoing atmosphere had disappeared. The only conversations that took place were those related to the situation. Most of the inhabitants had retreated into silence since their usual banter, jokes, and smiles did little to relieve the dense, choking tension that filled the air.

"Everyone has scaled back what they can," Fizz Reilly said in a low voice as she and Tess sat alone at a table in the dining room having a quick cup of coffee. "Ewan powered down the kitchen. The gas lines are secured. The knives are locked up. It'll be cold food—salads, sandwiches, and the like—until you say he can power it up again. Kendra is set up for triage. She and Mick have been turning the clinic into an emergency center. They're set up for whatever needs done: surgical supplies, oxygen, the odd straitjacket."

Tess looked at her in surprise and Fizz gave her the ghost of a grin.

"Sorry, gallows humor. The housekeepers and

Mick and I moved a lot of stuff into the growth station. That's the emergency shelter. It's got the water supply and an independent heat supply and it's next to the clinic."

"What did you put there?" Tess asked, having moved past exhaustion into overdrive hours ago.

"Blankets, heat packs, non-perishables, flares. It's near enough to the ready room so I didn't move the ECW gear, but we can bring that into the growth station if you'd prefer."

"We'll hold off until we need to do that. *If* we need to do that," Tess corrected herself.

"Dan tested the emergency backup power and ventilation systems. He tests them weekly anyway, but he did again. They're operational. What else do you want to know?"

Tess met the younger woman's eyes. "How are people holding up?"

Fizz gave her a tight smile. "Most of them are following the 'keep calm and carry on' method of dealing with this. We've had a few hissy fits and some tears, but most are just doing what needs to be done." She paused. "Everyone would feel better if the bloody power blips would stop."

Tess smiled. "It's been an hour or so since we had one. Maybe that was the last."

"It's been two hours, and I'll believe they've ended when a month goes by without one." Fizz put her hand around her mug and stood up. "I'll do another spin through the place to see what's what."

"Call me if you need me," Tess said, getting to her feet.

The women walked together to the corridor, then went in opposite directions.

Tess entered the sandbox quietly. The mood in TESLA's control center had been tense and somber for hours, the hush broken only by the sound of keys being tapped and the occasional profanity muttered under someone's breath. Everyone jumped when Ron slammed his fist onto the desk, shattering everyone's concentration.

He stood up, white-faced and looking faintly sick. Tess glanced at Nik, who rose to his feet.

"What's up?" she asked, feeling her voice break before she got the second syllable out.

"There's only one more in the queue, Tess."

"One what? Series?"

"One more command sequence. One more event. Looks like it might be another earthquake, but I don't know where. I've logged the similarities between this command and the others that I think triggered the quakes, and I think I've got it narrowed down to the southern hemisphere. Timing is soon."

"How soon?"

Ron shrugged and couldn't even fake casualness. The rest of the room had become as silent as a morgue.

"Real soon."

"That fucker." Nik was looking at them and breathing hard through his nose like a bull in a ring. "I'd give a lot to drag Greg's sorry ass in here and make him tell us what he's doing."

"Let it go, Nik," Tess said, her shaky voice betraying that she was barely holding it together. She turned to the rest of the people in the room. "Please, keep going. We have to stop this."

32

Ma'am, Ms. President, please. Please don't give those orders. Our support team is at the Pole. The Special Operations Team is—" Candy had to stop and swallow the rattle in her voice. "They're nearly at the drop zone. Once they go in, everything will be over quickly." Candy stood in the Situation Room, facing the grim woman at the table. The president looked like she'd aged years just in the last few hours.

"Candy, I understand where you're coming from, but this has gone on too long. I can't let it go on any longer. More events triggered since our last meeting. Heavy rains have begun flooding Southeast Asia. A massive earthquake hit near Anchorage, destroying the city and pulling HAARP out of commission. A volcano that's been dormant for decades blew in Peru with no warning, just a big boom followed by tons of ash clouds and lava flows. And since before dawn, temperatures are rising across Scandinavia and eastern Russia, and down into northern Europe just like they have been in Dallas. Above the Arctic Circle, a twenty-eight-degree rise in five hours *in April* is a catastrophe," the president said tightly.

Candy looked down at her hands. *Northern Europe. Glaciers. Tundra. Ice caps. Shit.*

"I've been on the phone so much in the last few hours, being shouted at and threatened, that I feel like a telemarketer. Everyone knows what's going on," the president said, her voice low and strained. "I can't hold back the tempers of the world. Even our staunchest allies believe I'd rather spare the lives of thirty-four U.S. citizens than stop Armageddon. They're threatening to take matters into their own hands—England, Australia, the Saudis, China: they're threatening to use military action against TESLA. And they don't mean troops, Candy, they mean nukes."

The president paused to take a breath and she stared at Candy with a hard look on her face. "Look, between you and me, this sucks, okay? The situation sucks and the decisions I have to make suck. But millions of people have died in the last twenty-four hours and millions more will die from the aftermath. Tens of millions have been left homeless. I can't wait any longer."

"Ms. President, *please*—" For the first time in more than a decade, Candy heard her voice break. "Please let our men do what they're trained for. Please. They're almost there."

The president locked her hot gaze on Candy's eyes; it seared, a trial by fire for her very soul. Then she turned to the man who stood next to Candy. "Admiral Hormann, we need to talk."

Greg sat in the center of the large conference room at FBI headquarters that was serving as his interrogation room. The chair was comfortable, an ergonomic design that rocked and swiveled. The room was a bit bland and filled with equally bland FBI agents and a few CIA interrogators, apparently there just for the entertainment value. They hadn't opened their mouths.

Some of the agents sat at the table, typing furiously into laptops. Others leaned against the walls and stared at him. Their eyes flicked from Greg's face to his hands and back again and, despite their relaxed postures, they were ready to leap at the first hint that he was about to move. Three more sat directly across from him and were doing their highly trained best to intimidate him into telling them what they wanted to hear. Which he had no intention of doing.

"I'm not quite sure why you fail to understand my position, Agent Dobson," Greg said with condescending patience to the lead interrogator. She was a petite woman, blond and green-eyed, with a cheerleader's smile and a Southern accent warm as honey.

But she's a lousy actress.

She'd been through the whole "nice cop" routine, and was now playing the "bored cop" role.

"Oh, I understand it, Dr. Simpson," she said, sitting diagonally from him with her hands folded in front of her on the table. "It's just that we need to move along and get to the part where you admit that you're behind all the tragedies the world has faced in the last few days. We have a nice cell all ready for you in a nearby federal detention center. If you'd rather sit there for a few days before we talk again, I can arrange that."

"I've asked for a lawyer. You haven't gotten me one."

"Well, I don't have to get you one because you're not under arrest. Yet. You're in custody, and you just might want to consider this protective custody because if any other country had gotten its hands on you—and believe me, they all want to—you'd be dog food already," Special Agent Dobson said with a friendly smile. "Now, keep in mind that we can arrange that. That's why our friends over here representing the CIA are present. They're better at those sorts of handovers than we are."

"Agent Dobson," Greg began, "we've been over this ad infinitum. I don't have to speak with you and I don't intend to speak with you. I have immunity and I would ask that you try again to contact Secretary Bonner."

"I know you don't like to be told you've got it all wrong, Dr. Simpson, but you do," she replied. "You're confusing the Fifth Amendment with immunity. You see, if you have immunity, then you're free to speak with us and tell us everything we want to know and you won't be prosecuted for any of it. The Fifth Amendment allows you not to answer our questions if the answers would incriminate you, but if you have immunity, you can't incriminate yourself so you can't take the Fifth. That means if you have immunity, you have to start talking to us. Now."

"Agent Dobson—"

"Actually, it's Special Agent Dobson, Dr. Simpson."

"—thank you for the lesson in constitutional law. I'm delighted that you were paying attention in school that day," he said with a sneer. "But I have no intention of answering any of your questions until you confirm with Secretary Bonner that I have immunity."

One of the male agents seated at the table cleared his throat. "Secretary Bonner," he repeated slowly, looking at the screen of the laptop in front of him.

"Would that be the same Secretary Bonner who's just announced his resignation as Secretary of Defense, according to CNN?"

Greg felt his stomach drop. Every eye in the room turned to him.

"My guess would be that it is," Agent Dobson said with a smile that had cooled considerably. "Maybe that's why his office has been too busy to get back to us about the little matter of your immunity, Dr. Simpson."

"Then try harder," Greg snapped. He could feel sweat begin to gather at his hairline as he glanced at the wall clock. He'd been here for several hours, and he'd witnessed the agents making several attempts to contact Bonner. They'd even let him use his own phone to call him. The call had gone into voice mail and hadn't been returned.

Bonner had never before failed to take Greg's call.

He's throwing me under the bus.

There was a small stirring among the agents working on their computers. They conferred in low voices, then one asked Special Agent Dobson to step outside for a minute. She came back in the room almost immediately and walked straight over to Greg. Her attractive face had changed to reveal a toxic mixture of fury and helplessness. She yanked the chair he was sitting on so that he spun away from the table.

"You son of a bitch," the agent whispered, her voice rough. With no warning, the agent drew back her arm and hit him with a closed fist so hard that everyone in the room heard the snap of his jaw as it broke, heard the crack of his head as it caught the edge of the small table behind him. The force of the blow made the agent take a stumbling step or two forward before she

caught her balance. Then she lunged at Greg. The chair
went over as her hands went around Greg's neck and
she began squeezing. Through a haze of pain from his
broken jaw, Greg began clawing at the vise-like hands
locked around his windpipe.

The reaction of the other agents in the room was
swift but not immediate, and Greg knew then that he
was no high-value asset. They'd let him die, given half
a chance.

His vision was awash with pinpricks of darkness
when the pressure against his throat suddenly abated
and the woman was pulled off him. Greg rolled onto
his side, gasping, awkward within the confines of the
fallen chair. He saw the agent, one arm twisted and
shoved up against her back, being moved away from
him.

"See, that's the trouble with immunity," he heard a
male voice mutter, and seconds later the speaker
moved into his line of sight and stood looking down at
him. "It only helps if someone isn't willing to kill you."

Two other agents moved into his line of sight and
Greg closed his eyes.

"Aw, hell, did he just die?" said the same voice.

"Go ahead and check, if you're that interested."

"I'm not."

"He better not be dead," came another voice. "He's
the only one who knows what's going on."

"Yeah, and he was just about to confess and tell us
how to fix it," the first voice said, dripping with dis-
dain. "How long you been around here, Morrissey?
Bad guys don't do that in real life. He's a psychotic
asshole, okay?"

The voice paused and Greg heard murmurs too
low to be distinguishable, then the harsh voice con-

tinued at a higher pitch of anger. "For Christ's sake, who gives a flying fuck if he has a concussion? Irreversible brain damage would be too good for him."

Greg felt a sharp thrust into his gut as he lay curled on the floor.

"Open your eyes, you pus-filled, motherfucking sack of shit." The shoe jabbed him again, harder. "I said, open your eyes."

Terrified, shaking, his jaw throbbing with white-hot pain, his throat scraped raw, Greg did as he was told.

"That agent who took you down? Dobson? She's from Alaska, where you made an earthquake happen a while ago. She just found out she lost her whole family. Courtesy of you. Asshole."

Greg stared at the men towering over him as he cowered, defenseless, on the floor. More faces moved into his field of view. They were all grim; some were flushed with anger, others were still and cold. The fury radiating from all of them was palpable, like the pulses from one of his arrays. It felt just as lethal.

I'm not going to get out of here alive.

The thought paralyzed him as he lay on the floor, waiting for he didn't know what.

"Oh crap. Oh man, oh man alive," Jonah, the youngest member of the science team, moaned in a voice thick with fear. As if pushed by an unseen hand, the young man fell against the back of his chair, his eyes squeezed shut.

"What?" Nik demanded, not looking away from his own monitor.

Jonah's only answer was another low moan. He was the quietest, most even-tempered person at the installation. It was a shock to see his face sheet white, his eyes huge and swimming with unshed tears.

"We're dead. He's killed us all," he said hoarsely, his voice choked with emotion. "I just figured it out."

Tess had risen at Jonah's first words. Now, she bent to see his screen and asked, "What are you talking about? What did you find?"

"I know what he did. Look. He reconfigured the array software. All of it. For every array." He took in a large, audible breath. "It's beginning to execute now. Every array is moving into position to fire simultaneously. Max power. He's sending one enormous pulse down. *Down,* at max power," the young man finished with a choking sob.

Tess felt a bone-deep chill settle over her as she looked at the code on Jonah's monitor. She looked up at Nik, who was at her elbow.

"Is what he said true?" Nik asked, his voice strangely quiet, yet almost booming in the too-still atmosphere. The sound made the skin on the back of Tess's neck crawl.

"Seems to be," Ron replied, more subdued than Tess had ever seen him.

"When?"

"Now. A few minutes," Jonah blurted in answer to Nik's hushed question. "They've started moving into position."

With hands that were shaking, Tess picked up her walkie-talkie. "I need everyone to the control room *stat.* I don't care what you're doing, get in here *now.*" She set the unit back into the holster clipped to her belt. "What's a few, Jonah?"

"Thirty-five."

Oh man.

She took a deep breath. "Plenty of time," she muttered.

The room had filled in what seemed like seconds. People crowded into every open space.

Tess cleared her throat and took a deep breath. "The situation is critical. We're in imminent danger of sustaining a catastrophic blow," she said bluntly, speaking loudly enough to be heard throughout the whole room. It wasn't difficult; you could have heard a feather drop. "The arrays are moving into a new position." She paused.

"Sorry if this sounds like a science lesson, but you guys need to know the scope of what we're facing. There's a theory about the effect of a specific combination of magnetic fields on the earth's gravity. Looks like Greg thinks he knows what the combination is and has decided to test it today." She took another deep breath. "The theory states that, when combined in the right sequence and magnitude, magnetic fields will momentarily release the earth's gravitational field in a very, very small area. That means for a few nanoseconds, that section of the earth's crust would be in zero gravity and fully vulnerable to the spin of the planet's magnetic core. Every fault line in that region would be able to move freely. And even though the gravitational pull would resume almost immediately, it would be too late; the crustal plates would be in motion."

"But there aren't any faults here, are there?" Fizz said. "This continent—"

"This half of the continent is one big seismic zone," Tess explained. "The ice sheet we're on is miles thick, but underneath all that ice is a large mountain range that's home to a lot of small, live volcanoes."

Fizz jumped as if someone poked her with a pin. "*Volcanoes?* Down *here?*"

Tess nodded, trying to remain patient. "About two and a half miles below us. The weight of the ice sheet keeps them from erupting into the atmosphere, but they have constant lava flows. Small icequakes happen every day down here. The ice sheet that covers the entire continent is moving slowly but steadily outward, toward the coast. The volcanoes aren't actually the biggest problem," she said after a slight pause, trying to keep her voice slow and measured so that the people listening, many with their jaws hanging open, could absorb it.

"The bigger problem," she continued, "is that the weight of all this ice we're sitting on has naturally, over the millennia, pushed the actual continent down. I meant that literally. So, in theory, the instant the gravity disappears, this ice we're living on will fracture, possibly explosively, as the crust rushes up. Then all that volcanism that has never had an outlet will erupt. There will be no way to stop any of it." She took a quick breath and went on.

"That's just the beginning. Earthquakes will trigger across the continent, further fracturing the ice sheet and shifting the pieces. Major ice shelves will break off, flooding every coast in the southern hemisphere and allowing the interior of the sheet to slide unimpeded until it hits the water. Once there, it will break into huge icebergs that will eventually drift into shipping lanes. As they melt natural forces will pull the excess water into the northern hemisphere, causing more flooding and rising sea levels. Meanwhile, the massive influx of freshwater will severely and irreparably compromise the thermohaline convection cycle and the global weather will begin to change." She shook her head, almost as if she couldn't believe what she was saying.

With a soft sigh, one of the housekeepers dropped to the floor in a loose-limbed heap. Kendra, the installation's physician, pushed through the crowd to her side.

"Let's get her straightened out. Somebody get something to elevate her feet." She looked up from the prostrate woman and met Tess's eyes.

"Is this for real?" the doctor demanded.

"Yes," Tess said simply.

"So let's get in the planes and fly out," Kendra demanded. "Let's get moving."

"It wouldn't help, Kendra. When gravity is disrupted, the last place you'd want to be is in the air," Nik said.

"But if we left now—"

"We wouldn't get far enough away," he snapped. "It's not an option, Kendra."

"So we just stay here and die?" Kendra said as she rose to her feet, with fear and fire blazing in her eyes, forgetting her patient, who was moaning slightly.

"No. We won't just sit and wait, Kendra. We need to stop the arrays from powering up, or at least from aggregating their frequencies." Tess looked around at the people in the room and her gaze came to rest on Dan Thornton. "Any ideas?"

"We don't have to worry about powering down, Tess, because the arrays can't be powered up like that. To get the arrays to do what you're talking about, getting all the arrays humming at full power at once, would require a hell of a lot of power and we don't have that kind of dedicated power," he said, arms folded across his chest. "Doing that would drain every fuel cell out there. And you'd need more to boot."

The group had begun to murmur, and Tess knew everyone liked what he'd said, and would believe him over her.

I wish I could believe him.

She frowned at him and held up her hands to quiet the crowd. "Dan, I don't want to contradict you, but the arrays are already powering up. Could they be programmed to pull extra power directly from the wind turbines?"

"Even if we had a Force Ten gale blowing out there, the conversion from the wind turbines wouldn't take place fast enough to provide the kind of juice you're talking about. Besides, have you been outside in the past few hours? There's practically no wind."

"Are you sure? I mean, about the power? Are you *absolutely sure*?"

"Never been more sure of anything."

She looked at Nik, who let the shadow of a smile cross his face, then at Kendra, who looked slightly less pissed off than she had a minute ago. Tess felt the weight of the world slide from her shoulders and she slumped, as she started to laugh. "Dan, I think I love you."

The tension in the room broke, and the sound of soft laughter mingled with pent-up sobs finally released. People held one another in fierce, silent hugs.

Kendra walked the few steps to Tess. "I'm sorry, I—"

"Don't," Tess interrupted her. "You were right to question me."

As she spoke, the lights flickered for nearly a full

minute. The room had fallen silent, except for a round of gasps.

Tess felt her knees begin to shimmy. She looked at Nik and saw true alarm on his face for the first time. Dan had gone pale and was already at a computer, key-stroking savagely. The lights flickered several more times, then blinked off. The emergency lights came on instantly, bathing the room in an eerie blue glow as a dozen alarms started sounding at once: the installation's emergency alarms, the backup power supplies for the computers. The door to the control room slid open and locked in place.

"Dan?" Tess asked shakily. "What's happening?"

"The power supply for the installation has been breached. It's being fed to the arrays," he said, not looking away from the monitor.

Tess felt her brain freeze for a second, as if all activity to the molecular level stopped as her mind absorbed the situation. "That can't happen, Dan. They're discrete systems with a one-way flow. We can pull power from the array power station, but the habitat can't feed power to it," she said, her voice raspy.

Shaking his head, Dan slowly looked up from the screen. "I know that, but it's happening. It's some sort of embedded override."

"Can you stop it?"

Dan held her gaze for a second, then returned his attention to the monitor without answering.

Tess turned to face Nik, who was at her side. "Greg is betting it all, Nik," she whispered hoarsely, trying and failing to keep her own terror in check. "When all that power goes to the arrays, they'll blow up. We'll have no life support. We can't let this happen."

"Tess, we don't have an option," he said softly. "We can't kill the power to the arrays. The system won't let us."

She turned then to the dozens of pale faces, many streaked with tears, that were focused on her with an intensity that was frightening. "Everyone needs to get in their survival gear and move to the growth station."

People who had already started to move toward the door stopped as another voice cut through the room.

"The arrays are starting to power up." Jonah's voice was strangled.

Tess knew the people in the room were stretched to their emotional limit; she was, too. She couldn't blame them for starting to lose it as the mutterings and sobs became higher and angrier. She turned to Nik and was about to speak when she met Dan's eyes—bright, furious, and full of a fighter's challenge.

"I don't know about you, Tess," he said quietly, "but I'm not quite ready to fucking die. I'd rather go out there and take an ax to the feed horn on the arrays or a fucking sledgehammer and kill the power station than sit here whinging until I freeze to death."

Kill the power station.

The room was still crowded but absolutely silent. Tess felt as if she'd been struck by lightning.

Her whole body was trembling, but she made her voice as steady as she could. "Dan, what's the biggest plane you have in the hangar?"

He stared at her in disbelief. "You want to fly out?"

"No. What's the biggest plane?"

"The Dash 7."

"Let's get out to the hangar."

He folded his arms across his wide chest. "What

the fuck are ye on about, Tess? I'm not leaving these people here to take you anywhere."

"I'm not asking you to take me anywhere but to the hangar," she said, her eyes boring into his. "We need to cut the power to the arrays. That's the only thing that will stop what Greg is planning. We can't do it using the computers. One man and an ax isn't, either. That leaves us with one option: we need to go to the source. The fuel cells. I'm going to drive the plane into the power station."

"*What?*" Nik demanded.

"It's the only way," she said. "The building was built to withstand gale force winds, Nik, but not a direct impact."

"Tess, it's suicide," he said, his voice nearly a whisper. "You can't do it."

She bit the inside of her lip hard against the sudden flood of emotion that swamped her. "Staying here and doing nothing is suicide, too, Nik. I have to do this. If I'm not successful, we all die. If I am successful, only I die. It's the only choice."

"No."

"Don't argue with me, Nik. You'll undermine my authority," she said with a shaky laugh through building tears. "I have to do this. The captain goes down with the ship." She turned to Dan. "On the way out to the hangar, you can tell me what to do. I know the power station for the arrays is the low building at the side of the far end of the runway. All you need to do is point me in the right direction and tell me how to hit the accelerator. Then you leave."

Dan, looking a little pale behind his cocky smile, set his gaze on her and shook his head. "There's no fucking way I'm letting *you* drive *my* Dash 7 into a fucking building full of fucking *hydrogen fuel cells.* In me arse, woman. *I'll* do it."

"No, you won't. Don't argue with me, Dan. That's an order."

"There will be a lot of fireworks. They'll see it at McMurdo." He paused. "There's no fucking way I'm missing a show like that."

"It'll be the first time I see fireworks from the inside," Tess said, forcing a tight smile. She turned to Nik and made herself meet his eyes, hating the pain she saw in them.

"I know this is a bad time for what-ifs, but you should have tracked me down in Moscow. I've always wondered what would have happened with us if we had half a chance," she whispered, then cleared her throat and addressed the group. "Ron, I want your guys to try to pull back the power that's being diverted from the installation. This place won't stay comfortable for long without it. The rest of you, get into survival gear. Nik's in charge." She turned to Dan. "Let's go, big guy."

Without another word or backward glance, the two of them left the room.

CHAPTER

Nik was stunned at Tess's decision. He turned back to the silent group and moved toward the desk she'd been using. "Ron, Lindy, let's try to get that power back. If we can't divert the flow, then we'll try to stop it. I don't care how. Etienne, you guys keep throwing everything you can at the arrays. Kendra, you get down there and follow Tess and Dan at a safe distance. Take someone with you. If they survive the crash and the explosion, they're going to need you. Fizz, you and the others go through the habitat and turn off everything that's not critical, even emergency systems. I want to have the lowest possible power load running when we pull this back."

"When?"

Nik turned to Fizz, who wore a vestige of her usual wide smile. "Excuse me?"

"You just said 'when.' I liked hearing that," she said as she turned to leave the room.

* * *

Teke sat in the first front-row seat of the sleek, narrow cabin of the Air Force's newest jet, the Peregrine Hypersonic Transport vehicle. The oddly shaped aircraft was made for exactly this type of mission, to get small, rapid-strike teams into place as fast as humanly possible. It flew higher, farther, and faster than anything else on earth, dropping altitude and speed only when it needed to be refueled in midair or to deliver its human cargo to a drop zone.

In four minutes, the team would begin to tumble out of the plane at 20,000 feet, dropping at a terminal velocity of well over one hundred miles an hour in approximately two minutes before opening their parachutes at 3,500 feet. They'd "hop and pop" their parachutes behind the installation's airplane hangar and cover one hundred yards of ground on foot to storm the habitat. As soon as they secured it, they'd send up a signal flare and a C-17 circling out of radar range would land to pick up whoever was there, friend or foe, dead or alive.

The Peregrine wasn't a quiet plane but it had been a quiet flight; the aircraft flew at such high altitudes that it typically avoided the weather variables conventional airplanes had to deal with. Teke was cautiously optimistic that the notoriously wild Antarctic winter weather would behave itself long enough for the guys to drop. The reports of the weather on the ground were surprisingly positive.

The entire jump team had been on oxygen since they'd reached 5,000 feet, just to ensure that their bodies would be able to handle the dangerous combination of extremely high altitude, rapid changes in air pressure, and temperatures as low as seventy degrees below zero Fahrenheit. The dangers they faced went far beyond the high-speed descent they'd endure. The change in air pressure as they fell could induce severe decompression and a shortage of oxygen could induce hypoxia. Either condition could lead to death if the jumper became disoriented and was unable to perform the rapid sequence of critical tasks that needed to be completed before the chute could be opened.

The aerospace physiology technician, or PT, was moving among the team, checking each person for the slightest indication that they weren't in peak form. The team members themselves checked and rechecked their equipment and reflexes. But despite the importance of their mission, the men sharing the cabin with Teke appeared as unconcerned as if they were a bunch of bureaucrats taking the rush-hour Red Line from Dupont Circle to Bethesda. Then again, taking on the worst, riskiest situations was what these guys trained for and lived for. Teke knew all about it. He'd spent ten years as a SEAL before opting to go political.

These guys usually take out Islamic jihadists who carry shoulder-mounted rocket launchers in their man-purses. Neutralizing a group of unarmed scientists should be a piece of cake.

Teke closed his eyes to get back into the mental zone he needed to be in; a few seconds later, a hand shook his arm and he looked into the face of the PT. She motioned with a jerk of her thumb that he should move toward the bulkhead. He picked up a handset attached to the wall and was patched into communications with the cockpit.

"What's up?" he said.

"We got trouble. Look out the window," said a voice.

Teke craned his head to peer through the small porthole. Stars were brilliant in a sky that was otherwise a dense, inky black. Then he spotted a small, brilliant, white-hot glow slightly ahead and far beneath them. It was shrinking as he watched.

"What is that?" he asked.

"A hydrogen fuel depot a hundred yards away from our drop zone. It just exploded. You'd need night-vision goggles to really see it. The stuff burns practically invisibly."

Teke's stomach dropped. Had they arrived a minute or two earlier, he and his team might have plummeted into the middle of that inferno. "So we're aborting?"

"I'd suggest it, unless you'd like to go down and take a look at Hell from up close. It's your call, admiral."

Smart-ass fly boy. "Can you patch me through to Washington?"

"Actually, sir," came another, only slightly less sarcastic voice, "I have them holding on line two."

Tess climbed up the steps of the plane behind Dan. She followed him into the cockpit, sat in the seat he pointed to, and looked around a little awkwardly. She'd looked into cockpits before, but she'd never actually sat in one or had a pilot's eye view of one. She was surrounded by dials, switches, lights, levers, and screens—at eye level, on the ceiling, on both sides of the seats. There were even banks of them on the walls behind the pilots' seats.

Dan busied himself flipping switches and positioning levers while Tess sat next to him, trying to nerve herself up to do what she had to do. Which was, basically, blow up a building full of explosives while attempting to avoid self-immolation.

Talk about conflicting goals.

The engines came to life and Tess craned her head to look through the side window. The propellers, hanging from the wings, which sat about halfway back along the plane's body, began to spin, first one way, then, it seemed, the other. She knew it was an optical illusion, but it had always fascinated her.

"Eyes forward, Tess. You can't afford to get dizzy or distracted," Dan snapped, and she immediately turned back to the huge dashboard in front of them.

"I wish you'd just tell me what to do," she said for the third or fourth time. "You're not supposed to stick around for the fireworks."

"If you're going to do this, I want you to do it right, lass. It's not like you'll get a second chance," he muttered as the plane began to move forward.

The Dash 7 left the safety of the hangar and lumbered slowly down the mostly windswept blue-ice runway. The sky was spectacularly clear, with hardly any wind. The sparkling canopy of stars above took her breath away.

"When I was little, my mother used to brush glitter through my hair on my birthday," she said, more to herself than to Dan. "I wanted it to look like there were stars in it."

"Oh, for fuck's sake!" Dan exploded, and Tess jumped.

"Don't be going all maudlin on me, Tess. You're the one who wanted to blow yourself to an early fucking heaven," he roared. "I don't want to hear your fucking last confession, either. Stay focused." He took a breath and tried to calm himself, but his voice remained harsh from emotion. "We'll try to get the old girl up to at least a hundred miles an hour. I don't think we'll be able to do more. The path is too fucking short. The hydrogen explodes at a fucking spark, Tess, and makes white-hot light. Don't look; it'll burn your eyeballs to a cinder. It burns at thirty-six hundred degrees, so you don't want to hang around, right? Keep the fucking night-vision goggles on your head, but don't put them on until *after* the boom. You'll blind yourself with the flash. But put them on right afterward, otherwise you won't know what you're walking through."

Tess stared at him. *"You think I'm going to survive?"*

"I'm going to do my damnedest to make sure of it," he snapped. "Jesus Christ in the manger, I grew up in Ireland. I've had enough of the scent of burning fucking martyrs to last me a lifetime."

They drove slowly along the runway. The fuel depot sat parallel to it, about two hundred yards away. Beyond that sat the radome-covered arrays, which surrounded the rest of the compound in a bizarre constellation.

Dan brought the plane to a near-standstill and slowly brought it around at a right angle to the runway. It now sat at the top of a service drive, also ice. The fuel depot was directly in front of them.

"Okay, you take the controls now," Dan said, and guided her hands into the correct positions. "Easy now. I know you think you're taking this for some sort of point-and-shoot joyride, but there's more to it than that."

Tess followed his guidance, the overwhelming sense of doom making her clench her hands much too tightly. It was better than throwing up, though, which is what her body really wanted to do.

Dan's voice was strikingly calm. "There's no room for error out here under the best conditions, Tess, and in the dark, it's more dangerous. There aren't any heat signals to pick up."

"The building has a glow to it."

"Barely."

"Dan, it's enough. I'm going to plow into it. I need momentum and mass, not precision," Tess snapped.

"Yeah, well, you need more information. Do you know what the fire suppression system is in that building?" he asked as he slowly increased the engines' power.

Tess caught her breath as she remembered the schematics she'd pored over just a few days ago. "Halon," she said, too quietly to be heard, then cleared her throat and repeated, "Halon."

"That's right. I'm not sure how effective the Halon will be, sucking all the oxygen away from the fire when we've ripped the shite out of the side of the building, but there's no point in assuming you'll have enough air to breathe," Dan said, twisting around in his seat. He handed Tess a gas mask with a small insulated canister of compressed oxygen attached. "Put this on now. Open the valve later. Get as far away from the fire as you can before you do it."

"Thanks," she shouted.

"Here's the plan. We now have a southerly heading. I'm going to go open the back door. I showed it to you, remember?"

Tess nodded.

"When I do that, it's going to get even colder and louder in here. Then I'm going to bring the engines up to full thrust, do the equivalent of popping the clutch, jam the steering mechanism, and drive this bird into that building," Dan said, pointing at their target at the end of the roadway. "When we get close to the building, we get the hell out of here. Remember to take the goggles off or the blast will fucking blind you. Tess, are you listening to me? We're both going to get up and run like hell out the back door. Jump, drop, and roll, but then get up and run like bloody hell. And keep running."

"I already told you, I'm going to do the driving. You go down to the back of the plane as soon as it's in motion, and I'll follow as soon as I can," Tess replied, her jaw aching with the tension of the last few hours. "There's no point in you getting hurt, too."

Dan stared at her for a minute, then shook his head slowly. "You're a fucking mad one, you are, Tess. Whatever you say. Now put that thing on," he said, pointing to the oxygen mask before getting up and walking to the back of the plane. Tess heard the back door open, then Dan returned to his seat and began to slowly bring the engines up to an ever higher pitch. The entire plane was vibrating and the engines were screaming before he released the brakes.

The sheer, brain-numbing terror that Tess had felt while Dan revved the engines was a mere dress rehearsal for what she felt as the empty, rattling plane began hurtling toward the power station.

It seemed to take no time at all before they were careening at a breakneck speed along the ice. Tess's entire field of vision narrowed to the solid wall of death rushing toward her. Her fingers, icy in the thick gloves she wore, clung painfully to the controls in front of her.

The building was getting closer and closer, looming before her like a harsh death. She was frozen in her seat, paralyzed with fear. Her brain snapped back to consciousness as she felt a hard hand grab her upper arm. Looking up, she saw Dan's face, creased with mingled alarm and anger. She wrenched herself out of the seat, awkward in her heavy clothing, and lumbered to her feet. Dan practically dragged her through the rushing plane and together they fell out of the open door as the unmanned aircraft slid and began to fishtail along the ground on its wide skis.

Tess had barely hit the ice when she heard the enormous crash as the plane slammed into the building. Instantly, a burst of blazing white light, brighter than anything she'd ever experienced, enveloped her. The force of the blast sent her skidding along the ice, tumbling like an inconsequential piece of trash. When she came to a stop, she gasped for air, not knowing for sure if she was alive or dead. Then pain, just as dazzling and just as hot, sliced through her.

Tess lay sprawled on the freshly shrapnel-pocked blue-ice roadway, staring at what she'd created. As Dan had said they would, the flames had died almost instantly to a nearly invisible blue, but the sound was like something from Hell. She reached up with a padded, shaking hand and pushed into place the night-vision goggles that were somehow intact and still on her head.

With the goggles in place, the scene before her was much different. The flames were vivid and achingly bright; calling the scene an inferno would not be an exaggeration. The sucking roar of the flames deafened her, the thunder and sparkle of steel beams crashing to the ground and the huge batteries exploding were magnificent in a horrifying way. It was the most beautiful, terrifying thing she'd ever seen. She didn't feel any heat, though, only the cold creeping through her, knifing her throat and lungs with every breath. She had to get moving.

"Tess?" The voice came out of the long, flickering shadows cast by the blazing building.

"Dan? Are you okay?" Tess struggled to a sitting position, hampered by the heavy clothes and a useless arm that sent vivid shards of agony through her at the slightest movement.

"No, I'm not fucking *okay*. My leg is killing me. I think it's broken, if it's still fucking attached. How about you?"

"I did something to my shoulder. I think I see the Delta coming toward us. Do you think you can get to me?"

"If I knew where the fuck you were, I might. I'm—oh, Sweet Jesus Christ in a handbag, this hurts," he yelped.

"Stay where you are. I'll help you." Tess struggled to her feet and looked around.

Dan lay ten feet away, one leg at an unnatural angle. Under other circumstances, seeing him like that would have made her sick. Right now, she was just glad to be breathing.

Tess limped to him and hunched down, using her good arm for balance. His face was contorted in pain.

"I'm getting cold. I think I'm bleeding," he rasped, breathing heavily.

Tess looked toward the installation and relief crashed over her when she saw the Delta drawing nearer to them. She cradled her injured arm and bit her lips against the pain as she stood up and began trying to flag it down.

The pain would pass. At least she was alive to feel it.

* * *

President Hernandez stood at the head of the table in the Situation Room. She was too tense to sit, and it was all she could do to keep herself from pacing. She turned to the group of senior intelligence and military advisors who were waiting silently, but with little patience, for her decision. They'd given her their input and pleaded their cases, but there was room for only one finger on the button.

Hers.

The submarine *Louisiana* sat in the southern Indian Ocean, ready and waiting. The Trident missile was hot and the captain was on standby. If Helena said "Go," the missile would be launched and approximately ten minutes later, the TESLA installation and its arrays—and all its personnel, and much of the East Antarctic Polar Plateau—would be obliterated. The threat posed by Greg Simpson's programming would be over.

If she hesitated, she ran the risk of other nations launching attacks—and the odds were that TESLA wouldn't be the only target. The nation she was in charge of protecting and defending would be on a fast track to oblivion. As might the rest of the world.

Helena looked away from the group of concerned yet professionally impassive faces and let her gaze drift to the large screen directly opposite her, which showed split-screen satellite views of the TESLA base. The enhanced video view showed a small, dark village, its structures barely visible; the infrared view showed a psychedelic welter of hot spots with one glowing brighter than the others.

"Ms. President, the Spec Ops team is about twelve minutes away from the drop zone." The voice was neutral, as if it had come from a machine instead of one of the many specialists lining the outer edges of the room.

There had been a small burst of activity just moments ago, three tiny dots, presumably vehicles of some sort, moving around on the screens. If those lights had not appeared, Helena wouldn't be hesitating. If all had been still, it would be easier to pretend that everyone there was already gone.

A new small slash of light appeared on the screen, growing slowly outward from the center.

"What's that?" Helena asked.

"It looks like doors opening, ma'am. I believe that's their aircraft hangar."

Helena didn't bother to identify the voice. Her eyes were riveted to the screen as a small but very bright light began to separate from the larger glow.

"That's some sort of a vehicle, ma'am. Big enough to be a plane. They have two onsite, a Twin Otter and a Dash 7."

"Are they going to fly out?" she asked, incredulous.

It was a question no one could answer.

Everyone in the room had their eyes riveted on the dot of light on the screen. It was moving very slowly in a straight line.

"Ms. President, the Spec Ops team is ten minutes away from the drop zone."

"Thank you." Helena's gaze was held in thrall by the small moving lights on the screen. "Who's the pilot at TESLA?"

"Daniel Thornton, Irish national, naturalized U.S. citizen. Eight years with the British Royal Air Force. Ten years with the British Antarctic Survey. Six years with Flint."

"What is he doing?" Helena looked at the nearest Air Force general.

"I don't know, ma'am. He's not moving fast enough for a take-off," was all he could say.

"What else would they use a plane for except to fly it?" the president asked, looking around the room in bewilderment.

"I don't know, ma'am," the general repeated.

Helena pressed her hands flat on the table and leaned on them to hide their tremors. Every muscle in her body was straining toward the image on the screen, waiting to see what would happen.

The dot stopped then, and its color rapidly intensified until it was a bright, hot red. After what seemed an eternity, the dot began moving again, perpendicular to its previous path. It was moving faster, too, its speed increasing as it traveled straight toward the largest glow on the screen.

"He's going to drive it into the building," someone said in disbelief.

The room went silent, as if everyone in it was holding their breath.

The dots merged then, the larger absorbing the smaller, and then, in an instant, the light grew exponentially larger and brighter, and much, much hotter.

The ultra-high-resolution streaming video showed a building at the edge of the village erupt in a fireball of light, the high, distinctive tail of a Dash 7 visible against the flames.

A wild cheer erupted around the table and Helena sank into the chair behind her, limp, drained, and shaking.

"The mission is now search-and-rescue. Candy, get your team in there," Helena said, putting as much force into her voice as she could summon.

She felt a soft hand cover hers, then grip it tightly, and looked up to see Candy Freeman's eyes brimming with tears. Neither woman needed to speak.

Nik was trying very hard not to think of Tess out there on the Ice, and trying equally hard to keep his focus on the race he and everyone in the installation was running: the one against the finite and dwindling supply of power the backup units were putting out.

"Got it," Ron said, quietly but with triumph in his voice.

"Got what?" Nik asked tightly, not moving his eyes from the screen in front of him.

The lights came on, causing everyone in the room to blink at the sudden brightness that replaced the gloom cast by the emergency lights and the computer monitors.

"I cut the diversion flow from the installation to the arrays," Ron said. "We're independent."

"Good job. Any news on the—," Nik began, only to be cut off by the roar of an explosion that shook the building they were in.

Everyone froze, staring at one another.

Jonah was the first to recover. He ran to the huge wall of windows and pulled back the heavy blackout curtains. In the near distance, a white-hot fireball lit up the pitch darkness. The body of the Dash 7 was thrown into silhouette for a moment before the light diminished to a faint, eerie blue glow.

It was the most horrifying, beautiful thing any of them had ever or would ever see.

Nik felt his body go limp and when he leaned his elbows on the desk to rest his head in his shaking hands, he realized that his face was wet with tears.

He felt a strong hand on his shoulder and forced himself to look up.

Lindy stood beside him, looking tortured. "Nik—," was all she could say, her voice thick with suppressed tears.

"They're out," Jonah shouted. "Both of them. They're moving."

Nik swung his head to look at Jonah, who was still standing at the windows, a set of night-vision goggles held to his eyes.

"They got out?" Nik demanded, grabbing Lindy's hand and pulling her to the window as fast as he could.

"It's got to be them," Jonah said, handing him the goggles. "Looks like Kendra is on her way. There are two Deltas on the move."

Nik held the goggles to his eyes just long enough to see for himself that there were two glowing figures out on the ice—one upright and one on the ground—and that both of them were moving, then he lowered them and handed the unit to someone—he wasn't sure who because everyone had clustered around them. Ron shoved his way through the crowd and the two men clung to each other in a tight embrace for a moment.

For once, the lead programmer had nothing to say.

Teke and his team had been ordered to divert to Amundsen-Scott South Pole base. The admiral had barely gotten off the plane when Dr. Jack Simon, the chief scientist wintering over at the base, entered the ready room. "We picked up some seismic activity from the plateau region where TESLA is."

Teke's brain froze for a split second. *The volcanoes.* "An earthquake?"

"No, no, it was very slight. The signature is more like an explosion," the scientist said as he turned around to lead the way into the base. "Come look at the tapes."

Teke turned to the Spec Ops team still divesting themselves of their gear. "I'll hook up with you in the common room. The support team is in there and we need to reconnoiter," he said.

He followed the scientist down the narrow corridor and into a large, messy workroom. The leader of the support team was already there. He and his crew had arrived more than an hour ago.

"Jack, a call just came in for an Admiral Curtis," one of the McMurdo guys said over his shoulder as Teke and the chief scientist entered the small, bare, practically makeshift office that housed four scientists and their files.

Dr. Simon had already made it clear that no one at the base had been particularly thrilled to be told they had to endure the dubious, if temporary, company of a dozen men who were so clearly not scientists. That was the support team. Then the Spec Ops team—unmistakably warriors—had arrived in the strangest-looking aircraft any of them had ever seen and the scientists' mood became even less hospitable.

Teke reached for the phone.

"Can you use the one on that desk? I'm working," the scientist said pointedly.

"Sure." *Because it's not like this call is important or anything, you dweeb.* Teke skirted the boxes of files to get to the other, currently unoccupied desk.

He grabbed the circa-1985 handset. "Curtis."

"It's Candy." Her voice sounded odd, sort of breathless and nasal, and not like her at all.

"What's up?"

"Did you see the explosion?"

"Yeah. It was the power plant."

"Someone drove a plane into it."

Wondering if he'd heard her correctly, Teke stared at the wall, which was covered in graphs and emails held up with pushpins and tape. "Say again?"

"Someone drove a plane into the power station at TESLA," she repeated, pausing for a delicate sniff. "I watched in real time, Teke. It was something to see, I tell you."

And those guys almost jumped into it at 126 miles an hour. "I can imagine."

"Your mission has changed to a rescue. We have no idea if there's still power in the installation. You and the boys have to get over there and evacuate them."

"Evacuate them to where?"

The scientists, openly eavesdropping, swung their heads in unison to look at him. "No room at this inn," Jack Simon murmured. "I don't care who it is. We can't handle any more people."

Teke ignored him. In his ear, Candy Freeman said, "TESLA has a blue-ice runway that will handle a C-17, and reconnaissance satellite images show that it's clear at the moment. I've been assured by Gianni that they have jet fuel and maintenance personnel on hand. There's a doctor and clinic at the installation. Between her and your PT, you ought to be able to triage any injuries. I'll let you know whether you'll take them to McMurdo first or straight to Christchurch. Just get over there. Power down whatever's left, lock the doors, and turn out the lights."

"Now?"

"Yes, now. Unless you have something else on your schedule," Candy replied.

Teke gave the thumbs-up to the leader of the support team, who nodded and left the room silently.

They'll be in their seats with the engines revved before I'm off the phone.

"What do you want us to do with the Peregrine?" Teke asked.

"Send it home," she replied crisply. "The fire at TESLA is still burning hotter than a Yankee's ass the day after a West Texas chili cook-off. The building had a Halon system inside, but something tells me that won't work too well when the side of the building is ripped open. So the fire might just have to burn itself out. Listen, sugar, I think the president wants to use this phone, so you and I can have that lovefest known as a debriefing when you get back on dry dirt. I'm heading to Christchurch on the next flight, so I'll meet you there in a day or so."

The line went dead and Teke replaced the handset, then turned to the pair of watching scientists.

"Thanks for your hospitality. Sorry to eat and run, but we've got to go," he said pleasantly.

"What happened at TESLA?" Jack Simon asked.

"You were right. It was an explosion," he replied nonchalantly. "That seismograph of yours is pretty sensitive."

"What exploded?"

Teke shrugged. "Couldn't say. I'm sure it will be in tomorrow's paper," he said as he walked out of the room.

"Is he really that stupid? There's no daily paper here," said a grumpy voice he hadn't heard before. Teke laughed as he walked down the hall.

"No. I think that was his way of telling us to fuck off and mind our own business," Jack replied.

Got it in one, doc.

Gianni stared through the dark window at all the moving lights glittering in the rain, which had lightened to a drizzle. Candy had called to let him know that TESLA had been put out of commission, if not destroyed outright, and there was a team heading there to evacuate his people.

My people. He shook his head in disgust. *What arrogance. What an unmitigated arrogant bastard I am.*

No. Was.

"That's going to change. Everything's going to change. I'm going to be different from now on. Less of an asshole, more of a human," he said to himself. "This is the only second chance I'm going to get. I refuse to blow it."

He knew he'd have to meet with Candy for a post-mortem and to discuss what was going to happen next. He had immunity from prosecution, so every avenue was open to him. Croyden and his heirs had died and the board had already been in touch with him, thanking him for taking charge and hinting at bigger things for his career. Their words hadn't thrilled him the way they once would have. The board's promises only assured him a spot in the scrum of corporate succession and a chance to fight his way to the top.

Or not.

It would probably feel better and be better for his physical and mental health if he just spilled the rest of the beans, accepted whatever was coming to him, and then . . . he'd figure out the future as it happened. It would have nothing to do with Flint, that's for sure.

Maybe I'll head back into academia. Teach Meteorology 101 and write papers no one will ever read on topics no one cares about.

He turned to walk toward the door of the hotel room, grabbing his suit jacket and coat on the way. The two agents on duty out in the hall got to their feet when he pulled open the door.

"You guys feel like grabbing a burger and a beer?"

They looked at each other, then back at him.

"The food here isn't good enough?" one of them asked with only a hint of a grin.

Gianni laughed, feeling lighter in his head and his heart than he had in months, possibly years. "I'm in the mood for guy food, something the Ritz isn't famous for. Are there any decent bars around here?"

The agents looked at him, clearly not sure what to make of him.

"We just made the world safe for democracy again," he said with a grin, shrugging into his suit coat and then his overcoat. "Let me buy you dinner. I'm not under arrest and I'm not going to try to ditch you. I just want to get out for a little while. Tomorrow is going to be hellacious."

The more senior agent shrugged. "Sure. There's a bar I know about two blocks away. It's small, but they do a decent burger."

"Great. Let's go."

The three men walked to the elevator and took it down to the lobby. They crossed the expensively understated space and made it onto the street.

"Left, and then a right at the lights," the agent said, and all three men began moving in that direction.

"It's a great night, isn't it? The rain makes the city smell clean," Gianni said.

"You want to let us know what you were smoking in there?" the other agent asked.

Gianni laughed as they came to a stop at the corner. "Not a thing. Some issues have worked themselves out and I feel better about things. It's just a good day to be alive, you know?"

The traffic light turned green and they started across the street.

Gianni heard the squeal of the brakes, but never saw the car. He wasn't even sure what happened. One minute he was on his feet, the next minute he wasn't. He was in the air, his body numb from a massive impact, and then he landed. His breath whooshed out of him in one motion, and he felt his head smash onto the street. People were bending over him. He could hear voices screaming and swearing, but they became softer as he lay there feeling nothing except his life fading softly away.

Two hours after she'd driven into the power station, Tess was back inside the installation. Her left arm was immobilized against her body and much of her torso was swathed in bandages. Nik was standing next to the bed on one side, unable to keep his eyes off her. She would have smiled but it hurt too much. Everything hurt.

In the next bed lolled a bruised and heavily sedated Dan, whose shattered leg had been set in a metal splint.

"That collarbone is going to be a challenge, Tess," Kendra murmured. "It's probably going to need surgery. You must have landed really hard for all that gear you were wearing not to lessen the impact. It's a really nasty set of breaks. We're going to have to get you evac'd somehow. Maybe we'll send up smoke signals."

"We already did. Too bad the fucking smoke is as dark as the fucking sky," Dan slurred. "Hope someone's watching us on infrared."

Kendra and Nik laughed. Tess would have if it hadn't hurt so much. She'd opted for only enough meds to take the edge off the sharpest pain. She knew she'd need a clear head to handle whatever came next.

"Me, too. Glad you're still with us, Danny boy," Kendra replied.

"Hey, doc, I feel pretty damned good, considering."

"That's the morphine talking," Kendra assured him. "You're going to feel like hell in a few hours. You're both insane, you know, throwing yourselves out the door of a moving airplane—"

"Better than the fucking alternative," Dan interrupted, pointing a wavering finger at her.

"I'll second that," Tess added. "Incineration is not the way I want to die. I want to go like that bumper sticker says I should: sliding sideways into the grave with a bottle of Champagne in one hand and a twenty-year-old surfer dude in the other."

"I don't think that's quite how the saying goes," Nik said, his eyebrows up, adding under his breath, "What have you got against forty-two-year-old geeks?"

She smiled. "Not a thing. Have we gotten the comms up yet?"

"Not yet."

"Maybe you should try blowing something up. It worked before," Dan slurred.

Kendra shook her head and was about to reply when an out-of-breath but perplexed Fizz came running into the clinic.

"We've got company," she said, panting.

They looked at her.

"What did you say?" Nik asked.

"A plane just touched down. A U.S. Navy C-17. It's taxiing toward the hangar."

Tess was swinging her legs over the side of the bed when Nik stopped her.

"You stay here. Whoever it is, I'll bring them to you."

"I don't care who it is," she called after him as he sprinted out the door. "Just make sure they have enough room on that plane to get all of us home."

Nik was in the first vehicle to reach the idling plane. Even before his Delta pulled to a stop, the plane's door opened and a metal ladder slid out, stopping a foot above the ground.

Nik climbed out of the Delta and reached the bottom of the ladder just in time to greet the first person, who landed on the ice easily despite the thick, shapeless layers of ECW.

"Admiral Teke Curtis, U.S. Navy," the mouth behind the balaclava shouted.

"Nik Forde, assistant director of research. Am I ever glad to see you." He motioned at the Delta and climbed in. The admiral climbed in behind him and Nik watched in mild amazement as people covered from head to toe in ECW with an arctic camo pattern streamed out of the plane, landing on their feet lightly with no loss of balance and immediately setting to tasks. The huge cargo ramp in the plane's underbelly was being lowered and what looked like brand-new tracked vehicles were being driven off it, headed toward the installation.

"What's all this?" Nik asked, motioning to all the activity.

"We brought a Special Operations team and a support team. We're evacuating you. All of you. Right now, we need to get refueled. I'd like to be airborne again ASAP in case the weather changes." The admiral looked closely at Nik. "I saw the power plant go up and heard that someone drove a plane into it. Hell of a thing to do. Any survivors?"

"There were two people in the plane and they both made it. Concussions, lots of bruises, some broken bones."

"What exactly did they do?"

Nik didn't answer right away, not wanting his voice to break. He still couldn't believe what Tess had done or that she had survived. "Just what you said. They ran a Dash 7 into the building at about a hundred miles an hour and threw themselves out the back door at the last minute."

"Damn. They're lucky to be alive."

Nik nodded. Talking about it was more difficult than he'd thought it would be. By the time the two men got back to the habitat, the Special Operations team and support team had already peeled down to their flight suits and were moving through the installation, gathering everyone into one area.

"They're going to freak people out," Nik told Teke as they stripped off their gear.

"They'll be okay. They know they're dealing with civilians. We're just here to get everyone out and turn off the lights."

Nik stopped what he was doing and stared at him. "Turn off the lights? You mean—"

Teke nodded. "We're pulling everything off line. Where is Tess Beauchamp?"

"She's in the clinic." Nik saw the admiral's eyebrows rise. "She was on the plane. She was driving."

The admiral's eyes grew wider. "She was? Can I talk to her?"

"Sure," Nik said. He showed the newcomer to the clinic and listened with mixed emotions as plans were made to shut down TESLA for good.

Tess's trip stateside was hectic. She'd insisted that all non-essential personnel be evacuated at once, that same day, but a few of them—Ron, Nik, and herself—had remained to make sure TESLA was brought down carefully and secured. She wasn't a whole lot of help in her semi-invalid state, but Teke had remained with them and they were able to leave within twenty-four hours of the others. The Flint board had sent the entire fleet of corporate jets to Christchurch to bring home the Teslans, sparing no expense in luxury and medical attention.

It was the least they could do, especially in light of the media blitz that awaited the personnel when they landed on American soil.

Stories of the devastation around the globe dominated the news cycles for weeks afterward; images of horrific injuries and destruction were seared onto Tess's brain.

As news of what had happened began to leak and trickle into the mainstream press, Greg became the living symbol of evil. His exploits and their aftermath resulted in global death tolls that rivaled those of Hitler and Stalin combined. The administration had

pushed for a speedy trial in the face of the incontro-
vertible evidence of the TESLA monitoring logs, the
diaries of Croyden Flint, and the testimony of Frederick Bonner. Greg had behaved callously in court, and
his outbursts were the rants of a lunatic, but even his
own legal team never raised the question of his sanity
and the trial had gone forward. Greg was now among
a new set of peers in the low-tech solitude of a super-
max prison.

The outcome for Tess had been different. The media
glare had focused on her even before she arrived in
the country, and her name had been linked with Greg's
in every imaginable way. It mattered to no one that
she'd been Greg's scapegoat, that she'd lost her parents in Greg's first salvo. She'd gone from having cameras shoved in her face to death threats in her email to
bricks thrown through her windows. Armed guards
had been posted outside her hospital room when she
had surgery on her collarbone, and she'd been moved
from safe house to safe house every other day for the
entire three months of congressional hearings.

By the time she was finally cleared of wrongdoing
and the talking heads began to call her a hero, the
public wasn't interested anymore. She didn't care. All
she wanted was to grieve in private for her parents,
for Gianni, for all the countless souls who'd died because of Greg's vindictiveness. As soon as she could,
she'd picked up what was left of her life, severed her
ties with everyone, and, leaving what remained of her
reputation behind, moved back to Europe.

34

CHAPTER

Tess sat in the early-spring sunshine on her tiny patio at the back of her house in central France. The fields came right up to the edge of her small space; they were her fields, but rented to her neighbors, who tended them as if they were their own.

Life was finally good again. No one knew about her past here and she had no complaints with being known as just another crazy *Americaine* with romanticized views of life deep in the French countryside. She had enough money to do what she liked, which usually entailed little more than reading, taking walks, eating, and surfing the Web.

Though good, life was also very slow in Lavoine. The high-speed Internet access she'd paid a small fortune to get had been a saving grace sometimes, keeping her informed about the world and her former colleagues. And Nik.

She stared at the screen of the laptop she had in front of her on the small table and felt prickles of both fear and desire run along her spine.

Nik was still in the business—after most of the furor had died down, he'd been offered and had accepted an endowed chair at MIT—and was speaking in Moscow in four days.

She rested her elbow on the table, set her chin on her cupped palm, and looked out.

Solitude is a luxury.

So is the company of an old friend.

And even if I chicken out and don't meet up with him, I'll at least have gotten out of the house for a while.

With a smile, Tess logged on to the Air France website and began to look for a flight.

Nik generally drove conference organizers crazy with his insistence that the lights in the hall remain lit. For one thing, he hated being in the spotlight, literally or figuratively. For another, he liked seeing who he was talking to and how many people were in the room. And that quirk of his was the only reason that, just after he was introduced, he saw the tall, blond figure in a coat and boots slip into the side door of the auditorium that had once been an opera house, and settle into the nearest open seat. After that, keeping focused on the notes in front of him had been a challenge, and he'd opened up the floor to questions earlier than he'd planned. He just wanted the damned lecture over so he could catch her before she left, in case she was thinking of sneaking out the way she'd sneaked in.

It would be just like Tess to do that. She had ignored his emails and phone messages and every other attempt he'd made to contact her since the congressional hearings had ended a year earlier. Most of the people involved had gone to ground to get out of the media's unrelenting eyes, but Tess had simply disappeared from the face of the earth.

Until now. In Moscow, of all places.

There's no way this is a coincidence.

Nik wrapped up the Q&A and waited patiently for the applause to subside. Miracle of miracles, Tess didn't bolt out of the room at her first opportunity. She hung around through all the applause and even lingered in her seat as various scientists, students, and members of the press came up to the stage to chat with him. Finally, all the others drifted toward the exits and she was the only figure left in the red velvet and gilt seats of the opulent but tattered auditorium.

And to think I was bitching about being the last speaker of the day.

Nik grabbed his jacket and managed to refrain from sprinting down the steps at the edge of the stage and up the aisle. In a moment, he was in front of her. She'd risen and moved into the aisle.

"Hi, Nik." Her voice was soft. Everything about her was soft—her hair, the sweater he could glimpse through the opening of her heavy coat, even her eyes. They didn't have that haunted look in them anymore. Not like the last time he'd seen her—the afternoon the congressional hearings ended. She'd stepped into the back of a waiting limo and disappeared without a backward glance.

"Hi, Tess," he said, not quite sure what to say or do next. It was a first. "You're looking well."

Her smile was the same, maybe a little hesitant. "Thank you. So are you." She paused for a second. "It was a good talk. Maybe a little rushed."

"That was for you."

Still smiling, she glanced away. "You've made the

Schlüchthofen band into a household term. Who knew it would capture anyone's imagination other than ours? I heard that one of its internal belts is named for you."

He gave a silent laugh. "Yeah, I guess that counts for the big time in this business."

She smiled, but didn't say anything.

"I'm glad you came, but I doubt you learned anything new."

"Well, to be honest, I already know everything about fractal clusters at the internal periphery of the Schlüchthofen band. I came to see you," she said.

The silence that built between them was heavy.

"You left without a trace, Tess. You didn't even say good-bye," he said at last.

She was silent for another moment, then met his eyes. "I know."

"I tried to contact you. A lot."

"I know that, too."

He let out a hard breath. "Tess, what happened to you? I—" He stopped as an unwanted blast of emotion threatened to crack more than his voice. He looked at the ornate ceiling soaring many feet above them and counted to five. Once more in control of himself, he continued, "I was worried about you, Tess. You just . . . disappeared."

"I was worried about me, too, Nik. That's why I left," she said quietly, looking away again and shifting on her feet. "I needed to be someplace where my face wasn't on the news every day, where I didn't have cameras following me and microphones shoved in my face and death threats overloading my email—where I wasn't called a mass murderer one minute and a hero the next." She let out a long breath and he could see tears glittering on her downcast eyelashes. "I'm sorry that I ignored you. I ignored everyone, if that makes you feel any better."

"It doesn't," he said with a short laugh. "Let's go somewhere. Get a coffee or a drink?" He glanced at his watch. "Dinner. Something."

She nodded, then slipped her arm through his. They walked slowly through the bustling, early-evening streets, dodging urban Russians headed in all directions. It was impossible to converse over the noise and, after a few blocks, wanting to get out of the teeth-rattling cold, they ducked into a small, crowded, too-warm bistro for a drink, which led to dinner.

With the soft lighting and languorous French music in the background, the setting might have been romantic if their conversation hadn't been so painful.

"So that was it," she said much later, pushing away the empty demitasse cup in front of her. "The hearings were over, I'd been demonized, my career was . . . I didn't know where my career was going, my parents were dead, and the world was in shambles." She shivered and shook her head as if to get rid of the memories. "All I wanted was to disappear, to go someplace where I could remember what 'good' was. So I went back to France, to a small town I'd driven through once."

Nik nodded as if he understood, though he didn't fully. "You didn't have to do that, you know. The public's attention never lasts too long. After a few months, we were all back to being ignored by store clerks and getting no recognition whatsoever when we said our names out loud."

Tess gave him a sad smile, brushed some of that long blond hair from her face, and flipped it over her shoulder. "I'm glad that for you it's that way. But you weren't the face of it. I was—" She shook her head again and forced a brighter smile onto her face. "Sounds like you've stayed in touch with the team."

Nik lifted a shoulder. "I worked with most of them for several years, so, yeah, we kept in touch."

"How is everyone?"

"Pretty well, for the most part. Ron got hitched. Well, eloped actually, but the party when they announced it was fun. Lindy married some admiral. Dan and Fizz got hitched, too—" He stopped and shook his head, watching the light from the table's lone candle flicker across her face. "So where are you living?"

"Outside of Lavoine in Allier. Central France. It's a tiny town that's not known for anything in particular. You'd have to look at a very detailed map to find it," she replied. "I'm surrounded by fields and vines and sheep and just a few people. We get four distinct seasons and very few tourists. It's great."

"But is it 'good'?" he asked lightly. "Did you find what you were looking for?"

She nodded. "It's very good."

"Any plans to get back into research or get on the lecture circuit?"

A shadow crossed her face. "I'm not making any plans, Nik, I'm just living in the present," she said after a moment.

He drained the last of his cognac, then rested his hands on the table near hers. She glanced at them, then at his face, and slipped one of her hands over his. It was smooth and cool and a very good sign.

"How long will you be in Moscow?" he asked.

"I leave tomorrow."

He could feel his eyebrows shoot up. "When did you get here?"

"This morning." She looked at him for a long moment without talking, and Nik watched her smile flicker and fade and reappear. "How long are you staying?"

"I'm leaving tomorrow, too."

"Are you flying through Paris?" she asked softly.

"As a matter of fact, I am."

"Any chance you might be interested in taking a detour to Lyon and then driving for about two hours to visit a little town in the middle of the country that's not even remotely a tourist destination and that doesn't have a whole lot to offer except its own brand of rustic charm?"

"I could be persuaded," he replied, feeling a grin steal over his face.

"How long could you stay?" She met his eyes, and let out a short laugh. "I suppose I should have asked you first if you're married or—?"

"I'm emotionally, legally, and financially unencumbered and I can stay until you throw me out. Did I mention that I'm not teaching again until August?"

She began to laugh. Nik cupped her hand in both of his and brought it to his mouth, not so much to kiss it as to just make sure it was real. "Let's get out of here," he muttered, taking one of his hands away to signal for the bill.

"And go where?"

"Where are you staying?"

"The Savoy," she said casually. "It's nearby."

And only the most expensive hotel in the city. He raised an eyebrow but said nothing as he handed over his credit card to the waiter. As soon as the transaction was completed, he stood and pulled her to her feet.

"To the Savoy. We'll have a nightcap in better surroundings than the last one we shared."

She gave him a questioning glance.

"My room at the installation. Your first night there," Nik added as they were handed their coats. He bundled her out the door and back into the cold, dark night. "It's strange to think that you were only there for three nights."

"Nik," she said, laughing at his hurry. "Slow down. I know it's cold, but the hotel is only a few blocks away."

"I don't want to spend any more time not looking at you than I have to," he said. "I want to get warm and comfortable and be able to—no, forget that. This can't wait." He whirled her to the edge of the sidewalk and then into a darkened doorway. He rested his forehead against hers. "Do you remember what you said to me before you went out to the plane, Tess?" he demanded, his voice rough from both the cold air and the fire inside him. "About if we had half a chance?"

She nodded, her eyes bright, her smile getting wider.

"Did you mean it? That given half a chance—"

"I meant it, Nik," she whispered. "That's why I came here. To see if we still had half a chance."

"We've got more than that, Tess. We've got the rest of our lives," he said, and brought his lips to hers, kissing her until the door behind him opened and a rough Russian curse jolted them apart.

Tess laughed, slipped her arm through his, and said, "On second thought, Nik, let's see if we can't catch a cab back to the hotel."

AUTHORS' NOTE

Who was Nikola Tesla?

There is no greater or more interesting scientist than Nikola Tesla. When you add it all up—his voluminous body of work, amazing scientific discoveries, electrifying showmanship, and eccentric personality—he was the "mega science star" of all time. In his day, scientists were like rock stars and he was "The King." Yes, there were other biggies, like Röentgen, Marconi, Sir Oliver Lodge, Hertz, Ampère, and that Edison guy, but Tesla, with his extreme height (he was over six feet tall) and even more gigantic personality, was astonishing.

Yet, now, Telsa is the unsung prophet of our electronic age. Without Nikola Tesla there would be no electricity as we know it, no power generation and transmission using alternating current, no radio or television, no ignition systems for cars and other vehicles, not even the remote control. To me, it's terribly disappointing that his life and achievements have all but vanished from public awareness. It's really a mystery to me why he has so vanished into the haze of the past. While I was researching and writing this book, I'd go to book signings and ask if anyone had heard of Nikola Tesla and usually no more than two hands were ever raised.

Tesla possessed a remarkable talent for charming

and astonishing his admirers while at the same time totally enraging his critics. His peers held him in high esteem—he was nominated for the Nobel Prize for Science in 1937. He did however have his harsh critics. Waldemar Kaempffert, science editor for *The New York Times*, branded him "an intellectual boa constrictor and a medieval practioner of black arts."

Tesla could also display streaks of cruelty. He was disgusted by people who were overweight and did nothing to disguise this. When one of his secretaries, who, in his opinion, was too fat, awkwardly knocked something off a table, Tesla fired her despite her pleading. He had a favorite joke about two of his aunts; the center of the story was that they were sublimely ugly. Even great men have their flaws and Tesla clearly had several.

Tesla was also a very cool man about town. He was one of Manhattan's social elite and a member of "the 400"—the most influential four hundred people in Manhattan high society (this group also included John Jacob Astor, Hamilton Fish, Jr., Peter Cooper Hewitt, Clement C. Moore, Cornelius Vanderbilt, and other notables from banking, industry, and the arts and sciences). He was also big-time friends with the writer Mark Twain, who was a frequent guest at Tesla's lab when Tesla put on his famous light shows.

Tesla fancied himself as the best-dressed man on Fifth Avenue. John J. O'Neill, the Pulitzer Prize–winning science editor of the *New York Herald Tribune* and Tesla's first biographer, said of him, "He was handsome of face, had a magnetic personality, but was quiet, almost shy; he was soft spoken, well educated and wore clothes well."

His secretary of many years, Dorothy Skerritt, wrote of Tesla, "From under protruding eyebrows his deep-set, steel grey, soft, yet piercing eyes, seemed to read your innermost thoughts . . . his face glowed with almost ethereal radiance. His genial smile and nobility of bearing always denoted the gentlemanly characteristics that were so ingrained in his soul."

Although he was quite the social butterfly, he never formed a relationship with any of the ladies—many of whom in "the 400" found him quite handsome, including Anne Morgan, daughter of the famous Wall Street financier J. Pierpont Morgan. There's been a good deal of speculation about Tesla's private life in recent years, some of which was the background for Nik Forde's history in *Dry Ice*.

While acquainting myself with the life of Nikola Tesla, I visited the sites of his old haunts here in New York City: the locations of his old laboratories on 40th Street and on West Broadway (formally South 5th Avenue); the many swanky hotels in which he'd lived—the Pennsylvania, the McAlpin, the Maguery, the Waldorf Astoria, and the place where he died, the New Yorker. I was married in another of Tesla's residences, the St. Regis Hotel. Tesla had a tremendous love for pigeons and somehow these luxury hotels allowed him to keep them with him!

I also went to Shoreham, Long Island, to look at the location of his ill-fated Wardenclyffe Tower. The building, minus the tower, still stands today. It was rather eerie to stand there and imagine Tesla, the supposed mad scientist, firing lightning bolts into the New York night. If you did that today, the EPA would sentence you to prison for eternity.

* * *

Nikola Tesla was born in Croatia to Serbian parents. His father was a minister of the Serbian Orthodox Church, a racial and religious minority at that time. Nikola came to America in 1884 and worked for Thomas Edison. He later became Edison's most hated rival. Nice career choice, right?

Tesla's crowning achievement was the invention of alternating current, A/C as we call it, the electricity we use today. He believed it was possible to wirelessly transmit electricity across the oceans using two towers, one on the East Coast of the United States and the other on the shores of England.

He also discovered wireless radio waves and invented radio. Exploring radio waves, he learned that radio waves of various frequencies could do many amazing and wondrous things, like shake a building down to its foundation (which he actually did). He proved that wireless transmission of extra low frequency waves (ELF) could shake the Earth to its core or affect the ionosphere of the planet, creating all types of phenomena. You could fry the electronics of an aircraft in flight . . . and you could make weather . . . which inspired *Dry Ice*.

Here's a list of only a few of Tesla's 250 patents:

The Rotating Magnetic Field
The Induction Motor
The AC Polyphase Power Distribution System
The Fundamental System of Wireless Communication (Legal Priority for the invention of Radio)
RF (radio frequency) Oscillators
Voltage Magnification by Standing Waves

Robotics
Logic Gates for Secure RF Communications
X-Rays
Ionized Gases
High Field Emission
Charged Particle Beams
Voltage Multiplication Circuitry
High Voltage Discharges
Lightning Protection
The Bladeless Turbine
VTOL aircraft

To me, Tesla was very cool because he played with electricity—and I do mean *played*—with millions of volts at a time! He amazed audiences at universities, science exhibitions, and World's Fairs with light shows of various-colored fluorescent tubes.

In playing and experimenting with electricity, he was almost killed on more than one occasion! Yet each time he managed to pull a Harry Houdini and escape. Lightning would dance all about him, zap metal fragments that ricocheted around his lab, yet he escaped without a scratch.

In his autobiography, Tesla wrote about these phenomena, which he believed started when he was a child:

*I was almost drowned, entombed, lost, and frozen.
I had hairbreadth escapes from mad dogs, hogs,
and other wild animals. I passed through dreadful
diseases and met with all kinds of odd mishaps. I feel
my preservation was not altogether accidental, but
was indeed the work of divine power. An inventor's
endeavor is essentially life saving. Whether he*

harnesses forces, improves devices, or provides new comforts and conveniences, he is adding to the safety of our existence.

There's no question that Tesla felt he was protected by the hands of God!

Hopefully for future meteorologists and inventive scientists, I've kindled a little interest in "mega science star" Nikola Tesla.

—BILL EVANS

Turn the page for a preview of

BLACKMAIL EARTH

•

BILL EVANS

Available in June 2012
from Tom Doherty Associates

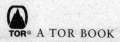
TOR® A TOR BOOK

CHAPTER

Jenna Withers could see more than fifty miles from the shotgun seat of *The Morning Show* helicopter. The farms and forests north of New York City had turned to tinder. Mid-October was as hot as mid-August had been, for the third scorching year in a row. Lakes and reservoirs were drying up and the rivers looked like they'd slunk away from their banks, thieves in the night.

It was just as dry—or drier—on the West Coast and across the Sun Belt. The hottest growing season on record. Much of the Midwest had been singed, too, with farmers in Iowa and Nebraska losing 80 percent of their corn crop. Food and fuel prices were rising fast as the mercury.

Minutes ago Jenna; her producer, Nicole Parsons; and their crew had choppered out of New York City, the heart of a drought emergency that had been declared two months ago. That was the second highest level of official panic, right below drought disaster—conditions so dire that they were bluntly unthinkable in a metro area of twenty million people.

No one in the Big Apple had escaped the vicious grip of the Northeast drought. Water for parks, golf courses, and fountains? Fahgeddaboutit. Let 'em brown, where they hadn't burned. Car washes? You gotta be kiddin'. Pools? You're still jokin'.

Not even sprinklers to cool off the kiddies, and fire hydrants were locked up tighter than Tiffany's. Most of the water for everything but drinking now came from the Hudson River, where crews worked twenty-four/seven to pump out tens of millions of gallons. The water level had dropped to historic lows.

Jenna, a meteorologist, didn't need the Ph.D. after her name to tally up the terror that could come from a cigarette tossed into the brittle brush down below, where a single spark could turn the region crisp as southern California when the Santa Ana winds wicked all the life from the land before burning the mountainsides black. Merely looking down at the devastation from the front passenger seat brought to mind the scores of scientific studies linking high temperatures and high-pressure systems to increased rates of homicide and the full spectrum of urban violence.

This classic summertime high had originated just east of Bermuda. For most of the past two months, it had driven the polar jet stream north, into Canada, and the subtropical jet stream south, below the Gulf of Mexico. That left the "Bermuda high," as it was aptly known, hunkered down above the East Coast like a bear at a beehive, far too content to move.

"You finding our reservoir? I'm getting nervous back here." Nicole's voice came through Jenna's headphones. In the seat behind Jenna, Nicci was the off-camera part of the weather team. She was as short and dark-haired as Jenna was tall and blond. They were the best of friends—real friends, not frenemies—which was good because they were virtually joined at the hip, "married" in the parlance of network television.

"I don't see it yet."

Nicci shot back, "We've got to land somewhere and go live in *nine* minutes."

The countdown, thought Jenna. *There's always a frickin' countdown.* Her stomach tightened as seconds flew by, relaxing only slightly when their pilot pointed to the huge empty bowl in the earth that was their destination, a reservoir wrung dry of every last ounce: all the water had burned into the sky.

Dust was rising now, engulfing the copter, swirling wildly like they were in Iraq or Afghanistan. Flying by instruments, the pilot landed them safely on the edge of the dry lake bed with the softest bump.

With the engine shut down and the AC off, the glass bubble heated up faster than a cheap lightbulb. Jenna started to sweat immediately. Her blouse and panty hose felt like warm, wet leaves plastered to her skin. Even the dust still eddying outside looked more appealing than sitting in this sauna. But as she reached for the door, the chopper pilot took her arm.

"I don't want that goddamn grit getting in here. It's hell on the instruments. Give it a sec to settle down."

Nicci said, in her most urgent voice, "we've got about five minutes to get out, get set up, and get on the air. *Five minutes.* Let's go." The producer shouldered open her door, rousing Andi, their camerawoman, from her open-eyed torpor. Andi cradled the high-definition digital camera in her arms as she climbed out of the helicopter.

Jenna sucked in one more breath before heading into the chest-choking air. Ducking as she hustled out from under the still whirling rotors, she spotted a man and his border collie in the drifting dust. The guy stood stiffly, rifle by his side. That made Jenna uneasy. She found little relief in glancing at Bowser. The dog was poised next to his master, staring at Jenna from a pair of unblinking blue marbles. Eerie freakin' eyes. *Doesn't the dust get in them?* Jenna's own eyes were closed to slits.

Squinting, she looked from beast to man. They looked like attitude squared, an opinion only confirmed when he roared, "You didn't even see us, did you?"

"I'm not the pilot," she said calmly, hoping to soothe him.

"You almost killed us."

"I'm really sorry."

"Everywhere we ran, that helicopter kept coming at us, and then we couldn't see a damn thing with all the dust. Four miles of open reservoir, and you just about planted that thing right on our heads. How stupid is that?"

Jenna glanced at the chopper. The pilot was staring straight ahead, leaving her to own up.

"Pretty damn stupid," Jenna agreed. "Look, really, I'm sorry. I'm Jenna Withers. I do weather for *The Morning Show*."

"I know who you are."

Now she noticed a pistol on his hip.

"Law enforcement?" she asked softly. Hoping. She'd grown up with guns—her dear departed father had been a hunter and marksman all his life—but years of city living had made her more wary of firearms.

But you're not in *the city,* she told herself.

Before he could answer, Nicci snapped, "Weather girl . . ."—only she could get away with that moniker—". . . three minutes. *Three.* Ready?"

Jenna nodded.

"Dairy farmer," the man said.

"Dairy farmer," she repeated. That sounded friendly enough: *Elsie the cow, right?* Reassuring. So was the lowered volume of his voice. Which was good because she needed to focus on the live update, now less than ninety seconds away. She pulled weather data up on her laptop screen, then checked temperatures for the region; this was a story on the Northeast drought so she didn't need to worry about the entire country on this go-round.

Pulling a tissue from her pocket, Jenna patted her face; sweat and dust stained the tissue when she was done. Or was that tan stuff makeup? She'd applied it during the flight, after all. Opening her purse, she drew out a small mirror in a sleek black leather case that looked like a notebook, then gazed at her face. The little case was a discreet way to check her appearance without reinforcing the narcissistic TV talent stereotype. The headphones had messed with her hair, so she straightened and fluffed it, then noticed that her eyes were red from the dust. *Murine* emergency.

Andi peered through her viewfinder, then snapped together a wireless microphone and clipped it to the inside of Jenna's blouse. The camerawoman kept eyeing the farmer and his border collie. Jenna understood the concern: loonies were known to mess with live shots in the city. *But you're not in the city,* she reminded herself a second time. And the dairyman didn't look like a loony. Actually, he looked kind of handsome, but she put aside his presence and turned her thoughts to the work at hand, though she figured that she could do an update in her sleep. And given the schedule of a meteorologist on *The Morning Show*— up at 2:00 A.M., on at 7:00 A.M.—she probably already had on numerous occasions.

Besides, what she would say would play second fiddle to the split screen that would be used as her backdrop: empty, dusty reservoir cheek by jowl with old footage of the lake brimming with cool water. The sweet "then," the sour—and *scary*—"now."

Cued, Jenna chattered to the camera, alternately smiling and serious as she boiled down the update to "hot and dry," the daily mantra for the last five weeks. The stagnant weather had shown no more inclination to move on than a two-ton boulder plopped on a trail.

She engaged in snappy closing patter with Andrea Hanson, *The Morning Show*'s visibly pregnant host, a darling of viewers and a mainstay of morning television for the past five years.

The dairy farmer and his furry pal watched Jenna sign off. She felt a familiar sense of relief when the camera went dark, then noticed that Andi was back to keeping a wary eye on the guy with the guns.

"Is the drought making dairy farming tougher?" she asked in her most empathetic "the weather really sucks" voice, hoping to charm away the tension. She unclipped the mike and handed it to Andi, who pocketed it before heading back to the helicopter. Nicci had already boarded.

"We don't need a drought to make dairying tougher, but the cows are okay. They're just moving a little slower."

"They free range?"

"That's chickens. Only thing free range these days are the roaches. They love the heat. Ever been to Puerto Rico? Cockroaches big as your fist. They're getting that way around here."

Who did he remind her of? Somebody appealing. Tall as she was, wiry, with smooth skin and sharp features. "What's your name?"

"Dafoe. Dafoe Tillian."

"Good to meet you, Dafoe." He shook her hand, and she knew that she had, indeed, charmed him; but try as she might, she could not place his face.

The rotors whirled faster. Jenna climbed aboard and belted herself in. Dafoe hurried away from the dust storm whipping up from the lake bed, then turned around so quickly that even through a hurricane of dust and heat he caught her staring. She wanted to look down, peel her eyes from his; but her body wouldn't obey, and a smile betrayed her even more.

As they flew away, Jenna closed her eyes, catnapping till Nicci asked her to join a call to *The Morning Show*'s executive producer, Marv Balen, or "the twit," as the two women called him in private. "He texted us a few seconds ago."

Up ahead, the city's skyline poked through the low-lying smog like quills through a dirty old quilt. Jenna turned on her headset.

"We're here, Marv," Nicci said. "Go ahead."

"We had three murders in the Bronx last night. Cops found the victims about an hour ago. They think they've got the shooter. Word is he snapped and started shooting his poker buddies when the air conditioner went on the fritz. So that makes three more heat-related homicides this week."

"So you want us to do the story?" Jenna said, hope as irrepressible as ever.

"Noooo. One of our correspondents will. But there's more gore out on the West Coast. Fresno's had a week of one-hundred-ten-degree weather and last night they had their fourth murder during that time. So you're going to be our resident expert on how weather affects behavior, Jenna."

"It's not really my area of expertise, Marv, but—"

"Yeah, I know," he interrupted, "but you can say that heat and high pressure systems are linked to higher murder rates."

The 101s of weather, Jenna thought.

"It's a lot cheaper than flying a crew up to MIT to get some professor to spew," Marv went on, "and you're an author. You can spout off."

He was referring, in his typically ham-handed way, to the book Jenna had had published seven years earlier on geoengineering—how technology could be used to combat climate change. There had been little interest back then, but the publisher had reissued it three months ago to great interest in both the academic and mainstream press.

"Talk about heat and murder, and don't throw in a lot of other stuff. Nicci, make sure she doesn't go yammering on about global fucking warming. We're keeping it supertight."

All stories had to be supertight these days: reports, live shots, updates, even the banter with Andrea Hanson. It was a presidential election year, and the news hole for everything but polls, politicians, and pundits had shrunk faster than a Greenland glacier.

They landed in Manhattan and raced back to the Weather Command Center where they were soon joined by a crew from the Northeast Bureau. The correspondent was an up-and-comer who was all smiles and good cheer, which Jenna appreciated. Life was too short for sneakiness and sarcasm—for people like Marv, in other words.

A cameraman set up quickly, positioning Jenna in front of *The Morning Show* logo. Product placement. As she finished answering the last question about heat and homicide, Jenna spotted Cassie Carter, the Weather Command Center's frizzy-haired assistant, waving frantically for her attention. "The White House is on the phone," Cassie said breathlessly.

"The White House?" Jenna asked. Nicci looked up from her laptop. "Is this a joke?" Jenna asked her. "Did you put Cassie up to this?"

"No, I didn't."

And she hadn't, Jenna learned an instant later when she heard "Please hold for Ralph Ebbing," the president's chief of staff.

"Good morning, Ms. Withers," Ebbing said a moment later. Jenna had heard Ebbing on the Sunday-morning talk shows often enough to know that it was really him.

"I'm sure you're busy," he said, "so I'll get right to the point: We'd like you to serve on the Presidential Task Force on Climate Change."

"I'm very honored. Very. But I'll have to check to see whether that's permitted. The network has rules about this. As you probably know," she hurried to add. Her heart was pounding.

"Absolutely. But I want you to know that we'd really like you to serve."

Jenna fleetingly thought about asking about *per diem* costs and transportation, but decided those pesky questions were best left to one of Ebbing's underlings—after she made sure that the network had no objections. "I should be able to get back to you in a day or two," she said.

"We'd appreciate that greatly. We believe your expertise could be helpful to your nation," Ebbing said. "The vice president will chair the task force, and if you could communicate with his chief of staff, that would be best." Ebbing gave her a phone number for his counterpart. "On behalf of the president, I want to thank you for considering this appointment, Miss Withers. I hope you'll serve."

And then the conversation was over. Jenna kept the phone to her ear after Ebbing hung up, savoring the request in silence for a few seconds because she was all but certain that as a member of the news division, she would be barred from taking the appointment.

After a breath, she cradled the receiver and passed the bulletin to Nicci and Cassie.

"Wow," Cassie said. "Big, big wow."

"The suits are never going to let me take it," Jenna said, shaking her head. "They don't want us doing that kind of stuff."

"Maybe you're right," Nicci said, "but you're a meteorologist, and that's a little different."

"I doubt they'll see it that way." Jenna shrugged. But she could take solace, scant as it was, that someone had seen her as more than the morning weather bimbo. Not many years ago, the joke in male-dominated newsrooms was that a woman's sole qualification for a weather job was whether her breasts reached from New York to Kansas when she stood next to the map.

The phones started ringing. Nicci picked up one and Cassie the other. The younger woman took a message, hung up, then handed the slip of paper to Jenna. "Just a guy who wanted to talk to you—"

Another one. It seemed to Jenna that half a dozen guys called after every show, most of them vowing to make her happy. Their means for accomplishing this were notably unmentionable.

"He said you almost landed on him this morning," Cassie finished.

"Really?" A lilt colored her voice. "What did he want?"

"He said just to talk." Cassie rolled her eyes.

Jenna stared at the name: Dafoe Tillian. Before she could do more than remember his rugged, pleasing appearance, Nicci cupped the receiver on her phone and said, "Rafan on line two."

"Rafan?" Jenna sat up. He was an old boyfriend, one of the few real loves of her life. "Where is he?"

"The Maldives, I guess. He says it's pretty important."

Jenna got on the line right away.

"I saw you on *The Morning Show,*" Rafan said in his accented English. "You do weather now."

Had it been that long since they'd spoken? She'd been doing the show for three years.

"Here, the weather gets hotter. The islands, they will disappear."

"I know, Rafan. It's so sad." She'd been aware of the threat to his country's archipelago of twelve hundred islands for ten years, since she'd started her doctoral work. The Maldives had been her home for several months of research. She'd look out and see nothing but islands and Indian Ocean all the way to the horizon. Now the Maldives seemed destined to become the first country to fall victim to global warming.

Seas rising much faster than the U.N.'s predictions were starting to claim thatched houses. To see your homeland washing away must be heartbreaking, Jenna thought.

In recent years, the Maldivian president and his ministers had strapped on scuba gear for an annual underwater cabinet meeting to dramatize the plight faced by the country's three hundred thousand people. To no avail. Most Americans, Jenna had found, had never heard of the Islamic nation, much less of its highly endangered status.

"Muslims here, they are angry. It's not like before. Remember? We would go to parties, have a good time. Here, it's changing, Jenna. It's changing very fast. People say the West, your country, is doing this to us. They say the decadence is killing us. Come see for yourself. I think they will strike back. Soon."

"What do you mean, 'strike back'? How?"

"How do you think?"

Jenna walked to the window and looked as far as she could to the right. She didn't do this often. It hurt too much. But now she let herself stare at the sky where the Twin Towers had once stood.

How do you think?

CHAPTER

I am now Minister of Dirt.

Rafan was a civil engineer in the Maldivian Ministry of Home Affairs and Environment, but at the moment he couldn't get that title—*Minister of Dirt*—out of his head.

He stepped into the throng hurrying down the narrow winding street of the Maldivian capital of Malé, where government officials huddled behind white walls and hatched crazy plans to pile dirt on an island to try to save it from the hungry sea.

That's if Rafan could find dirt. Millions of cubic meters of it. Not easy in the middle of the Indian Ocean. And these days that wasn't the only absurd plan afloat (though perhaps that was the wrong word for the circumstances). A real government minister—of development—had proposed building a towering skyscraper to house his country's people. Kind of a modern-day castle with the whole ocean as a moat.

A crazy country. Crazy. The president was even more ambitious: He was looking for an entirely new land where he could move everyone, as if a Xanadu were waiting just for them—the cursed Maldivians. Last night Rafan had heard a rumor that some of his government colleagues were feeling out Sri Lanka, India, and China to see if they wanted to buy the country's fishing rights. Testing the waters, so to speak. Or, perhaps more to the point, cashing in while they could. Maybe he should, too. Buy land in Asia or Australia and move, like others were doing. Every man for himself on a sinking ship.

But Rafan would never abandon his country, so he'd hunt for barges and try to pile dirt on an island faster than the waves could wash it away. Sisyphus in the age of global warming.

In his white ball cap and dark glasses, white pants and white shirt, Rafan looked too impeccable to be Minister of Dirt. He looked better suited, in the most literal sense, to working behind a desk while a Casablanca fan stirred the sweet tropical air above his salt-and-pepper pate.

He maneuvered toward an alley as a muezzin's call to prayer—*adhan*—quickened the crowd's pace. Five times a day the call rose from loudspeakers to remind the Islamic faithful of their beliefs and obligations. It reminded Rafan how much his country had changed in the past decade.

People peeled away to go to mosque, leaving men like him with the uneasy eyes of those who don't want to be seen ignoring the call. Ten years ago there had been no muezzin and no need to worry about snubbing the faith. Now, more and more Maldivians prayed with fervor, facing the loss of their homeland, a diaspora like the Jews and Palestinians and so many others had known.

The fever of faith had spread across the archipelago, along with anger hot as cook stones. Even the president and his ministers had made a show of praying underwater at their annual meeting in masks and flippers and oxygen tanks, all of them exhaling perfect bubbles of carbon dioxide and uttering "*Allah akbar*" before they signed hopeless proclamations with waterproof pens. But if God is so great, why do the pendanus trees bow to the sea, their roots eaten by salt, trunks by waves, until they lie facedown, limbs flattened and extended like worshippers heeding the muezzin? If God's so great, why does He let the lesser deity Neptune swallow us alive?

When Jenna had been with him, Rafan might have shared these inflammatory thoughts with her and other friends. Not anymore. Better to let the believers loudly implore the heavens while he quietly moved the earth, taking dirt from one island to another. Robbing Peter to pay Paul. *That's what Jenna used to say. We could make that the official slogan of the Maldives—if we weren't Muslim. We rob Peter to pay Paul all the time.* Rafan thought of the country's biggest moneymaker: the half-million vacationers lured to the Maldives every year by the Ministry of Tourism. Europeans, Asians, and North and South Americans flew thousands of miles to stay in isolated island resorts; each traveler churned out as much greenhouse gas in an average ten-hour flight as a Maldivian produced in a month. But Rafan's country needed money, so it welcomed the wealth of the developed world, and robbed the future—and the world's children—while wearing the smiley face of tourism.

The aroma of curried tuna drew Rafan's eye to a food cart by the entrance to the alley. Moments later he was leaning against a building, taking a bite of tuna when a bomb exploded a hundred and fifty feet away. He looked up, stunned by a horrifying ball of flame wide as the street. An oily cloud rose to the sky.

Rafan dropped his plate and ran toward the screams, dodging survivors. Through the pall of smoke he saw men, women, and children riddled with nails, scrap metal, and razor-sharp coral chips, their limbs twisted, charred, and melted like the bicycles incinerated by the blast. His eyes raced over the dead and injured—and he shouted in anguish at the sight of Basheera. She lay in a crater, smoke rising around her where minutes ago the muezzin's call had turned Rafan's thoughts to questions of devotion and diaspora.

His sister reached a hand to him, and he ran to her knowing, as he had with his first panicky step, that a second bomb might await the rescuers.

Khulood walked the sandy path that separated her thatched home from a seawall on the small island of Dhiggaru. The mass of concrete chunks and coconut shells rose as high as her chest, but held back only the refuse the sea tossed to shore, not the warm salty water that spilled through gaps in the structure. A week ago the ocean had touched her house for the first time, soaking the floorboards by the front door. A stubborn stain remained even now, as if the future had cast an inescapable spell.

Khulood had lived on Dhiggaru all her life, as her ancestors had. Her son, Adnan, had sailed the world and returned with pictures of wondrous places. He worked on ships bigger than many of the islands she could see from her house. But he hadn't left Dhiggaru for five months. The world, he'd said, was slowing down and didn't need so much oil. Maybe next year.

She spied him at prayer, eyes filled with Mecca. So much more devout than she. He turned when he heard her steps, smiled, then rolled up his prayer rug and tucked it under his arm. He'd begun to pray earlier this year when Parvez, his closest friend since childhood, had returned from four years of study of Islam.

Now a cleric, Parvez had chided her to pray like her son, but Khulood had declined. She wore a head scarf, not as a concession but to keep the sun off her scalp.

"I will cook fish and cassava," she said to Adnan.

He walked into the house with her and put away his prayer rug. "I'm not hungry, Mother. You eat. I must see Parvez."

He spoke his friend's name shyly, then kissed her cheek. She watched him walk away down the path which narrowed to a single set of footprints when it passed through a palm grove. Out there, in the gathering darkness, Parvez had made his home.

Rafan cupped the back of Basheera's head. Acrid fumes rose all around them, as if hell itself had exploded. Basheera's eyes were stark with shock. Blood poured from her mouth.

"They're coming," he said to her. *Doctors? Or the ones with more bombs?* he wondered.

He looked around frantically for help, nose burning from the smoke. Waves of heat drifted over his back, and he turned to see a flaming cavern that had been a tea shop. The dead and dying spilled at odd angles all around him, bodies lifted by force and dropped with fury. An old woman struggled to stand. A much younger man with sopping red pants tried to help her, agony in his eyes. They staggered away slowly, clutching each other.

Another bomb. Rafan's constant fear. He slid his arms under Basheera's back and legs and climbed to his feet. She was the last of his family, a young woman so slight that he couldn't feel her weight through his waves of terror. He held her so close that her heart beat against his chest; and he remembered her as a curly-haired toddler whom he had carried to bed.

As Rafan ran toward the hospital, he spotted two physicians in white jackets racing to the bombing. "Help her," he screamed, holding Basheera higher, like an offering.

The woman doctor stopped and opened Basheera's eyes; Rafan hadn't noticed that they'd closed. She checked his sister's pulse. The heart that Rafan had felt seconds ago had failed.

"No," he pleaded.

The doctor held his face in her warm hands and whispered *"Ma-aafu kurey."* I'm sorry. An instant later a second bomb tore apart everyone near the original explosion, and claimed the lives of those who'd tried to rescue the dying, including the doctor's colleague.

Rafan turned slowly. His tears fell to Basheera's burned and sodden dress, and he cursed the earth and all it held sacred. Then he looked up, shaken by the sight of the doctor, whose life had been spared by his sister's death, running fearlessly into a curtain of black smoke.

Tenderly, as if he could bruise her still, Rafan laid Basheera on the ground. *"Ma-aafu kurey,"* he cried to her before he, too, ran into the blackness.

* * *

Parvez shifted forward, speaking of an attack by Islamists in Malé. Twelve people killed. Three children.

"This is cruel," Parvez said. "The radio said they used an IED on our own people. Mohammed, peace and blessings of Allah be upon him, said this is always wrong."

"Is that what they taught you at school?" Adnan asked.

The cleric nodded without taking his eyes from Adnan, whose skin felt frighteningly alive in the presence of a man so steeped in the highest realms of Islamic thought. And to think Parvez had been his closest childhood friend.

"We must not shed the blood of our own, unless it is our supreme sacrifice." Parvez leaned closer in the dusky light, "Do you know what I mean?"

Adnan answered with a nod. Parvez rose, his robes swaying. Adnan followed him to a bamboo wardrobe. The cleric opened both doors. Adnan stared at the single item draped on a hanger. Parvez turned it so Adnan could view all of the vest.

"It can end the world as we know it." Parvez placed his hand on Adnan's shoulder and drew him closer. They stood side by side. "The man who wears this will know Allah's love."

"How?"

Parvez whispered his answer, shivery words that spoke of flame.

CHAPTER

Jenna boarded a train at Penn Station, joining an early Friday afternoon crush of commuters eager to flee the compressing heat and burgeoning violence of New York City. Two more murders had made the news in the past forty-eight hours, including the savage knifing of a twenty-two-year-old woman whose terrifying screams had been heard by hundreds of West Side residents.

Not that the dairy country she was heading to was any paradise: crops dying, water rationing, ugly struggles over state and federal disaster aid. Upstate New York looked as crispy as California's Central Valley, which looked as parched as Illinois, Iowa, Alabama, and Georgia. Drought, distress, and despair across the country.

At least it was cool on the train. Jenna lucked out with a stool at the bar and ordered white wine. She needed a cold drink, preferably cold enough for condensation. Few things felt better in the swelter than pressing chilly dampness to her brow.

She'd be riding plenty of trains over the next few days. This afternoon, she was meeting Dafoe, after phone calls during which she'd quickly sensed that she wanted to see him again. On Sunday, she'd return to Penn Station to board a train to Washington.

The network would have paid for a flight to the capital but the carbon footprint of train travel was a fraction of flying the same distance. She'd have to do some cramming on the train to be ready for the first meeting of the Presidential Task Force on Climate Change. She'd received word just that morning that the network had no objection to her taking the appointment, further underscoring her nonstatus in the news division. But she'd taken great delight in calling Vice President Andrew Percy's office to say that she'd be coming aboard. Percy himself got on the phone to tell her how much he appreciated her willingness to serve. There was that word again— "serve"—that made her feel so good about joining the task force.

She waved off the bartender's offer of more wine, wanting her wits about her when she saw Dafoe. She had returned his call on the theory that a few conciliatory words might save the network from a lawsuit and herself from endless depositions. The simple kiss-off had turned into a two-and-a-half-hour conversation marked by an easy give-and-take. Jenna had been impressed by the genuine interest Dafoe had shown in her, as opposed to the paint-by-number questions that so many guys felt obliged to ask before indulging in their favorite subject: themselves.

So it all came out: Jenna's family-farm childhood in Vermont, which had included a Guernsey cow called Hoppy; two acres of vegetable garden; chickens;

turkeys; rabbits; and two pigs, whose names and shapes changed, but whose number remained constant.

Dafoe had revealed that he'd spent his boyhood summers on his grandparents' farm in southern Illinois and his early adulthood as a notorious computer hacker.

During the call, Jenna realized he looked like Hugh Jackman in *Australia,* minus the star's facial scruff. Perhaps that was what had prompted her to say yes when Dafoe asked her out. He began to explain why it was tough for him to get down to the city this time of year, but she already understood.

"I'll come up there," she'd said.

Now she looked at the passing terrain—*his* turf, indeed—and wondered if she'd been a little rash. *What do I really know about him? Not much. At least I Googled him,* Jenna insisted to herself. She glanced at her watch. If the train was on time, he'd be meeting her at the station in less than five minutes.

Jenna carefully reapplied her lipstick, prompted by the stain on her wineglass. She wore little makeup away from the set of *The Morning Show,* and had kept her clothes to weekend-getaway casual: jeans, powder-blue top, and cream-colored ostrich leather cowboy boots. She'd had more elegant outfits shipped to her hotel in Washington.

But Jenna knew she would have looked striking in rags. With her white-blond hair and blue-eyed Icelandic heritage, she'd come up a winner at the genetic roulette wheel. And she was grateful. She had no illusions about the reason she'd succeeded so quickly in television, and it wasn't spelled "P-h-D."

On the platform, Dafoe looked more relaxed than

he had on their first encounter. A good sign. Jenna shut off her BlackBerry before she stepped from the train. No calls this weekend; Nicci could handle anything that came up. Dafoe took her hand, letting go after they hugged gently. Not *too* awkward, as such things went. Then he took her bag and did not attempt further contact while they made their way to his dusty old pickup, which sat right by the station, completely charming in its lack of pretense.

"What's your preference?" he asked once she was seated in the cab and he'd closed the door, resting his arms on the open window. "I can take you to the B&B, or I could take you to my farm, give you an icy beer, and show you around."

Decisions, decisions. If she went with him now, they'd have daylight for their first hours together.

"I'm not one to turn down a cold beer on a hot day."

"You're a wise woman," he shouted as he rounded the front of the truck, moving with ease. *Like an athlete,* she thought.

Despite the drought, the countryside looked pretty. Dafoe's twenty-two acres could have been a photo in *Sunset* magazine, the golden hues of the pastures so enticing that they almost obscured the tindery conditions. The truck rolled down a dirt and gravel driveway for a quarter mile, cattle fencing on both sides. Jenna oohed and ahhed at appropriate moments, appreciating his tidy and well-maintained operation—and hoping it wasn't evidence of obsessive-compulsive disorder.

His home sat on a slight rise; a classic square farmhouse with a veranda on the main floor and two dormers and a balcony on the upper level. Celery green with white trim and a white roof.

"Hey, that's smart. I was just reading about white roofs but I don't think I've ever actually seen one."

"I had to replace the old one," he said as they climbed out of the cab, "so I figured why not? Send some of that sunlight back up where it belongs. I should warn you that I don't have air-conditioning, so even with that roof the house might be a mite warmer than you're used to."

If so, she wouldn't find out till later; on the veranda, he grabbed two pilsners from a green minifridge that blended artfully into the wall. "Saves me from having to take my boots off every time I want something to eat."

Then Dafoe led Jenna on a leisurely stroll to a nearby pasture, reduced by the drought to dead grass and dust. His herd had congregated near the barn under the sparse shade of two withered maples. Bowser, as she'd dubbed his border collie at the reservoir, kept vigil by the cows, eyeing the two-legged intruder warily.

"I had those fields in hay," Dafoe pointed past the barn, "till the crop burned up two years running. Seedlings never got higher than half a foot."

"What are you doing for feed?"

"I'm buying hay by the truckload, and this year I started supplementing with alfalfa and flaxseed, which kind of mimics the wild grasses they used to get in the spring, before everything dried up. Their methane's down seventeen percent."

"You're putting me on."

"Not a bit, and they like it. They're hungry right

now. That's why they're hanging around near the barn. Bayou." He whistled to the dog and gave him a hand signal. "Watch this," he said to her.

Bayou darted through the cows to the gate, then rose on his hind legs and used his long, narrow snout to flip open a latch. Then the dog scrambled aside and the cows pushed the gate open and filed toward the barn. One calf failed to move until Bayou urged her on.

"You just get the one this year?" Jenna nodded at the reluctant calf.

"Two, and I almost lost that one. See the way her back leg is all wrapped up?"

"What happened?"

"Damn coyotes almost dragged her off. Bayou about went nuts with the pack of them. We were tracking those creatures"—he referred to the coyotes like a curse—"when your idiot pilot damn near killed us."

The force of his words startled Jenna; then he smiled and raised his hands as if to quell his own outburst.

"I'm not complaining anymore. People have met under stranger circumstances. I meant to tell you when we were on the phone that I don't usually carry a rifle and handgun. It was for the coyotes."

The news came as a relief. "You get any of them?"

"Nope. A big bird put a stop to that." He was still smiling.

When they turned back to the house, their hands brushed. A second later their fingers knitted a pleasing pattern. The simple act of holding hands with Dafoe felt better than a lot of kisses she'd known.

Trust your instincts, she said to herself.

He took off his boots in the mudroom and helped Jenna with hers. She was struck by the oddly intimate act of letting a man hold her leg so he could tug off her shoes. The house felt cooler than he'd suggested, a pleasure after the hard rays of late afternoon. She eyed an airy bathroom and slipped inside to wash up. Clean towels, floor, commode, and a newly enameled claw-foot tub. *Not bad.*

When she opened the door, Dafoe called, "In here," and she followed his voice to a dining room filled with natural light. The table was covered with a white cloth and laid with blueberry earthenware. "This is so nice. You do like your light colors."

"It's the farming," he replied. "You can go either of two ways, it seems to me. You can do what a buddy of mine did, which was take a sample of mud from his farm to the carpet store so he could match up the colors perfectly; or you can try to have a nice, clean place to come home to at the end of the day."

"Option number two for me," she laughed.

He gave her a thumbs-up on his way into the kitchen, returning with a smoked turkey salad. "Hope you like Gorgonzola. I traded a couple of gallons of milk to a cheese maker in town. Everything else," he filled her plate, "used to come from my kitchen garden; but there's no sparing water for that now. Another beer? Wine?"

"I'll stick with this." She was still nursing the pilsner. "So it's off to Safeway these days?"

"That's way too big city for us. We've got the Alverson Natural Food Co-op. But the turkey's mine. I've got a smoke shack back there." He glanced out a wide window but all she noticed was the strong line of his chin.

"The turkey's really good. So's everything. Thank you."

By the time they finished dinner, Jenna felt fully at ease. They cleared the dishes before moving—at Dafoe's suggestion—to the veranda to watch the sunset. The idyllic interval lasted about thirty seconds before Bayou stood up next to Dafoe's deck chair and barked as sharply as a car alarm.

Two attractive young women—early twenties, Jenna guessed—were climbing out of a salt-eaten Subaru wagon. Jenna hoped this wasn't about to turn weird; she'd experienced more than one jealous girlfriend in her time.

"Come on, join us," Dafoe called to the pair. The taller one, sporting black braids and a brilliant sunflower tattoo barely hidden by the shoulder strap of her fully filled tank top, greeted Bayou and rubbed his ruff.

Jenna drifted over, and Dafoe introduced Forensia as his "number-one farmhand."

"Your only one," she quipped.

"And Sang-mi is her friend," Dafoe added.

Forensia looked up from Bayou. "Hey, you really are Jenna Withers. You do the weather in the mornings."

"That's right," Sang-mi said with a Korean accent.

"Guilty as charged," Jenna said.

"Well, you're good at it," Forensia shook her hand. "I mean, even before you almost landed on my boss, we always caught your first weather report of the day. Working on a farm and all you kind of have to."

"Forensia's my chief troublemaker," Dafoe said.

"More like your chief slop hauler," the young woman replied.

"What's up?" Dafoe asked her.

"I left my pack by your computer and I'm going to need it for the weekend."

"And you wanted to meet Jenna?"

"Could be that, too," Forensia said good-naturedly.

"Go on, grab your pack. You're probably running off to a midnight meeting of your coven."

"It's not a coven," Forensia harrumphed playfully. Jenna sensed that this wasn't the first time they'd had this exchange. "It's a gathering, and we're not officially witches."

"Not yet," said Sang-mi in all seriousness.

"Pagans," Dafoe explained after the young women drove off and he and Jenna settled back on the veranda.

"Not your everyday belief system, at least not where I come from."

"Vermont? Are you kidding? There are lots of Pagans up there."

"Not when I was growing up."

"World's changing, but I'm fine with them. They care about the land as much as I do. And despite the rumors in this little burg, they're not sacrificing babies and goats."

"There's actually talk like that?"

"Oh, yeah, Forensia and Sang-mi aren't the only Pagans around. You'll find quite a few of them living on small farms or in town. Some are younger and still at home with their folks—who are freaking out, if the letters to the paper and what you hear around town mean anything."

"We're not that far from the city; it's hard to believe that people are getting so riled up about it."

"We've got more churches per capita in this county than anywhere else in the state, so this Pagan stuff is really stirring up the pot. There have been some harsh words thrown around. The police chief even held a town hall meeting to try to calm everybody down. Which is amazing because I would have pegged him as somewhere to the right of Attila the Hun."

Jenna canceled her reservation at the B&B, taking Dafoe up on his offer of a spare room. The arrangement felt comfortable and safe, and she luxuriated in waking to find her new beau priming the espresso maker.

Before she left, late on Sunday morning, they found themselves making out like a couple of teens. That's certainly how her passion felt: fresh and alive—a great unknown all over again.

She was tempted to go further, but told him that she wanted them both to get tested. Her words sounded breathless; and she held his hips firmly against hers, savoring the sweet pressure. When he started to speak, she put her finger on his lips and said "No arguments, Mr. Dafoe Tillian."

"You worried?"

"About you or me?" she asked.

"Either."

"I'm not worried about me but fair is fair."

Still aroused, and still sorely tempted, she belted herself next to him in the pickup, feeling like a cowgirl as he drove her back to the train station with his arm wrapped around her shoulders.

"Look," she said, once she'd unbuckled to face him, "I don't have a lot of time for games. I like you, Dafoe, so if you're serious, call me again, or email me"—she pecked his lips impulsively—"stay in touch. I'm putting it to you straight: I like you a lot."

With that last word, she put her finger on his nose. In the next instant he kissed it, and she was back in his arms till the train rolled in.

She waved until he passed from view, then leaned back in her seat, sighing with delight. *Our first weekend together.* She told herself to hold onto these memories. *So I can tell our kids someday.*

Aghast at the thought, she started leafing through a discarded section of the Sunday *New York Times,* finding little to engage her until she saw a story datelined the Maldives, covering the bombing two days earlier. When she skimmed down the column and spotted Rafan's name, she almost cried out; but he was described as a survivor whose sister had been killed by the first blast.

Basheera. Jenna had known her as shy girl of thirteen, smart and funny in her quiet, mischievous way.

Jenna thought of other terrorist attacks over the years, and all the times she'd sat in sad wonder, shaking her head over the enveloping tragedies. This was truly unfathomable—the Maldives had always been special. Not just to her and not just because of the precious months she'd spent there with Rafan ten years ago. The Maldives were special because they were paradise. Now paradise had been brutally wounded.

The Times quoted Rafan: "My little sister died in my arms on the way to hospital. I heard the second bomb and saw the others dying, too."

Jenna pulled her BlackBerry from her bag. She'd kept it off all weekend, and now knew another regret.

Tons of calls, but there was the message she was hoping for: Rafan's on Saturday morning. In a desperate voice, he'd pleaded with her to come, "Or send someone to do this story, or we'll all drown in . . ." A pause, and she was sure he'd say "the sea," that they'd all drown in the rising, frightening, murderous sea.

But when he regained his voice, it was so heartbroken that his words could have been pitted with shrapnel: ". . . in blood."

We'll all drown in blood. She said it to herself, head still shaking. And then her eyes pooled, salty and swelling like the waters of the world.

4

CHAPTER

Rafan turned from the row of fresh graves and the harsh glare of white headstones, lowering his eyes to where Basheera lay buried. Yesterday, under the same strong sun, his little sister had been shrouded in a white cloth and placed on her right side to face Mecca. In accordance with Islamic practice, the other eleven victims of the bombing also rested with their eternal gaze on Islam's holiest city, while their killers—men of renegade faith—took noisy credit for the carnage, promising more blood with every breath, and claiming that God Himself had anointed their mission.

Muslims murdering Muslims. Rafan shook a fist at the burning sky.

They would have murdered him, too, if he'd been seconds slower walking down that crowded street. If he hadn't tried to carry his dying sister to hospital. If he hadn't hurried.

He sank to his knees. The newly settled dirt received him softly, and he tried to pray, as he'd tried at the burial with seven men beside him, all staring into her open grave. None of them had known Basheera well. For her sake he'd cast prayers to heaven, trying to reel in grace, forgiveness, hope.

Basheera's three dearest friends, fellow teachers at the English Language School in Malé, were not permitted at her grave site, for "Allah has cursed women who frequent graves for visitation," a quote attributed to the Prophet Mohammed.

Basheera would have hated the ceremony, so male and mannerly, though she might have laughed, as she had many times, at the irony of her life as a Muslim woman: torn by her faith, troubled yet true—and scorned by extremists whose anger stifled debate and silenced dissent.

Do you know you killed one of your enemies? Rafan had wanted to scream yesterday as dirt darkened the shroud that covered Basheera. *She hated what you do. What you say.* But to shout would have granted them a greater victory, and he never would have done that.

Instead, he would defy them—and honor his sister—under the quiet cover of darkness. He would usher Fatima, Musnah, and Senada—the dark-eyed, dark-haired married woman whom he loved dearly—to Basheera's grave. The three women planned to scatter petals of the pink rose, her favorite flower

No one guarded the cemetery. No one would stop them when night came. Even prying stubborn eyes had to sleep.

Hours away, on the small island of Dhiggaru, Adnan took his first clumsy steps in a pair of black flippers. *Like a seal on a beach,* he thought. He turned to look at his impressions in the sand, so big he could have been a giant. *Or a monster?*

Just nine steps to the water. The strip of sand had
narrowed and trees had fallen to languish in the gentle surf, shifting side to side with the thrust and parry
of the sea.

Parvez had loaned him the mask, snorkel, and fins.
"You must see for yourself," he'd said.

"But I know about it."

"*See* it," the religious leader had insisted. "*Touch* it.
It is not only sand that disappears. The reef is dying."

The warm water swirled around Adnan's legs; in
the distance the ocean appeared flat and still, reflecting the sun's blinding rays like a mirror.

He rinsed the mask before he put it on, and swam
with his eyes on the ocean bottom, watching the scal-
loped sand slowly recede as the water deepened. He'd
swum with sea turtles as a boy, once shadowing a
turtle as large as himself. The creature had glided
fathoms below him, fins lifting and falling in unison,
effortless as palm fronds in a breeze. For many minutes he'd trailed the turtle, mesmerized by a hard shell
so alive in the soft embrace of sea. He'd felt buoyant
and free, unfettered by land or air or need.

Now he swam the last few meters to the coral reef,
white and lifeless as sand, killed by an invisible gas that
spilled from the sky and formed a deadly ocean acid.

"They have played God with our world," Parvez
had said when he'd handed Adnan the snorkeling gear.
"They took all of creation in their hands and squeezed
it like a lime until no more juice ran into their bowls."

Adnan had listened. Now he placed his hand on the
coral. *Dead.* He'd never known that a reef could feel
so devoid of life. The silent heartbeat of the ocean's
hardest growth had vanished. He remembered an admonition of his youth—"Don't touch the reef"—be-

cause human contact killed it, but Parvez had told him that you can't kill the dead, and Parvez was right. Adnan could touch this reef for hours and he'd never harm it because . . . *you can't kill the dead.* Parvez had pointed to the resort islands, where tourists stayed in sprawling beach bungalows. "You can only give them rest. Let them dream. Let them sleep. We are coming."

Starlit, Rafan crept alongside Fatima, Musnah, and Senada to within whispering distance of the cemetery.

"Wait behind there." He pointed to two towering palms that rose inches from each other.

The three women, all in headscarves, crouched down. Rafan took a steadying breath and walked to the entrance. An Islamic inscription had been chiseled into the arch centuries ago: ALLAH GIVES LIFE, AND ALLAH TAKES IT AWAY.

He headed directly to where Basheera's body salted the earth with minerals and blood. He did not sink down, as he had earlier that day. Instead, he listened with the ears of a sentry as his eyes studied the commanding stillness, looking for those who would condemn him and the three women by the palms.

Slowly, he walked back to the gate, hanging his head as a bereaved man. But he was still searching for what he did not want to find.

Fatima, Musnah, and Senada stepped away from the palms. None of them spoke, but Rafan saw light, and thankfulness, in Senada's moist eyes. Basheera had been at Senada's side when she gave birth to a stillborn son; and his little sister, who had always been the quiet one, had stood up to Senada's husband when he had screamed at his grieving wife, "Murderer. Murderer."

To be out at night with Rafan and two women was

dangerous for Senada. "You are sure no one is there?" she asked.

"I am sure," Rafan said, though certainty was never possible with so many followers of Allah searching for the sins of others.

They did not pass under the arch. Rafan walked them along the perimeter, four hunched, hurrying figures moving through starlight and shadows until he turned and led them to Basheera's grave. The women gathered side by side. Rafan stepped back to keep watch.

A murmur of prayer arose. Rafan's surveillance revealed not a trace of movement in the cemetery. A stillness as absolute as death.

Fatima, Musnah, and Senada reached into a woven bag and released handfuls of lush pink petals. They glittered and floated to Basheera's grave like the snow the women had never seen. A blanket, luminous and pure, covered the freshly dug earth.

Adnan stared at the massive tiger shark and tried to tread water with the slightest movement possible, torso and legs dangling in the water like bait from the great hook of heaven. Dozens of shark species lived in the seas around the Maldives, most no more threatening than a squid, but tiger sharks attacked swimmers, divers, even boats.

It swam so close that Adnan felt water shift against his stomach, then moved on.

No, it was turning back for another pass. Hunting. The shark circled the man lazily. Any second it might bump him, see if he was a living creature.

Adnan prayed for Allah to save him, and imagined

his God saying "For what? What shall I save a such a sinner for?"

Adnan gave Allah the first answer that came to mind, repeating what Parvez had whispered in his ear: A life for a life.

Rafan led the three women from the cemetery, forsaking care for a hasty retreat. It was essential to escort Senada home before her fisherman husband returned from the sea. When they stepped back on the street, Musnah, dark hair cascading from under her head scarf, breathed loudly in relief. Rafan smiled to himself, for he felt the same freedom. They moved a few more steps before a voice ordered them to stop.

Imam Reza walked up to them. He'd conducted Basheera's funeral and burial, always keeping his back to the young woman's body, his eyes on the faithful, though Rafan knew he would question their faithfulness now. *If he knows.*

"You have been to the cemetery," Imam Reza said. His beard was a dark bush that brushed his chest, and in the sparse light his turban could be glimpsed only in outline.

"Yes," Rafan said. "I took a message from Basheera's friends to her."

"We watched him go," Fatima said

"You have no faith that your prayers can be heard in paradise?"

"Yes, Imam Reza, I'm sure they can," Musnah spoke without looking up. "But we miss her so."

Rafan noticed that all three women kept their heads bowed. Senada stood behind her friends, almost cowering. Imam Reza would like that.

"What prayer did you take to your sister?" Imam Reza asked him. It was a test.

"The prayer of forgiveness for all my sister's sins," Rafan answered. "The prayer of hope for all the faithful. The prayer of memory, that she would never be forgotten."

Imam Reza's eyes moved over the headscarves that faced him. "Did you enter the cemetery?"

"No, they did not," Rafan said "Only I—"

"I asked them."

"No," answered the women, keeping their heads low.

He doesn't believe us, Rafan thought. *But this isn't Iran or Waziristan. Not yet.*

Imam Reza walked toward the cemetery, leaving Rafan chilled.

"Did he believe us?" Musnah whispered after they'd moved some distance away.

"I do not know what he believed or what he saw." Rafan looked over his shoulder. "I know only that these imams never forget."

Senada stepped lightly toward the back door of her home, sticking close to the wall, away from the starlight. What would she say if Mehdi was waiting inside? She touched the door's handle, wondering if her husband had left a trace of his heat, if he'd gripped it so hard in anger, twisted it so violently that she could sense him . . .

But the metal was cool and when she opened the door, the room was black. Silent. She struck a match and held it out like a frightened child, peering into the pitch. Her bed was empty. She did not smell fish.

She climbed under the covers and said a prayer of gratitude: for safety, for friends, for Rafan.

"Allah saved me," Adnan told Parvez, who stood in the door of his one-room house on the north end of Dhiggaru. A lantern burned behind him, illuminating a simple desk and an open Koran. "He drove the shark out to sea after I made a vow."

Parvez asked which vow. Adnan spoke without moving: "The vow of paradise."

Parvez took the lantern and walked him along the path through the palm grove still teeming with their secrets. He didn't stop until he brought Adnan to the end of the seawall, where he placed the lantern before putting his arm around his friend's shoulder.

"If you could see through the darkness for many miles," Parvez said, "you would see diamond island."

Not its real name—what the Maldivians called the richest resort island. Adnan's mother took a boat there every weekday to make sure that the rooms were cleaned and that every toilet was scrubbed till it shined. Then, on Saturdays, a small supply ship picked her up on its way back from Malé. She usually added a big bag of locally grown limes to the hold, already heavy with cases of champagne, caviar, chocolates, and the other everyday luxuries of diamond island. Her job, though she wasn't paid for the crossing, was to watch the seamen for pilferage. Not a lime, not a single dark chocolate truffle, could be missing when they docked. Bags and cases had to be sealed tighter than a hatch in a storm.

His mother had been astonished the first time she'd seen the resort. The "bungalows" were larger than

any house she'd ever known, almost as big as the
presidential palace. Each was lavishly appointed with
silver, gold plate, marble, and exotic hardwoods, and
came with a staff of three, a private pool, and a yacht.
Ten thousand dollars a night. More than his mother
earned in four years of hard work.

"Your mother could put the dead to rest," Parvez
said in the quiet that had fallen.

"No," Adnan shook his head. "You said I would
do this. I would put the dead to rest."

"So you will. But your mother can do what you
cannot: she can go to the heart of diamond island and
stop their sins forever. Every hour of every day they
slap Allah in the face."

Liquor, sex, drugs, parties with unmarried girls.
Muslim girls corrupted by the West. *Muslim* men corrupted by the West. *And she worries about their truf-
fles and toilets.* That thought—and Parvez's words
about Allah—stung sharply.

"You can bury the gift of paradise in a bag of limes,"
Parvez said. "She'll carry it to them. She'll never know.
We can time the arrival."

"But this is what they did in Malé. They made a
bomb." *And you said it was wrong.*

"No, they killed many brother and sister Muslims
in Malé. Out there," Parvez turned his gaze seaward
again, "the dead still wait for their rest."

"But what about me? The vest?" So much more
willing to take his own life than his mother's.

"The vest will be filled, and when the time is right
and Allah speaks, you will wear it. You will see your
mother in paradise. Someday, you will see me, too."

Parvez turned away, leaving Adnan trembling in
the sultry tropical night.

CHAPTER

President Victor Reynolds gripped Jenna's hand in both of his, looked directly into her bright blue eyes, and thanked her profusely: "Your president and your nation deeply appreciate your service."

She was impressed. He was the *president*, after all, even if he was afflicted with that annoying, self-important tic of referring to himself in the third person. Indeed, his warm welcome might have overwhelmed Jenna, if she hadn't already heard him repeat the very same words to nine other members of the newly assembled task force. And there were still a half dozen in line behind her.

Little matter, she was proud to shake the chief executive's hand and enter the Oval Office. They'd been herded here by Vice President Andrew Percy, who was well positioned to succeed his boss in four years. The press corps had dubbed him "Hair Apparent" for his wavy black locks; at sixty-three, they remained suspiciously unstreaked by gray, à la Reagan, and rose like a crown above his handsomely weathered face. It was as if every hair were straining to reach the nation's highest office, openly betraying the man's scantily clad ambition.

Jenna glanced around the Oval Office. *How great is this?* she asked herself. *Very great.* By joining the task force, she'd plunged right into the fiercely unpredictable currents of history.

The president began his official welcome speech.

"All of you are about to embark on a task critical to our nation's future, and to the future of our children and our children's children . . ."

She tried to focus—she really did—but clichés always sent her thoughts reeling. She tuned back in as Reynolds concluded his mercifully brief remarks with "And may God bless each of you and guide you on this momentous journey. Now, I have to go down to the Situation Room, and you've got your own duties to attend to."

A White House aide ushered the task force out of the Oval Office. As she left the room, Jenna took a final look around, noting the portrait of George Washington above the fireplace. And Abraham Lincoln, to her left as she headed out the door.

Jenna trailed the other task force members to a conference room where carafes of coffee awaited them. She didn't need caffeine to get jazzed, not this morning.

The vice president, in his role as task force chair, moved to the head of the long mahogany table. As he perused his notes, another aide, as clean-cut as a pine plank, handed out confidentiality agreements that each member signed.

Though Jenna recognized a number of scientists on

the task force, the person grabbing her immediate attention was Senator Gayle Higgens, who'd represented Texas until two years ago. "Tossed out with the other rascals," was how she'd described her defeat to *The Washington Post*. In that interview, Higgens did not mention how deeply she'd been bankrolled by the petroleum interests so dominant in her home state, or her controversial six-figure "speaking fees." They had become such a scandal that in the end, most voters in Texas went for the other guy . . . a landslide defeat that made Higgens even more memorable.

Two environmentalists of note sat to Jenna's right. She nodded and smiled, and had to look away when the one with a white goatee—old enough, and then some, to be her father—stared too intently into her eyes. *No, I'm not trolling for a date. Jesus.* She thought of Washington's strange sexual charge, where power— and access to power—was the dominant aphrodisiac.

Across the table she spotted two scientists who wrote immensely popular blogs on climate change. One of them, Ben Norris—balding, freckled, jowly—had been an outcast at NASA during George W.'s regime. Jenna was glad to see that Norris had finally been granted a seat at the table, literally and figuratively. She gave him a quick smile, pleased that the panel was dominated by men and women of his caliber.

"It has become painfully clear," the vice president began, looking over the assembly, "that we are nowhere near the level of reductions in greenhouse gases necessary to prevent disastrous consequences from climate change. That's the overwhelming scientific consensus, which is no longer in serious dispute . . ."

Jenna sat up, astonished to hear such direct language

from the VP, who was speaking far more frankly about
global warming than any administration official in history.

*Of course, all of us just swore to keep our mouths
shut.*

"Even if we had managed to convince the American people of the need to make dramatic changes in
the way we live," Percy went on, "which we've utterly
failed to do, the developing world—especially China,
India, and Brazil—has shown a tragic unwillingness
to make more than nominal attempts to cut back."
Percy shook his head sadly; it didn't look like an act
to Jenna.

She shot a glance at Gayle Higgens, wondering
what "Senator Fossil Fuels," as the greenies called
her, made of the vice president's shocking admission.
Higgens—Jenna could scarcely believe this—was
smiling and nodding.

Have I just walked through the looking glass, she
wondered, *where nothing is as it appears?*

The vice president paused, looked meaningfully
around the room, and said "We have to see what science and technology can do to lower the earth's ther-
mostat. We have to move forward aggressively with
geoengineering. I want you to consider everything
that's feasible, from CCS"—carbon capture and storage, usually underground—"to launching sulfates into
space to reflect sunlight. We want to hear about whatever you think will work."

Whoa. Jenna had assumed that geoengineering
would be on the agenda—why else would they have
invited her?—but not that it would *be* the agenda.
And to talk so causally about using sulfates, in particular, was sobering. She'd had a nightmare about sul-

fates being blasted into the atmosphere. Desperate to awaken, she'd dreamed she was standing at a window watching a beautiful sunny day turn bitter cold. Her reflection in the glass showed frost coating her face, and she felt her heartbeat slowing. Then she heard it stop, which awakened her, ironically enough, in a sweltering pool of perspiration.

"That's what all of you have in common," Percy said. "You're acknowledged experts in your fields, and you've all expressed deep skepticism about our country's willingness to take the steps required to reduce GHGs." Greenhouse gases. Percy nodded at Norris, the prodigal son from NASA, who sat grimacing with his arms crossed. "You need to understand that we basically agree with those of you who have been most critical of your government's efforts in this regard."

"Hold on, Mr. Vice President," NASA's own said. "What you're telling us—let's cut to the quick here—is that there's no real commitment to reduce GHGs, so now we're going to tinker with the planet's incredibly fragile heating and cooling system. Do you have any understanding of the risks? This could kill all of us. Miserably."

"We do, of course. But we think that doing nothing will be much worse."

"But you won't address the risks publicly?"

"No, we won't. We recognize that this is the most serious crisis ever faced by any administration, but talking publicly would only set off panic."

"If you'd spoken openly five years ago—"

"That was then, this is now. Ben, let's not squabble over what's done. There's no time. Look," Percy pushed aside his notes and leaned forward, "we've tried complicated international agreements, and no one, including us, has ever lived up to them. And it's not just climate change by itself that has us worried: the CIA has just completed a two-year research project investigating the impact of what's happening with the planet on national security. The conclusions are dreadful: in Africa alone, warming is expected to make civil war as common as drought."

No coincidence there, thought Jenna.

"And none of us should think that we'll be able to write those wars off as 'just another African tragedy,' because the carnage will happen in the world's most critical oil- and mineral-rich regions. Think of it: civil wars waged around the world's biggest oil spigots. It's happened before, and it's going to happen a lot more in the future."

The vice president held up a document from the stack in front of him. "This is the actual CIA report. It says we'll risk being buried by defense spending because countries all over the world will be in open conflict." He read from the report, "'Nations will engage in armed conflicts over rapidly diminishing arable land, because of drought, floods, windstorms, and rising oceans; rapidly diminishing fresh water; rapidly diminishing food; and rapidly diminishing oil supplies.'" Percy looked up. "The Agency says we're in for an unprecedented period of what it calls 'social and climate chaos.' So we must consider *all* our options."

Jenna put down her pen. She'd planned to take notes but she'd already written the book from which the vice president could have been quoting.

"Most of you have highly specialized knowledge. A few of you, like our well-known colleague, Ms. Jenna Withers, are highly educated generalists."

"Hey, me, too," Senator Higgens chimed in. "I'm all

about generalities," she added with a self-deprecating laugh that drew smiles from most of the people at the table.

Since losing her Senate seat, Higgens had become executive director of the United States Energy Institute (USEI), the oil and coal industry's powerhouse lobbying group. She'd reportedly written more than three dozen energy bills in the last session alone, and found plenty of former colleagues—beneficiaries of USEI largesse—to introduce them under their own names. A boisterous, robust presence, Higgens had long been a favorite of Sunday-morning interview shows: a plain-talking Texan whose twang-tinged homilies belied a superior intellect and political savvy widely respected inside the Beltway, where cunning counted as a virtue, not a vice.

"The esteemed senator," Vice President Percy said with a smile, "is not giving herself proper credit, but I'm sure she'll agree that it's vital for us to come up with a plan that will really deal with global warming. If we don't, we're . . ." And here Percy paused, maybe for dramatic effect. If so, Senator Higgens usurped the tension entirely:

"Toast, Andy. We're toast, baked, bar-bee-cued." The senator guffawed, spurring surprised laughter around the room.

But Jenna sat in startled silence, shocked by what the senator appeared to endorse: wholesale acceptance by the oil and coal industry of the impending peril posed by climate change. Amazing. Momentous. Even bigger than when some of the oil industry giants finally stopped funding institutes that denied climate change with pretend science.

"We *are* warming," the vice president agreed wryly

with the senator. "Evan Stubb," Percy's chief of staff, "will coordinate your efforts to come up with the cheapest, most efficient means of sharply reducing temperatures and GHGs. In other words, the president wants a short list of the most promising geoengineering options, and he'd like it in the next sixty days, along with your recommendations on how to proceed."

"Planning on being reelected?" asked the goateed environmentalist who'd leered at Jenna. The election was only ten days away.

The vice president just grinned and directed one of his aides to pass out the memo his office had prepared on geoengineering. Jenna skimmed the first page quickly. Under "Most Feasible" she saw a short section on increasing cloud cover, which noted tersely: "Will cool earth by reflecting sunlight back into space. Will not remove greenhouse gases."

Sure won't, she thought. Increasing cloud cover would only make it possible to live with higher levels of the gases . . . in the short run. Carbon dioxide would still be absorbed the by oceans, generating ever more carbonic acid, which killed sea life. This was no theoretical threat: in just the past nine years, vast stretches of ocean in which algae had died and disappeared had grown by 15 percent. And every scientist, including Jenna, knew that algae was overwhelmingly important: it was the source of much of the earth's oxygen and was the beginning of the food chain for many animals. Far more visible than the loss of algae was the destruction of half the world's major reef systems, dying from carbonic acid overload. The human species was not likely to survive if life vanished from three-quarters of the planet.

Under a separate "Feasible" category, the vice president's memo included "underground sequestration of carbon dioxide." *Might work,* Jenna agreed, but she knew that it would lower temperatures only *slowly.* Geologic sequestration, or GS as it was called, entailed injecting huge amounts of CO_2 from manufacturing or power plants into rock formations deep within the earth. Over time, the rock would eventually "wash out" the carbon. But "eventually" meant centuries, and the amount of CO_2 being produced even in just the U.S. was overwhelming. Plus, if this was to work, there would have to be a sea change in attitudes at the EPA because the agency had approved only a few rock formations for sequestration. Meantime, glaciers would continue to melt at record rates. Already, the lives of one hundred million people in South America were threatened by the loss of their chief source of drinking water: low-lying Andean glaciers.

As the author of a celebrated book on geoengineering, Jenna might have been expected to have been in a celebratory mood as she left the White House: her time had come, along with a great deal of attention. Clearly, the executive branch had given up on making any additional efforts to try to get people to change how they lived, ate, traveled, and worked. But she felt deeply ambivalent about this surrender. She wondered what would happen if people were given the real, painful reasons—or real incentives—to modify their patterns of production and consumption. Geoengineering, even at this late stage, felt like giving a heart patient quadruple bypass surgery instead of putting him on a low-fat diet. It *might* save the patient, but it could just as easily kill him.

Jenna no longer wondered why USEI was on board: as long as geoengineering muscled its way to the forefront of climate change efforts, the fossil fuel industry could argue that it was okay to burn every last barrel of crude oil and bucket of coal.

Exiting the White House, Jenna was escorted to one of a fleet of electric cars that would ferry away the task force. As she climbed into the backseat, she was unable to think of a viable geoengineering technique that did not threaten lethal consequences for humanity. But as the car eased past a regiment of reporters hurling questions that nobody on the task force rolled down their windows to answer, she also knew that political impotence—and widespread public skepticism of global warming—had sent the earth cartwheeling down a precipitous slope.

The car had no sooner turned on to Pennsylvania Avenue, the White House looming in the background, than she realized with a start that geoengineering truly posed the most daunting question ever faced by humankind: Do you embrace a dangerous technique that could save the planet—or, with a single miscalculation, plunge it into a final frozen collapse? Or do you soldier on with potentially safer solutions that lacked political support and had failed to arrest the devastating climate changes taking place on land, in the sea, and, most crucially, in the tender skin of sky that protected us all?

Quadruple bypass surgery, or low-fat diet?

After one meeting of the task force, Jenna knew the White House answer: welcome to the operating room for planet earth.